Praise for Susan Elliot Wright

'Passionate, intriguing and beautifully written . . .
A powerful and talented new voice'
Rachel Hore

'If you love Maggie O'Farrell, you will love this'
Veronica Henry

'Exquisite storytelling, full to the brim with authentic characters, family secrets and an emotional weight'
Isabel Ashdown

'A brave and moving story about how much can be lost and what happens next'
Alison Moore

'[A] tense and emotional drama'
Daily Express, **Best Summer Reads**

'I was swept along by Elliot Wright's assured storytelling'
Katie Ward

'Two intertwined stories explore a past filled with terror and grief, and a heartbreaking present, in writing as smooth and bittersweet as fine dark chocolate'
Jane Rogers

'Compelling and deeply moving . . .
this is superb storytelling'
Jane Rusbridge

Susan Elliot Wright grew up in Lewisham in south-east London. Before becoming a full-time writer, she did a number of different jobs, including civil servant, cleaner, dishwasher, journalist and chef. She has an MA in writing from Sheffield Hallam University, where she is now an associate lecturer, and she lives in Sheffield with her husband.

To find out more,
visit her website: http:/www.susanelliotwright.co.uk
or follow her on Twitter @sewelliot.

Also by Susan Elliot Wright

What She Lost
The Secrets We Left Behind
The Things We Never Said

the flight of cornelia blackwood

SUSAN ELLIOT WRIGHT

SIMON & SCHUSTER

London · New York · Sydney · Toronto · New Delhi

A CBS COMPANY

First published in Great Britain by Simon & Schuster UK Ltd, 2019
A CBS COMPANY

The paperback edition published 2019

Copyright © Susan Elliot Wright, 2019

The right of Susan Elliot Wright to be identified as author of this work has been asserted in accordance with the Copyright, Designs and Patents Act, 1988.

1 3 5 7 9 10 8 6 4 2

Simon & Schuster UK Ltd
1st Floor
222 Gray's Inn Road
London WC1X 8HB

Simon & Schuster Australia, Sydney
Simon & Schuster India, New Delhi

www.simonandschuster.co.uk
www.simonandschuster.com.au
www.simonandschuster.co.in

A CIP catalogue record for this book is available from the British Library

Paperback ISBN: 978-1-4711-8342-3
eBook ISBN: 978-1-4711-3455-5
Audio ISBN: 978-1-4711-8084-2

This book is a work of fiction. Names, characters, places and incidents are either a product of the author's imagination or are used fictitiously. Any resemblance to actual people living or dead, events or locales is entirely coincidental.

Printed and bound by CPI Group (UK) Ltd, Croydon, CR0 4YY

For all the mothers

The Flight of Cornelia Blackwood is set on the outskirts of Sheffield, on the borders of the Peak District. The geography is, I hope, reasonably accurate. The exception to this is the village of Castledene, which, while it has similarities to a number of Peak District villages, is a made-up place.

CHAPTER ONE

Now

I only open the back door for a moment to let the smoke out, but it is enough time for the creature to walk in, its black, claw-like feet clicking on the tiles. I grab a wooden spoon from the earthenware jar next to the hob and throw it at the crow, jolting my back and missing the crow by a mile. The bird flutters its feathers and caws twice at me before flying back outside. I slam the door shut, hands shaking as I turn the key in the lock, and as I toss the burnt toast in the bin, I realise my legs are trembling violently. I steady myself against the worktop and concentrate on my breathing until I feel calmer. It's not unusual for crows to be out there on the grass, or even for them to come up close to the house to peck around the plant pots looking for snails, but they've never tried to come inside before. Does this mean I can't ever leave the back door open again? My fingers twitch for a cigarette, but I promised myself I wouldn't smoke in the house when Adrian was home, and if I'm going to give up properly I need to stick to it. I can't resort to a cigarette every time something upsets me, or I'll be chain-smoking again in no time.

I start to get to my feet, but the pain makes me stop sharply mid-movement. When it's this bad I have to go back to using my stick, and I hate doing that – it makes me feel more like eighty than forty. Most of the time now I can manage without the bloody thing, but my back is really stiff today, probably because of all the sitting I did yesterday. Throwing that wooden spoon wasn't too clever – I'll probably be in pain for the rest of the day now. Leaning on the stick, I walk to the other side of the kitchen and switch on the coffee machine, but even that movement, reaching out and pressing the switch, sends a twinge down my spine, through my hip and into my leg. I should have been more careful yesterday – done my exercises at lunchtime, or at least taken a walk. The first tutorial was early so I'd hit the rush hour, which meant the drive into town took longer than usual, then three tutorials back-to-back before lunch and another two in the afternoon. But it's not often I have a day like that, and I'm grateful to the university for being so flexible. For having me back at all, really, after all that's happened.

I listen to the floorboards creaking overhead as Adrian moves around in the bedroom, packing for another conference. I hate waiting for him to leave the house. There's something about the sound of him preparing to go that makes me hyper-aware of his going, as if he's even more absent as he's getting ready than he'll be when he's gone.

The coffee machine whirs and clunks as I walk slowly to the kitchen door. 'Adrian?' I call up the stairs. 'You got time for coffee?' He can't hear me. I could go upstairs to ask him, but my back's killing me, and he'll probably want to get going anyway. I take my coffee into the sitting room and lower myself carefully into a chair by the window facing the garden. At least in here I can't hear him moving around so much. I light a cigarette and draw the toxins into my lungs, despising myself. Usually I open the door to the garden while I'm smoking, but that crow walking into the house completely freaked me out, so I leave it closed.

There's a breeze blowing up outside, and the trees in the woods beyond the fence are moving, the odd leaf floating to the ground. The leaves are beginning to change colour, and in a few weeks they'll fall from the trees, covering the grass in a carpet of russet, copper and gold. Start of the Autumn term. After two years of working solely on a one-to-one basis with final year students, returning to my old role is a bit scary. It's only a couple of days a week, and I can cope with the work-setting, marking, departmental meetings and awaydays, but the thought of standing up in front of a full lecture theatre ... Even the thought of being back in the department is daunting, but if my life is ever going to return to anywhere near normal I need to start interacting with people again. Mike, my line manager, has been great – really supportive. He tells me several times that colleagues will be pleased to see me back, but I'm not convinced.

I hear Adrian hurrying down the stairs, and then immediately bounding back up again. He's so heavy-footed when getting ready to go anywhere that my senses are on high alert, every nerve ending waiting for the next sound or movement. I squash out my cigarette. I *must* stop soon. He's been great about it, but he shouldn't have to put up with this. It was a stupid thing to start doing. I look at the pack on the coffee table, a plain white box with the words SMOKING KILLS in stark black letters. I wonder what my undergrads would think if they knew, given how I used to have a go at them when I came across little groups on campus, puffing away outside the library or the lecture theatres. *You've got away with it so far,* I'd say, *but what if you knew for sure that the next cigarette was the one that would trigger lung cancer? You'd stop, wouldn't you?* It was so straightforward. Who knew I'd end up relying on the bloody things to help get me from one hour to the next?

Adrian is coming down the stairs again. It sounds like he's lugging his suitcase this time. I take a swig of coffee. It's cold, but it'll tone down the taste of smoke on my lips when I kiss him goodbye. He appears in the doorway just as I reach it, laptop bag over his shoulder. He opens his arms and pulls me gently into them, his lips resting against my hair. We hold each other for a few seconds before he releases me. 'Bad timing, really, isn't it? If it was next week, you'd be back at work and too busy to notice being on your own.' He sweeps back my fringe. 'Will you be okay?'

'Yep – course I will.'

'How's your back?'

'Not too bad. I can take more painkillers soon, and when they've kicked in, I'll do my exercises.'

'Good. What will you do while I'm away?'

'Get ready for next week, I suppose. I've done all the reading, I just need to get my thoughts together. And I might start making some notes for the Hardy lecture.'

'Lecture? I thought you said you wouldn't be lecturing straight away?'

'No, I've got a few weeks, but it's such a long time since I've done it, I really, really need to be prepared. You know what they say.' We say it together. '"Fail to prepare, prepare to fail".'

'You'll be great. I know you're nervous, but at least you've been in and out for tutorials, so it's not like you'll be facing everyone for the first time.'

I haven't told him that I arranged the majority of my tutorials off-campus to avoid bumping into colleagues.

He kisses me on the lips and picks up his suitcase. 'And if it turns out to be too much, you can always go back to supervision only.'

I nod. 'Yes, true.'

'You just need to get that first seminar out of the way and you'll feel better.' He pauses, touches my face again. 'I know it's hard to move on, but somehow—'

'I know. Now go on, or you'll be late.'

'Sorry, I didn't mean to . . . you know.' He picks up his car keys. 'I'll phone you later.'

'Aren't you getting the train?'

'Yes, but I've left it too late to call a taxi. I'll leave the car near the station.'

'Why don't I drive you?'

No, he assures me, he's ready to go now so there's no point in me coming out. I won't argue. Driving can be difficult when my back's this bad.

'If you're sure. Go on, then,' I stand on tiptoe to kiss him. 'Get going. I'll talk to you tonight. Drive carefully.'

He closes the door and the empty house settles around me. I hate it when we're apart – always have. It's how I knew I loved him, right from the start.

CHAPTER TWO

Then

My stomach did a somersault as Adrian opened the door, grinning widely and smelling of shower gel. 'Leah.' His gaze flickered over me. 'You look fantastic.'

'So do you.' Oh God, did that sound too keen? He was more tanned than when I'd run into him a couple of weeks ago at a friend's wedding. Although I vaguely remembered him from uni, it was only at the wedding that we really got chatting, and I'd been amazed when he invited me over for dinner. He really did look great tonight. His dark, almost black hair was still damp from the shower, and it was sort of tousled. He was wearing light blue jeans and a plain white t-shirt, not too tight, but not thin and baggy either. It looked as if it might have been new, and I wondered if he'd gone out and bought it specially for tonight.

'I brought these.' I handed him the chilled wine and the freesias I'd bought on some mad impulse on my way here.

He put his nose to the flowers. 'These smell nice. I think this is the first time anyone's ever bought me flowers.'

I could feel myself going red. I'd never given a man flowers before. What was I thinking of? Why couldn't I have just brought wine and chocolates, like any normal person? 'I just . . .' I shrugged. 'I thought they were pretty.'

'They are. They match your dress.' His eyes lingered on me for a second. 'Come on up – I haven't finished unpacking yet, so it looks a bit sparse.'

I'd forgotten he'd only just moved here. He was about to take up a research post at the university, he'd told me. Educational studies. After several years of teaching in secondary schools, he'd become interested in educational theory. I'd wondered if we might be working in the same place, but it turns out he'll be based at the other campus.

There was a wonderful garlicky smell that got stronger as I followed him up the stairs and into the flat.

'Come and talk to me while I'm cooking.' He led me into a galley-style kitchen that opened out on to a balcony overlooking the park.

'Ooh, what a lovely view.'

'Yeah, probably the main reason I went for this place. When the traffic dies down you can hear the little river that runs through the park.'

'What are we having? It smells gorgeous.'

'Coq au vin.' He lifted the lid of a heavy-looking orange

pan and there was a lovely warm waft of wine and garlic. 'I know it's old-fashioned, but it's hard to beat that chicken/red wine/garlic combo, and everybody likes it.' He turned to me, still holding the saucepan lid, and I saw a slight flicker of anxiety in his eyes. 'I hope?'

'Sounds lovely.'

I was touched by how relieved he appeared to be. He poured us both some wine, and we clinked glasses. I'd forgotten how amazing his eyes were, especially when he looked right at you – they twinkled. He held my gaze and I suddenly felt like a schoolgirl. I wondered if I was blushing.

'I'm so glad we ran into each other again,' he said, more serious now.

'Me too.' I wanted to say more, but I had a sneaking suspicion I might stutter or muddle my words up or something. So I sipped my wine and gave what I hoped was an attractive smile. The evening sunshine was pouring through the open door and adding to the warmth of the kitchen, and during a lull in the traffic, I could hear the gentle movement of the river below. I leaned against the worktop and watched as he chopped parsley on a little wooden board. It felt natural, being here; comfortable.

'So: coq au vin, rice and green beans, then chocolate tart – I cheated and bought that from Waitrose. But I made the starter myself. Sorrel soup.'

'Sorrel soup?' I was on a date with a man who had made me *sorrel soup*. 'I'm deeply impressed. Where did you learn to make sorrel soup? Honestly, the last time a man made a meal for me it was spag bol with sauce from a jar.'

He laughed.

'Actually,' I confessed, 'I can't do much better myself. I do cook, but it's all jars and packets. I admire people who do it all from scratch.'

'Really? It isn't that difficult, you know. Do your parents cook?'

'Not really. My dad can do basic stuff, but my mum died when I was seven, and from what my dad says, she didn't like cooking much. I don't really remember her, although I do remember my friends being jealous because we used to have fish fingers and chips a lot.'

'I still like fish fingers and chips.' He smiled. 'Sorry to hear about your mum, though. Growing up without a mum is shit – mine died when I was fourteen.'

'Oh, I'm so sorry.' I could tell we were both thinking about the coincidence.

'My dad was brilliant. Well, after the first few months, anyway.' A faint lemony scent wafted up as he lifted the lid of another pan and I could see the vibrant green of the sorrel soup. 'He'd never made more than a slice of toast before then, but he threw himself into looking after us – my brother and me – trying to make up for us losing our mum. He taught himself to cook by reading books and trying stuff out. He was really good at it in the end – still is.'

'So he taught you to cook?'

'A bit, but mainly he drummed into us that anyone can do

it if they're not afraid to try. "If you can read, you can cook", he always says. He had a few disasters – one Christmas he roasted the turkey with the plastic bag of giblets still inside. We ended up having sausages instead but with all the trimmings – me and Chris thought it was the best Christmas dinner we'd ever had.'

I laughed. 'Your dad sounds great.'

We talked a bit about our families, which, it turned out, were both quite small.

We ate outside on the balcony, watching the sun sinking down behind the trees in the park. It led on to woodland, he told me, which you could follow right out into the Peak District. 'Do you like walking? Maybe we could do a walk one day, have a picnic.'

He did want another date, then. A thrill ran through me. 'That sounds nice. And I love walking.' The evening was still warm enough, but the faintest of breezes began to move through the trees, lifting my hair now and again. 'This is really, honestly the nicest meal I've had in ages,' I told him as I put my cutlery together. 'The coq au vin is the best I've ever tasted and that sorrel soup – it was *amazing*.' I lifted my glass and clinked it against his a second time. 'It's all so lovely. Thank you.'

His eyelashes flickered and he looked as if he might blush. I knew it was a weird thing to think when this was only our first date, but I was suddenly aware of a powerful desire to stay close to him. Even the thought of leaving him to go home tonight caused a huge swell of sadness in my chest. What on earth was wrong with me?

'I nearly asked you out when we were at uni, you know.'

'Seriously?' I was genuinely amazed. We hadn't even been on the same course. We took a couple of the same modules and we had some friends in common, but we barely spoke. 'I didn't think you even noticed me.'

'Of course I noticed you.' The corners of his mouth twitched. 'Everybody did – you had very short, stripy hair, for Christ's sake. Pink and blue, if I remember.'

'Oh my God, don't remind me – what was I thinking of?'

'Were you making some feminist point about gender stereotyping? Or sexual ambiguity, perhaps?'

For a moment I was tempted to try and sound clever and cool and pretend that was it, but then I covered my face with my hands and mumbled through my fingers. 'No, I just wanted to be different, and I liked the colours.'

He laughed.

I took my hands away. 'Is that why you didn't ask me out?'

'No, I didn't ask you out because I thought you and that Danny bloke were an item.'

'Danny? You're joking!'

'I saw you jogging along by the canal with him a few times, and the two of you always arrived places together and left at the same time, so—'

'No, Danny and me? Never in a million years. He was one of my housemates, that's all. Nice guy, but—'

'I know that now, but by the time I got round to asking anyone what the deal with you and Danny was, you were going out with that guy with the ponytail.'

I could hardly believe this – he'd actually bothered to ask someone about me. I thought back to the few times our eyes had met in a seminar or across a crowded pub. How I'd looked away quickly, certain he wouldn't be interested.

'What was his name?' He frowned. 'Mike?'

'Mark.'

'Mark. That's right. So I take it that didn't work out in the end?'

'No, not once we left uni. He went back to Bristol, and I moved here to do my master's.' I shrugged. 'It wasn't serious. How about you? Weren't you seeing that girl on your course? Really tall girl with long red hair?'

'Ginny. Yeah, for a while. Same thing, really – it wasn't serious.'

I wanted to say *good*, but I stopped myself. I sipped my wine and gazed out across the park, over the rooftops and out to the hills and moorland in the distance. 'It's lovely here,' I said eventually. 'Gorgeous view. And peaceful now the traffic's stopped – all I can hear is birdsong and the river.'

He nodded, took a languid swallow of his wine and looked around.

'I love the—' I said, at the same time as he said, 'It's great to—'

We laughed.

'You first,' he said.

'Okay. I was just going to say how much I love hearing the birds in the evening. They sound slower and sleepier than in the morning. Even the crows sound as if they're just cawing goodnight to each other.' I lowered my eyes. God, that sounded so childish. He'll think I'm a total moron. 'What were you going to say?'

'Funnily enough, I was just going to say how much I like waking up to the sound of the river. And the birds, of course. The first thing I hear after the alarm is the dawn chorus and the water running along down there beneath the window. It's even better at the weekends when there are hardly any cars.'

'That must be so nice – my flat's opposite an auto repair centre, so the noises I wake up to aren't quite so charming, even on Saturdays – in fact, I think that's their busiest day.'

He didn't say anything, but the silence felt like it was about to burst – a definite pregnant pause. Was I imagining the sexual tension?

'Saturdays,' he said slowly. 'That's what you're likely to wake up to tomorrow morning, is it?'

I nodded, unable to speak. Were we each thinking about the other lying in bed, naked? I took another sip of my wine. Could he hear my heart thudding? I wanted to look at him, but if I did, he'd see exactly what was going through my mind. I never usually slept with anyone on the first date, but this was different, wasn't it? I could feel him looking at me. What should I do? What should I—

'So,' he said, and there was something so sexy about the way he uttered that tiny word, I felt absolutely certain he was going to ask me to stay the night. I turned my face towards him. He fixed my gaze and looked right into my eyes. 'Can I tempt you to some shop-bought chocolate tart?'

'Oh . . . oh yes, yes please,' I spoke quickly, too loudly and far too brightly. Then, in my hurry to take another sip of wine to cover my embarrassment, I knocked the glass and it rocked sideways before I managed to grab it, but not before I'd slopped Sauvignon Blanc all over the table. 'Oh God, sorry . . .' I rummaged in my bag for tissues and to hide the shame that was burning my face.

'Don't worry about it,' he said. 'It's only a drop. Here, let me top you up.' As he filled my glass, I noticed that his hand trembled slightly.

He went into the kitchen for the tart and brought it to the table with a pot of double cream. Neither of us said much as we ate, and the sexual tension that I'd been so certain was there had evaporated – if it was ever there in the first place. The silence was not so much charged as empty. Gaping, in fact. And I couldn't think of a single bloody thing to say.

'Coffee?' He didn't meet my eye this time. He was bored. Shit. I was boring him. Or maybe I'd scared him off; maybe it was written all over my face.

'I'd love some. Thanks.' I cringed at how formal I sounded, how polite.

He went back inside to make the coffee while I stacked the dessert plates, then carried them and the remainder of the chocolate tart in through the French doors. 'Shall I put this in the fridge?'

'Oh, yes please, thanks. The box is on the side there.'

I glanced at him as I slid the tart back in its box. He seemed anxious and he kept running his hand through his hair, making it stick up at the crown. For an awful moment I thought he was going to say something to end the date, or at least to make it clear there wouldn't be another. This was crazy; I'd only really got to know him over the last few hours, and now I couldn't bear the thought of life without him.

'Leah,' he said, and as I braced myself for the brush-off, I realised he was reaching for me, and the next thing I knew we had our arms around each other – me still holding the chocolate tart behind his back – and we were kissing and kissing and kissing. 'Stay,' he murmured when we eventually pulled apart. 'Don't go home tonight.'

CHAPTER THREE

Now

Shit. I forgot to turn Adrian's alarm off last night. I stretch across the cold expanse of empty bed and hit the button. When he's away, I'd rather sleep late so I'm less aware of him not being here. I miss the sounds of him getting ready for work in the mornings – I like hearing him shave in the bathroom, whistling in the shower, Radio Sheffield on in the kitchen while he makes his scrambled eggs. I ease myself out of bed, but my back feels a bit better today. I shower and dress, grab my stick just in case and make my way down to the kitchen. I switch on the coffee machine and throw the last two slices of bread into the toaster. We're low on butter, too, and milk, so as soon as I've eaten I grab my coat and my keys. It's chilly today, and though it's not actually raining, there's the sort of drizzle that you barely notice until you realise you're actually quite wet.

Our local convenience store is pretty good for the bits you need between online shops, and I grab milk, butter, feta cheese, cherry tomatoes, a loaf of wholemeal and a bottle of Cabernet Sauvignon. There's only one checkout open today, and my heart sinks when I see who's operating it. Surely the woman should have retired by now? But maybe she isn't as old as she looks. Her hair, which this time is an improbable blue-black, is fiercely permed and rigid as a helmet. She smiles at each customer and her puffy chin wobbles as she comments on the weather, or on what the customer is buying, or about the rumoured introduction of self-service checkouts which, apparently, will put everyone out of work and is *the thin end of the wedge* and *a slippery slope*. Personally, I can't wait. I watch her numerous gold rings flashing on her pudgy fingers as she scans the barcodes and helps to pack items into carrier bags. When I get to the front of the queue, she says, 'Morning, duck,' automatically before looking up and meeting my eye. I see the recognition and distaste fluttering across her features simultaneously.

'And forty Marlboro Lights, please.'

Her blatant scorn sharpens my embarrassment at the public acknowledgement of my addiction. She slides open the door to the tobacco cupboard, takes two packs of cigarettes from the shelf and tosses them onto the counter.

'Thank you,' I murmur as she scans the contents of my basket, banging each item down on the counter with unnecessary speed, including the wine bottle, which she sets down hard enough for it to make an alarming sound but not quite hard enough to break. Then she sweeps the basket off the counter and throws it clumsily but with infuriating accuracy onto the stack next to her. 'Thirty-three twenty-eight.' She holds her hand out while looking over my left shoulder at the next person in the queue.

I'm struggling to pack everything into the canvas bag I've brought with me, but when I ask if I can buy another for five pence, she tuts pointedly before tearing one of the flimsy bags off the roll and dropping it in front of me.

'Thanks.' I delve into my bag for my purse, realising I didn't check that I had it with me. *Please let it be here.* I can feel sweat starting to prickle my underarms as she sighs and drums her fingers on the edge of the till. I hook my stick on the counter so I can search with both hands, but it immediately slips and clatters to the floor. *Shit!* An elderly man stoops to pick it up for me. 'Thank you so much.' I return his smile but, aware of the assistant's stony expression and intimidating outstretched hand, I carry on searching in my bag. I still need to finish packing, too. Ah! My hand closes around my purse – thank God. When I hold out my debit card, she sighs theatrically and nods towards the chip and pin reader. 'Put your card into the machine, please.' Her voice is cold and hard.

'Oh, okay. Sorry.' I decided ages ago that the best way to deal with hostility is to ignore it, stay polite and remember it could be worse. A memory flashes into my head: waiting in the chemist's for my prescription soon after I came out of hospital, the pharmacist calling my name, and then as I reached for the bag of medication, someone grabbing my wrist. Startled, I turned round to see a blonde woman of about my age with a tattoo on her neck, pursing her lips. I honestly had no idea what was happening until the woman's spit landed on my chin. Then she turned and wheeled her pram away while I stood there, wiping my chin with the sleeve of my jacket. A shudder of revulsion passes through me.

As I lean over to slide my card into the slot, the half-filled carrier bag that's hanging open over my arm catches the wine bottle and knocks it to the ground. It smashes spectacularly, splashing red wine over my boots and sending a puddle spreading across the shop floor. 'I'm so sorry,' I say to the checkout woman, who is now shaking her head as she rings the bell. The customer behind me is bending down, wiping red wine off her very new-looking Hunter wellies with a wad of tissues. 'Oh no, did I get you, too? I'm really sorry.'

'It's okay,' the woman mutters, 'no harm done.' But she can't hide her irritation.

I stoop to start picking up the jagged bits of glass that are sticking up like sharks in the sea of wine. 'Just leave it,' the assistant snaps. She rings the bell again, calls loudly for everyone to move down to the next till and then, still without making eye contact, says, 'Enter your pin number, please.'

I shouldn't let her get to me, but my hands are visibly shaking as I tap in the numbers.

CHAPTER FOUR

Now

Maybe even just a bit further into Sheffield, I think as I type *Rightmove* into the search bar, nearer the city centre where people are busy, where they have other things to get on with and are less interested in the lives of their neighbours. Or maybe it should be somewhere completely different, like London. That's about as anonymous as you can get, isn't it? I'm not sure what we'd be able to afford down there, but it wouldn't be much. Maybe the coast would be an option – we both love the seaside. I click 'Property for Sale' and type in *Brighton*. There are some lovely houses there, places we could definitely afford. But after twenty minutes or so of looking at dream houses by the sea, I sigh, close all the windows on my screen and shut down the computer. The truth is, I don't really want to move. In spite of everything, I still love this house. Yes, it holds memories I'd rather escape, and the idea of living somewhere where no one knows what happened is appealing, but there are good memories here, too, memories I don't want to leave behind. Adrian hasn't mentioned it for a bit, but I know he'd be happy to move away. Maybe I'll want to go somewhere else eventually – I'd love to do something to make him happy after everything I've put him through, but it doesn't feel right, not yet, anyway.

While Adrian's away, I focus on making sure I'm as prepared as I can be for the lectures and seminars that are coming up in the next few weeks. I'm so absorbed in what I'm doing that time passes quickly, but although it's been okay here on my own, I'm glad when Thursday comes around. I'll make something nice for dinner, stick a bottle of Sauvignon Blanc in the fridge. He'll want to tell me all about the conference when he gets back. I love the way he stores up little things to share with me, bits of the conference he knows I'll be interested in, or funny stuff people have said.

I spend the morning straightening pictures and plumping cushions, then I go outside and cut the last of the sweet peas, some lavender and a few Michaelmas daisies. I like to make the house look nice for when he gets back. Upstairs, I vacuum the bedroom, make the bed and straighten the rug, then I vacuum the landing and the study. We don't use the other rooms any more, so there's nothing else to do up here, but instead of going straight back downstairs, I hesitate by the door that leads to the attic. I like to go up there sometimes to look through the boxes. Adrian thinks I'm torturing myself, but it isn't like that.

I'm just making a cheese sandwich when Adrian calls. I'm surprised, because he'll be home tonight.

'Leah, sorry, I forgot to tell you last night – I won't be late, but I won't be home in time for dinner. I'm going for a quick drink with Richard and some of the other delegates.'

'Oh, okay.' I try not to sound disappointed; after all, he hardly ever goes out without me. 'So what time do you think you'll be back? Shall I pick you up from the station? If you're going to the pub . . .'

'No, no need for you to come out. I'll probably only have one. It'll be nine-ish, I should think. No later than nine thirty, anyway. In time for a glass of wine with you.'

There's a softness in his voice, and I'm suddenly aware of how much I've been looking forward to this evening, to us having a nice dinner together, sharing a bottle of wine and chatting about the last few days. But why shouldn't he go out for a drink with his colleagues for once? 'Look, don't rush back. I honestly don't mind picking you up. Have a few drinks and—'

'No, don't worry. It's horrible out – damp and foggy, and it's getting worse by the hour. You stay inside. If I have any more than one or two, I'll get a taxi and pick the car up tomorrow. Okay?'

'Okay.'

There's a pause. 'Sure you don't mind?'

I *do* mind, but I don't want to mind. I hate that my life has shrunk to something so small and insignificant that I'm in real danger of becoming one of those women who depend on their partners for everything, even their own identities. It's one of the reasons I'm determined to start proper teaching again. It would be easy just to stay home and rely on Adrian, but I can't let myself do that any longer; I'd be letting him down, apart from anything else. I take a breath. 'No, of course not.' I force a smile, hoping it'll seep through into my voice. 'Have a nice time, and I'll see you when you get back.'

'Great,' he says. 'See you later.' There's a pause. 'Leah?'

'Yes?'

'Love you.'

We don't automatically end every phone call with those words like some couples, so it feels like it really means something. 'Thank you,' I say. 'I love you, too.'

I need to pop out for a few bits before Adrian gets home but I can't face the convenience store, so I decide to drive a bit further to the Tesco Express. The dashboard clock says it's a quarter past two when I get in the car, so I won't have to worry about the school traffic. Adrian was right about the weather – it's horrible. It's cold and drizzly, and what was just a mist this morning is thickening into proper fog now. I put the headlights on full and follow the golden beams that cut through the whiteness, driving carefully at little more than twenty miles an hour. When I see the Tesco sign, I swing into the car park. The staff here are mainly students.

I recognise the boy with the dyed black hair and eyebrow rings who does his usual flirtatious thing of asking me for ID before he scans my bottle of wine, then grins and blushes. If only this was in walking distance, I'd never have to go to the local shop again. I drive back slowly through the fog. The sky has clouded over and it's starting to feel quite gloomy. It's only a couple of weeks before the clocks go back, I realise. I don't mind the lead up to Christmas as the nights draw in, but I can't bear the prolonged darkness that makes winter feel endless. As I turn into the drive, I spot a police car parked on the road outside. That's unusual around here. I wonder what's going on?

CHAPTER FIVE

Then

I wasn't sure I'd heard him properly. 'Sorry?'

We were lying in bed at his flat having spent a whole wonderful week together, lazing around in the sunshine, going for walks along the river, drinking pints in pub gardens and having sex in the afternoons. He didn't start his new job until September, but I was due back to work today, although my first seminar wasn't until eleven. I didn't want to go; he didn't want me to go. I'd never pulled a sickie before, but I was sorely tempted to call in and pretend I had a stomach bug or something. I just didn't want to be away from him. We'd barely been apart this week, even going to the corner shop together every time we needed a pint of milk or a loaf of bread.

'I said, part of me wants to marry you.' His tone was deadly serious.

'Which part?' I half-laughed. It wasn't an appropriate moment for a joke, but I was so gobsmacked by what he'd just said that I didn't know how else to respond.

'Well,' he turned his head towards me on the pillow, smiling, 'definitely the bottom half. But . . .' He tapped his head. 'Up here, too. And here, obviously.' He put his hand on his heart. We'd done the *I love you*s that first night we spent together, both laughing and saying how crazy it was, and how surprising, but how completely and utterly truthful. We both felt it, and we couldn't stop saying how lucky we were. How lucky that somehow, in a world full of billions of people, we'd found each other.

'Hmm.' I pretended to think about it. 'I don't think I'm doing anything on Saturday . . .'

'Shall we do it, then?' He took my hand and pulled it across so it rested on his stomach. His skin was warm and still slightly damp with sweat.

I laughed as I turned onto my side to face him. He was still grinning, but I could see in his eyes that he was serious. 'I don't think you can get a licence in five days,' I said, 'unless you're about to drop dead.'

'How long does it take?' He lifted my hand to his lips and kissed my palm. 'Shall we go down to the town hall and find out?'

I tried to think of another funny comment, but Adrian sat up, then turned and looked at me again. 'Can you think of a single reason why we shouldn't get married? Apart from the horrible truth of my real name, of course.'

He'd been named Clive after his granddad, he told me last night, but no one really liked it and he'd always been known as Adrian. I laughed. 'If that's your only dark secret, I think I can live with it.'

'Well then? I'm serious, Leah. I can hardly believe I'm saying this, but when you think about it, is there actually any reason why not?'

I sat up, too. 'I ... no, I don't think so. But we've only known each other two weeks. Shouldn't we—'

'We've known each other for years.'

'*Technically*, yeah. But ...' Why was I saying 'but'? I loved this man; we were really, truly in love. We were the other half of each other and we knew it. 'No, you're right. But shouldn't we, I don't know, maybe find out a bit more about each other first?'

'Like what? We've talked about films, music, sport, our families. We know about each other's previous relationships – Christ, we even know how many other people we've shagged.' He ran his hand through his hair and pulled a face. 'Though I sort of wish we hadn't talked about that now.'

'Yeah, me too. Tell you what, let's not talk about our past sex lives from now on.'

'Done.' We shook hands. Then his expression became all serious again. 'Leah, maybe we should wait until we know more about each other.'

I started to feel my heart sink until I saw that little flash in his eyes that told me he was joking.

'I mean, I have absolutely no idea what your favourite colour is.'

'Blue. And I don't know your favourite food.'

'Toast.' He threw back the duvet and jumped out of bed. 'Sorted. Come on then, let's get down there now and see what the deal is. Wonder if we can arrange our wedding and still have you at work for half eleven?'

Half an hour later, we were striding hand in hand across the Peace Gardens towards the town hall. We were both smiling; we couldn't *stop* smiling. I'd had two serious relationships before. One was my first love, David. We were together for three years, then I went to uni in Manchester and he went to Exeter and that was that, really. No big rows, no drama, just a gradual fizzling out. Then there was Leo, the guy I lived with for two years before I got the post here in Sheffield. We had a good time and we rarely argued, but I don't think I ever really loved him, and when I saw him in a wine bar one night with his arm round another girl, it was almost a relief. The break-up was hard, though – we'd built a home together, and dismantling it made me sadder than I'd expected, even though I'd known all along that my life with him was temporary.

But now I was going to marry this man I'd known for two weeks, and I had no doubts. I loved him and he loved me. The sun was hot and bright and the Peace Gardens were busy. Students were lying stretched out on the grass, some reading, some just dozing. Office workers sat on walls drinking coffee, and children in swimming costumes ran in and out of the water fountains, squealing with delight as frothy jets of water shot up out of the ground.

I stopped walking and put my hand on Adrian's arm. There was one thing we hadn't discussed, and as I thought about it, my insides felt cold and the euphoria began to evaporate. 'Adrian,' I looked over to where the mums with prams and buggies were clustered around the fountains. 'We've not talked about . . . about children.'

'What about them?' he said. But then his face changed as he realised what I meant. He looked serious, worried. 'Do you want kids?'

I nodded. It was a deal-breaker. I loved him, I knew that absolutely, and I wanted to spend the rest of my life with him. But I also wanted to be a mother, and if he—

'Good,' he said. 'I always assumed I'd have kids. We'll start with four or five and then see how we feel about more.' He glanced at me and laughed. 'Your face! Maybe just one or two, then? How does that sound?'

'Perfect,' I said. 'Maybe even three.'

CHAPTER SIX

Now

I'm putting the wine in the fridge, still in my coat, when the doorbell rings. The image of that police car flashes across my mind. I grab my stick from the kitchen because even though I don't really need it today, I like the feeling of security it gives me. I feel vulnerable without it, like when you forget your phone. As I go to open the door, I think back over the journey I've just done to the Tesco Express and back. I couldn't have hit something without realising it, could I? I'm sure I didn't, but it *is* quite foggy, and this did happen once before. I'd pulled over too sharply to let a van pass and I'd hit a parked car. I genuinely couldn't see any damage and I thought I must have just bumped the mirror. Then later that evening, the police came round saying I'd 'failed to report an accident'. Fortunately they believed me when I explained, so I paid for the repair and it was all fine. But I'm sure nothing like that happened today.

There are two police officers on the doorstep, a man and a woman, both a bit younger than me, late twenties, early thirties perhaps. The woman is slim, not very tall, but the male officer is big and bulky, and his uniform looks too tight, as if he's struggled to button it over his bulging middle.

'Mrs Blackwood?'

Some dark fear blows through me at the sound of his voice. I try to nod, but find myself unable to move.

The woman speaks now. 'I'm PC Lindsay Jacobs,' she says, 'and this is PC Andy Davies. May we come in?'

Why are they telling me their names? Why do they want to come in? *What's happened?* I stand back and hold the door open. They both remove their hats and wipe their feet on the mat. My stomach feels as if it's filling up with iced water as I show them in and invite them to sit down. PC Davies puts his hat on the arm of the sofa, whereas the woman is turning hers round and round in her fingers. I sit in the armchair opposite. 'Nasty weather, isn't it?' I can hear the oddness in my voice. 'Can I get you some tea? Or a coffee?' Some distant part of me reasons that the more I talk now, the longer I can delay hearing what they have to say. The male officer clears his throat. 'I'm sorry to have to tell you there's been a road traffic accident involving a Mr Clive Adrian Blackwood. Is that your husband?'

'No.' I shake my head. 'Sorry, I mean, yes, Adrian is my husband. He doesn't use Clive – he's always hated it. But, no, it can't be my husband – Adrian left his car at the station. He's at a conference in Leeds.'

The officers glance at each other.

'I only spoke to him an hour ago. He's there all day, then he's going for a drink with some of the others.' Aware that I'm talking to the police, I add, 'He'll probably only have one, then he'll get the train back. And if he has any more than that, he'll leave his car at the station and get a taxi home, or I'll go down and pick him up. He—'

'Mrs Blackwood,' the woman interrupts. 'Mrs Blackwood, your husband was carrying his driving licence. The accident was on the A621, just outside Castledene.'

'No, Adrian wouldn't have been anywhere near Castledene, even if he *was* in the car, which, as I say, he isn't, because he left it at the station – or near the station. So that's where he'd be coming from. It can't be him.'

PC Davies sighs as he flips open his notebook, reads out the registration number, then glances up at me. 'Black BMW. Do you recognise the registration, Mrs Blackwood?'

I have a powerful sensation of something shifting away from me, of any semblance of normality moving out of my grasp as I realise that it *is* Adrian they're talking about, that somehow he's been involved in an accident. *Please don't let it be too bad*, I think, although it must be quite serious or the police wouldn't be here. I stand up, ready to look for my car keys. 'Where is he? I need to get there.' Or maybe they'll take me to the hospital in a police car. 'Is he badly hurt? Was anyone else injured . . . ?'

'Your husband was alone in the car, Mrs Blackwood. Or can we call you . . . ?'

'Leah, yes, please call me Leah.'

'Thank you, Leah. There was no other vehicle involved, and it looks as if your husband's car skidded in the fog, left the road and crashed into a tree. Visibility was poor, and driving conditions—'

I nod. 'Yes, he said it was getting thicker when we spoke on the phone. Where is he now? I know he must be hurt, but can you just tell me how badly? I need to know.'

'Maybe you should sit down again, Leah,' PC Jacobs says, standing up and crossing the room. She takes my arm and gently steers me back towards the chair. 'And if you can point Andy to the kitchen, he can make us all a cup of tea.'

Somehow, the evening passes and it's almost two in the morning. I keep thinking they must be wrong, it must be a mistake. But if it wasn't him in that car, who was it, and where is Adrian? I indulge myself with possible explanations – he changed his mind and took the car after all; was taken ill and decided to stay in Leeds; sent me a text that wasn't delivered; lent the car to a colleague . . .

But deep down, I know.

I get into bed without undressing, and I just lie there, staring at the ceiling. After about an hour, I go back downstairs and sit in the kitchen, smoking. They're sending a car for me at eight thirty. As soon as it's light, I go up to shower and brush my teeth. I shouldn't have sat still for so long – my back is killing me. But even after I've showered and dressed in clean clothes, it's still only just gone eight.

I smoke three more cigarettes as I wait for the car. It makes me feel a bit sick, but smoking is about all I'm capable of at the moment. The doorbell rings on the dot of eight thirty, and for a few seconds I can't make myself move. If I don't formally identify him, he can't be dead. But then the bell goes again, longer this time, louder, so I drag myself upright and walk slowly across the hall to open the door.

As the soft-voiced policewoman leads me into the room, I realise that there's still a small part of me that is convinced it won't be Adrian's face under that sheet, but some other poor man whose car skidded off the road in the fog. Then they turn the sheet back. It's a cliché, I know, but he doesn't look dead. Slightly paler than usual, maybe, but his features are undamaged and there's no blood on his face, no horrible mangling of his limbs. It's only when I lean down to kiss him that I see the dark mass of blood-matted hair at the side of his head. I hear myself gasp and my fist flies to my mouth. The policewoman makes soothing noises and gently rubs my back.

A few minutes later I'm sitting in a small, carpeted room with a cup of tea on the coffee table in front of me. The policewoman is sitting opposite, her face settled in a sympathetic expression. This one is older than me, I think. There are wrinkles around her eyes and she looks tired, and I wonder how many times she's had to do this in her career.

She's put a box of tissues within easy reach, I notice, but I can't seem to cry, even though I want to. 'Is there anyone who can come and be with you, Leah? Anyone you'd like me to call?'

'No, there isn't anyone, really.'

'Not your mum or dad?'

I shake my head. 'My mum died when I was a kid and I lost my dad a couple of years ago.'

'I'm sorry,' she says. 'Do you not have—'

'Paul! Oh God,' I say aloud. 'Adrian's dad. I'll have to call him.'

'We can do that for you, if you like.'

I hesitate. 'No, it's okay, but thanks.' And there's his brother, Chris, and Richard, his oldest friend, and I'll need to call his colleagues . . . a wave of sadness engulfs me and I almost reach for a tissue, but I still can't let go of the tears.

CHAPTER SEVEN

Then

The day after we booked the wedding, we went to meet his dad. My dad was away on a painting holiday, so we couldn't tell him until the weekend anyway. I was so nervous, I hadn't been able to eat a thing all day and my stomach had rumbled throughout two seminars and four tutorials, to the amusement of my students.

The house was lovely. It was in a little crescent in Nether Edge, set back from the road with a long, sweeping drive and surrounded by a pretty walled garden. Adrian had already told me his dad was sixty-five and had taken early retirement a few years ago. He'd taught history and politics, but now spent his time painting, playing guitar and walking in the Peaks. He was also learning jazz dance, apparently. He sounded fun.

'Is that your dad's car?' I asked as we pulled up next to a

low, sporty-looking red car parked right outside the house.

He turned off the engine. 'Yes. It's new – I think he's trying to pull some woman at his dance class and he thought that would impress her.'

I checked my appearance in the rear-view mirror, tugging at a few wayward strands of hair.

'You look great,' he said, opening the car door. 'Come on. Let's go and give him the shock of his life.'

'Adrian,' I said as we walked up to the front door. 'He is expecting us, isn't he?'

He shook his head. 'Nope. It's a surprise.'

'Oh no, really? Is that a good idea? Don't you think you should call him first?'

'No, it'll be fine.' He rang the bell. 'He likes me just turning up. I never use my key without asking him, though – I don't want to walk in and find him in flagrante delicto.'

The door opened to reveal a tall, good-looking man with a shock of white hair, wearing a loose flowery shirt over faded green cords. Unmistakably Adrian's father – the features were identical. He looked from Adrian to me and back again. 'Well, well,' he said. 'This is a nice surprise, I must say.' He shook my hand warmly. 'And whom do we have here?'

'This is Leah, Dad. Leah, my dad – Paul.'

'Lovely to meet you, Mr—'

'*Paul*, please.' He smiled. 'It's a pleasure to meet you, Leah.' He turned to Adrian and did that half-hug, half-handshake thing that men do.

'Leah Moore, soon to be Leah Blackwood.'

His dad's eyes widened and his grin spread across his face. 'You're engaged?' He looked from one to the other of us again. 'Now, you're not teasing, are you?'

'Nope. As of yesterday morning, Leah is officially my fiancée.'

Fiancée. I hadn't thought of us as *engaged*, but I supposed we were. I tried it out in my head: *This is Adrian, my fiancé.*

'In that case, congratulations!' He patted Adrian's back. 'This is wonderful news. Come in, Leah, come in.' He guided me into the house. 'Adrian – see if there's a bottle of something nice we can crack open, would you?'

I could feel myself smile, becoming more relaxed. His dad was lovely – why had I been nervous?

'So, how did you two meet?' He gestured to a chair.

I sat opposite him and explained how Adrian and I had been at Manchester at the same time, and how we'd met up again at Lucy's wedding and had become close since then. Adrian came back with champagne in an ice bucket, but no one minded that it wasn't properly chilled, so his dad opened it and poured us all a glass. We stood in the middle of the room as Paul cleared his throat and raised his glass. 'Here's to the two of you,' he said. 'And to a long and happy life together.' We all took a sip and then sat down.

'Now, have you thought about where and when? If you're thinking of next year, you'll need to get your skates on from what I hear.'

I glanced at Adrian. He was swirling his champagne

around in his glass, a smile pulling at the corners of his mouth.

'Christopher and Judy,' his dad continued, then turned to me. 'Have you met Adrian's brother and his wife?'

'Not yet, no.'

'They married a little over a year ago, and if memory serves, they had to book almost two years in advance. Mind you, they had the ceremony at Kew Gardens, so it was quite—' He stopped and looked at Adrian. 'What is it?' he said. 'I know that expression. You don't want to get married in a bloody football ground or something, do you?' He turned to me. 'Leah, I hope you'll be a civilising influence on this boy of mine.'

At which point Adrian couldn't contain himself any longer. 'We've not only thought about the time and place, we've arranged it already. All booked up, deposit paid.'

His dad looked stunned for a moment, but then he took a mouthful of champagne and nodded. 'Well, good for you. I suppose you've considered all the options.'

'Yes,' Adrian said. 'We've considered all the options, waiting, not waiting—' He caught my eye and I willed him to just say it. He must have read my expression, because then he said, 'Sorry, I *am* teasing you a bit now. Thing is, we don't want to wait a second longer than we have to, so we're getting married in four weeks' time.'

His dad spluttered, spilling champagne all down his shirt. Then he had a coughing fit. It would have been funny if it was some sitcom on the telly, but it wasn't funny at all.

Adrian let go of my hand and we both jumped to our feet. 'Are you all right, Dad? Shall I get you some water?'

'Let's just get some – where's the kitchen?'

'It's okay, I'll get it.' Adrian hurried out of the room and I stood there, feeling awkward. I went over to Paul and put my hand on his back, wondering if I should thump him between the shoulder blades, but it wasn't as though something was stuck in his throat, so I just patted his back gently. By the time Adrian came back, the coughing had begun to subside, but Paul was very red in the face as he sipped the water. 'Gosh.' He thumped his chest with his hand a couple of times. 'Must have gone down the wrong way.'

'Are you okay now?' I leaned forward. 'We didn't mean to give you such a shock.' I hoped he'd make light of it, laugh even. He nodded, touched my hand briefly in acknowledgement, then excused himself and went upstairs to change his shirt.

'That went well.' I slumped back in my chair.

'Don't worry.' Adrian reached for the champagne and topped up our glasses. 'He just needs some time to digest it, that's all.' He sounded so confident that I relaxed again. Paul came back a few minutes later in a fresh shirt, but when he sat down he didn't pick up his replenished glass, nor was he smiling.

'I thought you said you only met again at this wedding recently?'

'That's right,' I said. 'It turns out we have quite a few friends in common.'

'Yes,' Adrian chipped in. 'It's surprising we haven't bumped into each other before, really.'

'But this was just two or three weeks ago, wasn't it?'

We both nodded.

His dad picked up his glass then and took a sip. 'And you've arranged a wedding for four weeks from now?'

'Yes, four weeks today.' Adrian's voice had lost its light, everything's-going-to-be-brilliant tone. 'I know it's a bit quick—'

'A bit quick?' His dad was looking only at Adrian now. 'That is an understatement. So you will have known each other for a total of what, six weeks? Seven?' He held up his hand to stop Adrian interrupting. 'You're going to argue that you met at university, but you know damn well that's not relevant. The fact of the matter is that you have only really known each other for a few weeks.' He took a swig of his champagne and plonked the glass back down, then ran his hand through his hair in exactly the same way Adrian did. 'Look,' he sighed, then leaned forward, arms resting on his knees and hands clasped together. 'Adrian, Leah, I don't want either of you to think that I have any objection to you marrying – I'm delighted, in fact. But this . . . this *haste*. Surely you can see why I'm concerned?'

'Yes, of course I can,' Adrian said. 'But we've thought about it a lot—'

We'd only had the idea yesterday! He caught my eye and I knew he was thinking the same thing.

'And we just can't think of a reason why not.'

'Why don't you move in together, see how things—'

'Dad, trust me, okay? We're not teenagers, we don't want to "see how it goes". We want to make a proper, public commitment.'

His dad sighed. 'I wish your mum was still alive. I wonder what she'd have thought?' He turned to me. 'What do your parents think, Leah?'

I explained that it was just my dad and that he was away this week, but that I was sure he'd be pleased once he understood how we felt. I mentally crossed my fingers as I said this.

Paul sat up straight again. 'You're grown adults, both of you, and of course you must make your own decisions. But would you do one thing for me, Adrian?'

'Probably – depends.'

'Talk to your grandma. She's a wise woman, and she's always been remarkably astute when it comes to knowing what's best for you and Christopher.'

'Of course,' Adrian said. 'I'll call Chris later, too.'

'Good.' Paul nodded. 'Good.' He turned to me. 'I hope you don't think I'm not pleased for you both, Leah, because I am, but—'

'I understand,' I assured him. 'My dad still worries about me, too.'

He smiled, a little sadly. 'I'd probably worry less if my wife were still around to share these concerns. I'm sure your father feels the same.'

I felt flat as we got back into the car, despite the fact that his dad had genuinely seemed to like me. He clearly thought we were out of our minds to be getting married so early in our relationship, and he probably wouldn't be the only one. We'd been so caught up in the excitement and romance of what we were doing, we hadn't really considered that other people wouldn't be as ecstatic about it as we were. For the first time I felt a pinprick of doubt. Not about Adrian – I had no doubts about being with him – but maybe we *should* wait a while. On the other hand, we were in love, we were inseparable – I already resented every moment we spent apart.

I could feel Adrian looking at me as he started the engine.

'Leah, what is it? You're not going to let my dad's reaction bother you, are you?'

I turned to face him. 'We're not being stupid and we just can't see it, are we?' The moment I said it, I wished I hadn't – what if he said yes, perhaps we are being stupid?

'Oh, Leah.' He took my hand. 'Is that what you think? No one can be certain what's going to happen in the future, but being together for years before you get married doesn't stop things going wrong, does it? My cousin Emily – the one I told you about who's just got divorced? They lived together for four and a half years, had a big fancy church wedding that cost a fortune and now, two years down the line, they can't stand the sight of each other.' He leaned over and kissed me softly. 'I'm prepared to risk it if you are. I *want* to risk it.'

'It doesn't sound stupid at all when you put it like that.'

'I honestly don't think it is. I suppose no one ever knows for sure, do they? Marriage doesn't come with a guarantee. All I know is, I want to be with you.'

'I want be with you, too.' One thing I knew for sure was that I wouldn't be happy at all if we weren't together, and I also knew my feelings wouldn't change in the foreseeable future. So why wait?

He smiled again now. 'Not stupid,' he said. Another kiss, a peck this time. 'Clever!'

I laughed. Everything was upbeat again. He turned the music on and we set off.

'Right,' he said, his tone as cheery as it had been earlier. 'Let's go and tell my granny.'

CHAPTER EIGHT

Now

I go through the motions in a daze. When Diane next door touches me lightly on the arm and mutters how sorry she is, I'm so surprised that all I can do is nod. She doesn't linger, though. I carry on moving around the room thanking people for coming, accepting condolences and handing round the plates of sandwiches that Judy, my sister-in-law, spent all morning making. It seems slightly absurd that people are standing here eating sandwiches when my husband has just died, and for a split second I have an urge to throw the plate at the wall. I still can't quite take it in. I pour myself a whisky and drink it neat, in two swallows. The fiery hit is instantly soothing and it occurs to me now, as it has in the past, how easy it would be to abandon myself to alcohol.

Not everyone who was at the crematorium has come back to the house, but more than I expected. Adrian's dad is sitting on a hard chair in the corner, red-eyed and somehow smaller. He's wearing a white shirt and black tie, and the same charcoal-coloured suit he wore to my dad's funeral, but it swamps him now. His woman-friend, Helen – Adrian told me off for calling her his girlfriend – had planned to come with him, but her daughter went into labour this morning and she's had to go and pick up the older children from school. Helen is fairly new on the scene, but already Paul looks lost without her. 'Paul.' I pull up a chair so I can sit next to him. 'How are you doing?'

He shakes his head and sighs, then reaches into his pocket, pulls out a huge white handkerchief and wipes his eyes. 'Never mind me,' he says. His voice is hoarse and I suspect he's been crying. 'It's you I'm worried about.' He places his age-spotted hand over mine and I nod in acknowledgement. I can feel my own tears brimming, but they won't quite spill over. We sit like that for a few minutes, watching Judy and Chris topping up drinks and bringing in trays of tea. They've been brilliant. I don't know how I'd have coped without them.

Reluctantly, I leave Paul so I can carry on circulating, making sure I've thanked everyone, though I have to keep slipping outside to smoke a cigarette. I can't get through this otherwise. There aren't that many neighbours here, although I put notes through several doors. Diane appears to have gone home already, but I feel disproportionately grateful that she came and that she actually spoke to me. She's barely been able to look at me these last few years, and I miss her friendship.

I just wish I'd said something in return instead of staring at her like an idiot. Most of the people here are Adrian's friends and colleagues, and it's clear that some of them prefer to share their memories of him with each other rather than with me. There are a few unfamiliar faces who are happy enough to talk to me, though, and as I listen to the glowing tributes, I'm touched by the genuine warmth that people clearly feel for him. I'm not surprised, of course, but I have to keep reminding myself that I can't tell him about it later.

'Leah, I'm so sorry.' Richard Clarke, Adrian's long-term friend and colleague. 'I don't know what to say. I still can't believe it.'

'Me neither.'

He puts his hand on my arm. 'How are you? Are you coping?'

'I'm not sure I've really taken it in yet. I still feel numb. I've been hoping today would . . . you know.'

He nods. 'That's what funerals are for, isn't it? Let's hope that once this is over, you can start to . . .' He looks at me. 'Christ, as if you haven't been through enough.'

I can feel my eyes filling with tears. Sometimes, hostility is easier to deal with than kindness, but Richard has always been kind. Adrian said it was Richard who held him together during the time I was in hospital. And then later, after I came home from the unit, he was there for both of us, cooking meals, taking us out for days in the country or by the sea, showing us it was possible to carry on, letting us see that we still had each other.

'Leah, I hope you don't mind me asking – tell me to sod off and mind my own business – but do you have . . . well.' He shifts to the other foot, looking uncomfortable. 'The support to get you through this?'

'Don't worry, Richard. I'm still taking the tablets.'

'Sorry, I didn't mean to pry.'

'It's fine, really. I'm not offended. My GP's very good. I've got sleeping tablets if I need them, and a number to call about bereavement counselling.'

He nods and then sighs. 'I know it's a cliché, but I mean this: if there's anything I can do, just shout, okay? I mean . . .' He shakes his head. 'This is so fucked up. Anything at all, Leah. Promise me you'll let me know.'

'Thanks, Rich, I appreciate that.' I hesitate. 'Actually, there is one thing. You were at the Leeds conference, weren't you?'

He nods. 'He talked about you, you know, when we went for a drink.'

'Did he?' I feel a flush of warmth in my chest. 'What did he say?'

'Oh, just how pleased he is that – shit, sorry. I still can't get used to talking about him in the past tense. He was saying how pleased he was about you getting back into teaching, how he thought it was the right thing to do. He worried about you, you know.'

'I know.' My eyes swim again as I remember how he'd often call me from work, even in the middle of a day packed with meetings, or when he was trying to finish a paper.

And his gentle hints about things that might help me make new friends or reconnect with old ones. I dab at my eyes. 'Richard, come out here for a minute, will you?' I lead the way out into the hall, away from everyone else. 'Look, I don't want to put you in an awkward position or anything, but do you know where Adrian was going when he had the accident?'

Richard appears surprised. 'He was on his way home, wasn't he?'

'No, that's the point. He was on the A621, halfway between Castledene and Baslow.'

He looks blank, and I remember he doesn't know the area. 'Thing is, there was no reason at all for him to be on that road, or near those villages.'

'Maybe he took the long way round, to avoid traffic.'

I shake my head. 'No. And it's not just that.' I swallow. 'He lied to me.' Saying it out loud for the first time makes it more real.

'What, Adrian did? What about?'

'He told me the conference finished at six and that he was going out for a drink with you and some of the others afterwards.'

It's clear from Richard's expression that this is news to him. 'Well, er—'

'But I've since found out it finished at noon.'

'There must be an explanation.' His face colours with discomfort. 'Maybe he was ... I don't know, maybe he just wanted to look at the scenery after being shut in that stuffy conference centre . . .' His voice trails off, but then he shakes his head. 'There's bound to be some reason.'

'He told me the car was at the station and he'd get a taxi home and pick it up the next day. Why would he do that?'

Richard sighs. 'I don't know. But listen, does it matter? I don't know what you think he was up to, but you know Adrian adored you. He's proved that these last few years, surely?'

There is an edge to his voice now. Could he be covering for Adrian? Maybe I'm reading too much into it.

'Leah.' His voice softens again. 'Is it really important whether he changed his mind and decided to drive after all? What matters is he's . . . he's gone.' I hear the emotion catch his voice. He clears his throat. 'Any more of that Scotch?'

I pour us both another drink and assure Richard that yes, I'll be fine financially, and yes, I'll let him know if there's anything he can do.

Back in the sitting room, a group of Adrian's colleagues are standing near the window. I spot Angela, and then John and Tony, all of whom I know were there in Leeds. I move nearer to them, gradually joining their conversation. As soon as it feels right, I ask if they remember whether Adrian had happened to mention to any of them what his plans were after the conference finished. They all say no, and they seem genuinely puzzled. 'I reckon he was planning a surprise,' Angela says. 'Do you have a birthday coming up? Some sort of anniversary?'

'No, nothing like that. Surprises aren't really an Adrian

sort of thing.' It's usually me who arranges things like that. We didn't go out at all for a couple of years, but recently we'd started having the odd meal out again, choosing a nicer restaurant for special occasions. But it was always me who booked the table. The nearest Adrian ever came to surprising me was to bring me flowers when I was feeling particularly low.

I've been standing for too long now and my back is beginning to ache quite badly. I glance at my stick tucked in the corner behind an armchair, but if I started using it now it would feel like I was waving a banner, so instead I walk slowly to the kitchen so I can take some painkillers. When I return, a few people are gathering bags and scarves and saying polite farewells. Judy is fetching coats from the hall. There's a couple standing at the door, and as the woman kisses Chris politely on the cheek while her husband kisses Judy, I realise who they are – Adrian's old schoolfriend, Rob, and his wife Alison. I didn't notice them at the crematorium. Alison hitches her bag further up her shoulder as she and Rob look around the room. I walk over, ready to apologise for not having spotted them earlier. They turn towards me, faces open and expectant. Rob takes a step forward and leans down to kiss my cheek. 'I'm so sorry, Leah,' he says. 'I don't know what to say.'

'Thank you. And thank you so much for coming – I know it's a long way.' I turn to Alison. 'I really appreciate it.'

Alison's eyes flicker and she looks away as she mutters her condolences. Then she puts her hand on her husband's arm. 'We really ought to make a move.'

Rob nods. 'Yes, we should, I suppose.' He smiles at me again. 'The M1 can be a nightmare this time of day. Anyway, nice to see you, Leah, but sorry it's in such unhappy circumstances.'

'*Rob*,' Alison says, frowning and hitching her bag up onto her shoulder again.

'Well, thanks again for coming.'

Alison gives a tight little nod and hurries out into the hall, followed by her embarrassed-looking husband.

CHAPTER NINE

Now

Judy insists on helping me load the dishwasher and tidy the sitting room before she and Chris head back to Cambridge. They offer to drive Paul home – he's had a couple of large whiskies, so he'll have to leave his car here – but I can see he isn't ready to be on his own just yet. 'Don't worry about your dad,' I tell Chris. 'I'll make up a bed for him here, or if he doesn't want to stay I'll put him in a taxi. And thanks for everything, both of you – you've been fantastic.'

After they've gone, I try to persuade Paul to stay the night. He says he prefers his own bed, but I suspect it's more that he thinks he's imposing. 'Stay for a bit longer,' I urge, sitting down next to him at the kitchen table. 'See how you feel. It'll take me two minutes to make up a bed.'

He sighs heavily and then nods. 'All right, dear. If you're sure you don't mind, I think I will stay for a while.'

'Of course I don't mind. I could do with the company.' I'm glad he's staying. I'm fond of my father-in-law. He looks exhausted. Older, too, and still slightly bewildered, as if he can't quite believe this has happened.

'Thank you.' He pats my hand and sighs again. 'You're a good girl, Leah.'

At that moment, his phone rings. His face softens as soon as he answers. I go back into the sitting room to give him some privacy, but after a minute or so he follows me in. 'I've got Helen on the phone – she's wondering if it's too late to come over. I think she wants to offer her condolences.'

'That's nice of her, and of course it's not too late, but I thought she was . . . I mean, how is everything? With her daughter?'

His gaze flickers and he breaks eye contact. 'I gather it all went smoothly. Her son-in-law and his mother are there now as well, so she's free for the time being. She said she'll drive me home later, and bring me back in the morning for the car.'

'Oh, okay. And is her daughter all right? What did she have?'

'Yes, both well.' He turns back towards the kitchen, and I only just hear him mutter, 'Little girl, I believe.'

'Tell her congratulations,' I call after him. He's trying to protect me, but he doesn't need to. It's hard for me to hear about people's new babies, but I'm used to it now. Life goes on, as they say. Even Adrian said that once.

When I open the door to Helen, she reaches out and immediately pulls me into a hug. I haven't seen her since a couple of weeks before the accident, and I'd only met her a handful of times before that. Adrian and I both liked her as soon as we met her. Her warmth is so genuine that I find myself choking up again.

'You poor, dear girl. What a terrible thing to happen. I can't tell you how sorry I am.' She holds me for a good few seconds before releasing me.

'Thank you,' I say, touched to see that there are actual tears in her eyes.

'I lost my husband six years ago, and I've never known such grief.' Then she puts her hand on my arm and squeezes. 'And you have known far too much already.' At that point, Paul comes out into the hall to greet her and I wonder how much he's told her. They embrace each other tightly, and when they pull away, they both wipe their eyes.

She's tiny, about Paul's age, maybe a bit younger, dressed in expensive-looking blue jeans and a red fitted jacket. Her salt-and-pepper hair is short and prettily styled, and her make-up and jewellery are subtle and flattering.

I congratulate Helen on her new grandchild and I ask after her daughter but, like Paul, she seems afraid of upsetting me so we quickly move on. I offer her tea or coffee or a drink. 'Tea with one sugar would be lovely,' she says. 'And maybe a teeny sherry if you have any?'

Judy was right about sherry being essential at funerals. I can't remember the last time I even drank sherry, never mind bought any, but we've gone through almost two bottles of the stuff today. I decide to have one myself, and Paul agrees we should probably slow down on the whisky, so he pours three glasses while I make the tea.

We spend the next hour or so talking about Adrian as we drink tea or sip sherry – it's sickly-sweet but oddly comforting. We don't talk about the crash, or why he was on that road, or the fact that he's gone, but about *him*. Things we remember about him; things he did or said, often funny, sometimes sweet, occasionally annoying. Like the way he couldn't stop himself from telling you the whole plot of a film or book, including the ending, even if you intended to watch it or read it yourself. There are a few stories I haven't heard, and I carefully store away the details to take out again and pore over later. I didn't know about him climbing out of his bedroom window when he was sixteen to go to a party after he'd been grounded, for example. And I didn't know he'd once gone missing during a family holiday on a farm in Devon when he was four. 'We had the police out and everything,' Paul says. 'And all the time he was fifty feet away, curled up asleep with the pigs. How the hell he wasn't crushed to death we'll never know.'

Helen sits there, smiling good-naturedly, and I wonder whether she's itching to get back to her daughter and new grandchild, but she seems content to listen to these stories about a man she barely knew.

'He was like that, though, wasn't he, Leah? If he got it in his mind to do something, he'd do it, no matter what, and the sooner the better.' He smiles and turns to Helen. 'Have I told you about the day he brought Leah to meet me?'

Helen shakes her head, and he goes on to tell her about our 'whirlwind romance', and how we'd come and told him we were getting married the following week.

'It was four weeks, actually,' I say.

He brushes the words away with his hand. 'Something like that.' He's enjoying himself now, clearly pleased by Helen's widening eyes, her obvious delight at the romance of the story. 'I told them they were potty, told them to wait a year at least. But what did I know? Turned out they were right all along.' He smiles at me, and I feel a rush of affection for him.

'Don't forget what else you advised us to do,' I add.

He looks puzzled for a moment, then his face brightens. 'Ah, yes. I told them to go and talk to his grandma – my mother. I always turned to her for advice after Audrey died. She lived nearby and she doted on the boys. A clever woman, my mother, with considerable wisdom and common sense.'

As Paul is relating the story to Helen, I let my own memory wander back to that day. Adrian had described his grandma as a 'formidable old lady', so I was extremely nervous about meeting her. I thought she'd be deeply suspicious of me, and protective of her beloved grandson. I remember perching rigidly on the edge of an armchair in her flat while she moved slowly around in her kitchen making a pot of tea and cutting slices of a home-made marmalade cake. When she came in and sat down, she looked at Adrian with a rather stern expression. 'Well now, to what do I owe this unexpected honour?'

Adrian came straight out with it. 'We're getting married in

four weeks' time and we want you to come to the wedding.' The silence rang around the room.

She looked at me, then back at Adrian, still straight-faced. 'Are you each in love with the other?' We both nodded and Adrian said, 'Yes, Grandma, we absolutely are.'

Her response was a slight inclination of the head. 'And at what point did you become aware of this deep affection?'

She hates me, I thought.

'Within about an hour,' Adrian said with a grin. He didn't seem remotely concerned at her tone, and appeared relaxed as he leaned back in his chair and stretched out his long legs.

For the first time I saw the ghost of a smile taking shape on the old lady's face as she turned to me. 'And you, young lady? Did you feel the same instant certainty about this rather reckless young man?' Her tone had changed; I wasn't entirely sure, but I thought I detected a hint of playfulness.

'Yes,' I said. 'I did, actually.' I hadn't intended that slightly defiant note, but it slipped out. To my astonishment, she put her hands together and almost squealed with delight. 'Then I shall give you my blessing. Oh, Adrian, I am *so* pleased. Is your father happy? Your mother would have been, I'm quite sure. We must celebrate. Leah, my dear, open the left-hand door of that sideboard. You'll find some sherry. Ignore the one in the green bottle, it tastes like furniture polish – cheap and nasty. We'll have that rather nice Portuguese one. Adrian, fetch some glasses.'

'See?' Adrian whispered as he walked past me to go to the kitchen. 'Told you so.'

I smile now at the memory, vaguely wondering if that was the last time I drank sherry. I can feel Paul looking at me. 'You tell her the rest,' he says.

I turn to Helen. 'Dorothea was a firm believer in love at first sight, it turned out. After she'd finished grilling us, she told me about the day she met Adrian's grandad. Apparently she was having tea with her mother at a posh hotel in London – it was her sixteenth birthday and the tea was a birthday treat – when he walked in with a couple of friends and sat at a nearby table. She said she glanced over at him because she thought he had a nice laugh, but as soon as she did so, their eyes locked and she felt an immediate connection. She leaned over to her mother and said, "See that man with the big moustache and the black umbrella? I'm going to marry him one day". And two years later, she did.'

'What a lovely story,' Helen says. Her eyes are shining and I wonder if she's remembering the husband she lost a few years ago. 'How long were they married?'

'Sixty-six years,' Paul says. 'And they were devoted to each other all their lives.' He looks thoughtful for a moment, then reaches over and pats the back of my hand. 'You and Adrian . . . it was right. I'm glad he had . . .' He swallows and shakes his head. 'Shouldn't have been cut short like this. All you went through, the two of you, but you never gave up. You got through it together.' His voice has gone hoarse again and he clears his throat to disguise it. In less than a minute, the mood in the room has changed from borderline cheery to, well, *not* cheery. I think we're all thinking the same thing – that for the last hour or so, the fact that today was Adrian's funeral has almost slipped into the background.

It's clear that we're all quite tired, and soon we move to the hallway for their coats. I thank Helen again for being here when it's such an important time for her own family. 'Oh, don't worry about that,' she says. 'I've got three daughters and seven grandchildren – oh, eight now – so a new baby isn't any big—' She stops and I see the sudden discomfort breaking out on her face. Her voice trails off. 'I mean, well, it, um . . .'

At least that answers one question: Paul must have told her about what happened. Her distress is obvious, and I feel awful for her. I give her a hug. 'I expect you must be getting used to it now.' I make a fair attempt at a smile.

She looks so grateful, I almost want to hug her again.

After they've gone, I can't settle. I keep having this odd feeling that I've forgotten something to do with the funeral. It's as if it isn't quite complete, as if there's something else that needs to happen now everyone's gone. Then I realise what it is. I'm waiting for Adrian to stop being dead. For him to come back so I can talk to him about it all, find out what he thought and ask him what we're going to do now.

CHAPTER TEN

Now

I've been avoiding going through his things. I like seeing his jackets hanging in the wardrobe and his iPod on the dressing table where he left it. But when Paul and Helen offer to help, I realise I can't put it off any longer. Paul goes out to deal with the garage and shed, while Helen follows me up to the bedroom to sort out his clothes. 'Moral support,' Helen says. 'It's tough doing a job like this on your own. How about if I take everything out of the wardrobe and lay it on the bed, then you can have a good look through? Some people seem to think it's just a matter of bagging it all up and taking it to the charity shop, but I know it's not that simple.'

'It's not, is it?' I'm relieved she understands.

'So, wardrobe first?'

I nod, and she puts her hand on my arm. 'This'll be hard.'

As I go through the pockets, it flips into my mind that I

might find some clue as to why he was out near Castledene that day. I try not to think about it – as Richard said, *what matters is, he's gone.* But the question keeps creeping back in. I'm not sure if I'm relieved or disappointed each time I find nothing but a half-pack of chewing gum or an old train ticket. I find myself checking the destinations and dates, though: Leeds, April – that was another conference; Derby, a few weeks ago – football with Richard; and there's one to Cambridge in August. That'll be the weekend he went down to help Chris lay the new terrace while Judy took the boys to Norfolk. When I've finished, I look at the things I've retrieved. There's a pencil sharpener, a couple of elastic bands, a few coins, four ballpoint pens, paperclips, a page from a memo pad with the name of a book and a publication date scrawled on it and half a packet of fruit pastilles. I pick these up and hold them for a long time. I feel my eyes filling up. I am oddly moved by the thought of him going into a shop to buy sweets like a little boy, and then popping a fruit pastille into his mouth and sucking on it while his mind wrangled with educational theory. These are the things that are hardest to throw away, the things of no consequence; things he slipped into his pockets day-to-day without even thinking.

'What about this?' Helen hands me a smallish cardboard box with a lid. I don't recognise it, but it looks like it might have once contained stationery – paper, or envelopes. 'It looks personal – cards and photographs, and so on.'

I lift the lid and am touched to see some of the cards I've

made for him over the years. I knew he'd kept one or two, but there are quite a lot here. 'Where did you find it?'

'It was at the bottom of the wardrobe, under all those pairs of trainers.'

Was this just forgotten, or had he hidden it? My heart is pounding again – could this box contain a clue as to what he was doing on that particular road that day? 'Thanks.' I replace the lid and put the box on the dressing table to take downstairs. 'I'll go through it properly later.'

We agree that Chris would probably like the CDs of bands the two of them used to be into. There are a couple of good guitars, and I remember Judy saying something about the boys having lessons. Maybe one of the boys would like the iPod, too. We take everything that's to go to Chris and Judy's downstairs, and I pack it all in a box in the hall for Paul to take down next weekend. As I straighten up, a pain catches my spine and shoots down my leg, causing me to cry out. Helen comes rushing to my side. 'What is it? Are you all right?'

I nod. 'I'm okay. I moved without thinking, that's all. I just need to take some painkillers and sit down for five minutes.' I walk carefully into the kitchen. I haven't used my stick for days, but it's easy to overdo it or make a careless move. I swallow a couple of painkillers with a mouthful of cold coffee, then I sit at the table and wait for them to kick in. I feel another wave of sadness as I look at the table, the first piece of furniture we ever bought together. It was the only thing we bought for years because every penny we had – the proceeds from the sale of my flat, all Adrian's savings – went into buying this house. The place was a total wreck when we moved in, and even the money our dads gave us as a wedding present just disappeared when we started doing it up, but when we found this table in one of those warehouse-damaged clearance sales, we both loved it. The damage to one of the legs was barely noticeable and anyway, we wanted the inevitable marks and scratches to help build its character. We wanted this table to be a tangible reminder of the joys of our lives together, from those first days, to when we became parents and perhaps even grandparents. I trace my finger round the little dents, chips and grooves on its surface. There are not enough of them, not nearly enough.

Helen puts her head round the door. 'How about his personal things, toiletries and so on?'

I don't answer straight away. Getting rid of the little travel kit he took to the conference with him was easy, because everything was miniature and disposable – bought specifically for travel and not really personal to him. But the things that are here in the bathroom are so *Adrian*. There's the electric razor I bought him last year, still plugged in; his sandalwood deodorant and aftershave on the shelf; the Ocean Fresh shower gel he likes – liked – so much. And his slightly worn toothbrush, still at the back of the basin where I got annoyed with him for leaving it. It is these things that nearly fold me over with grief, and yet the thought of them not being here . . .

'I felt the same when I lost my husband,' Helen tells me.

'Left all his bits and bobs there for weeks, which was daft, really, because it made it all the harder to clear them out. My sister got rid of it all for me, in the end.' She puts her hand gently on my shoulder. 'Would you like me to do it?'

I nod. I feel that familiar tightening in my throat that I keep expecting to turn to tears, but which always stops just short. I'm sure I'd feel better if I could cry. The sense of loss is definitely physical. I can feel it right in the centre of my gut, a cold, dull ache. I wonder what Paul and Helen must make of my absence of tears. There can't be many women who still haven't been able to cry properly six weeks after their husband's death.

It's almost half past one, I realise. I don't feel like eating, but Helen and Paul must be getting hungry. I take a block of frozen leek and potato soup out of the freezer. Adrian was alive when I made that. Again the tears clot in my throat. I put the soup on to heat, pick up my cigarettes and unlock the back door. I can hear Paul moving around in the garage, so now is probably a good time. I've only had three today – I try not to smoke when there are other people here. I'm halfway through the cigarette when I hear Helen's voice behind me. 'Do you think I could pinch one of those?' My astonishment makes Helen giggle. 'Goodness, the look on your face!'

I close my mouth. 'Of course you can.' I offer her the pack. 'But I'm a bit surprised.'

'Once in a blue moon, that's all. I gave up properly years ago, but a bereaved lady shouldn't have to smoke alone.'

I like having company while I smoke. It's the reason I started in the first place. I'd become friendly with a few of the other patients and at one point, I was the only one in a group of six who didn't smoke. Once I'd started, I found it surprisingly easy to overcome my horror at what it was doing to my body, and I liked the comforting repetition, the way cigarettes became a sort of punctuation to the day.

When Paul and Helen have gone home, I open the box Helen found in the wardrobe and start to sift through the contents. There are a handful of photographs of Adrian as a child, one with him and Chris and both parents, a few of him with his mum. There's one of him at about three years old on a seesaw with Chris, his mum holding him in place so he doesn't fall. Then I find one of me sitting on a bench with a glass of wine in my hand, shielding my eyes from the sun. I remember that day – we'd had a picnic in the park. We'd only been together about a week. As well as the photos, there are loads of cards – birthdays, anniversaries, Valentines – possibly every card I ever made him. The earlier ones were quite elaborate – proper white card and with bits of ribbon and other things stuck on the front. Some are no more than a folded piece of paper with a badly drawn heart and a few kisses dotted around. I have some like this that he made for me, too, and I treasure them just as much as the others. I pick up a folded piece of thin green paper. For a moment I wonder why he has one of my old pay claims in this box, but then I see the writing on the back and I remember. *Good morning, husband, and happy first day of the rest of our married lives. It looks like we've missed breakfast, so I'm going out to look for some rolls or croissants. Love, your wife xxxx*

The first day of our honeymoon in Lyon. My vision blurs and I blink to clear it.

I look up at the picture on the wall. Adrian smiling and tanned in a light grey fitted suit, the rose in his buttonhole drooping a little in the heat. And me in a floor-length burgundy dress with spaghetti straps, hair pinned messily on top of my head, grinning and holding a tied bunch of white roses with wispy trailing ribbons. We invited about forty people, and even though some of them thought we were mad, most people got caught up in the excitement of arranging everything in just four weeks. It was touch and go, but we got there. There was a simple lunch of cold poached salmon, potato salad and asparagus, followed by strawberries and cream, with plenty of wine and champagne to go with it. And thanks to Adrian's grandma, who still had a weekly 'baking day', we even had a small wedding cake which she iced herself. It was the most amazing day, and even the sceptics admitted it was possibly the happiest wedding they'd ever been to. We couldn't get a photographer at such short notice, but Paul, Richard and Abi, my friend from work, all took lots of pictures, and in every photograph of that day there's not a single person who isn't smiling or laughing. We were so ridiculously happy that it just spilled out onto everyone else. We knew we were meant to be together; we just *knew.*

I take the picture down from the wall and wipe the dusty glass with the sleeve of my t-shirt. I search Adrian's face for some clue, and as I look into his eyes I ask him silently, *Where were you going?*

I'm too tired to go through the desk tonight and my back is aching quite badly, so I swallow some painkillers and climb into bed. Automatically I reach for Adrian's t-shirt, which I bunch up against my face, burying my nose in the fabric. At first, the smell of him was so close and warm that I could fall asleep almost believing he was lying next to me, but now his precious scent is fading, and soon it'll be gone completely. A few tears leak from my eyes and I let out a small sob as I whisper his name into the pillow, but my tears don't last and I'm left with that dull ache behind my eyes. If only I could cry properly, loudly, like a child. I take his watch from the bedside table and settle down to sleep with it clutched tightly in my hand. It still works, although the glass casing was damaged in the crash. As I lie there in the dark, the watch face cool against my cheek, I am comforted by the sound of it ticking, by hearing the wheels and cogs of the mechanism continuing to go round even though his heart is no longer beating.

CHAPTER ELEVEN

Now

The evenings are the hardest, because the house feels so much emptier now Adrian is gone for good than when he was simply somewhere else. It's as though when he was alive, his presence, his *aliveness*, was palpable even when he wasn't here. I try to do some reading for next semester, even though I'm still not sure if I'll be up to taking on the point three contract after all, but I find I'm reading the same paragraph over and over.

The house is making noises as if it's restless. There's the knocking sound, which is only the central heating pipes cooling down but which seems louder and more insistent than it did before. There are creaks and cracks as the floor-boards settle, and the wind, which wasn't particularly strong when I put the rubbish out, is whistling loudly under the back door and through the gaps in the old window frames.

I pour a glass of wine and turn on the television, flicking through the channels until I find some old episodes of *Frasier*, Adrian's favourite sitcom. Amazingly, I find myself laughing out loud, and it distracts me for a while. Then there's a documentary about Elgar and I try to focus on it, but before long, the dark thoughts begin to creep in and that same question starts to niggle away at me – what was he doing out there on the A621 that day? Where was he going? It's driving me nuts. I turn the television off, pour more wine and make my way up to the study, where I switch on his laptop again. I don't know why – I've already searched his emails a couple of times. His work account is full of reminders about meetings and briefings, marketing stuff from educational suppliers and invitations to attend conferences or subscribe to research journals. There's nothing unusual in his personal email, either. Maybe I should go further back. Or maybe I'm missing something.

When the screen comes up, I click into his personal account. There are new emails, but nothing of interest – a reminder to renew his phone insurance, spam purporting to be from Microsoft, a notification that his bank statement is ready to view. Nothing significant at all. As an afterthought, I click the trash folder. I scroll down, reading everything that isn't obviously junk. I hate doing this, especially the personal stuff – from his dad, or from Chris, or Richard – but I read every one, searching the innocent lines for a clue. This is ridiculous. I'm about to close the programme when something catches my eye. I didn't spot this before, but I notice it because the subject is *Invoice and delivery details.* Adrian rarely buys anything online. It's from an online gift company. *Item: Wooden Farm Animals Set – a beautiful hand-painted farmyard set, perfect for little farmers. An educational toy, suitable for age 2+.* Further down the page it says, *Recipient: Oliver Simpson.*

Simpson. Who do we know called Simpson? I stare at the screen. Oliver. I can't think of anyone with a little boy called Oliver. Maybe it's a colleague. But if he was friendly enough with them to send the child a birthday present, surely he'd have told me? I scroll down to the bottom of the invoice for the delivery address. Castledene. My heart starts crashing against my ribcage. I click print, and as the paper comes out of the printer I notice something I didn't spot before – at the bottom of the page, underneath the boxes describing the item, the cost, (*£24.99 plus next day delivery £4.95*) and the delivery address, is a box headed, *Your personal message.* The small type inside reads: *It was nice to meet you, Oliver. You are a fine boy and I can see that your mum is very proud of you. I know it's not your birthday or anything, but I thought I'd send you something. I hope your mum doesn't mind, and that she'll read this to you. Tell Mummy I'll be in touch, and maybe I can come and see you one day. Love, Adrian xxxx*

I lie in the darkness staring at the ceiling and trying to make sense of that email. Is it possible that I know who Oliver Simpson is but I've forgotten? The medication sometimes affects my memory, especially when I'm tired. It dulls things, pushes them to the back of my mind, so I'm not aware of them for long periods of time, but I don't think it's ever wiped out a memory completely. I sigh and turn over. It must be a colleague's little boy. He probably told me when I was distracted and I just didn't take it in. But the note said he was planning to see the child. Or hoping to. There's something odd about the wording. Or am I being paranoid? But I can't ask him, so how am I supposed to get it out of my head? I turn over again, then I move over to Adrian's side, but I still can't sleep. If I hadn't had a couple of glasses of wine I'd take a sleeping tablet, but I don't want to be sluggish and muzzy in the morning. I haven't taken my other pills yet, I remember. I sit up and switch the lamp on. I hate having to take so much medication: two different lots of painkillers; drugs to keep my mood stable; drugs to stave off the depression. I feel like an old lady as I open the plastic pill container with compartments for each day of the week. The consultant said I might have to take some of these indefinitely, but how am I supposed to know whether I still need them? In the last few years, I've been on a range of meds at different doses and in varying combinations. It can be hard to get right, the consultant explained, because some people respond better than others. 'With some patients,' he told me, 'and you appear to be one of them, we have to go through a whole series of different medicines, waiting for the body to adjust and the side effects to settle down, before we find a combination that works. It's trial and error, I'm afraid, an imperfect process but it's the best we have.'

When I was at my worst, I was so heavily medicated I was barely conscious. What followed were dark moods and hopelessness, and at that point I wasn't really aware of the numbness, although I remember other patients on the unit talking about it – saying it made them feel 'blunt' or 'shut down'; some said it could make them almost catatonic. I didn't care at the time. I welcomed the inability to feel.

I look at the tablets in my palm. What's the worst that could happen if I were to stop taking them? They're probably not doing much now, and even if they *are* doing something, is it really worth feeling like this, as if I'm not properly bereaved? I'm fairly sure I'd be able to think more clearly if I wasn't chucking all this shit down my throat. I *want* to feel the grief. My soulmate is dead and I want to cry my eyes out.

I throw back the covers and get out of bed. I take all the little boxes and blister packs from my bedside drawer and toss them into the wastebasket, then I take the pill dispenser into the bathroom and flush all the pills down the loo.

CHAPTER TWELVE

Now

It's nearly five thirty by the time I arrive home. The house is in darkness. Why hadn't I left a light on when I went out? At least the heating will be on. This is the first time I've been out for more than about an hour since Adrian died, so it feels a bit strange anyway. I had to force myself to go out today – I agreed to do a tutorial, but I was so tempted to cancel it at the last minute. I know it's stupid, but I feel that if I leave the house for more than a few minutes, Adrian might come back while I'm out and I might miss him.

As I let myself in, the sadness of the empty house sweeps over me. I switch on the lamps in the hall to kill the darkness, then I hang my stick on the hook and dump my bag on the floor so I can take my coat off. This afternoon's tutorial went well, and just that hour of thinking about something else has helped me feel a bit lighter. My line manager's been brilliant – he's agreed to postpone my return to lecturing until at least after Christmas, and he said he was prepared to allocate my students to another supervisor if necessary, but I don't think he'll need to do that. After all, I've coped with supervision for the last two years, often in an emotionally ragged state, especially at first. I hang my coat up and head to the kitchen, where I can see a red light flashing on and off. I assume it's the cooker, but then I see that it's the house phone, and the display says there's one new message. How bizarre – no one calls the landline these days. In fact, I'm not even sure why we still have it. I press the button to listen to the message, and my heart stops as I hear Adrian's voice, cheery as always: *Sorry we're not here to take your call at the moment, but if you leave your name and number after the tone, we'll get back to you as soon as we can.* And then there's a message about huge discounts on solar heating panels. I delete it, then pick up the handset and go through the menu until I get to, *To listen to your greeting, press one.* I press one, and lean against the dresser as Adrian's voice pours into me, soothing as balm. Then the female voice says again, *To listen to your greeting again, press one.* I press one, cradling the handset against my cheek. I pull a kitchen chair towards me and sit down. *To listen to your greeting again, press one . . .*

By ten o'clock, I can barely keep my eyes open. I consider plugging the landline in next to the bed so I can listen to Adrian's voice just before I go to sleep, but I know it's a false comfort, so I resist the temptation. I don't know if I'll ever be able to wipe that message, though.

I fall asleep quickly, for once, and sleep right though until the alarm goes off. There's a beat or two before I remember that Adrian isn't away for a meeting or a conference; he's dead and he isn't coming back. At first this happened every morning, but it's not so often now. But the next thought that comes into my head has been the same every single day: why was he on that road, and why did he lie about the car? And since I found that email last week: who is Oliver Simpson and why did Adrian buy him a present?

I get out of bed cautiously, my back stiff from being in the same position for too long, and make my way downstairs. Ibuprofen wrecks my stomach if I haven't eaten, so I make toast and eat it quickly, standing at the kitchen counter. I look out of the window at the miserable greyness as the coffee machine does its thing. It's starting to snow. Not heavily enough to settle, just a few soft flakes falling lightly from the sky. There are two crows and a magpie in the branches of the old plane tree, pecking at the bark and occasionally opening their beaks to call their strange, harsh call. Horrible creatures. I shiver as I remember the crow that walked in through the back door a few weeks ago. It dawns on me as I take the first sip of my coffee – that was the day Adrian went to the conference, the last time I saw him alive.

Once the painkillers have kicked in, I go back upstairs to do my exercises, then shower and dress. As I stand by the window towelling my hair, I watch next door's children playing in the garden, no doubt enticed by the snow. They run around shrieking in delight as they try to catch the snowflakes. I love seeing them all wrapped up in scarves and bobble hats, the toddler in a puffy snowsuit that makes him look like a little Michelin man. They're doing their best to make snowballs out of the light dusting of white. The little one is wearing pea-green mittens, but the others have bare hands that are red with the cold, as are their noses. They must be freezing. My eyes start to fill as I watch the children playing. Would I cope better with losing Adrian if I were watching my own children playing out there? At least there would still be a tiny part of him left, something for me to love. Even though I know there would never – *could* never – have been another child, the pure scientific fact of it now is hard to take.

I remember standing here at this very window a few days after I had the miscarriage, staring out at the garden where we planned to put a swing and maybe even build a tree house for when the children were older. It was earlier in the year than this – autumn – when the trees were at their best, all reds and browns and golds and russets. The doctor had said there was no reason we couldn't start trying again straight away, and when I told Adrian, he looked so pleased that I burst into tears. He put his arms around me immediately, holding me while I cried. When it first happened, he'd cried, too, but a week later, he was coping and I was still a mess. I'd been growing that baby inside me for almost ten weeks. I hadn't felt it move but I'd felt its presence, I'd talked to it, connected with it. He kissed my head. 'I know you're still devastated,' he murmured as my tears subsided, 'but it *is* good news, isn't it?'

I nodded, feeling in my pocket for a tissue. 'I know it is.' I stepped back from him to blow my nose. 'But I wanted *this* baby.' More tears leaked out.

'I know,' he said softly, putting his arms round me again. 'So did I.' We stood there for several minutes, and silent tears ran down my cheeks as he rocked me slowly back and forth, almost as if we were dancing.

When I gave a shuddery sigh and mopped my face, he turned me gently towards the window. 'Ten years from now,' he said, standing behind me with his arms around my waist and his head resting against mine, 'we'll have half a dozen kids running around out there.'

I turned to look at him, raising my eyebrows and managing a small smile.

'Oh, all right,' he said, kissing my cheek. 'Two or three kids, then.'

So within a few weeks, we started trying again.

CHAPTER THIRTEEN

Then

Being almost eight months pregnant in the height of summer was no fun, especially when you were working in a building with dodgy air conditioning – and we couldn't open the windows because of the noise from the building works going on around the university. Would it all be done by the time the students came back in September, I wondered? Then I remembered I wouldn't be here anyway.

I picked up a cardboard file and fanned my face. It really was unbearable in here today. I made a mental note to try to plan it better next time I got pregnant. Not that I was complaining, really. Part of me would always mourn my lost baby, even though he or she was not much bigger than a Brazil nut, but now we were only a few weeks away from meeting our new son or daughter, I couldn't be happier. I looked at my watch – ten past three. I might as well start packing things up now. I'd been feeling great – once we'd got past that scary twelve-week point, at least. Before that, it was hard to enjoy being pregnant, even though I had virtually no morning sickness this time. But since then, I've felt better and better with each passing week. I'd planned to work up until thirty-eight weeks, but now they said my blood pressure was a bit high, so today was my last day in the department.

I was still slightly in shock that everything had happened so quickly, to be honest. I fell pregnant straight away this time, whereas before we'd been trying for seven months before I conceived. Last time, we were doing the usual thing of waiting until the twelve-week point before we told anyone, so as not to jinx it. But when I lost the baby, I was in such a state we couldn't possibly have kept it to ourselves, so I ended up having to say, *Actually, I was pregnant but we lost it.* Whereas if people had already known, I think it would have been easier just to tell them the sad news. So this time we told people straight away – well, when I was six weeks. Everyone was thrilled, but it was clear most of them thought the early announcement was a bad idea, especially after what happened last time, and there was a collective sense of relief around us when we got to twelve weeks.

My maternity sundress was sticking to my legs, so I tried to hold it out away from my body and waft the cotton fabric about a bit to get a draught going around my legs. I could feel the sweat gathering under my breasts and prickling at my armpits and the backs of my knees. I took the cap off a bottle of water and stood by the window under the air conditioning while I drank. The humanities department was on the eleventh floor, and there was a brilliant view from up here – you could see all across Sheffield, over the rooftops and church spires of the city centre, right out to the hills and moorlands of Derbyshire and the Peak District. The sun was glinting off windows and cars, making everything look silvery, and there was even a bit of a heat haze. You couldn't see the Peace Gardens from here, but when I walked back that way at lunchtime, the grass was covered with people sunbathing or watching children run in and out of the fountains. I wasn't sure if it was cooler near the water, or if it just seemed cooler, but I fantasised about going down there now, sprawling on the grass and maybe catching some of the spray from the fountains. I couldn't, of course. If I sat down on the grass, I'd never be able to haul my bulk back up, for one thing. I'd have to be content with a cool shower when I got home.

I'd been treated like a queen since the moment I walked in this morning, and I'd been showered with presents and cards. I managed to pack most of the smaller gifts into a couple of big supermarket shopping bags. Then there was also a changing mat, a baby bath and a bouncy chair that played music and vibrated to soothe the baby. All these lovely things. I was so overwhelmed by everyone's generosity, I kept having to stop to wipe away a tear.

I probably wouldn't get it all in the car, but if I took most of it now, Adrian could pop back for the rest of it later in the week. I was hoping someone would help me take it all downstairs, but there didn't seem to be anyone around. It was always quiet on campus at this time of year – exams were over, the marking was done and there was a lull before it all kicked off again. I opened the door and looked out into the corridor. Where was everyone? The department was deserted. It was a bank holiday weekend, though, so perhaps they were all drifting off early. I was trying not to mind that everyone appeared to have buggered off without saying goodbye, when Carol, the course administrator, poked her head round the door. 'Could you pop up to the top floor, Leah? Little surprise for you.'

My heart lifted. Not everyone had gone, then. 'Another surprise? You're spoiling me.'

Carol grinned. 'Come on.' I followed her to the lifts, and when we got out at the top floor, she beckoned me along the corridor and into The Top Table, the restaurant for staff and postgrad students and definitely the nicest place to eat on campus. Abi was there, and Eliza and Liam. Then I saw Kitty and Rebecca, and Adam. It was unusual for so many of my colleagues to be in the same place at the same time, but there they all were, standing around in groups and sipping cava. It was only when I noticed that the room was decorated with white and silver balloons and bunting that it dawned on me this was all for me. Tears rushed to my eyes – ever since I'd been pregnant I seemed to cry at the drop of a hat. As I groped in my pocket for a tissue, I spotted Phil, the head of humanities, coming towards me. 'Leah.' He beamed and put a fatherly arm around my shoulder. I hadn't realised he even knew my name. 'Come and sit down. Let's get you a drink.'

'Orange juice, please.' I smiled. 'Or sparkling water.'

'Oh, a tiny drop of fizz won't hurt, will it? Just this once?'

'Probably not, but I'd rather the orange juice.' I could see his disappointment. Probably thought me a party pooper, but I was so relieved to have hung onto this pregnancy, there was no way I was taking any chances. Phil banged a spoon on a glass to get everyone's attention, and then launched into an incredibly flattering speech about how I'd made such a mark here with my first full-time teaching position, how impressed he'd been with my achievements over the last five years and how well liked and respected I was among staff and students. For a few seconds it genuinely didn't register that he was talking about me, and as soon as I started properly taking it in, I felt myself tearing up yet again.

Then everyone was clapping and smiling and he was handing me an envelope. I stood up to shake his hand and take the envelope. 'Thank you, everyone. Thank you so much.' I tried to beam my smile around the whole room. 'I'm so touched by—' I began, but Phil was pointing to the envelope. 'Open it, then.'

I was thrown for a second. I assumed it contained gift vouchers, and looking at them in front of everyone felt a bit mercenary, like counting money. But Phil looked quite excited, so I slipped my thumb under the flap and took out the paper inside. It was a picture of a beautiful wooden cot.

'It's being handmade,' Phil said. 'A family firm in Buxton. It converts to a toddler bed when the baby's old enough.' He smiled. 'I know it'll be a while before you'll need a cot, but it's all paid for – just call them and say when you want it delivered.'

I felt the tears start spilling down my face. Someone produced a tissue and there was a chorus of *aah*s from around the room.

'I'm sorry,' I managed to say between blubs. 'I knew today would be emotional, but . . .' I paused and buried my face in the tissue. 'I can't think why I bothered to put make-up on this morning.' Everyone laughed, and I was struck by how much I was going to miss them all, even if it was only for six months.

By the time the little presentation was over, someone had taken everything except the bouncy chair down to my car and loaded it in. Carol was going to drop the chair off later. As I drove home in the sunshine, the boot laden with gifts, I was aware that I was still smiling. I was surrounded by love and happy thoughts, and I felt buoyed up by it, as if I was floating. It was a beautiful day, and I kept all the windows down so I could feel the warm air puffing into the car. Adrian had suggested going out to eat tonight, but I didn't really want to be inside some stuffy restaurant on such a gorgeous evening, so I decided to stop on the way and pick up some bits and pieces for a barbecue – Adrian would like that, and it meant he could have a drink. Maybe we could invite a few of the neighbours over. As I pulled into the supermarket car park, I was picturing the evening, Adrian in charge of the barbecue, swigging from a bottle of beer and chatting with Richard and Andy as he turned sausages with the giant tongs. I could almost hear the sizzling, and I could see the clouds of smoke that would fill the air with the delicious savoury scent of flame-charred meat. I made a mental shopping list: chicken, prawns, sausages, maybe some mushrooms and peppers for veggie kebabs, some salad leaves, tomatoes, crusty bread. Nice and simple. I wasn't sure if we had enough tea lights to dot around the garden, so I added those to the list. I parked the car and turned off the ignition, idly wondering if Diane next door would bring a bowl of her famous coleslaw. I'd pop in and invite her as soon as I got back. I hauled my bulk out of the car and started to walk towards the entrance. I felt suddenly light-headed and a bit unsteady on my feet. I'd got out of the car too quickly, most likely. But then a surge of nausea stopped me in my tracks. It was probably just the heat, but I had to lean against one of the cars to stop my legs from buckling. I waited for the nausea to pass, one hand automatically supporting my bump, the other resting on top, and I tried to recall when I'd last felt the baby move.

As the nausea enveloped me a second time, I was acutely aware of the hot tarmac beneath the soles of my sandals and a tingling sensation as the sun burned the tender skin at the back of my neck. There was an increasing sense of chill in my stomach, and a second later, I felt the blood in my veins start to turn to ice.

CHAPTER FOURTEEN

Now

It's still snowing when I leave the house, but it's only light and the roads aren't too bad. I throw my stick on the back seat in case I need to walk any distance, then I check the email printout and set the satnav according to the postcode. It's just gone eleven, so there's no rush hour, but I forgot to allow for the fact that it's the last Saturday before Christmas. I haven't exactly *forgotten* about Christmas, it just hasn't really registered. That reminds me, I must call Paul – he's still trying to persuade me to go with him and Helen to Chris and Judy's. Maybe I should make the effort.

The shopping traffic thins as I head further out into the Peaks. It's been falling more heavily up here – it's quite a bit higher. There's a frosting of snow across the moors, and the fields beyond are a vast tablecloth of white. The road is fairly clear, though, and I'm in Castledene in less than twenty minutes, by which time the snow has given way to a light drizzle. The satnav tells me that my destination is on the right. I pull up outside a church, opposite a small terrace of grey stone houses with big front gardens.

There's a Christmas tree to the side of the bay window of number nine, but the lights aren't switched on, although there's a flickering blueish light from a television further back in the room, so it looks like they're in. The garden is well kept – a lawn, a couple of small trees, raised flower beds and a few shrubs. A low wall separates the garden from the street, and a crazy-paved path leads up to the front door. I strain my eyes but I can't see much more from here, so I start the car again and drive further into the village, passing a newsagent's, a hairdresser's, a DIY store and a post office. There's a Co-op further on with a small car park, so I pull in and manoeuvre the car into one of the few free spaces. I pick up my stick from the back seat, then change my mind and put it back – I'll be less conspicuous without it.

The Co-op is reasonably busy, thank goodness. Some of these Peak District villages are so small that everyone knows everyone else, and if you haven't lived there for about thirty years, you stand out like a beacon. There's nothing I really need, but I buy a few things – cigarettes, teabags, muesli, pasta, a couple of jars of pesto – enough to fill a carrier bag. Then I walk as purposefully as I can back in the direction I came. As I approach number nine, I slow a little and glance through the glass as casually as possible. The television is still on, cartoons of some sort, but there doesn't seem to be anyone watching it. A dark-coloured sofa takes up one wall and there are a couple of huge red beanbags against the other. I can see a large mirror over the fireplace, a Picasso print in a clip frame and a few framed photos on the wall opposite the window, though I can't make out the details. There's definitely no one in the room, but at least that means I can take another look on my way back to the car without being spotted.

I walk on for another few minutes until I come to a patch of grass where there's an ornate wooden memorial bench. I need to rest if I'm going to be able to walk back to the car without being in pain, so I pull my coat tightly around me and sit huddled on the damp bench while I try to decide what to do. It's either keep walking past until whoever lives at number nine makes an appearance in their sitting room, or come back later. It'll be almost dark by half past three, and maybe that time on a Saturday afternoon is when a small child is likely to be watching television. If I come back then, maybe I could just sit in the car across the road without being seen. I sigh. Why am I even doing this? What am I hoping for, exactly – that I'll recognise the child and suddenly remember who he is?

The bench is cold and I'm aware of the drizzle settling on my skin and wetting my hair, so I pull up my hood and get to my feet, picking up my shopping with one hand and automatically reaching for my stick with the other. Shit. I left it in the car. My back is starting to hurt now, and there are twinges down my leg, so there's no way I'll be able to keep walking back and forth past the house. I get to my feet and start making my way to the car. If there's still no sign of life in that front room, I'll come back later.

As I near the house, I see the front gate swing open and a small child wearing a mustard-yellow anorak step out onto the narrow pathway. I only catch a glimpse of his face before he squats down to examine something he's spotted on the ground. 'Oliver!' A woman's voice comes from behind the hedge. 'You naughty boy, I said wait for me.' The child glances back through the gate at his mother before turning back to whatever it is he's studying on the ground. My instinct is to cross to the other side of the road, but there's virtually no pathway on that side so it would look odd. The woman is wearing a big, dark coat with a hood, her face almost completely hidden. As I get nearer, I drop my gaze in case she tries to make eye contact, then I take out my phone and pretend I'm checking a message. As I pass, the child stands up, the hood of his anorak falling back and revealing a full head of thick, dark hair, sticking up a little at the crown. He looks up at me, and it is as if I am hit by a thunderbolt that paralyses me, pins me to the ground. A chill engulfs my whole body, like someone has thrown cold water over me. Then, just as suddenly, I feel hot and dizzy and faint and there's a buzzing in my ears and . . . oh, my God, I'm going to be sick. I manage to take a few steps so I can lean against the low wall that fronts one of the houses. I close my eyes and concentrate on my breathing. Thankfully, the nausea passes, but my hands are sweating and trembling and my legs have gone shaky.

In that split second before the child took his mother's hand and trotted off in the other direction, I saw that I *did* recognise him; his features are as familiar to me as if they were my own.

CHAPTER FIFTEEN

Now

Somehow, I make it to the car. I collapse in the front seat and slump over the steering wheel before breaking into loud, uninhibited sobs. I'm not sure how long I cry for, but one thing's for certain, I'm not feeling numb any more. Oliver. My husband's child, his face a newer, fresher, unspoilt version of Adrian's. There is no mistaking this child's dark, soulful eyes, the slight upward tilt of his nose, the full, perfectly shaped mouth. And the hair, the child has Adrian's thick, near-black hair. It even sticks up at the crown.

The car park is getting busier now, and I'm aware of one or two people glancing in my direction. I must have been making more noise than I realised. I pull down the sun visor and check my face in the mirror. Blotchy skin, red, shiny nose, wet eyelashes and eyelids already swollen beyond recognition. As I examine my reflection, I feel the tears rising again. My face starts to crumple and my eyes fill once more. I manage to find a tissue at the bottom of my bag, and as I hold it over my face for a moment, I try to calm myself again. I remember reading something about how in some cultures, it's normal for widows and bereaved mothers to wail and rend their clothes; that's what I feel like doing right now, wailing, tearing at my clothes. How could Adrian have a child, when I – we – have lost our babies? I put my head back down on the steering wheel as more sobs overtake me. Slowly, I become aware of a tapping on the window. A wide-faced man with a beard and a purple drinker's nose is leaning down and looking through the glass at me with concern. 'Are you all right, love?'

I wipe my face again. 'Yes,' I say without looking at him. 'Yes, thank you. I'll be fine in a minute.'

'I say,' he says, louder this time. 'Are you all right in there? Do you need any help?'

Oh God, I'm going to have to face him. Taking a deep breath, I press the button to lower the electric window a couple of inches. 'Sorry, I've had some bad news, that's all. I'll be all right – thanks for asking.'

'Are you sure you don't need—' But I wind the window up again and start the engine before he can finish.

I'm not even really aware of the drive back, and as I turn into our road it crosses my mind that I may have inadvertently driven through a red light. There's no way I'll be able to concentrate enough to back the car into the garage, so I leave it parked outside the house. How I've managed to drive home without hitting anything, I don't know. Diane next door is in her garden putting bottles into the recycling. She glances in my direction and then quickly turns away and for once, I'm glad. I don't want anyone seeing my red, puffy face and swollen, pig eyes. My hand is trembling so much that it takes me a few moments to get the key into the lock, but when the front door swings open and the familiar smell and warmth of my home rises up to greet me, I feel momentarily comforted, although the feeling is as fleeting as a baby's breath.

I go straight up to the study with the intention of going through Adrian's things again. There must be some other evidence of his connection to this child – *his* child – apart from a deleted invoice, but as soon as I'm standing in the room, I know there's no point – I've been through everything several times already. My mind is in turmoil, the thoughts crashing against each other. Adrian, having an affair; it doesn't make sense. I remember that old song my dad used to play all the time after my mum died – Dusty Springfield singing, 'I Just Don't Know What To Do With Myself'. That's exactly how I feel. I start to pace the room, but pain shoots up and down my back and leg and I'm forced to sit. I shove things around on the desk roughly, then I deliberately knock a pile of papers off the edge before realising that they're my own lecture notes. Shit! What a moron. As I gather up the notes I feel hot rage bubbling up inside me. It's made much worse by the fact that Adrian isn't here, so I can't even vent my anger. There isn't much of his stuff left in here, but there's the little pot with his pens in, so I sweep that onto the floor, then I pick up the green reading lamp he was so fond of and, with as much vigour as I can muster, I hurl it at the wall. The shade smashes with a satisfyingly loud crack and I watch as the shards of green glass spray out and fall onto the rug, then I stand again, walk calmly out of the room and close the door behind me.

After drinking the last of the whisky, I feel a little better. I go back up to the study. There are so many questions to answer. He was obviously on his way to or from Castledene when he had the crash, but he can't still have been seeing the mother regularly, because I almost always knew where he was – with the obvious exception of the day of the accident. The conferences were only every three or four months, so not often enough to provide cover for a full-on affair. And I'd know if he was supporting the child, because I've been dealing with the household finances again for more than a year now. I'd have noticed any odd payments from the joint account. I take down the black folder from the shelf and go through the statements from his personal account, transaction by transaction – he keeps paper statements for a year or so – but there's nothing. I couldn't be wrong about the child, could I? No; I'd be deluding myself if I tried to pretend that the likeness was a coincidence. I sigh as I make my way slowly downstairs. We've been together almost ten years; all those years with a man I thought was the other half of me, a man who loved me, even during the darkest moments when I was unable to love him back. A man who kept me afloat while almost drowning in his own grief, who held me as we both sobbed, raw and needy in the chill of early morning. Who, when we slowly began to live again, whispered, we *are* each other, as we made love.

And now it seems I didn't really know him at all.

It's almost five o'clock. Sod it. It's still early, but today has been about as shitty as they come. I take a bottle of Shiraz from the wine rack, selecting it because it's the first one I spot with a screw top and now I've decided to have a drink, I want it immediately. I take out one of the large goblets – they were a wedding present, and we used to call them the VBD – very bad day – glasses. I slosh in a generous amount of the ruby-coloured wine and, feeling consciously reckless, I take two good gulps. I don't have the medication to worry about any more, so I fully intend to get drunk.

I spend the next hour sitting at the kitchen table, chain-smoking, knocking back the strong, spicy wine and crying. I must have cried almost as much in these last few hours as I've done in the last few weeks; maybe it'll do me some good. My eyes are starting to feel sore, though, and I can feel myself becoming dehydrated. I take a pint glass out of the cupboard and fill it with tap water, but it sits undisturbed on the table while I take another bottle from the rack.

Half an hour later, as I'm pouring yet another drink, I remember I have a card somewhere with the number for Jan, the community psychiatric nurse I used to see after I left the unit. I find it in the kitchen drawer eventually and, finger swaying as I try to focus on the number – I'm so pissed now that my vision is blurred – I press the buttons on the keypad. It's late, but maybe Jan will be on duty and answer her mobile. It goes to voicemail. I do my best to sound sober, but I can hear the slur in my voice as I try to explain. 'I know I've had a drink, Jan, but I've got to talk to someone. You said I could call you if I needed more support, right? Well, I really fucking need support now. Did you know that my husband has a child? He's called Oliver.' I pause as another sob comes, and by the time I've composed myself by lighting another cigarette and drawing on it deeply, the beep has gone. 'Fuck,' I mutter, and press the redial button. 'S'me again. And you know what? I worked it out. He must have been shagging her while I was ill. Probably while I was still in hospital. How could he do that, Jan?' I start to cry again. 'Why should she, that woman, whoever she is, why should *she* have his baby and I can't? It's not fair. Not fucking fair.' The beep goes again and I'm not sure how much I managed to say before it did, but Jan will call back anyway.

The sensible part of myself, the part that knows I'm very drunk, is appalled by my behaviour and slightly fearful of what'll happen when Jan picks up the message. I've always been a model patient, but even in my drunken state I know that this is not model patient behaviour.

It is only when I wake the next morning with a searing pain in my head and nausea rising in my throat that I see the text that came through in the middle of the night. *I don't know who you are, and I'm sure you called this number by accident, but I do not appreciate receiving drunken, obscene messages on my voice-mail. Please delete this number from your phone NOW!!* 'Oh God,' I say aloud. I was so drunk last night I could barely see the numbers on the card, let alone copy them into the phone. I immediately start to type an apology to this disgruntled stranger, but that makes me feel even more nauseous, so I just do what the person says and delete the number. The only silver lining is that I didn't manage to get through to Jan after all.

A few days later, Judy calls again to ask about Christmas. 'It's kind of you, Judy,' I say, 'but I don't think I can face a family Christmas just yet. I'm probably just going to take a bottle of wine and a box of chocolates up to bed with me and crawl under the duvet until Boxing Day.' I realise that sounds a bit bleak, so I add a little laugh, just to show I'm not suicidal.

I hear Judy sigh. 'If you're sure that's what you want.' She pauses, but I don't say anything. 'If you really can't face it, then of course we understand, but if you change your mind, just come, okay?'

'Okay. Thanks, Jude. By the way, I'm afraid I haven't got round to doing any proper Christmas shopping this year, but I've put a couple of gift cards in the post for the boys. I hope—'

'Honestly, you needn't have worried, Leah. Not at a time like this. But thanks all the same – they'll be thrilled.'

CHAPTER SIXTEEN

Now

It's unusually mild and sunny for March, and after the long, dark winter, a bright day like this makes everyone feel better. It's a bit too mild for this coat, really. I've been relying on the hood to cover my head, but I'll need another way to disguise myself as the weather gets warmer. Not that Oliver or his mum ever seem to notice me, but it's nice to have the freedom of being able to watch this child without alarming his mother. All I need is to catch a glimpse of him now and then, take pleasure in seeing him smile or laugh, see how quickly he grows taller. I park the car in the road behind the church and switch off the engine. They won't be out for another fifteen minutes.

I'm supposed to be at my bereavement support group today. I joined a few weeks ago, and if I'm honest, it probably has helped. Turns out I'm not the only one to be angry with a dead spouse, although I *am* the only one to discover my partner's infidelity as a result of his death. Pushing it to the back of my mind doesn't work; it comes creeping in insidiously like a fog while I'm brushing my teeth, or making coffee, or marking a student's work. Adrian cheated on me and he had a child. How dare he give another woman his child! And how dare he go and die so I can't even talk to him about it. This is what I talk about mainly at group – how upset and angry I am with him. Maybe I'll go to another meeting, or maybe I won't.

I glance at my watch again. They'll be out soon. There's no way I can get away with keeping my hood up today, so I tie my hair back with an old rubber band and put on the glasses I usually only wear for driving. I still have a few minutes, so I light a cigarette as I walk through the cemetery at the rear of the church and along the narrow path to the smaller churchyard at the front. With the sprinkling of snowdrops and crocuses, it looks particularly pretty today. Sometimes while I'm waiting for Oliver to appear, I wander around reading the ancient headstones, but as it's so mild today, I sit on the bench in the middle of a sea of daffodils. Here, I have a good view of the house, and I'm almost completely shielded by the holly and hawthorn that grows by the wall. I squash my cigarette underfoot and settle down to wait. After a few minutes, the front door opens and out comes Oliver, clutching his Shrek lunchbox. My heart contracts as I watch him bouncing down the path while his mother locks the door behind them, then grabs the little boy's hand

and hurries him into the car. She lifts him up and straps him into his child seat before jumping in the front and starting the engine. The woman is always in a hurry.

It's Wednesday today, so she'll drop Oliver at nursery, then drive straight to the café where she works. Once a week, after dropping him off, she drives to a big, double-fronted house in Dore where she spends exactly two and a half hours, then drives home again. It was only when I saw her come out to the wheelie bin, still wearing rubber gloves, to empty a couple of wastepaper baskets that I realised it's a cleaning job. But that's only on Fridays. On the other days, it's straight to the café. Her shift must finish at three. Oliver finishes nursery at a quarter past, but it's often almost ten past by the time his mother emerges from the café and hurries to her car. Sometimes I watch the nursery instead, and all too often the poor child is one of the last, if not *the* last, to be collected. She should be more organised where her son is concerned. The car is a silver Renault Clio, quite old by the looks of it, and it's clearly had a few knocks and bangs. I hope those didn't occur while Oliver was strapped in the back. The car pulls away and accelerates too quickly and I have to suppress a wave of panic as the image of a crash flips through my brain.

They told me Adrian lost control of the car in the fog. It skidded off the wet tarmac and down a slope, where it crashed into a tree. I wanted to see where it happened – God knows why – so just before Christmas, I drove there and saw the actual tree. It was the only tree that stood anywhere near the road. If it had happened five seconds earlier or later, he'd simply have come to a stop in a muddy field. I got out of my car to inspect the tree, gratified to see its bark scarred by the impact. *Good*, I thought. *I hope you're scarred for life. I hope you die.* Now, having seen the damn tree, I can't unsee it, and I am haunted by images of the moment of impact. *Drive carefully*, I urge silently as I watch the Clio disappear over the hill.

Oliver's nursery is about halfway between their house and mine, a ten- to fifteen-minute drive away. Sometimes I watch from the car when the children are playing outside, but today I drive straight to the café, assuming she'll have dropped Oliver off and then gone straight to work for her shift – ten until three. Sure enough, at just after ten, the silver Clio turns into the car park and Oliver's mum jumps out, hurriedly locking the car before dashing across the road to the café. I park my car and put enough money in the machine to cover two hours. I'll have a wander round the shops first, buy something so that I can be carrying a bag or two when I go in. I *will* go in today; I've chickened out three times already, but I *have* to do this; I have to make some sort of contact.

At a quarter to eleven, I push open the door. At first I only see an older woman behind the counter, cutting a chocolate cake into slices ready to go under its glass dome. But then I spot her, Oliver's mother. Adrian's lover. Nausea ripples through me at the thought. She's smiling at a customer as she takes his order. There's no queue, but there are a few customers working on laptops, studying their phones or reading newspapers. A teenage boy is wiping tables and topping up the pots with sachets of sugar. 'Morning,' I say as I reach the counter. My voice sounds high and tight, and I hope it doesn't betray my nerves. I'm relieved to see that, close up, the woman isn't particularly gorgeous, although she *is* attractive in a clean, wholesome sort of way. She's probably a bit younger than me, though not more than two or three years. Her face is friendly and open, with pretty hazel eyes, a smattering of freckles across her nose and cheeks and reddish, shoulder-length hair pulled back in a ponytail. It looks like the only make-up she's wearing is mascara and a touch of bronze lipstick. There's a silver chain round her neck with a letter 'C' on it, hanging at her throat. Charlotte? Carrie? Cat? Carly?

She smiles at me. 'What can I get you?' It's hard to tell if she has a Sheffield accent, but her voice is soft and pleasant, the words well formed.

'Latte, please, and a flapjack.'

'Coming up.' She lifts one of the glass domes and uses tongs to pick up a flapjack, which she puts on a plate with a folded serviette and hands it to me. 'Take a seat, and I'll bring your latte over in a sec.'

'Thank you.' From my table, I watch as she operates the coffee machine, each movement confident and efficient. She's slim, not very tall, and under the long red apron bearing the café's logo – a spray of white daisies – I can see she's wearing skinny black jeans with a floaty, bottle-green top. She smiles brightly as she brings the coffee over. 'There we are. Anything else I can get you?'

'I don't think so, thanks – I'll shout if I need anything. By the way,' I say quickly as she turns to walk back to the counter, 'I like your top – gorgeous colour!'

She flushes. 'Thank you. I have to make myself wear colours – I tend to live in black – it's so easy, isn't it?'

'I know what you mean. I usually go for black, too. But that green really suits you.'

'Thanks.' She smiles again and goes back to the coffee machine. I take out my book and drink my latte slowly as I pretend to read, surreptitiously watching what's happening behind the counter. I'm not even sure why I'm doing this; why I'm sitting here, trying to imagine my husband and this woman together. Maybe it's some form of self-punishment. I don't want that image, obviously, but I have to try to understand or at least accept the situation. More importantly, I have to find out more about Oliver, and the only way I can do that is to strike up a conversation with his mother. It may not help, but what else am I supposed to do? Now I know that her son is Adrian's child – Adrian's flesh and blood – I can't just pretend he doesn't exist.

CHAPTER SEVENTEEN

Now

I park outside the nursery and pretend to talk on my phone as my eyes scan the playground. After a moment, I spot him on a small wooden climbing frame, clambering across the top with his little bottom in the air, hair sticking up in tufts just like Adrian's. He's wearing a blue and white striped sweatshirt and blue jeans, with red lace-up trainers. He looks so healthy, so *clean*, like a child from one of those 'perfect mother' washing powder ads. He stops and looks at the little girl who is climbing up the ladder behind him, then he swings round into a sitting position and gives her a broad, white-toothed smile. He is such a beautiful child, and so like Adrian it makes my heart ache. My eyes swim for a moment. Oliver is climbing down the other side, more carefully now. It's not particularly high, and all the playground equipment is set on special soft-landing material, but I still wait to see him safely back on the ground before I put my phone away and drive off.

My back is playing up today, so I'm using my stick, and as I walk up to the door of the café, a man coming the other way hurries ahead so that he can hold the door open for me. I always feel touched and humbled when people are kind to me. I nod my thanks as I go in and take my place in the queue. This is my fifth visit now, and coming here has quickly become something I look forward to, partly because I'm getting nearer to having a proper conversation with Oliver's mother, but also because of the simple pleasure of drinking coffee in a nice café and occasionally exchanging a 'good morning' with other customers. Apart from the two days a week that I'm at the university, I don't really speak to anyone else.

There are two of them behind the counter, Oliver's mum and the girl with the rings in her nose and lip. As I get near to the front of the queue, I calculate that it's likely to be the girl with the piercings who'll serve me, so I pretend to be deliberating over which cake to choose and I let the man behind me go first. When my turn comes, I smile at Oliver's mother. 'Latte, please. And a piece of the lemon and coconut cake.'

'Ah, no flapjack today, then?'

'You have a good memory.'

The woman smiles. 'We get to know our regulars.'

I feel a little leap of pleasure. 'Thought I'd try something different – it looks so nice.'

'Good choice.' She lowers her voice. 'That one's my favourite, as it happens, and it was fresh out this morning. Take a seat – I'll bring it over in a sec.'

I hang my stick on the edge of the table and take out my phone and book. There's a text from Paul: *Hope you're ok, dear. I don't want to intrude, but we haven't heard from you for a couple of weeks and I just wanted to check all ok. Would be lovely to have a chat when you have a minute.*

I feel a pang of guilt. I've been avoiding Paul, worried that I won't be able to stop myself from blurting out what I've discovered. He'd be so disappointed in Adrian, and I don't want to do that to him. It wouldn't make me feel any better, either.

I type out a reply. *I'm fine, just a bit busy with work – exam time coming up. Will call at the weekend, L xx*

Oliver's mum appears at my side with the cake on a gold-edged china plate. She sets it down on the table along with a folded serviette and a cake fork.

'Thanks. Pretty plate. And I love eating cake with a proper cake fork.'

'Definitely. No point in doing something nice if you don't do it right.' She nods towards my stick. 'What have you done to yourself, then?'

'Oh, nothing. Well, not recently. It's an old fracture, and it plays up every now and again. I hate using this, but it helps take the pressure off.'

'You poor thing. Isn't there anything they can do?'

I shake my head. 'Not really. It's something I need to

manage. I have a set of exercises I'm supposed to do every day, but I'm not always that good at doing them.'

'I know what you mean. I broke my arm a few years ago – did the exercises for the first few days and then,' she shrugs, 'well, you know. Probably why it still hurts sometimes.' She points to my book. 'How are you getting on with that?'

'I'm not sure, to be honest. I love the set-up, but . . .' I pick the book up and check the page number. 'I'm sixty-odd pages in and I'm not enjoying it as much as I'd hoped.' I bought this novel after a couple of my colleagues and one of my supervisees raved about it. It's been well reviewed, apparently, and it was shortlisted for one of the big prizes, but I'm struggling to get into it.

The woman nods. 'Hmm. I won't say a lot, then, as you haven't finished it.'

'You've read it?'

'Yes, a few weeks ago.'

'Do you read a lot?'

'Yes. Well, when I have the time, anyway.'

It's a relief to find that Adrian isn't the only thing we have in common. At least it should make conversation easier. 'What sort of thing do you usually like to read?'

'Oh, all sorts, really. I like historical stuff. I'm not really into whodunnits, but I like a good thriller, and I quite like sci-fi, too.' Then she laughs. 'You look surprised.'

'A bit. I don't know why, though – you can't ever guess someone's reading tastes. I should know – I teach English literature. One of my mature students – she's in her seventies – is doing her dissertation on Jane Austen, but I asked her the other day what sort of thing she reads on holiday, and she said her first choice would be "a bloody good western".'

She laughs. 'Brilliant. I'm not that bothered about Jane Austen, but I've read some of the Brontës – I did *Shirley* at A level, but I read the others through choice. I prefer modern stuff, though. It must be nice, teaching literature, although I suppose there's more to it than getting paid to read all day.'

'Yeah, but it's good, and I'm only part-time now.'

She nods towards the book on the table. 'That had brilliant reviews.'

I nod. 'That's mainly why I bought it. But you didn't like it?'

'I didn't hate it, but . . . I shouldn't say any more – you might love it, and I don't want to put you off.' She glances towards the counter. 'I'd better crack on, I suppose.'

'Nice to talk to you . . . what's your name, if you don't mind me asking?'

'Cassie.' She smiles. 'What's yours?'

'Leah.'

'Leah. I'll remember that.'

CHAPTER EIGHTEEN

Then

'It doesn't have to be more than a line or two,' Gillian, the woman on the helpline, said. 'It doesn't even have to be coherent. What's important is that you release all those feelings you're holding in. Just try it once or twice, see if it helps.'

'Okay, I will. Thank you.'

'And call the helpline as often as you need to, okay? We all understand. We've all been there.'

I did feel a little better after talking to her. She wasn't a 'proper' counsellor, she told me, just another mum whose baby had died before birth. We had an appointment with a bereavement counsellor next week, but when I called the helpline number it was because I didn't know how I was going to get through the next five minutes, never mind the next week.

I'd had to deliver him. We knew it was a him by then, because they had to scan me to see why he wasn't moving. We decided to call him Thomas. The moment I saw that frozen image on the screen, I knew. I knew before anybody spoke; before Dr Winter held my hand; before I saw the realisation on Adrian's face. I asked about a caesarean, but they said it could affect future pregnancies, so the only option was to go through labour.

After I said goodbye to Gillian, I went into the study to find the thick white writing paper, the stuff we hardly ever used but thought we ought to have to hand, just in case. I made some coffee and sat at the sun-warmed table in front of the big window overlooking the garden. I picked up my pen and began. *My dear, sweet Thomas . . .*

But I had to stop there, because just writing those words made me cry. This was the second child that had died inside me. Hundreds of thousands of women gave birth every year, sometimes women who didn't even want kids. Teenagers, schoolgirls who knew nothing, who did all the things you're not supposed to do, but they still had healthy babies, didn't they? I'd taken my folic acid and given up alcohol as soon as we started trying to get pregnant, and I'd never smoked, not even when I was younger – why couldn't I produce one live baby? I followed Gillian's advice and allowed myself to sob, then I blew my nose and tried again.

My darling baby boy, it is two weeks today since you were 'born sleeping'. I still can't quite believe that you're never coming home. I have loved you since the moment I knew you existed . . .

I paused again and bit the end of my pen.

It was so quiet now that Adrian had gone back to work. I hadn't been alone for more than an hour since it happened, and I felt self-conscious all of a sudden, as though the house was listening to my thoughts, but I carried on.

. . . and the fact that you are not here with us now doesn't change that. That short – much too short – time we spent together after you were born is so precious to me, even though you never took a breath. I rewind it in my head like a film, over and over again. I miss you so much, sweetheart.

With all my love, Mummy xx

I'd thought I might feel silly doing this, but I didn't. I felt like I was actually talking to him. I picked up the page. It was like a proper letter, good-quality paper and rich, dark blue ink. I stood up, stretched and rubbed the back of my neck. I felt slightly – very, very slightly – lighter as I held the letter in my hand.

'Some mums keep what they've written,' Gillian had told me. 'You may want to look back on it later. Others feel they won't want to revisit such a painful time, even though pouring out what they feel now is important, so they burn it afterwards. Have a think about what feels best for you. Some mums say that burning the letter makes them feel as if they've sent it off to their baby, and they find that a great comfort.'

I decided I wanted to 'send' the letter to Thomas, so I rummaged in the kitchen drawer for the gas lighter, but it was empty and I hadn't got round to buying the stuff to refill it. I was sure there must be some matches here somewhere. After more rummaging, I found an almost-full box. I put them in my pocket and, with the letter in my hand, slipped my shoes on and opened the back door. It was warm and sunny and the birds were singing. It was what most people would call a beautiful day, but it just made me even sadder that Thomas wasn't here to see it. I walked down the garden to the gate at the bottom that opened onto the woodland path. I wanted privacy while I did this. I didn't want to be observed from someone's window. I walked a few metres along the path that ran behind the gardens until I came to where it widened, then separated and branched off. As I turned to go deeper into the woods, I recognised the strong, musky smell of fox. It was so powerful and distinctive; it always reminded me of a line from a Ted Hughes poem: *a sudden sharp hot stink of fox*.

The only people you tended to bump into out here were dog walkers, and there weren't many of them at this time of day, so as soon as I got to a little clearing among the trees, I took out the matches. I didn't think there was any breeze at all today, but as I struck match after match only for the flame to die instantly, I saw that I was wrong. I was about to strike another when the thought hit me that maybe Thomas didn't want me to do this; maybe it was my baby's breath that was blowing the matches out. I flicked my head, told myself not to be ridiculous. I'd never believed in that sort of thing, and if I allowed myself to start believing it now, it'd drive me crazy. I made a mental note to tell the counsellor about this when we saw her next week. Perhaps it was normal. Even so, as I took the next match from the box, I told myself that if it too went out immediately, I would give up. I struck the match and as it flared into life I almost dropped it, partly because I half-expected it not to light, but also because it was tricky holding the paper and the lit match at the same time. As soon as I held it to the corner of the page, I realised this wasn't going to be as easy as I thought. Although the flame caught quickly each time, it struggled to eat through the thick paper and it took no fewer than five matches to burn down to where I was holding it between my thumb and fingertips. I let go at the last moment, then knelt down to look at the little pile of soft, charred flakes at my feet. It didn't seem right to leave them here, and I wondered whether to try to gather them up and then scatter them, like we'd scattered Thomas's ashes at the weekend. But when I touched a blackened curl with my finger, it disintegrated immediately. There was a rustling in the trees above me and a definite breeze lifted my hair and rippled the grass at the edge of the path, then it caught the black flakes of my letter to Thomas, and in no time at all they were gone, disappeared; dissolved in the wind.

I hadn't been bothering much with lunch, but maybe my appetite was returning. I opened the fridge and peered in, surprised that there was so much food inside. Things in dishes, labelled with instructions for freezing and reheating – a chicken and asparagus quiche, a lasagne, a mixed-bean casserole. These were all from Diane. We were lucky to have such lovely friends and neighbours. I'd barely cooked since it happened. I hadn't been able to concentrate enough to plan meals. Adrian had cooked a few times – comfort food: macaroni cheese, shepherd's pie, pasta bake – the sort of thing my dad used to give me when I was little. I took out eggs, mushrooms and cheese. I fancied an omelette. I actually fancied making something decent to eat, instead of just putting bread in the toaster or shovelling down endless bowls of cereal. I made the omelette, I sat down and ate it, I even quite enjoyed it, but as I was putting the plate and cutlery in the dishwasher, I started to cry again, because I suddenly remembered Judy saying, 'Make sure you stock up on eggs because once you're home with the new baby, they're the only thing you'll have time to cook.'

CHAPTER NINETEEN

Now

The café is quiet today. Cassie brings over my coffee and cake and, as there's no one else to serve, folds her arms and leans against the windowsill, ready to chat.

'I love coming here,' I say. 'It's not just that it's good coffee – and cake – but there's such a nice atmosphere, even when it's quiet like this.' I mean it. There's something about the sound of the coffee machine in the background and the gentle hum of friendly conversation that I find soothing, especially on days like today, when I'm feeling a bit down. Sometimes, I feel I'm coming to terms with losing Adrian, but every now and again the grief surges up inside me, dragging anger in its wake. I miss him; I don't want to be angry.

'It's a good place to work,' Cassie says. 'Everyone's friendly and nice, and most of the customers are lovely. Do you live near here?'

I wondered if she'd ask that. 'Not that near, no. I found this place by accident – I used to see an acupuncturist not far from here, but I'm not sure it was really helping.' I cut into the cake with the fork. 'So, do you work here full time?' I try to sound casual, as if I have no idea of Cassie's movements when she isn't here in the café.

'No, unfortunately. I'd love to, but I think I mentioned I have a little boy, Oliver?'

'Oh, yes, I think you mentioned him.'

'Well, he's just started preschool, so I have to fit work round that, really, and the dropping off and picking up can be a nightmare.'

I nod. Then, heart thumping, I ask, 'What about his dad? Or does he work full time?'

Cassie's expression flickers. 'It's just me and Ollie. His dad isn't on the scene.'

I turn my head away so my face doesn't betray my thoughts. I'm bursting to ask her what she means by that, because I know he was on the scene a few months ago, or he wouldn't have been near Castledene that day. 'Sorry, I didn't mean to be nosy.'

'No, it's fine. We're not in touch.'

'Really? He doesn't . . . he doesn't support Oliver, then? Financially, I mean?'

She looks up sharply. My heart is hammering so hard I feel sure she'll be able to see it leaping about in my chest.

'No, he doesn't, but we're fine on our own. We manage.'

I go to reach for my coffee, but my hand is shaking, so I

put it back in my lap. I swallow. 'That's terrible. Sounds like he's avoiding his responsibilities.'

She looks at me oddly and I know I've gone too far. 'Sorry. I don't know what comes over me sometimes. I really must learn to mind my own business.' I smile to try and make light of it, but part of me wants to tell her; part of me wants to scream at her that he's dead and she won't ever see him again. I feel tears threatening, so I swallow them back. Another part of me feels sorry for her, and the strange thing is, I quite like her, this woman who slept with my husband. Did she know he was married, I wonder?

'Don't worry. It's not a secret or anything, and it's not like he's some horrible man who's run out on me.' She shifts position and refolds her arms. 'It was my choice, you see. I didn't want . . .' She pauses. 'Oh, never mind. It's a boring story.'

'I'm sure it isn't – I like hearing about other people's lives.' Does that sound weird? 'It must be tough for you, bringing up a child on your own.' I gesture around the café. 'This is lovely, but I'm guessing it doesn't pay that much, not if you can only do part-time.'

'No, it doesn't. But my parents help out when they can – financially, I mean. They live in Cornwall, and I think they feel guilty that they can't babysit. But it's fine, because I'm banking on winning the lottery very soon – like, this Saturday. Or maybe next.' She smiles. 'So all this will be a distant memory, but in the meantime, I cope. I had a cleaning job as well up until a couple of weeks ago. Only a few hours a week, but it was quite well paid.'

'You do cleaning? Oh, my god, you don't want another job, do you? I'm serious. I could really do with a cleaner. We had one for a while, but she was a bit scary, to be honest – she'd been cleaning for forty-odd years and she liked things done her way.'

Cassie laughs. 'I know the type.'

'It would be much easier if it was someone like you coming to the house . . .' I pause. 'That's if . . . I hope I haven't embarrassed you by asking.'

'No, no, it isn't that. I'd love to clean for you, but it's tricky now. Thing is, Ollie's just moved up from nursery to preschool, but it's only Monday to Thursday so he's home on Fridays, which used to be my cleaning day – it's the only day I don't work here. I thought I might be able to swap things around a bit, but it didn't work out.'

'Bring him with you! Fridays are perfect for me. Morning, afternoon – whatever suits you.'

Cassie smiles. 'That's a very kind offer, but I'm sure you don't want a manic three-year-old running around your house.'

'I love children. He's three, your little boy?'

'Just. And I suppose I'm not being fair to him, really. He can be a handful at home sometimes, but he's very well behaved when we're out.'

'Well, there you are then.'

Cassie is looking at me. 'You're serious? About me bringing Oliver, I mean?' She glances at my wedding ring. 'Is your husband at work during the day?'

'I . . . I'm on my own now. And I'm totally serious. It would be lovely to have him – if he's happy to come, of course. He could bring some toys to play with while you're working.'

Cassie nods thoughtfully. 'He's a good boy, so he wouldn't be any trouble. Can I think about it?'

'Of course. There's no hurry. I'd pay you the same as you were earning before, if you're happy with that. I've let things go a bit lately, and I could really do with the help. And I promise you'd get a decent coffee break.'

'You're absolutely certain it's okay to bring Ollie?'

'Definitely! It'd be great to have him around. The house is far too big and quiet, especially now that . . .' I almost use his name, but stop myself just in time. 'Now that my husband's gone.'

Cassie nods. 'How long have you been on your own?'

But before I can answer, the door opens and three women who I vaguely remember seeing before come in, smiling and chatting, and Cassie goes off to serve them. It's a long time since I've been out for coffee with friends. Or lunch, or a drink. Odd how, when I had friends, I took them for granted, often neglecting them in favour of Adrian. He was my best friend from the moment we met. At least, that's what I thought. My eyes swim briefly and I blink away tears. To think he was cheating on me all the time. Well, not all the time, but even so. I drink the last of my coffee, more to break the train of thought than anything else. If I linger on this for too long, the pain is almost physical, like a steel rod being pushed through my very centre. I watch Cassie serving the women, smiling, remembering their usual orders, laughing at something with one of them. Cassie is just the sort of person I'd go for a drink with if I could.

The women settle themselves at the bigger table in the window and carry on talking and laughing, occasionally glancing at their phones. Cassie brings their drinks and cakes over on the tray. 'Yes,' I hear her say. 'That's my favourite, too, as it happens.'

The same thing she said to me. What if her friendliness is an act? Simply part of the job? I'm surprised at how much this idea bothers me, and when I look at the table and see that yes, she's referring to the lemon and coconut cake, I am disproportionately relieved that it wasn't only a sales technique. I'm beginning to realise just how much I need a friend.

As usual when I have a coffee, my fingers twitch for a cigarette, but I'm not going to go and stand outside to smoke. I probably would have done a year ago, but I'm determined to cut down this time. I make a firm decision: if Cassie agrees to bring Oliver with her to the house each week, I will stop smoking. There, I've made a pledge. It takes a moment for me to register the enormity of it. My addiction to nicotine happened bizarrely and quickly, and I still don't completely understand it. Maybe if I have something else to think about, even if it's only to solve the mystery of my apparently loving husband's infidelity, I'll no longer need the security of always having a packet of cigarettes to hand.

I don't want to go home yet, and I'm about to get up and

order another coffee when Cassie catches my eye and mouths, *Same again?* I nod and a few minutes later, she brings it over and sets it down on the table. 'This one's on the house,' she says quietly. 'So, what were we talking about?'

But at that moment, the door opens again and a young man with a laptop bag slung over his shoulder comes in. He holds the door open for an older couple, who are quickly followed by another group of women.

Cassie makes a tutting sound. 'Sorry, Leah, I thought we were going to be dead quiet today, but it looks like the lunchtime rush is on after all.'

I glance at my watch. It's well past noon, so the café's bound to start filling up now. 'Don't worry,' I say quickly. 'I shouldn't monopolise you anyway.'

'You're not monopolising me.' She looks over to the man at the counter. 'Be right with you,' she calls, then turns to me. 'I'll definitely think about what you said, and I'll let you know. You're in next week, are you?'

I smile and say I will be. I like that all the staff recognise me now, although Cassie is the only one who uses my name. They expect me to be here on Wednesday mornings, and they don't seem surprised when I pop in at other times.

As I drive home, I think about the possibility that Cassie might decide not to accept my offer. I push away the dark cloud. There's no point in worrying about that now. I'll just have to deal with it if and when it happens.

CHAPTER TWENTY

Now

Waiting until the following Wednesday for Cassie's response is unbearable, and I have to stop myself from going to the café before then. If I pressurise her into making a decision before she's ready, she'll probably say no. When I offered her the job, I thought it would help me get closer to her and Oliver, but now that there's the possibility of her actually bringing him with her, the whole thing has become even more important.

When Wednesday finally comes round, I force myself to wait until my usual time before driving out to the café. As soon as I go in I can see that it's much busier than usual. Cassie is in the middle of doing a big takeaway order, and there are three other staff serving today. I recognise Pam, the older lady; Lena, with the piercings; and Sam, a tall, fresh-faced and relentlessly cheery student who beams at me as I reach the front of the queue. 'And what can I get for you on this lovely sunny day?' I'm so used to Cassie knowing what I want that I have to think for a second before ordering my usual latte and a flapjack. As Sam keys my order into the till, I keep my eye on Cassie's back, hoping she'll turn round and give me some clue as to what she's decided. 'Okey-dokey,' Sam says. 'Sit yourself down and I'll bring it right over.'

'Thank you.' I deliberately speak loudly so she'll know I'm here, but she doesn't turn round because she's concentrating on marking the lids of the takeaway cups and fitting them into the cardboard carrier.

A minute or so after I sit down, Sam appears to my left and sets my coffee and flapjack in front of me with a flourish. 'Enjoy,' he says. 'Anything else I can get for you today?'

'No, thanks.' I say. *Just bugger off so I can catch her eye.* But by the time Cassie finally spots me and waves, I've finished my coffee and I'm waiting for a lull in the queue so I can go up and order something else.

I wave back, but she still doesn't come over. Oh God, it must be a no. Or maybe she's too embarrassed to tell me. Or perhaps she's going to pretend that conversation never happened. I push down that thought. Maybe I should go up to the counter as soon as it quietens down and just ask her, *Did you give some thought to what we talked about the other day?* She'll have to answer then, surely? I don't realise how much I'm fiddling with the little paper cylinder of demerara sugar until it splits and the amber crystals spill out onto the table. As I'm attempting to sweep the spilled sugar into my hand,

Cassie appears beside me. I look up. 'Sorry, I've made a bit of a mess here.'

'No problem,' she says.

I look at her expectantly.

'Um, you know what you said the other day? About me maybe coming to clean for you?'

'Yes.' I smile.

'You said . . . Well, I just wanted to check again about my little boy. Would it definitely be all right—'

'Yes, bring him with you. Honestly, he'll be no trouble, and it'll be lovely to have him. He can watch TV or do some colouring – I'm sure I've got some coloured pencils from when the boys – my nephews – were little. And there's quite a big garden, so he can play outside if the weather's nice.'

Cassie's face breaks into a grin. 'If you're absolutely sure, then yes, that would be great. Did you say two hours a week?'

I nod. 'As a minimum. Extra hours as and when?'

'That sounds perfect.'

'It'll need a good going-over to start with. I only go in to work on Mondays and Tuesday afternoons at the moment, but if my back's bad, it's hard to keep on top of the cleaning, and I've really let things slip since my . . .' No, maybe I'm saying too much. I clear my throat. 'Any chance you could start this Friday?'

'As a matter of fact, I can – my mother-in-law was supposed to be coming over, but she's cancelled, so—'

'You're married?' Everything seems to tilt, and for a moment I wonder if I've made a massive mistake.

Cassie is shaking her head. 'Widowed. Five years ago. But I stayed in touch with his mum. She likes to see Oliver.'

'But I thought . . . How old is Oliver?'

Cassie looks puzzled for a minute, then smiles and shakes her head again. 'Sorry, it must be confusing. Ollie isn't my husband's child, but Joyce – David's mum – is fond of him, and—' She glances over at the counter, where the queue is building up again. 'Sorry, I'd better go and give them a hand. I'll have to tell you all about it another time.' She starts to walk away, then turns back, taking a pen and notepad from her apron pocket. 'Here's my phone number.' She tears off a sheet and puts it on the table. 'Can you text me your address?'

'Yes, sure. What time should I expect you?'

Cassie looks at me oddly and laughs. 'I think you're supposed to tell me, aren't you?'

CHAPTER TWENTY-ONE

Now

I go round the house, opening all the windows to let in some air. They've been closed for so long that I have to force some of them. There aren't many photos of Adrian on display, but I check in every room. I take down the wedding photo from the wall in the bedroom, choking up as I look at Adrian's smiling face. I remember how his eyes glittered as he made his promises, how his voice cracked with emotion. We both meant what we said, I know we did, so how could he have done this to me? And a child. After everything; a *child*. As I stand there on the verge of tears again, I have an unexpected urge to throw this picture at the wall. But I'll only end up picking bits of glass out of the rug, probably end up cutting myself, too. And all that would be different afterwards would be a Band-Aid around my finger and splinters of glass in the carpet. I sigh as I wind bubble wrap around the picture so I can store it away on the top shelf of my wardrobe.

In the kitchen, I tear the cellophane off the pack of colouring pencils I bought yesterday, then rip the first few pages from the sketch pad. I take a few of the pencils and scribble roughly over the paper to wear down the ends, then I take a few more, sharpen them, then break the ends off and sharpen them again. Why on earth didn't I say I had felt pens instead? There: at least they no longer look like they've just come out of the packet. I don't want it to look as if I've made too much effort.

I glance at the kitchen clock. Ten fifteen. They'll be here soon. I've bought pains au chocolat for myself and Cassie, and a gingerbread man for Oliver. We've agreed on a three-hour session today, just to get on top of it, so maybe she'll want to start straight away and have coffee later? I realise I have no idea whether she prefers tea or coffee. What if she's one of those people who only drink cold drinks? Bugger. I should have bought some Coke, or something. All I have is the summer fruits squash I bought for Oliver. I sit down, but stand up again, restless. My hands and lips strain for the feel of a cigarette.

Five minutes before they're due to arrive, I have a sudden memory of seeing Adrian's old staff photo card in the dressing table drawer. What if she opens it? It's natural to be curious, after all. I hurry out into the hall and climb the stairs as quickly as I can, which isn't very fast. I'm not using my stick at the moment, but I still need to be careful and it's frustrating, having to go so slowly. Before the accident, I'd have run up these stairs two at a time. But there's no point in thinking about that. I was a different person then.

I scan the bedroom again to check there are no more photos on display, then I slide open the shallow drawer in the dressing table. Yes, there it is. The picture is five years old, but it's unmistakably Adrian. I shove it in my jeans pocket for now. My heart is beating harder, partly from climbing the stairs and partly from recognising what was – or could have been – a near miss. The last thing I want is for Cassie to find out who I am by stumbling on a photo of Adrian. I suppose I'll have to come clean at some point, but I haven't thought that through yet. I haven't really thought any of this through. All I know is that Oliver only has one parent when he should have two, and as Adrian isn't here, I can be that other parent. I can help Cassie, and I can give Oliver all the love I've built up inside me.

Cassie tells Oliver to say hello, but he just smiles shyly, remaining glued to his mother's side as we stand in the kitchen having the obligatory discussion about the weather. 'So,' Cassie says, 'do you want to show me what you'd like me to do? And where you keep your cleaning stuff and so on?'

I talk her through where to find things, open the cupboard under the sink to check what's there and then cross the room to show her where I keep spare cloths and bin bags. As she moves nearer to have a look, Oliver clings to her hand. It's hard to see how she's going to be able to leave him while she cleans, but somehow, this *has* to work out. 'Oliver,' I say, crouching down to his level and ignoring the tight pull in my back, 'Would you like to do some colouring?'

Oliver appears to give this some thought before shaking his head. 'No thanks,' he says. This is the first time I've heard him speak, and his voice is so sweet I want to reach out and hug him. 'Tell you what,' I straighten up and smile at Cassie, 'how about we have coffee first? Then he might relax a bit; feel more comfortable.'

Cassie glances at her watch. 'Only thing is, I'm a bit tight for time today because Ollie has a party to go to at two.'

'That's fine. I don't expect you to work for the whole three hours, you know. I was factoring in coffee and a chat.'

'Well.' Cassie smiles. 'If you're sure. That would be lovely, thank you.'

There's a subtle difference in the way we're talking to each other now, I notice. In the café, she was more at ease, more confident. 'So,' I smile at Oliver, 'you're off to a party today, are you? That's exciting, isn't it, Oliver? Or is it okay if I call you Ollie?'

He looks at his mother and then back at me and he nods, a smile touching the corners of his mouth but not quite manifesting fully.

'Whose party is it?'

'Harry's.'

'I see. And is Harry your best friend?'

He shakes his head. 'No, him is just my friend. My best friend is Edmund. He's three. I did went to his birthday on a different day. He did get a Spiderman suit and a Spiderman lunchbox and I gived him some Spiderman pyjamas and a Spiderman mask.' He looks up at his mum. 'Didn't I, Mummy?'

'You certainly did.'

'Really?' I say. 'Does Edmund like Spiderman, by any chance?'

He nods earnestly.

'And do you like Spiderman, too? By any chance?'

Again, the serious nod.

I catch Cassie's eye and we laugh. 'What would you like, Cassie? Tea or coffee? Would Oliver like some squash?

'Oh, black coffee, please. I've got Ollie's drink here.' She rummages in her cavernous bag and brings out a cup with a lid, which she hands to Ollie. 'Now sit at the table and drink that like a good boy.' Then she pulls out some miniature figures and a couple of plastic cars.

'If it hadn't been so wet recently he could play in the garden.' It occurs to me that there isn't really anything for a small child to play with out there, although there's a lot of space to run around in. I remember seeing him in the playground at the nursery kicking one of those smaller-sized footballs designed especially for young children. I make a mental note to buy one. I switch the coffee machine on. 'Americano okay?'

'More than okay – I'm used to instant at home.'

I bring the coffee to the table along with the pains au chocolat and the gingerbread man.

'My goodness, look at this, Ollie! What do you say?'

'Thank you,' he says obediently, not taking his eyes from the enormous biscuit. Then he looks at his mum. 'Am I allowed—'

'Go on,' she says. 'Special treat.'

'Sorry.' I look at Cassie. 'I didn't think – I should have checked with you first.'

'It's fine. We're careful about sugar, but that doesn't mean he can't have the occasional treat.' She nods towards the pastries. 'You're spoiling me as well – this is so kind of you, Leah. Honestly. I'm perfectly happy with a cup of instant and a custard cream.'

'You might be,' I laugh, 'but I'm bloody not.' I slap my hand over my mouth. 'Oh, God, sorry.' What is the matter with me? I've dreamed of getting to know Ollie since I first laid eyes on him, and then I go and spoil it by swearing in front of him.

'Don't worry,' Cassie says. 'I'm sure he's heard worse from me.'

'It won't happen again, I promise.'

We'd agreed on eleven pounds an hour, and when I hand Cassie thirty-five pounds, she starts rummaging in her purse for change. 'Oh, for God's sake, don't worry about that – it's only a couple of quid.'

'But I've hardly done anything today. By the time we got Ollie settled and sorted out what needed doing, well, I can't have done more than two hours at the most.'

'No, you've been here for three hours, so I pay you for three hours.'

Cassie looks hesitant. 'Well, if you're sure. Thank you, thank you very much.' She packs Oliver's toys back in her bag. 'Next time, I'll bring your stepladder up from the cellar so I can do the tops of the pictures and mirrors. I'll have a wipe round the picture rails, too.'

'That would be great,' I say. 'Climbing ladders is tricky for me now, so anything above eye level is probably filthy.'

'Does it cause you a lot of pain?'

I pause, wondering if she'll ask. People tend not to. There's something about accidents and injuries that everyone seems to recognise as being private. It's another taboo – if you don't ask what happened, you keep it out of your consciousness; it's not part of your world and therefore it can't happen to you. 'On and off. Some days are worse than others. Anyway,' I smile and look around, 'the house looks lovely – it must have been dirtier than I thought.'

'No way. Between you and me, your house is considerably cleaner than some of the houses I've worked in.'

'Really?'

'Oh yes, especially the last one. Massive place it is, even bigger than this. They've got a big long drive at the front and huge gardens at the back – even have a gardener twice a week. You'd think they'd try and keep it nice, wouldn't you?' She kneels down to help Ollie with his trainers. 'They've got three teenage children. And, well, their bedrooms . . .' She wrinkles her nose and fans under it with her hand. 'Even the daughter – and I thought girls' bedrooms were supposed to smell nice!'

We laugh conspiratorially. 'Sorry,' Cassie says. 'You must think I go blabbing about every house I clean, but honestly, I'm not usually this indiscreet.' She lifts Ollie and sets him back on his feet, then stands and hoists her bag onto her shoulder.

'Cassie, I think I know you well enough now to know you're not a gossip.'

She hesitates. 'Leah, don't take this the wrong way, but it feels a bit weird, you know? Working for you after we've talked so much in the café? I'm really grateful for the job but, well, I hope we can still, like, chat when you come in for your coffee?'

'Of course we can! Have I put you in an awkward position? That's the last thing I want to do. It's just that when you said you did cleaning as well, I got quite excited because, like I said, the only cleaners I've come across before have been . . . I don't know, I'm not sure how to put it without sounding like a stuck-up cow, but, well, you're not your average cleaning lady, are you?'

Cassie laughs. 'I suppose not. Although when you think about it, what *is* your average cleaning lady? I know several intelligent, educated women who clean other people's houses because it's the only thing that fits in with school times. One of the other mums at the preschool cleans four mornings a week and she's doing a PhD.'

'Now you think I'm a snob.'

'No. But let's be honest, it's not exactly a career choice. Nor is the café, although I do enjoy working there.' She glances at her watch. 'Oh God, I'd better get Oliver Cromwell here to this party.'

'My name is not called Oliver Clomwell.'

'Joking, mister,' Cassie says. 'Leah, sorry – I must go. But I'll see you at the café on Wednesday as usual, yes? We can catch up properly then.'

I smile. *Catch up properly.* Like old friends. 'I'll look forward to it. Unless … unless you want to pop back after you've dropped Ollie off? I could do us some lunch.' Am I being too pushy? 'Only a sandwich, or some cheese on toast, maybe. It's just as easy to make enough for two.'

Cassie appears to consider this before shaking her head. 'It's ever so nice of you, Leah, but I need to get some shopping done while he's at his party. Thanks, though. Maybe another time?'

'Great. I'd like that.'

'Say bye-bye to Leah.' She takes Oliver's hand and leans down to whisper in his ear.

'Bye, Leah. Thank you for the gingerbed man.'

'My pleasure, Ollie. Enjoy the party.'

CHAPTER TWENTY-TWO

Now

Five minutes or so after they've left, the doorbell rings. I'm not expecting anyone, so I almost don't answer it, but as soon as I step into the hall, I recognise Cassie's outline through the glass. She must have forgotten something.

'Leah, I'm so sorry to bother you, but the car won't start. I've called the AA, but they said it'll be forty minutes to an hour, and I was just wondering if you'd mind if I leave my car keys with you in case they arrive before I get back. We're going to hop on a bus.'

'Where's the party?'

'Oh, it's not that far. If we weren't in a hurry, we could probably walk it, but—'

'Let me drive you.'

'No, I couldn't possibly ask you to do that. It's only, like, a ten-minute bus ride.'

'Cassie, it's no trouble at all – really. If it's not that far, it won't take long. Then I can bring you back here for a cup of tea while you wait for the AA.'

'Well, if you're sure. It's ever so kind of you.'

'No problem. Let me grab my keys.'

Cassie takes the child seat out of her car and fits it into mine before lifting Oliver into it, chatting to him all the time, *There we go, Ollie, let's get you strapped in, that's it, good boy, isn't it kind of Leah to drive us to Harry's party?*

'Okay, where are we heading?'

I drive according to Cassie's directions, and we go past Oliver's little nursery. 'Look!' he says, excited. 'That's my preschool.'

'Is it?' I say, making a point of looking out of the window. 'It looks a very nice place, Oliver. Do you like going to school?'

'Preschool.'

Cassie laughs. 'He's a bit pedantic because he's just moved up from nursery. It's the same place, he's just in a different room with different teachers, and he's feeling very grown up about it.'

'Ooh, I see. Sorry, Oliver, I mean, do you like going to preschool?'

There's no reply, then Cassie laughs. 'It's no good nodding, Ollie. Leah's driving – she can't turn round to look at you.' She turns to me. 'He used to do that all the time when he was on the phone to my mum or David's mum. He's getting the hang of it now, though.' She points straight ahead. 'If you can take the next right, then it's the second turning on the left.'

The house is decorated with balloons and there's a Happy Birthday banner stretched across the bay window. The front door is open and I can see children milling around inside.

'I'll just get him settled,' Cassie says. 'He's been here to play loads of times, so I shouldn't be long.'

'No hurry. Have a lovely time, Ollie.' I wave as he walks up the path holding Cassie's hand, and the smile he gives me as he waves back makes my own mouth stretch into a broad grin.

'I can't tell you how much I appreciate this,' Cassie says as we drive back. 'I'd have got him there on the bus, but it would have been a mad dash to get back for the AA, and then I'd be worried about picking him up again. Bloody car.'

'Let's hope it's something simple.'

'Yeah, hope so. I totally took the car for granted when David was alive. He was good with engines. If it broke down, he'd tinker around with it and either fix it immediately or go off and buy some second-hand part and fit it himself. If anything goes wrong now, it costs me a bloody fortune.'

I don't say anything for a moment. 'Remind me how long ago it was that you lost your husband?'

'Nearly five years now. We'd only been married two years.'

'Oh, that's terrible. So sad. If you don't mind me asking, how—'

'He was diabetic, and he used to do his own insulin

injections. He went to a party one night – normally, I'd have been with him, but I'd had the flu and I still felt weak, so I didn't go. I'm not sure what happened, whether he was careless or whether someone thought it would be funny to get him drunk, but anyway, he missed his insulin, and—' Her voice catches.

I glance at her and, seeing that she's struggling not to cry, reach over and touch her arm. 'I'm sorry, I didn't mean to upset you. I shouldn't have asked.'

'No.' Cassie sniffs, then sighs. 'No, I don't mind talking about it, it just gets me now and again, that's all. I'm thirty-seven years old and I'm a widow. I just think it's shit, sometimes.'

'I'm really sorry,' I say again. 'That's something we have in common – both too young to be widowed.'

I see Cassie turn her head sharply. 'Oh, my God, I didn't realise! When you said you were on your own, I don't know why, I just assumed you meant you'd split up. Shit, Leah, I'm so sorry.'

I find I can't speak. I intend to shrug and say something along the lines of, *I'm coping*, or, *I'm getting used to it*, but my throat is clogged with tears. Now it's Cassie's turn to put a comforting hand on my arm. I bite my lip and nod in acknowledgement.

'How long ago?'

'Not long.' I slow down as I approach the house, flick the indicator and turn into the drive. 'October last year. He was killed in a car accident.'

Cassie gasps and both hands fly up to her mouth. 'Oh, my God,' she says again, 'how awful. I don't know what to say.'

I turn off the engine, rest my hands on the steering wheel and sigh. 'No, it's hard to know what to say. I think ... Sometimes I think I still haven't quite taken it in myself. I keep thinking he's going to walk back in one day.'

'I used to think that about David. I couldn't believe he was never coming back.'

We sit in silence for a few moments, then I take the keys out of the ignition. 'Come on, let's go in and get a cup of tea.'

We're both subdued as we drink tea at the kitchen table.

'How old was your husband?' Cassie asks.

'He'd just turned forty-two.'

'David was thirty-six. We used to talk about "the future", as if it was this long period of time stretching out in front of us that we could fill with ... Oh, it felt so *unfair*, apart from anything else.'

I nod. God, I want a cigarette. 'I know what you mean. Did you feel angry? I did. Angry that he'd gone, angry with him for dying, and angry ... Oh, I don't know. Just generally very, very angry.'

'Yes, me too. Sometimes I used to walk round the house crying and shouting at him for leaving me so soon, before we'd even had a baby. Mad, isn't it? But I think grief can make you go a bit loopy. What was his name, by the way? Your husband?'

'Oh.' There's a beat before I say, 'Clive.' It crosses my mind too late that he might have told Cassie his real name rather than the one he used, but she doesn't react.

'I expect—' She stops as her phone vibrates. 'Hang on, this might be them. Hello? Yes, brilliant, see you in a bit.' She gets to her feet. 'They're just round the corner. Thanks again, Leah. For driving us, and for the chat. It's good to talk to someone who knows what it's like.'

I nod. 'Yes, I agree.' This is unexpected, this bond I sense starting to form between us. I take a breath and swallow the lump that's rising in my throat. 'I hope they can fix your car, but if not, come and let me know and I'll drive you back to pick him up.'

As soon as she's gone, I go upstairs to the bedroom, from where I might just be able to see what's happening. Sure enough, there's the AA van pulling up behind Cassie's Clio. If it can't be repaired on the spot, I'll drive her back to collect Oliver and insist on driving them home. She's bound to invite me in, and then we can talk some more.

I stand there, peering round the curtain like some nosy neighbour for about ten minutes, but my back doesn't like me standing still for long. I was so excited about them coming today that I didn't do my exercises this morning.

I go back down to the kitchen for painkillers. If I don't take something now, I won't be able to drive; but just as I swallow them, a text comes through: *All done – blockage in the fuel pipe. Thx again for all yr help Cxx*

Disappointment washes over me. The rest of my Friday, which half an hour ago held the promise of more time with

Oliver and another conversation with Cassie, now looks the same as most of my other days – food of some sort, wine this evening, probably too much, and an attempt to distract myself with something on Netflix.

Oliver seems more relaxed the second time, trotting in happily with his rucksack full of toys and colouring books. The house is starting to look sharper, more definite, and the kitchen gleams. As Cassie tackles the spills on the cupboard doors, the spattered, greasy tiles, smeary taps and stained sink, I realise how badly I've let things go.

It's a nice day, so Oliver takes his toys into the garden and plays happily on the grass where I can see him through the window. At eleven, I call to him that Mummy and I are having a coffee break, and would he like a juice break. He runs in from the garden and clambers up onto the kitchen chair, swinging his feet back and forth as he sips at his cup of blackcurrant and apple squash. He seems distracted. 'I'm hungry,' he says, and before I can say anything, Cassie says, 'Oliver, come on. You had a huge bowl of Cheerios before we came out, not to mention toast and peanut butter.'

'But I'm *starving*,' he whines.

'You can't possibly be hungry already.' Then her face changes. 'Wait a minute, I get it.' She looks at me and mouths, *He's remembering last week.*

Really? I mouth back. Then I turn to Oliver. 'Ollie, I'm afraid I don't have any gingerbread men this time, so sorry about that, but—'

'Don't apologise, Leah. Ignore him. He's being outrageous. And Ollie, don't think we're not on to you, buddy.'

'Well,' I say quietly, 'I do have something – if it's okay with you? It's only sponge cake, I think, with a little jam and buttercream icing.'

'Oh look, you shouldn't have. I don't mind him having sweet stuff now and again, but don't let him manipulate you into buying cakes and things. He's not as hard done by as he makes out.'

I laugh. 'I'm sure he isn't, but I couldn't resist this.' I open the cupboard and take out the Spiderman cake I paid ten pounds for yesterday. 'I was in Waitrose last night when they started reducing things, and this was down to two quid – I know he likes Spiderman, and . . . well, it was such a bargain, I thought, why not?'

Oliver's eyes widen at the sight of the cake.

'Two quid?' Cassie says. 'You're kidding.' She leans over and looks at the spidery *Happy Birthday* written in red and black icing across the middle. 'Although I suppose it's not the sort of thing they can shift easily once it's at its sell-by date.'

'That's what I thought.' I make sure I keep my thumb over the date as I slide the cake out of its packaging and cut him a big slice.

CHAPTER TWENTY-THREE

Now

Ollie has become increasingly used to me over the last few months, and he's so comfortable here now that he makes a beeline for 'his' cupboard as soon as he comes in – I keep some colouring books and a few toys here for him. Only bits and pieces I've picked up in charity shops, but he likes to have something different to play with. 'Hey, Ollie, where's my hug? Did you have a nice time at Nana's?'

He nods as he comes and gives me a quick hug. They've been down in Cornwall for two weeks, but it seems longer since I've seen him. He's unusually quiet, so while Cassie's in the sitting room washing the windows, I sneak him a few Smarties and ask him what's wrong. At first, he won't answer, but then he mutters that he wanted to play with Gemma and Georgie.

'Are Gemma and Georgie in your class?' I ask.

He shakes his head.

'Oh. How do you know Gemma and Georgie, then?'

He looks puzzled. I'm only just learning the complexities of conversation with a three-year-old. 'I mean, if they're not friends from nursery—'

'*Preschool*,' he corrects me.

'Sorry, preschool. Are they friends you used to play with before you started at preschool?'

He shakes his head again. 'I gotted them . . .' He thinks for a moment, then climbs down from his chair and runs into the sitting room. 'Mummy, what day did I get Gemma and Georgie?'

I hear Cassie answer him, then he comes running back in. 'I gotted them on Thursday. Mummy says they might get dead when they're two. Or maybe three.' He shrugs. 'Something like that.'

I look at him. Did he say what I thought he said?

'Gerbils.' Cass appears in the doorway, smiling as she peels off her rubber gloves. 'Got any vinegar, Leah? I've rinsed them, but they're still a bit smeary.'

'Vinegar. Yes, I think so.' I open the cupboard next to the cooker. Cass comes up behind me and whispers, 'He wanted a kitten, but I managed to persuade him to go for the gerbils. The bloody things stink the house out, but at least they won't live too long.'

'Ah, I see.' A thought creeps into my head, but I need to assess it properly, so I take my time finding the vinegar. It's quite a big decision, but I can't linger; it needs to be now.

'There. Knew I had some somewhere.' I hand the bottle to Cass. 'Good move on the gerbils. Weird coincidence, though.' I lower my voice. 'I've been thinking about getting a pet myself since . . .' I swallow. 'Since Clive died. I'd more or less decided on a kitten. I was looking online last night, believe it or not.'

'Spooky! Did you find one?' Cass glances at Ollie, who is now engrossed in his Peppa Pig jigsaw and is humming the theme tune. 'I feel mean, not letting him have a cat, but it's just too much of a tie, not to mention the cost.'

'Don't feel guilty. Maybe you can get one when he's older. Anyway, no, I haven't chosen one yet. But maybe I could get Ollie to come and have a look with me now – might help pass the time until he can get back to his gerbils.'

'He'd love that,' she says. 'You'll be his friend for life.'

'Great. I was planning to make up my mind today, so this'll make me get on with it.' I walk over to the table. 'Ollie, listen, there's something you might like to help me with.'

As I scroll through the photos of cute seven- or eight-week-old kittens for sale or 'free to a good home', I find myself becoming quite excited about the idea of having a pet again. We had a lovely black cat called Louis when we were first married, but we were both so upset when he got run over that we never got another one. Oliver is drawn instantly to a four-week-old tortoiseshell, but when I explain that it'll be a few weeks before it's old enough to leave its mother, he goes for an adorable little grey tom with a white bib and paws. A brief phone call later, and I've arranged to pick the kitten up on Thursday. 'So he'll be here next time you come.' I ruffle Ollie's hair as we go back downstairs. 'And you'll be able to play with him straight away.'

He nods, but I can see he's disappointed that we can't have the kitten immediately.

I go to the café on Thursday afternoon instead of Wednesday. 'Hi.' Cassie smiles. 'You're messing with my head – it's Thursday today, isn't it? Missed you yesterday.'

'Oh, God,' I laugh, 'am I that predictable? Thing is, I'm picking the kitten up this afternoon, and I was wondering whether Ollie would like to come with me? If you don't have other plans, that is. We'd need to pop his child seat over into my car, but if I take him to pick up the kitten then back to mine for an hour, you could grab some "me" time and I could drop him back to you, say, five thirty-ish? How does that sound?'

Cassie's face brightens. 'Leah, that would be fantastic! I had a bit of a domestic crisis this morning and it's going to take some sorting out when I get home, so it would be brilliant if you could occupy Ollie for an hour or so. If you're sure you don't mind?'

'Of course I don't mind. What happened?'

'Bloody water tank in the loft burst and the water came through the ceiling in Ollie's room – it was dripping onto his bed.'

'Oh, no! Was he okay?'

'He didn't even wake up! I thought he'd wet the bed, but then I saw the hole in the ceiling. It's the second time I've had a flood in this house – it was the washing machine last time, but at least that was just the kitchen floor.' She shakes her head. 'Had to get an emergency plumber out first thing, so that cost a bloody fortune. I seem to be prone to leaking pipes and burst tanks.' She gives a half-laugh. 'In fact, that's how I met Ollie's dad.'

I feel my pulse rate shoot up and my face going hot. 'Oh yes?' I try not to show how desperate I am for more detail.

'Yes, a pipe burst in the flat above the shop – I used to have a little florist's business – the shelves were coming down, and . . . Oh, it's a long story.' She glances back at the counter where the queue is lengthening. 'I'd better get on.'

'You'll have to tell me another time.'

'Yeah, okay. Are you sure about today? There's quite a mess to clear up, and I could really do with Ollie being out of the way.'

'Of course I'm sure. And I'd love to hear more about the florist thing sometime.'

'You're a lifesaver.' Cass looks at her watch. 'I finish in an hour. Shall I meet you at the preschool? I'll text you the address and we can pop in together to pick him up.'

'It's okay – I know where it is.' There's a beat before I add, 'We drove past it that day, remember? When I drove you to the party. See you there.'

*

Preschool finished five minutes ago, and there's still no sign of Cass. I drum my fingers on the steering wheel as I watch the stream of parents thinning out, their children skipping along beside them clutching lunchboxes and paintings. It's another four minutes before I see Cassie's car pull up opposite. 'Sorry,' she says as she dashes across the road. 'It's always so bloody hard to get out of that place. Didn't mean to keep you waiting.'

'It doesn't bother *me*,' I say. 'I'm just worried about Ollie.'

'He'll be fine. He probably won't even be the last one there.'

In fact, he is the last one there, but only just, and he looks happy enough when he sees we've both come to collect him. If the teacher is pissed off, she doesn't show it, and smiles pleasantly when Cassie introduces me.

When Cassie explains the plan to Ollie, a grin stretches across his face and he slips his hand happily into mine while Cass walks on ahead to move the child seat over.

Oliver grips my hand tightly as we wait on the doorstep. 'What do you think we should call him?'

'Spiderman,' he says without hesitation.

'Hmm. Let's see what we think when we see him.'

There's a distinct whiff of cat litter as the door opens, but the woman is big and smiley, and Ollie relaxes his grip as we follow her along the hallway and through an enormous, shambolic kitchen dominated by cats. A large wooden

Siamese serves as a doorstop; ceramic cats in all colours look down from cluttered shelves; the cushions on the battered sofa are appliquéd with cat faces, and the walls, cupboard doors and fridge are festooned with feline photos. It takes me a moment to register that there are also five or six actual live cats in the room, perched at various levels on shelves or chairs. A large black and white with a tattered ear rubs briefly round my legs. We follow the woman through the kitchen and out into a long, narrow extension, where the cat litter smell is even stronger. The floor is covered with newspaper, and there are wet patches here and there. 'They think the litter trays are for playing in,' the woman says, smiling at a ginger kitten who is leaping about, scattering litter all over the place. There are several cat baskets along the side wall and two large cages at the end, both open. I can see a bundle of sleeping tabby fur in one of the cages, though it's impossible to tell how many kittens it consists of. 'We have two litters at the moment,' the woman explains. 'But I think you said you were interested in the grey and white? The little boy?'

'That's right,' I say, then, 'Are you still keen on the grey one, Ollie?'

Oliver's eyes are wide as he looks around at the bundles of fluff in varying colours, and I wonder if he might change his mind, but he nods solemnly.

'Right you are, duck.' The woman puts her hands on her hips and looks around. 'Just have to find the little tinker.'

'*Tinker.* How about that as a name, Ollie?'

'Ah, there he is,' the woman points to a threadbare armchair where a tiny white paw is just visible poking over the top. 'He likes climbing, does this little lad.' She turns the armchair round to reveal the grey kitten spread out like a starfish across the back, claws clinging to the upholstery and tail flicking back and forth. 'Come on, young-fella-me-lad.' She carefully unhooks each claw and then buries her nose in the grey fur before gently placing the kitten in Ollie's arms.

We go back through into the kitchen and I count out the cash as the woman goes through the kitten's routine and hands over his vaccination record. Ollie is kneeling on the floor, grinning as he draws his finger up the front of the sofa to encourage the kitten to climb after it. 'Now, I'm sure you're very excited, Oliver,' the woman says, 'but you must remember that kitty is still a baby, so although he'll enjoy playing with you, you must be very gentle, and you must remember that kitty needs his rest, too.'

Oliver giggles as the kitten bats at his finger with its paw, but then he glances up and nods. 'Okay.'

'It might take kitty a few days to get used to his new home, so you'll have to—'

'Oh, Oliver doesn't live—'

But the woman continues, '. . . be patient with him, and make sure you listen to Mummy when she—'

I hesitate before interrupting a second time. Ollie is so engrossed in the kitten, he isn't paying much attention anyway. I've been a mother; will always think of myself as one, but I'll never be 'Mummy' again. 'I'm not his mum, actually. But he'll be having quite a lot to do with the kitten, I hope.' I brush my hand through Ollie's hair. 'You're going to come and play with him at my house, Ollie, aren't you?'

He nods, not taking his eyes from the kitten.

'Oh, sorry, I just assumed. Well, Oliver, still bear in mind that you mustn't tire him out when you visit him, okay?' She looks at me. 'Have you decided what to call him yet?'

'What do you think, Ollie?' I've made it his choice, so if he insists on Spiderman . . .'Spider,' he says. And the cat is named.

Ollie pleads to be allowed to stay a bit longer, even though Spider is now sound asleep in the red tartan basket we bought from Petland on the way home. 'I told Mummy I'd have you home by teatime, but maybe . . . What's your favourite tea, Ollie?'

He thinks about it. 'Sausages and beans.'

'That's amazing! That's my favourite, too. In fact, I was thinking of having sausages and beans tonight. I wonder if Mummy would let you have tea here? Then you can play with Spider for a bit longer and I could take you home after. Would you like that?'

Ollie is bouncing around by this time, and I wonder whether the Fanta and chocolate fingers I gave him the moment we got back have anything to do with it. He's dancing around the kitchen. 'Yes please, yes, please, yes pleasy-weasy, Leah-leasy.' Then he's overtaken by giggles.

'Okay, let's call Mummy and see what she says.'

Cassie is still cleaning up after the flood, she says, so if I'm sure I don't mind . . .

We sit together at the kitchen table, Ollie swinging his legs and chattering away as he eats his sausages and beans, and I find myself staring at him, at the way one of his eyebrows arches slightly higher than the other, just like Adrian's; the way a little tuft of hair sticks up at the crown. I think about my babies.

Oliver plays with the kitten again after we've eaten, and when it's time to go home, he looks almost tearful until I remind him that he's coming again tomorrow because it's Friday. By the time we pull up outside Cassie's, he's so nearly asleep that his eyes are glazed and half-closed. 'Come on, sweetheart.' I unclip him from the child seat and lift him out, settling him against my hip. He lays his head against my shoulder and puts his thumb in his mouth, and for a few blissful moments, I rest my head against his before locking the car and carrying him into the house.

CHAPTER TWENTY-FOUR

Then

We were in bed by ten o'clock most nights. We both started yawning at about nine, so there didn't seem much point in fighting it. Grief was tiring. Adrian reached for his book, and I picked up my notebook and rested it against my knees. I wasn't using proper writing paper this time, because I'd decided to stop 'sending' my letters. I was thinking of this more as a journal now, even though I still wanted to write in letter form. I'd tried writing a journal before, but I wasn't very good at keeping it up. It didn't matter this time, though, because it wasn't for any other purpose than to help me to come to terms with losing Thomas.

My darling baby boy,

It's now more than three months since we said hello and goodbye to you on the same day. I still think about you every single day and night and I miss you more than I thought possible. I am back at work now, and in some ways it helps, because when I'm thinking about my lectures, or writing my comments on a student's essay, it means there's a purpose for me, a reason to be here. For the first few weeks all I could think about was that the thing I was meant to do was to be your mummy, but that I'd never be able to mother you like I was supposed to. It's so hard to accept. I am trying, though.

Daddy and I talked about you last night, and we looked at the photos we took of you in hospital. You were so beautiful, so peaceful. You really did look as if you were asleep, about to open your eyes at any moment. We found some pictures of Daddy when he was a baby, and you look exactly the same.

Then I found myself writing, *Did you get my last letter?* I crossed it out quickly. Idiot. I felt so stupid I almost laughed at myself. I didn't think setting my letters alight and allowing them to burn was silly, though. And I suppose I *was* 'sending' them, in a way, in that I was releasing my expression of grief and love out into the ether rather than keeping it all inside. But if I started thinking I was actually sending them to Thomas, and that he was going to read them, well, that was borderline nuts. Some of the women on the baby loss forum talked about feeling as if they were going crazy, or being 'mad with grief'. And sometimes it did feel as if I was only just holding onto my sanity.

Sweetheart, I write. *I'd give anything to hold you in my arms and look into your eyes. I love you so much. Mummy xxx*

I closed the notebook and put it on the bedside table. Adrian yawned and shut his book. 'I don't know why I'm bothering,' he said. 'I've just read three pages and haven't taken in a word.'

'Tired?' I asked. 'Or were you thinking about Thomas?'

'Bit of both, I suppose.'

Part of me was glad it wasn't just tiredness that was stopping him from reading. I knew he'd been devastated at the time, but after the first few weeks it seemed as if he was getting over it, and while I didn't want him to be as bogged down by grief as I was, I didn't want to be left behind, either.

He gave a big, deep sigh. 'It was hard today. At work.'

My first thought was that I really couldn't give a toss whether he'd had a hard day at work. My baby was stillborn, for Christ's sake! I must have made some sound that gave away what I was thinking because he turned sharply to look at me.

'I wasn't going to tell you this, because I know it'll upset you, but . . . Well, the thing is, now you're back at work, too, the same thing's bound to happen to you at some point, so I thought I'd—'

'Stop talking in riddles. What happened?'

He sighed again. 'Toby – you remember Toby? Got married Christmas before last – we went to the evening do?'

'Yes, of course I remember. What about him?'

'They've had a baby.'

The room seemed to shift. My throat closed up and although I tried to speak, nothing was coming out. I took a breath, then let it out slowly. 'I . . . I see.'

'I'd forgotten they were pregnant, then he rang in to say she had the baby at two o'clock this morning, and of course I had to congratulate him, say what wonderful news it was.'

'Did he know? About Thomas?'

Adrian shook his head. 'I don't think so. He's been working at Loughborough. Only came back last week, so I don't suppose anyone would have told him, not with his wife about to . . . In any case, I certainly didn't.'

He reached for my hand. We sat there for a good few minutes, not saying anything, just thinking. I wanted to put my arms around him, or even just move nearer to put my head on his shoulder, but I felt frozen.

He sighed. 'Well, I just thought I'd tell you, you know? So you're prepared for it if the same thing happens at your place.'

I nodded. It was quite likely, given that I had a lot of female colleagues. And students, of course. I couldn't believe it hadn't occurred to me. 'I'm sorry. It must have been upsetting.'

'Yeah,' he said. 'It was shit.' There was a hint of anger in his voice, then another silence. 'Oh, well, I suppose we'd better get some sleep.' He leaned over and kissed me briefly, chastely, on the lips. 'Night,' he said, and reached out to switch the lamp off.

'Goodnight,' I murmured, and then we turned our backs on each other and tried to sleep, our bodies not even touching.

I wondered how this had happened to us. And I wondered how long it would last.

CHAPTER TWENTY-FIVE

Now

Ollie wakes again as soon as we're inside, bursting with news of the kitten and the name he's chosen and the nice lady with the smelly house full of cats. It isn't long before his chatter subsides, though, and he's soon yawning. Encouraged by the novelty of sleeping on a camp bed in his mum's room until the ceiling is repaired, he trots off to bed without argument.

'Out like a light,' Cassie says when she comes down from tucking him in. She opens the fridge and takes out a half-full bottle of Chardonnay. 'I know I said stay for a cuppa, but shall we have a glass of wine instead? I bloody deserve it after the day I've had. And you deserve it for helping out with Ollie.'

'Just a small one, then. Honestly, he's no trouble. And it was lovely to see him with the kitten.'

'I'm knackered.' Cassie raises her glass and clinks it

against mine. 'I've had to move everything out of his room so the guys can get to the ceiling to repair it, and as you can see, there's not a lot of space here, so I've had to be creative. The flooring's ruined as well – I put laminate down, thinking it'd be more practical. I hope the insurance pays up quickly.'

'Good luck with that.' I take a sip of my wine. 'You said you've had trouble with flooding before?' *That's how I met Ollie's dad.* I have to consciously steady my hand as I put the glass down.

'God, yes. This is the third time. At least last time the only damage was in the kitchen – I had to replace the floor tiles, but that was it.'

'You said something about meeting Oliver's dad because of a flood?'

'Yes, that's right. Seems like another life now. David – my husband – and I ran a little floristry business. I did the flowers, he did the deliveries and managed the contracts and we both worked in the shop.'

'I didn't know you'd been a florist.'

'Yeah. Went to horticultural college and everything. I loved it. Still miss it, in fact.'

'I'm impressed! So you know all about plants and stuff?'

She smiles and nods.

'Remind me to ask you about my garden at some point. So what happened? With the flood?'

She sighs. 'Things started to cave in after David died. Fortunately, his insurance paid off the mortgage on this place, but I still had to try and earn enough to cover food and bills, pay the rent on the shop, buy in the stock, and so on.'

I nod, try to look encouraging.

'As you can imagine, I was in a bit of a state. I was thirty-two and I'd lost my husband, just at the point when life had started looking up – the shop was doing well, and we were trying for a baby. But after I lost him . . .' Her voice catches, and she takes a gulp of wine.

I know I should say something, tell her not to carry on if it's upsetting her. But it's too important. *Please tell me what happened*, I urge silently.

'I closed the business for a couple of weeks, but I couldn't afford to take any more time off, and there wasn't anyone who could help out in the shop. My mum came up for a while but she wasn't much help, to be honest. Anyway, I let things slip and the takings went down, and then, about three months after David died, there was this flood in the flat upstairs. A pipe had burst, and it started coming through the ceiling. I ran up and knocked on their door but there was no one in and the water just kept on coming. I was trying to move stuff out of the way, but then a bit of the ceiling came down, smashed onto the shelves and sent the plants crashing onto the floor.'

'Oh no, that's awful.' *What does this have to do with Adrian?*

'Then I noticed that one of the other shelves was starting to tip forward – the water was running down the wall and soaking the plaster – which wasn't all that stable in the first place, and I could see the bracket was coming loose. This shelf had a lot of expensive stock on it – china plant pots, and so on – so I was up the ladder, frantically trying to support the wood with one hand and take stuff off it with the other, when the door opened and this guy came in.' She picks at the label on the bottle.

My heart thuds. Do I really want to hear this? But I can't not. I have to know.

'He could see he'd walked right into a crisis and he went straight into action. Helped me get all the stuff down, then took the shelf off the wall so it didn't crash onto the other plants. He was brilliant. He stayed to help me clear up the mess and get everything into the back room so it wouldn't get damaged – the water was still coming through at this point. It stopped eventually, and we got everything as in order as it possibly could be, but for some reason that was when I burst into tears. I think it just suddenly hit me. David was gone, and I was completely on my own. So this guy – Adrian, he was called—'

I know, I want to shout, *I bloody know.* But I just nod to show I'm listening.

'He was so sweet, so sympathetic. He gave me a cuddle, found a loo roll so I could mop my face and then insisted on taking me for a drink. It was one of those weird things, you know? He was married – he told me that immediately – and I was still grieving for David, but somehow . . .' She shrugs.

I grip the stem of my glass so tightly to stop my hand from shaking, I worry it might snap. I'm sure my face and neck must be turning red. I wait, but she doesn't say any more. 'So how did you end up with Oliver?' I'm aware of the confrontational edge to my voice, but Cassie doesn't notice.

'Well, one thing led to another, as these things do.'

I take a mouthful of wine but my throat feels paralysed and I struggle to swallow. 'A one-night stand, then?' I try to make it sound light, as though I don't really care.

'More or less. A two-night stand, in this case. We got quite drunk that night, and we came back here . . .' She pauses. 'Are you sure you want to hear all this? I'm going on and on about myself, and it must be quite boring.'

'No, it isn't. So, this – what was his name? Adrian? Did you say he was married?'

'Yes, but his wife – I'm not making excuses here, but she was ill, apparently. Very ill, although he wouldn't say what was wrong. My sister said it was probably a load of bollocks, but I believed him.' She meets my eye as if expecting me to challenge this. 'And it wasn't like I was looking for a relationship.' She looks thoughtful for a second. 'He wasn't, either. In fact, the reason he'd come into the shop in the first place was to buy some flowers for his wife – she was in hospital, and he was supposed to be going to see her the next day, although of course he didn't because he ended up staying here. I felt guilty about that, but he said she probably wouldn't even register that he wasn't there, so she must have been quite bad.'

So he did sleep with her while I was in hospital. The thought of it hurts almost physically. I don't remember much about that time – I'd still have been out of it at that point, and even when I began to surface from the medication-induced stupor I was in for so long, I didn't have any real sense of time. It felt continuous, with no defined separation of one hour or one day from the next. There was no day and night, no light and shade, only darkness.

Cassie has stopped talking. 'You disapprove, I can tell.'

I give an unconvincing shake of my head and reach for my wine, surprised to find I've nearly finished the glass. I'll have to slow down or I won't be able to drive home.

'I wouldn't blame you – I'm not proud of what I did, but . . .' She looks down at the table and shakes her head slowly. 'It's hard to explain, but that couple of days . . . Oh, I don't know.' She picks up her glass again, drains it and goes back to the fridge for more. 'Sorry, I must be boring the arse off you.' She holds up the bottle. 'Drop more?'

'Just a dribble.'

She sloshes the rest of the wine into my glass before I can stop her, then opens another bottle and refills her own.

'Thanks. And you are definitely not boring me! So what happened? Did you fall madly in love?' Again, I try to sound light and flippant, but although I'm aware of a wobble in my voice, Cassie doesn't seem to notice.

'Oh no, it was hardly the grand passion. It was just . . . God, it sounds like such a cliché, but we were two lonely people. I'd lost David, and he . . . well, he hadn't lost his wife, but I think he was afraid that he might – she was obviously very ill – and I suppose that bonded us together for a short while. He stayed two nights, and that was it.'

'But you got pregnant.'

For a moment, Cassie doesn't speak, then she sighs deeply. 'It was deliberate. I lied. Told him I was still on the pill.' Her voice is barely a whisper.

'But why? Why would you—'

'I was desperate, Leah. David and I had been trying to get pregnant when he died, and ... Oh, I wasn't thinking straight, but the idea of having a child to soak up some of the love I had left, love I'd never be able to give David ...' Her eyes glitter with tears and she brings her hand up to her mouth. 'Sorry. God, I sound so mushy.'

My own eyes are brimming. I shake my head. 'No, not at all. I ... I can understand that. I know what it is to long for a child. To have all that love and ...' I can't continue.

Cassie reaches across the table and lays a hand on my arm. 'So we have that in common, too. Were you trying to get pregnant when your husband died?'

I try to swallow, but my throat has closed up and there's a roaring in my ears. *Breathe*, I tell myself. *Breathe*. The surface of the wine in my glass shivers, like wind blowing across a lake, and I realise my hand is trembling. 'No. We ... we lost ... I had a miscarriage first, and then ... and then ... a little boy, but he wasn't ... he didn't ... he didn't live.'

Cassie scrapes back her chair and is at my side, her arm around my shoulders. 'Oh God, Leah, I'm so sorry. I shouldn't have asked.'

I'm crying now, real, full-on sobbing. I've definitely had too much to drink, and the tears keep coming. Not being able to cry was horrible, but right now it feels like I can't stop. The memory of that day is still sharp and clear.

Everyone in the delivery suite was very kind. Dr Winter, on the verge of tears herself, kept her voice crisp and professional as she asked if we wanted to see Thomas as soon as he was born. It hadn't occurred to me that I wouldn't, but Adrian had reservations. 'Will it be upsetting?' he asked, running his hand through his hair. 'I mean . . . will he look . . .'

'Some skin changes can occur after a baby dies in utero, but we think Thomas's heart stopped within the last twenty-four hours, so in his case, these should be minimal.'

'I want to see him,' I cut in. 'I've been carrying him inside me all this time. I've been talking to him. How could you think I wouldn't want to see him?'

Labour seemed to go on for ever. They gave me an injection that made me feel separated from myself, and at first I didn't realise that the whimpering I could hear was me. There was no other sound in the delivery room, so I could hear what was happening in the room next to ours. 'Sorry,' our midwife, Sally, said. 'We were hoping you'd be on your own up here tonight, but it's suddenly gone mad.'

The voices in the next room were encouraging and excited, and then came the high, outraged cry of a newborn, followed by an explosion of joy. *Shut up*, I wanted to scream at the wall. *Please, please, shut up.* Sally carried on bustling around, doing her best to drown out the happiness next door.

Listening to all that joy only intensified the horrible silence around me, and as I started to push, Sally was the only one who spoke, her voice barely more than a whisper. 'That's the way,' she said. I could feel her awkwardness and distress, and I wondered if this was the first time she'd delivered a stillborn. 'Good girl. Nearly there now.'

When another violent contraction gripped me, I pushed so hard I let out a prolonged grunt.

'That's the head. One more push now,' and almost before she'd finished speaking, I felt him slither out. I caught a glimpse of him as they whisked him away, the blueish colour, the spots of blood. On television, babies often looked like this when they were born, and for the briefest of moments, I thought maybe it was all a mistake. Maybe the heartbeat we heard on the monitor *hadn't* been mine, like they said, but Thomas's, steady and strong, undetectable because it was beating in rhythm with my own. But then I remembered that rigid, unmoving image on the screen.

The room was still silent but for the faint rustling of sterile packs and the odd clink of metal instruments as they prepared to stitch me up. I closed my eyes for a few seconds and when I opened them, Sally was standing next to me with Thomas, wrapped in a white blanket. For the first time, I felt a flicker of apprehension. But then Sally leaned over and put him in my arms. 'I am so sorry for your loss,' she said, her voice catching. 'He's beautiful. Six pounds, two ounces.'

He looked just like Adrian – thick, dark hair, long, curled eyelashes. He even had that same little whorl of hair at the crown. His skin was pale and greyish, but apart from that he looked completely normal. As I kissed his forehead, I registered the strangeness of his cold skin. There was nothing repugnant about him at all, and I was filled with love as I gazed at him. He would always be my beautiful firstborn, my precious, longed-for baby, even though he wasn't born alive.

'Look,' I said to Adrian, turning Thomas towards him. 'Isn't he exquisite?'

Adrian touched Thomas's cheek with his finger, too moved to speak.

CHAPTER TWENTY-SIX

Now

Cassie holds me with both arms and rocks me like a child. My head rests against her chest and I can smell a fabric softener that makes me think of the sea. The last person who held me like this – apart from Adrian – was one of the nurses on the unit. With the help of a few deep breaths, I manage to control myself so that my sobs turn to shaky sighs.

'My sister's little girl was stillborn,' Cassie murmurs after a while. 'It was almost ten years ago, and she says she's never really got over it, even though she has two other kids now. I can't imagine what it must be like to lose a child.' Cassie gives me a gentle hug, then steps back to examine my face. 'Are you all right?' she asks softly. 'Is it something you'd like to talk about? Or would you rather not?'

I shake my head and blow my nose. 'No. Thank you, but no, I don't think . . . not yet, anyway. But thanks for asking, and sorry for blubbing all over you. I don't know what came over me.'

'Come on, surely we know each other well enough by now? Sometimes you just need a bloody good cry.' Cassie opens the fridge and takes out the wine. 'Get this down your neck.' She fills my glass again, almost to the brim.

'No, I can't,' I say. 'I've got the car. And I've totally brought the evening down now anyway.'

'Nonsense. We're friends, aren't we? And if you can't talk to me about stuff like that, well . . .'

I nod. 'Thanks, Cass.'

'But listen, you're already over the limit, and you're in no state to drive. Stay here. That sofa's quite comfortable, and I've got plenty of spare bedding. I usually put guests in Ollie's room, but if you don't mind roughing it.'

'I don't know . . .' It's tempting to stay and abandon myself to the wine, but the surge of grief and the ferocity with which my tears forced their way out has shaken me. Not to mention the fact that I was on the verge of telling her far too much. If I were to start talking about Thomas, who knows what would pour out. And I'm not sure I can trust myself to remember to refer to Adrian as Clive. I don't know how much I've had to drink, but I know I'm not thinking straight. What would Cass think if she found out now that I was married to Adrian? A tremor passes though me. God, what a mess I've got myself into. And how have I managed to get drunk on such a small amount of wine? When I scroll back through the last few hours, I realise that I've barely eaten anything since the toast I made at about half nine this morning. That's when I remember the kitten. 'Spider,' I say aloud. 'I almost forgot about the kitten.'

'Oh, shit – me too! What a shame. Tell you what, why don't you get a taxi, then at least you can stay for one more. I'm cleaning tomorrow, aren't I, so I could drive you back to pick your car up when I finish. Go on, stay and have another drink.'

'Oh, all right then. Just one.' I take the precaution of ordering a taxi to pick me up in half an hour.

Cassie tops us both up and we clink glasses. 'Cheers,' I take a swallow and wait a beat or two. 'Before I started blubbing all over you, you were telling me about when you got pregnant with Ollie. Did the dad not stick around?'

'I didn't tell him. Like I said, it wasn't a *relationship* or anything. I wanted a baby, not a partner.' Cassie swirls her wine in her glass.

I bite my lip to stop myself from blurting out the hundred questions that are bubbling around in my head. Instead I sit back in my chair. 'So,' I speak slowly. I want to sound casual but I need to choose my words carefully. 'Are you saying he . . . he doesn't even know Ollie exists?'

She shakes her head. 'No, he knows now. I didn't want him to, but he found out by accident.'

How? What happened? When? 'Oh yes?'

'Yeah. You see, Oliver looks very much like him. More than I'd realised. We bumped into him one day and as soon as he saw Ollie, he guessed.'

'Really? He must be the image of him, then.'

'Yep. Carbon copy.'

'Wow. That must have been weird. Was this recently? What happened?'

'Last summer. You know I meet my sister for lunch once a month?'

'Yes, I think you told me – did you say she lives in Leeds?'

She nods. 'We usually go for pizza because it's not too expensive and they're very kid-friendly. So, she was already there with her two, and as I pushed the buggy over to her table, I saw this bloke do a sort of double take. It was Adrian. He was with three other men – some sort of work meeting, I think. I could tell he recognised me because he half-smiled, but he didn't say anything and then I saw them pay the bill and leave, so I thought that was that. But then a few minutes later, he came back in because he'd left his sunglasses on the table – deliberately, I think. This time, he came over. He was all smiles and he said hello and how are you, as if he was an old friend. I could see it register on my sister's face as soon as she saw him. And when he looked at Ollie, it was like, well, it was obvious he knew. He said hello, and asked him what his name was.'

She stops and I can see her focusing on the memory.

'For a minute he seemed to be mesmerised by Ollie, and I thought he was never going to leave. But then he straightened up and started chatting, you know, really casual, asking me if I still had the shop, and if I was living in the same place – I didn't think anything of it at the time, so I said yes,

I was still living here, but that I'd had to close the shop.' She pauses. 'God, I miss my little business.'

I know she wants me to ask about the florist's but I'm longing to hear the rest of the story. 'So, did he—'

'I don't know what made me think I could carry on running the shop. I had this mad idea that I could get a part-time assistant to help with the customers and the deliveries, and I'd make the wreaths and arrangements while the baby slept. Ha!'

For the first time I see a flash of, not resentment, exactly, more like disappointment, cross her face. She takes a big gulp of her wine. 'Then he said goodbye, and it was only as he was walking away that he said he'd be in touch.'

'What did you say?'

'Nothing. He sort of tossed it over his shoulder on his way out. I think he knew I'd say no. He hadn't asked for my number or anything.' She picks up the wine bottle, holds it up to the light and frowns, then tips a bit more into each glass. 'About a week later, I'm sitting in the garden watching Ollie splashing about in the paddling pool, and I see a car pull up opposite. I knew it would be him, somehow. I just knew it, like a sort of sixth sense. Do you ever get that?'

Her speech is slurred now. She's in full flow and I probably don't need to prompt any more, but I don't want her to go off the point. 'Sometimes. Weird, isn't it? So what did he say, then? When he turned up?'

'I told him I didn't want anything from him – after all, I'd deliberately got myself pregnant, and I'd managed perfectly well up until then. But he seemed genuinely keen to have some sort of relationship with Oliver. Said he wouldn't interfere with our lives, but that he wanted to contribute something – he had quite a good job, I think, so he wasn't broke. But I couldn't make a decision just like that, and with Ollie running around and wanting ice lollies and drinks and stuff, it was all too much to deal with, so I said I'd think about it. Ollie and I were going to Cornwall to see my mum and dad in a few days, so I agreed he could come again in a couple of weeks to talk about it properly.' She sways slightly as she looks at me. 'All my instincts were saying *no, stick to your guns*, you know? Anyway, three days after that, a present turns up for Ollie with a nice little note, and I start to think, well, maybe it would be nice for him to have his dad in his life, as long as it doesn't affect anything I want to do in the future, like if I wanted to move or anything.'

'You're not thinking of moving, are you?'

'Not now, but I'm not going to stay in this house for ever, am I?' She shrugs. 'But it's irrelevant, because after all that, he never turned up and I haven't heard from him since.'

I try to find my voice. 'Did you try calling him?'

'No, never took his number – he was married, remember? Although I'd have needed it eventually, if he was going to be in Ollie's life. Maybe that's why he didn't show up; maybe he saw that it wouldn't have worked. He'd have had to tell his wife, wouldn't he? Assuming she was still alive. I never asked.' She picks up her glass and finishes her wine in two swallows. 'Ah, well.'

I don't say anything for a few moments. This isn't what I expected. Not that I know what I expected. 'So . . . does Ollie know this bloke was his dad?' I realise I've used the past tense, but Cassie doesn't notice.

She nods. 'I've been up front about it, but I don't think Ollie remembers much about him – they only met twice, and Ollie wasn't even two and a half at the time. But I didn't want him starting school thinking he hasn't got a dad. He seems to accept it, but he's still only little, isn't he?' She looks at me, clearly struggling to focus. 'I think I'm a bit pissed.' Then she giggles. 'I've been talking about myself non-stop.' She leans towards me. 'Right, missus. Tell me about you.'

Before I can say any more, my phone rings and a text appears to tell me the taxi is outside.

It all goes round and round in my head. The pain of Adrian's infidelity tangled up with the relief that he hadn't fallen in love with someone else, that I hadn't driven him to a long-term affair. And that those first years before – and maybe even these last few years – weren't a sham; that we *were* soulmates, just as I always believed. But the bottom line is, he became a father without telling me. Of course I understand *why* he didn't tell me, but that doesn't change the fact that he made another woman his child's mother. It isn't fair, isn't fair, isn't fair.

CHAPTER TWENTY-SEVEN

Then

I was loading the dishwasher when Adrian came into the kitchen. I looked up, surprised. He usually went straight into the study after dinner to deal with emails and work on whatever paper he was delivering next. He'd told me about this one, but I hadn't taken it in.

'Let's go for a drink,' he said.

'A drink?'

'Yes.' He smiled. 'A drink. In a pub. It's ages since we've had a night out.'

'I don't know. I've got marking to do.'

'I thought you finished that last night?'

'Almost, but I've still got a few more.'

'But you're not teaching again until Wednesday, and you've got the whole weekend.'

I hesitated. We used to go out once a week, either for a

drink or, when I was pregnant, to have a meal or see a film. 'I don't really feel like it, to be honest.'

'Oh, go on.' He stood behind me and put his arms around my waist. 'It'll do us both good.'

'But what if someone in the pub asks—'

'We don't have to go to the Crown. We could try the Fox and Hounds. Or the Black Horse? Or if you don't mind a bit of a walk, we could—'

I shrugged him off so I could finish loading the dishwasher. 'No, I don't think so. Maybe another night.'

He sighed and turned as if to go, but then he turned back. 'Leah, it's been over six months now. I know it's hard, but we have to start learning how to carry on with our lives. I get that it still hurts – it hurts me too, you know.'

'I know. I wasn't suggesting it doesn't.'

'Then come for a drink with me. Please.'

'Oh. So you're going anyway, are you? Whether I come or not?' I said it like a challenge, as though I was trying to start a row. Why was I doing this? Why, when I needed him close to me, was I pushing him away?

He looked steadily at me for a moment then lifted his chin and said, 'Do you know what? Yes, I am. I would really, really like you to come with me, but yes, I am going out for a drink.'

We stared at each other for a minute and then he looked away. 'Right,' he said. 'See you later.' He pulled the kitchen door closed behind him.

What the hell was I doing? I ran across the room and opened the door. 'Wait! I'm sorry. I'll come.'

He didn't say anything. He still looked, not angry, exactly, but borderline. I couldn't bear what was happening to us; I needed to pull this back, make it right again. I made myself smile. 'If I'm still allowed?'

I saw something like relief in his eyes. His expression softened. 'Come on,' he said. 'We'll have one drink and then see if we want to stay longer, okay?'

This time I smiled properly. 'Okay.'

It was almost eleven when we got home. Adrian automatically put the kettle on. 'Tea?'

I still had the rich, spicy taste of red wine in my mouth, and I didn't want to lose it just yet because it reminded me of happy times – Christmas, birthdays, celebrations. I shook my head. 'No thanks. I'm not really in the mood for tea.'

He turned the kettle off again. 'Neither am I. It's just force of habit. Sod it, let's have another drink.' He took a bottle of red from the wine rack, then stopped and looked at me. 'Is this okay? Or did you want an early night?'

Early nights used to mean sex, but now they tended to mean something different, usually something along the lines of *I'm going up early so I can be asleep – or pretend to be asleep – by the time you come to bed. That way, we don't have to acknowledge the fact that we've gone from being unable to keep our hands off each other to barely even touching.* 'Yes, I mean no, I don't want an early night. Another glass of wine would be lovely. Thanks.'

We took the bottle and glasses through into the sitting room, which was still warm from earlier, the embers in the wood burner still glowing. I settled myself in the armchair with the table next to it where I could rest my glass. I took off my boots and curled my legs under me while Adrian knelt in front of the wood burner sorting out more newspaper and kindling so that within a couple of minutes, the flames were strong enough to take another log. He moved over to the sofa and stretched his long legs out in front of him. 'It's been nice tonight, hasn't it?'

'Yes,' I agreed. 'I've had . . .' I hesitated. 'I know it's silly, and I feel guilty saying it. But I'm going to say it: I've had a nice time. I'm glad we went.'

It was a quiet, old-fashioned pub with lots of dark wood, an open fire and a big friendly collie called Guinness. He sat by our table, wagging his tail and nudging Adrian's leg with his nose. We spent most of the evening throwing crisps for him, which made us both smile. And when he stuck his muzzle into the empty packet for the last crumbs, we actually laughed. It's been a while since that happened.

It was only the second time we'd been out since we lost Thomas, but at least we were able to talk about him tonight, wondering what he'd look like at six months, whether he'd have cut his first tooth, whether he'd be crawling. We wondered if he'd suck his thumb like Adrian had when he was a child, whether he'd be laughing yet. So many wonderful moments we'd never see. Thank God we had that brief, precious time with him after he was born. Maybe it was a strange thing to think, but even though that day was tragic and devastating, there was something beautiful, almost magical about those few hours, and I would always treasure those memories.

They moved us to a special 'bereavement suite', a cosy room, no windows but soft lighting, abstract paintings on the mushroom-coloured walls, armchairs. And a cold cot, so we could spend time with Thomas and say goodbye properly. We opened the pack they gave us. A disposable camera, a kit for taking hand- and footprints and a tiny outfit – a gown made of white silk and netting, a knitted white bonnet and bootees and a little cloth nappy. We took photographs of him, of each other holding him, and then we set the timer and we took some of the three of us together, our little family. I thought it sounded macabre at first, but they said that having beautiful new baby photos, just like every other new mum and dad, was often a comfort to bereaved parents. It was proof that your child had existed. There was something reassuring about doing the same things other parents would be doing, taking photos, making memories. I laid out the gown, bonnet and bootees, then I unwrapped the hospital blanket and dressed him for the first and last time, talking to him as I did so.

All too soon, there was a light knock on the door and Sally came in with another nurse. 'How are you doing?' Sally rested her hand softly on my shoulder. 'I'm afraid it's time.'

'Time? No, you can't take him now, not yet.' I was on my feet, making a barrier between them and the cot. 'You said we could have a couple of hours.'

'It has been almost three hours,' Sally said quietly.

'It can't be.' I looked at Adrian for support, but he looked at his watch and nodded, then he put his arms around me again.

'I know this is terribly hard for you both, but—'

'Okay,' Adrian said, still holding me against his chest. 'Just give us five more minutes.'

I didn't hear the door close, but I knew they'd gone because that was when Adrian started to cry. We clung to each other for a few moments before pulling apart. Adrian leaned into the cot and kissed him first, then it was my turn.

'I can't.' I shook my head. 'I can't leave him here. How can we go home without him?'

Adrian gently pulled me to him again. 'We have to, Leah. You know we do.'

It was a few moments before I could move, but then I took a deep breath, picked Thomas up and held him against my cheek. 'I love you, sweetheart,' I whispered, kissing his cheek. 'I love you, I love you, I love you always.' As I laid him back in his cot, I didn't even bother to wipe away my tears and one of them rolled off my chin and fell onto his cheek. I reached out and smoothed the tear into his cold skin with my thumb, and I felt a little better, because I knew that part of me would always be with him.

One of the logs in the burner cracked loudly, bringing me back to the present. Adrian looked down into his glass as he swirled the dark red wine around inside it. 'I know what you mean about feeling guilty. I keep catching myself not being sad, joining in with some of the banter at work or laughing at some silly thing on Facebook. And then I feel like crap because I remember that our baby died.'

I nodded. 'I still think about him every day. Do you?'

'Probably. Not as much as I did to begin with, but yeah, probably every day.'

For a while, I'd thought Adrian had moved on, so I was reassured. Tonight was probably the most we'd talked about it since it happened, and I was glad. But we still hadn't talked about what had happened to *us*. 'Do you think we'll ever be able to laugh again without feeling guilty?'

'Of course we will,' he said. 'Let's try and make it happen. I know things will never be quite the same again, but we've had such a nice evening. It's made me think there's hope that we'll be able to get back to some sort of normal.'

Some sort of normal. 'Yes, maybe that's what we should aim for – some sort of normal.'

'Come and sit over here for a change.' He patted the spot on the sofa beside him.

I picked up my glass and padded over the warm wooden floor to join him.

He slid his arm around me and pulled me close, but it felt a bit awkward. 'We used to do this all the time, didn't we?'

'When we were younger, yes.'

He laughed. 'Bloody hell, Leah – we're still in our thirties! What you mean is, we used to do this before our baby died.'

I felt my body go rigid, but he was right. It was just that everything that happened before that seemed like a lifetime ago.

'Sorry, I didn't mean to upset you.' He rested his lips against my hair and kissed the top of my head. I let my body relax against him. 'Come on, Grandma.' He put his wine glass down and encircled me with his arms. 'Let's canoodle.'

'Okay.' It came out as a whisper, but I put my arm around his waist and squeezed.

'You know what we were talking about the other night,' he said, his voice suddenly more serious. 'About trying for another baby?'

I nodded, my skin scraping against the roughness of his jumper, but I didn't say anything. We'd stumbled over the conversation and had ended up abandoning it.

'Well?' he whispered. 'Have you thought about it any more?'

'Yes, but I'm scared,' I murmured. I looked up at him. 'And not just about being pregnant again; about us. About *getting* pregnant.'

'Me too,' he whispered, and it looked as if he had tears in his eyes. 'It's been a long time, hasn't it?' Then he lifted me to my feet and held my face in his hands, and as he kissed my eyelids, I felt the faintest stirrings of desire. 'Come on,' he said. 'Let's go up. Let's be close to each other.'

I'd been going to write another letter tonight, but after only a moment's hesitation, I decided it could wait.

CHAPTER TWENTY-EIGHT

Now

When I open the door, Ollie is grinning, despite the torrential rain. He pulls back his hood and jumps in onto the mat. 'I've got new wellies,' he says, proudly putting his foot out so I can admire the frog faces on the toes.

'Wow! Those are fantastic. What a lucky boy.'

'It's absolutely chucking it down out there,' Cassie says, hanging up her coat, which is already wet, even though she's only walked from the car.

Ollie drops his rucksack in the hall and allows me to help him off with his dripping mac and boots. 'Can I play with Spider?'

'Of course you can. I think he's on the windowsill in the sitting room.'

As Ollie skips off to find the cat, I turn back to Cassie. She looks different. Her skin looks brighter and clearer, her eyes are shining and she's done something to her hair. 'Cass! You look amazing! What have you done?'

Cassie flushes and her eyes sparkle. 'I went to the hairdresser's. I thought it was about time I had it done properly. I just had some layers put in. And a few highlights.' Her hand strays up to push a wisp of hair behind her ear.

'It suits you.' It's an understatement. 'It looks lovely – really flatters the shape of your face.' It isn't just her hair, though. She looks sort of . . . softer. Something is different. 'Shall we have coffee now? Then we can have another one when we've done upstairs.' We often work together these days, me vacuuming while Cassie dusts and wipes, or vice versa, depending on how my back is. I was uncomfortable about the cleaner–employer relationship even at the start, but now we're definitely friends it seems even more wrong.

'Let's have one now.' Cassie grins, looking pleased with herself. 'Got something to tell you.'

'Oh yes? What?' I lead the way into the kitchen.

'Coffee first. Have you got anything nice to have with it? I know it was my turn to get the cakes but I couldn't park anywhere near the shop, and what with this sodding rain . . .'

'No worries. I'm sure I can find something.' I switch on the coffee machine and open the cupboard a few inches so Cassie can't see the selection of cakes, biscuits and sweets I keep for Ollie when I look after him. I always give him a little treat before Cassie picks him up. I take out a box of Mr Kipling French fancies.

'Ooh, Ollie'll be pleased – these are his favourites, especially the yellow ones.'

'Are they?' As if I don't already know. I slide them onto a plate, then take out a bottle of squash and the plastic cup I keep for him.

'Don't call him just yet,' Cassie says, her voice lowered. 'Let me tell you my news.'

'Hang on a sec.' I bring the coffee to the table, pull out a chair and sit down. 'Okay. What is it?'

'I've met a man. And he's a very nice man.'

I carry on smiling, but it's clear Cassie is expecting more of a reaction. For some reason, it hadn't occurred to me that Cassie might start seeing someone, although now I think about it, why wouldn't she? 'Come on then,' I try to inject some enthusiasm into my voice, 'spill! What's his name? Is it that really tall guy with the blond dreads?' He's a regular at the café, and he's always eyeing Cass up when he thinks no one's looking.

'Who? Oh, I know who you mean. No, not him.' She pulls a face. 'He smells funny. No, his name is Luke, and we met through . . . Well, it was weird, like it was fate or luck or something. Bad luck turning into good luck, I suppose.'

'How do you mean?' I can hear Ollie in the hallway, laughing and talking to Spider and flicking a ping-pong ball up and down the floorboards for the cat to chase. I love hearing Ollie playing here in this house.

'You know I put that big mirror on eBay?' Cassie bites off a chunk of cake, chews and swallows, then takes a sip of coffee. 'Ooh, that's hot. Well, this guy bought it for twenty-six quid, but the only time he could pick it up was Monday afternoon before three, so that was going to be tricky. You're not around Mondays, and after I've finished at the café and picked Ollie up, it'd be quarter to four by the time I got home. So I left the mirror in the hall and arranged for Jean next door to let him in. Basically he should have been and gone by the time I got back, so we shouldn't even have met.' She giggles, then raises her eyebrows and puts on a melodramatic voice. 'But then, spookily, fate intervened.'

I manage what I hope is an encouraging smile and take a bigger mouthful of coffee than I mean to, burning the roof of my mouth.

'So anyway, I get home with Ollie, and there's this drop-dead gorgeous bloke on his knees on my front path. For a minute I thought it was some leaflet delivery guy who's collapsed, but then I realise what's happened. He's dropped the mirror he's just paid me twenty-six quid for, and he's on his hands and knees trying to pick up all the slivers of glass off my path. He remembered me saying I had a child, and he didn't want to risk him hurting himself. Wasn't that sweet?'

'Yes, I suppose so.'

'So I went in and got the dustpan and brush, told him not to worry and that I'd finish clearing up, but he wouldn't let me – said he'd never forgive himself if me or Ollie cut ourselves. Then he asked me about some of the things I'm growing in the front garden – knew the Latin names and everything. Turns out he's a gardener! So then we were off, talking about plants and stuff, and how the rain's affecting everything. He went to the exact same horticultural college as I did. How spooky is that?'

'Small world, as they say.'

'Yeah. And you know what? All the time I'm standing there chatting to him, I'm thinking, this guy is *soooo* nice. So I invite him in for a cup of tea, and he ends up staying for a drink.' She takes another sip of coffee. 'Oh, Leah, we got on so well – it feels like I've known him for ages. He asked if he could see me the next night, so I'm like, yes, obviously. He brought some wine and we got a pizza delivered, and then the next night I said I'd knock up some pasta, and he came with wine *and* flowers *and* chocolates, and he even bought a little book for Ollie.'

I don't like the idea of this stranger buying presents for Oliver.

'Cut a long story short, he stayed the night, and it was . . .' She closes her eyes. 'It was wonderful. He's . . . Do you know what, Leah, I think he's someone I could fall in love with. He's certainly the first person I've been seriously interested in since David died.'

'What about Adrian?' It is out of my mouth before I even know I'm going to speak.

Cassie looks startled. 'Adrian? What on earth has he got to do with anything?'

'Oh . . . I . . . I don't know, really. Just,' I shrug, 'you must have been a *bit* interested in him. He was Ollie's father, after all.'

'Yes, *was* being the operative word. And anyway, I said Luke is the first person I've been seriously interested in since David died.' She's looking at me oddly. 'I have to say, it feels a bit weird, you bringing Adrian up.'

Shit. Shit! My face and neck are turning red, I can feel it. 'Sorry, I don't know what made me think of him. Maybe it's because we were talking about him the other week and you said he'd wanted some contact. I just thought . . .'

'Yes, but he never showed up – I told you. I haven't heard anything from him since then and that was, like, a year ago.' She takes another mouthful of coffee. 'And I told you, didn't I, that whole thing . . .' She sighs. 'It's something I still feel embarrassed about – and ashamed of. I used him to get Ollie. I wasn't even attracted to him, and I don't think he was to me, either. If you want the truth, it was a disastrous couple of days of mediocre sex and crippling guilt.'

Good, I think. But I wish I hadn't blurted out his name like that. It shocked me almost as much as it did Cassie. 'Well.' I'm dangerously close to tears and there's a crack in my voice. I swallow. 'Sorry again for bringing him up.' I take a few deep breaths as I go to the sink for a glass of water, then I turn back to Cass with what I hope is a more cheerful expression. 'So tell me more about this gorgeous man you found in your garden, presumably dropped there by the Boyfriend Fairy.'

Cassie laughs and her smile returns. 'He's just turned forty, and he's a freelance landscape gardener, like I said. He was married for four years but he's been divorced for three, no kids, no contact with the ex. He was seeing someone but he split up with her just before Easter, so he's properly single.'

'How does Ollie feel about it? About you having a boyfriend?'

'I haven't made any big deal of it, like, "this is my boyfriend" or anything. But Luke's very good with him, and Ollie seems to like him.'

I nod slowly. 'That's good.' I don't like the idea of a strange man being so close to Ollie, but I know it's not really anything to do with me. 'You sound very keen.' I give a half-laugh. 'You're not *in lurve*, are you? You've only just met him.'

Cassie grins. 'True, but didn't you tell me you and your husband had only been together for a few weeks when you got married? That you just *knew*?' She smiles almost dreamily. 'I don't want to jinx it, but I think he might be *the one*.'

CHAPTER TWENTY-NINE

Then

Adrian held my hand as the blood pressure cuff tightened around my upper arm.

'Perfect,' Dr Mason said, unwrapping the cuff. 'Now hop up onto the bed so we can see how things are doing.' She placed the stethoscope over my bump, and as she did so, we could all see an area of flesh rising up as a hand or foot glided under the skin. She laughed. 'Well, I certainly don't need to ask you about movement.' A second later, I felt that strange, intimate shift within me and another little mound appeared. 'My goodness, he's lively today. Or she.' She stretched the tape measure over my enormous stomach and down to my pubic bone. 'Spot on.' She smiled. 'All is exactly as it should be. I'm very happy with the way things are progressing. Come and sit down when you're ready.' The extreme cheeriness made me slightly nervous, but I could see she was trying to keep us positive.

Adrian helped me up off the examining table and once I'd straightened my clothes, I sat down next to him. Dr Mason scribbled something on her notes, then put her pen down and turned her attention to me. 'How are you feeling about the birth, as we're getting nearer to the date?'

'Nervous, obviously. But not too bad, I suppose. I'm glad to be past the thirty-six-week point.'

'Understandably.' She looked from me to Adrian and back again. 'Is there anything at all that you're concerned about, either of you?'

'Apart from the obvious,' Adrian said, 'no. I think we're both feeling optimistic, aren't we?' He squeezed my hand. I smiled, but I knew that my optimism was as fragile as a bird's wing.

'Leah? Anything worrying you specifically?'

'No, not specifically. At least, not while I can feel the baby moving around.'

'Good. Let us know if there's anything you're worried about, okay?'

'Thanks,' Adrian said, and I could feel the appointment coming to a conclusion. I should have been getting to my feet, but I hesitated. Sod it, I know what we said, but I had to ask. 'I was wondering whether there's any chance of bringing it forward at all.'

'Leah,' Adrian said, 'we talked to Rhona about this, and she said—'

'I know, but I just want to check . . .' Rhona was the midwife. She said they don't like doing caesareans early unless it's an emergency, but she wasn't a doctor, after all. I looked hopefully at Dr Mason. 'The waiting, you know, after last time. It's so hard.'

'I understand your anxiety, of course I do.' She was looking at the notes. 'You're thirty-seven and a half weeks,' she said. 'And as I think the midwife explained when you raised the issue before, we don't like to deliver before thirty-nine weeks, not unless there's a sound medical reason.' She took her glasses off and arranged her face into a sympathetic expression. 'I know this must be a difficult time for you both, but I hope I can reassure you that there is no cause for concern with this pregnancy.'

I tried to look grateful for the reassurance, but the trouble was, there hadn't been any cause for concern last time, either.

'Your baby is the right size,' she continued, 'and in the right position, with a strong and healthy heartbeat. There's plenty of movement still, so it's all good. Now, your section is booked for . . .' She put her glasses back on and peered at the notes. 'The third of Feb, so there's really not long to go. She smiled again. 'Try not to worry, both of you. I know that's easy for me to say, but we're looking at a perfectly straightforward C-section.'

We nodded our thanks and exchanged a brief comment about the weather before heading home. It was cold today, and windy, and there was a gale blowing as we stepped out of the surgery. Adrian took my arm as we walked across the frosted tarmac to the car – my bulk made me a little unsteady. He squeezed my hand, and I squeezed back, aware that he needed reassuring too. He'd coped with the miscarriage. Oh, he was upset, of course, but I don't think he regarded it as an actual baby, whereas losing Thomas had nearly destroyed us both.

'I'll drive,' I said as we reached the car.

'No,' he said, 'let me. You're far too big to be driving at this stage.'

'It's okay. I drove into town yesterday and it was fine. It'll do me good to have something else to think about.' I heard the slight catch in my voice, and so did he. We both knew I was thinking about Thomas, and if I was driving, I'd have to concentrate, whereas if he drove, I'd sit staring out of the window, wishing away the next eleven days until they could get this baby safely out of my uterus and into my arms.

'Okay,' he said. 'If you're sure.'

We were almost home when there was a movement to my left, a tiny black thing from nowhere. I braked automatically, even though I was sure it was just a leaf or a piece of rubbish blown into the road, but I pulled over anyway.

'What's the matter?' Adrian said as I unclipped my seat belt.

'I think I hit something.'

'No,' he said. 'We'd have felt it.'

'I want to make sure. Won't be a sec.' The wind was so strong it took me a moment to push open the car door. I heaved myself out and walked back along the road, hair whipping around my face. At first I couldn't see anything. Maybe it was just a twig blown down from one of the trees that were swaying and rustling above me. Then I saw the little dark lump in the road. I wondered if it was a blackbird, but it was too fluffy and its beak was black. Then I realised it was a baby crow, more fluff than feathers, beak still too big for its head. As soon as I crouched down, I could see it was dead. 'Oh no, you poor, poor thing,' I murmured. 'I'm so sorry.' I could hear another car approaching, so I picked the bird up to move it out of the way. Its soft, fragile body was still warm in my hands, and I felt my eyes fill with tears as I thought of the mother crow returning to her nest and finding her baby gone. Maybe even spotting its still body by the side of the road. I wondered if birds went looking for their babies if they couldn't find them.

'Leah? What's up?' Adrian appeared next to me. 'Ah, poor thing,' he said as he saw what I was holding. 'Is it still alive?'

I shook my head. 'I hit it. I knew I'd hit something.'

'It's very young.' He stroked its soft feathers. 'Probably fell out of its nest.' He put an arm around my shoulder. 'Come on, put it down and let's get back to the car.' I stroked the little bird with my finger and as I laid it gently on the kerb, I noticed a smear of blood on my nail.

'You all right there, love?' An elderly woman with two bulging carrier bags leaned forward to see what we were doing. 'Bird, is it?' She lifted her glasses and looked more closely. 'Ah, that's a baby crow, that is.' She turned to me. 'Filthy creatures, them crows.'

'Yes, well.' Adrian nodded at her and tried to steer me back to the car. 'Come on, let's go home and get some coffee.'

I didn't move. Why hadn't I let him drive? His reactions

were quicker than mine, and if he'd been driving we probably wouldn't have hit the poor creature. I looked up, half-expecting to see its distraught mother hovering in a tree or on a telephone wire above me, but there was just a wood pigeon clinging to a branch as it bounced in the wind.

'Leah? Come on.'

'I wish I could see its mother. I hate leaving it there.'

He sighed. 'I know, poor thing. It's sad, but there's nothing you can do. Just one of those things.'

I felt myself fill up with tears. We both knew the few weeks leading up to the birth were likely to be emotional, but I was surprised it had hit me now and with such force.

The old lady was shaking her head. 'Harbingers of death, them crows,' she said. 'Full of germs and parasites. You want to wash your hands when you get indoors, lovey.' She moved off on her way again.

'We'll do that.' Adrian nodded at her, then leaned towards me and whispered, 'Ignore her. I'm sure she means well, but don't take too much notice.' He lifted my hair away from my face. 'Leah, you're crying! What is it?'

'It's . . .' I could barely speak. 'It's just . . . the poor little crow.'

He squeezed my hand. 'It wasn't your fault, it wouldn't have felt anything, I'm sure.'

As I allowed him to lead me to the car, I heard the old woman tut and mutter under her breath, *it's only a bloody bird.*

Which was true, but I was the one who bloodied it.

CHAPTER THIRTY

Now

I press the buzzer on the intercom and wait for the response. 'Hi,' I say into the silver box on the wall. 'It's Leah, picking up Oliver.'

The metal gates swing open and I walk across the playground to stand outside Ollie's classroom. I'm early – I always am. I can't bear the idea of him having to wait, and the thought of him sitting on the bench with his coat on and his little lunchbox in his hand is enough to choke me up. Cassie says he'll be coming here full-time after Christmas, but I think it's too soon. It's not just that I'll miss him on Fridays, it's that he's still so young. The four days a week he does now tire him out, and he won't be starting proper school until this time next year, so I don't see what the hurry is.

A few other parents arrive, and one or two of them nod and smile in recognition. When I was picking him up last week, I got talking to a mum whose child had just started. Ollie came running out while we were chatting, grinning from ear to ear and chattering away about what he'd been doing. The other woman smiled and said, 'Your son seems happy here,' and I felt my heart skip with pleasure. I should have corrected her, but instead I nodded and said, 'Oh, Ollie loves it here. I'm sure your daughter will, too.' It was such a small, harmless pleasure. Of course, she's probably met Cassie by now.

At exactly three fifteen, the class door opens and, as always, the sight of all those innocent little faces brings a lump to my throat. Stacey, the teacher, smiles at me and turns back to the room. 'Oliver!' she shouts. 'Leah's here.' Ollie comes trotting towards me, clutching a drawing. I crouch down to hug him. 'Hello, sweetheart. Had a nice day?'

'Uh-huh,' he says. 'I drawed a owl, look!'

'Wow! That's fantastic. Aren't you clever?'

He nods, smiling.

'Bye Ollie, see you tomorrow.' Stacey touches him gently on the head before turning back to the queue. 'Paris! Daddy's here. Felix! Grandma's here . . .'

Ollie automatically slips his hand into mine. 'Where's Mummy?'

'Mummy's working late today, so you're coming to my house for tea and then Mummy and Luke are going to pick you up later, okay?'

'Yeah!' He grins happily, making me wish I'd told him the two things separately so I could gauge which bit he's so pleased about. Maybe it's both. As I strap him in, it occurs to me that we really ought to buy another child seat. It's a hassle having to keep moving this one from Cassie's car to mine every time I drive Ollie anywhere.

'I'm hungry,' Ollie says, ten minutes or so after leaving half his toast and Marmite. I told Cass I could easily give him dinner, but she said not to. 'Please can I have some crisps?'

'I thought you were full up?'

'I was, but now I'm hungry.'

'Would you like some more toast?'

He shakes his head. 'No thanks. I'm just hungry for crisps.'

At least it's honest. Maybe I shouldn't let him have so many treats when he's with me, but I love the way his face lights up when I offer him crisps, biscuits, sweets or ice cream. Cassie gives him healthy meals and snacks, so a few treats now and again can't hurt, can they? I take a packet of cheese and onion from my 'Ollie cupboard' and toss them gently enough for him to catch. 'There you go.'

He looks at the packet. 'Can I have the blue ones?'

'I thought cheese and onion were your favourite?'

He shakes his head. 'I used to like cheese and onion, but that was before I met salt and vinegar.' He pronounces it 'vigenar'.

I laugh as I go back to the cupboard. I should write down some of the funny things he says, though I'm hardly likely to forget. I spend a lot of time thinking about him, wondering what my babies would be like at this age, what cute things they'd say; what their paintings and drawings would look like stuck all over the fridge like Ollie's are at Cassie's house.

The doorbell rings while we're watching *Shrek* on DVD. 'That'll be Mummy and Luke.' I must make an effort to be nice to this Luke person, despite the wave of apprehension I feel as I see the two silhouettes through the glass.

Cassie is smiling, as is the blond man standing next to her. 'Leah, this is Luke,' she says. 'Luke, Leah.' He's shorter than I'd imagined. For some reason, I'd pictured him as tall and broad-shouldered, but he's neither. Nice enough face, though. I make myself smile and take the hand Luke offers. Even his hand feels small for a man, but he has a decent handshake. 'Come in.' I try to sound friendly. 'It's nice to meet you at last. It's a cliché, but I really have heard so much about you.'

'Likewise,' he says. 'Nothing wrong with clichés – if some phrases are overused, it's probably because they're good phrases.'

'True.' And that's another bloody cliché.

'Where's his lordship?' Cassie asks. 'Watching telly?'

'Yes. *Shrek the Third* – again.'

Cassie turns to Luke. 'He must have seen that film about twenty times. He even says some of the dialogue along with the DVD.' Then she calls Ollie to come and get his coat on.

'Do you have to dash off? I wondered if you . . .' I flick my eyes towards Luke. 'I thought you might like a quick drink.'

I see Cassie look at Luke, and the almost imperceptible

movement of his eyes that says *no, let's not stay – I want you to myself.*

'Thanks, Leah. We would normally, but we're taking Ollie to Pizza Hut and we don't want to be too late getting him back to bed. But listen, thanks ever so much for having him today. I really appreciate it.'

I swallow back my disappointment. 'You're welcome. I'll have him any time, if I can, you know that.'

'Actually, I've got another favour to ask.'

Thinking it'll be more babysitting, I smile. 'Go ahead, you know I'll help if possible.'

'I was wondering if I could clean on Saturday instead of tomorrow? I won't even need to bring Ollie with me because he's got a party to go to at the Play Place on Saturday morning and he's having a sleepover with Max tomorrow night, so Max's mum is going to take them. I know it's short notice, but the thing is, Luke's got tomorrow off, and as that's the day Ollie's not at preschool . . .' She glances up at him, smiling. 'He wants to—'

'I thought I'd take them both out for the day,' Luke says, pleasantly. 'Thought we might go to the Yorkshire wildlife park or something. If it fits in with you, obviously.' He looks around. 'I have to say, this house doesn't look as if needs cleaning at all to me, but then I'm just a bloke.'

I can feel the smile falling off my face. 'Of course!' I try my best to sound cheerful. 'Not a problem.' I suppose it's inevitable that they'll have other stuff to do occasionally, but I so look forward to having the two of them here every week that the thought of them not coming is hard to take. I look down to pick at an imaginary thread on the hem of my t-shirt. 'You don't need to come on Saturday, though, Cass, not unless you really want to. It's not that bad, so it can wait until next week.'

'Are you sure? I wouldn't mind skipping this week, if that's really okay?'

'No, it's fine.' I could get Cass to come on her own, but there doesn't seem much point, especially as it's clear she's keen to spend some time with this new man of hers.

'Thanks, Leah. You're a star.' Cassie slips her hand into Luke's. 'Oliver,' she calls. 'Come *on*.'

When Ollie comes out into the hall, his face breaks into a grin when he sees Luke.

'Hello, champ,' Luke ruffles his hair. I try to ignore the flash of irritation that stabs at me.

I can't sleep. I turn over to look at the clock – almost two. Luke seems nice enough, if I'm honest, but I don't like the way he talks to Ollie as if they're old mates. And I wish Ollie didn't seem to like him so much. I suppose I'd be more worried if he *didn't* like him, and anyway, maybe the fact that he's taking them to the wildlife park might have something to do with it. I'm not stupid; I know that one of the reasons Ollie loves coming here is the treats I keep for him, and the surprises I try to come up with every few weeks so he doesn't get bored. He's still besotted with Spider, but that could change. That cat is amazingly tolerant. The other day he let Ollie dress him up in a Spiderman cape, and waited a good minute before wriggling himself free, then he washed himself furiously before ambling away as if he wasn't really bothered. I'm becoming attached to Spider, despite the dead birds he keeps bringing into the kitchen. But there's every chance Ollie will lose interest in favour of something more entertaining. He talks a lot about Max, his new best friend at preschool – Max has 'awesome stuff', apparently – remote-control cars, and a truck that lights up and beeps and says 'reversing' when you push it backwards. I lean over and turn on the bedside lamp, then I swing my legs out of bed, wincing as my back twinges. I head downstairs to make some hot chocolate, but instead of taking it back to bed, I somehow find myself wandering along the landing and into the study, where I switch on the computer. I sit looking at the screen for a moment before opening up Google and typing into the search bar *electric train sets.*

CHAPTER THIRTY-ONE

Now

I hum to myself as I move around the supermarket aisles stocking up on crisps, chocolate buttons, Smarties and jelly snakes. It's the first time I've had him overnight, and I want to make sure he has a brilliant time, especially as I'll have him all day tomorrow as well. It was Luke's idea. He wanted to do something special for Cassie's birthday, he told me when they collected Ollie the other day. Dinner at a nice hotel on Saturday night, then a spa day on the Sunday – would I be able to babysit from Saturday afternoon until Sunday teatime?

I put sausages, frozen chips and a tin of spaghetti hoops in my basket for tonight, but what will he want for breakfast? There's plenty of bread, and I have Marmite, honey and peanut butter, but the only cereal in the cupboard is muesli, so I go for one of those breakfast selection packs my dad used to buy as a treat when I was little. I add a couple of pots of instant porridge, and my hand hovers over the Pop-Tarts – I bet Cass never lets him have these. I drop two packs into my basket, one strawberry, one chocolate. We'll need lunch as well. He definitely likes pizza, but which type? Pepperoni? Ham and pineapple? I put one of each in my basket, then take them out again. We'll go out for pizza; that'll be more exciting. As I'm walking towards the checkouts, it occurs to me that he might prefer a cooked breakfast. I have eggs and baked beans in the cupboard, but I'd better grab some bacon, just in case. If he's anything like his dad . . . I stop moving, shocked by a sudden upsurge of grief. It doesn't hit me every day now, and I'm not angry with Adrian any more, because if he hadn't slept with Cass, I wouldn't have Ollie. Somewhere, way back in the recesses of my brain, I know that I *don't* have Ollie; all I have is a tiny share in his affections.

After I've unpacked the groceries, I head out again, this time to the big shopping centre at Meadowhall. It doesn't take long to find a Spiderman duvet cover and matching curtains, and as I'm about to pay for them, I spot a bedside lamp with a Spiderman shade, so I buy that as well. On the way home, I pop into B&Q for a frieze to brighten up the box room's darkish, blue-green walls. When I've made up the bed and hung the new curtains, I carefully fit the frieze, and once the brightly coloured jungle animals are scampering around the walls, it looks much more like a child's room. I pick up the cellophane-wrapped box containing the new Hornby train set. I paid almost seventy pounds for this. Maybe Cassie won't realise how expensive it was. Or maybe I could say it's an early Christmas present? But then I won't be able to buy him something lovely at Christmas. I could say I bought it cheap. Or second-hand? Yes, that's it.

I manage to find a battered cardboard box in the cellar. I pile in the train carriages and the other bits and pieces, and then I throw the lengths of track in on top so it looks haphazard. I'll say I spotted it in a charity shop. Cass is unlikely to look at it properly, and Ollie won't know any different. It won't be as much fun as giving him the big, colourful shiny new box, but at least he'll know there's a train set here for him to play with every time he comes. I feel guilty about not putting the Hornby box in the recycling, but I can't risk Cassie seeing it, so I squish it up with the cellophane and the plastic moulding and push it to the bottom of the black bin.

Something still isn't right with the room. Maybe it needs a rug on the floor next to the bed, something bright and colourful – I'll get one for next time. If only he wasn't so keen on Spiderman. I'd prefer a design more suited to a younger child. After all, Ollie is only three – well, three and a half, as he keeps reminding me – and he still takes a teddy bear to bed with him. That's it! That's what's missing. I open the door to the attic and make my way up the narrow staircase. It's a while since I've been up here, and as soon as I push the door open I'm aware of the change in temperature, so I bend down to turn on the radiator, tweaking my back. I'll never be able to use this room again for anything other than storage, but I still like to come up here sometimes to go through the boxes. I like to hold my babies' things in my hands, to try to recapture my fleeting moments of motherhood.

Both boxes are wooden, painted white and decorated with tiny silver stars. Adrian had them made specially. Thomas's is tiny, because there weren't many things to put in it. After the miscarriage, we were so afraid of jinxing his birth we hardly bought anything before he was born. All it contains is three babygros, a tiny blue teddy, the photographs we took at the hospital and the condolence cards, most of them plain white with black or silver lettering, maybe a white flower here and there.

The other box is much bigger, tucked in under the shelves. I don't look in this one very often. In fact, it was a long time before I was able to open it at all. I slide it out and take the lid off. A familiar wave of sadness washes over me. Adrian had this made for when I came home from hospital, so that we could fill it together. The birth congratulations cards are all here, hidden underneath the babygros, her little red snowsuit, the dresses she'd just started wearing. Those cards covered every surface in the sitting room and dining room, a sea of pink, with ribbons and lace and pictures of balloons and bubbles and sweet-faced cherubs. There were condolence cards, too, Adrian said, but he didn't keep those. He couldn't bear to look at them at the time, he told me afterwards, and it hadn't occurred to him that I might want to see them later. He was in such a state, he wasn't really thinking.

I'm tempted to pull out one of the babygros, to bury my face in the fabric and kid myself that I can still detect a hint of that heavenly baby scent. But it's a fantasy, and I don't want red, puffy eyes when Ollie arrives. What I'm looking for is right on top anyway – a big, golden-coloured teddy bear wearing tartan pyjamas. My eyes are full as I put the lid back on the box.

After I've placed the teddy bear on Ollie's pillow, I stand in the doorway to look at the room again. That's better; the teddy makes all the difference. I feel the tiniest pang of guilt for giving it to Ollie, but I know I'm being silly. It isn't as though he'll be taking it home, after all. It's just for when he's here overnight, which I hope will happen more often now, assuming all goes well this time.

About an hour before they're due to drop Ollie off, my phone goes. It's Cass. 'Change of plan,' she says. 'Sorry it's so last-minute, but Ollie's not feeling well. I thought he was just a bit snuffly, but he's got earache now, and he's really miserable.'

I swallow. 'Oh, poor Ollie. Does he need the doctor?'

'No, he's had some Calpol and I've made him up a poorly bed on the sofa. He'll probably be fine by tomorrow.'

'Shall I come over to yours instead, then? I could be there in—'

'No, it's okay, but thanks for offering. I'm sure it's nothing, but I don't really want to leave him, not when he's feeling like this.'

'But what about all the arrangements? Hasn't Luke . . .'

'I know, it's a shame, but it's one of those things. Luke understands – he's fine about it. He called the hotel and they can't refund the deposit, but they said if we want to book it again after Christmas, they'll just carry it over. So maybe we could arrange his sleepover for then, if you're not busy?'

'Yes,' I mutter, disappointment thickening my throat. 'Yes, of course. Just let me know.'

'Luke's going to pop out and get us a curry and a bottle of wine, so we'll still have a nice time.'

'Good,' I say. 'Let me know how he is tomorrow, won't you? And give him my love.'

The black gloom that descends after I've said goodbye almost folds me in two. Reality is screaming at me. Ollie isn't mine, and he never will be. I have no control, no say in his life. I am nothing.

CHAPTER THIRTY-TWO

Then

Adrian and I held hands as we waited to go down to theatre, and I was conscious of feeling less nervous, more relaxed. The tension of the last few months had been almost unbearable, but we'd made it to today, and although I couldn't pretend I wasn't scared, I was no longer convinced it was all going to go wrong. It helped that the baby was moving a lot this morning, almost as if it knew that today was the day. As soon as we arrived, Adrian checked with the midwives that they knew our history. I'd ended up in tears before now at a perfectly innocent and well-meaning comment. It was always hard when another expectant mum asked if this was my first baby, because how could I say to another pregnant woman, *My first was stillborn*? On one of my appointments here, I was called in to have my blood pressure checked. The midwife was very young, possibly still a student and not one of my usual care team, and she'd somehow picked up that this wasn't my first pregnancy but not that Thomas was stillborn. 'So,' she said as I sat down, 'I bet your first one's excited about having a new little brother or sister. What have you got already? A boy or a girl?' Adrian wasn't with me that day for some reason, and I couldn't think what to say. I just sat there staring at her like an idiot. She was looking at me expectantly with her bright, friendly smile. I eventually managed to make my voice work, but it was barely more than a whisper. 'I had a little boy the first time, but he . . . he didn't live.' The poor girl was devastated. Her face coloured and her eyes filled with tears. 'I'm sorry,' she kept saying, over and over again, 'I'm so sorry.'

So now, we checked. We made sure everybody knew.

'Look.' Adrian pointed to the window. 'It's snowing.' As we watched the flakes falling softly, a huge black crow landed on the windowsill. It tipped its head sideways and looked at me, and for the first time since we arrived, I felt a surge of apprehension as I remembered that poor little baby crow I ran over a couple of weeks ago. I read something once about crows being super-intelligent, that they can recognise and remember human faces, and although I knew it was a ridiculous thought, it came into my head that this adult crow might be the baby's mother. At that moment, the midwife came in to say we'd be going down to theatre in a few minutes. How were we feeling, she wanted to know? Adrian said something, but I wasn't really paying attention. Then he mentioned the snow, and she moved over to the window to look. The crow was still there and the midwife tapped on the glass. 'Shoo!' she said. 'Nasty birds. We get a lot of them here, scavenging round the hospital bins. 'Go away.' She tapped again, more forcefully this time, and the crow flew off.

Somehow, after all the months of anxiety, all the extra antenatal visits, all the what ifs, here we were in theatre, about to meet our baby son or daughter. Adrian had been relaxed and chatty all morning, but now he'd gone quiet. 'All set, Cornelia?' the surgeon said. I nodded.

'Leah,' Adrian told him.

'It's okay. I don't mind.' Usually I much preferred Leah, but today there was something comforting about him calling me by my full name. Maybe it was because the only other person who called me Cornelia was my dad. And my grandma, before she died. 'Okay, Leah, we'll make a start then.' He smiled and his eyes twinkled.

I sent a silent message to my baby. *Hold on, sweetheart. Everything's going to be all right.*

I wasn't supposed to be able to see what was going on – there was a screen of green drapes across my middle – but I could see the reflection in the huge silver light on the ceiling. I felt lots of pressure on my bump and then suddenly, the silver light flooded red and I gripped Adrian's hand more tightly. The surgeon said something but I didn't hear it properly. I felt the oddest sensation, like someone was doing the washing-up in my stomach. Then there were suction noises, and then everyone was talking to me at once. *Nearly there, Leah. Any second now. Got any names yet? Do we know what we're having? Boy or girl?*

I knew this was a crucial moment and that they were trying to distract me. I was touched by how much they seemed to care, these strangers who were delivering my precious baby. I wasn't sure who to answer first, or if I could even remember the questions. I was still looking up at the silver light, and I could see a thatch of darkish hair. For a moment I was overtaken by a powerful wave of longing for my mum. Strange, given that I barely remember her, but I had exactly the same feeling after Thomas was born. I hung onto Adrian's hand as the surgeon lifted her out of my belly like a little bruise-coloured bird coming out of an egg. There was a fleeting moment of quiet before the surgeon's voice rang out. 'We have a little girl!'

'Why is she that colour?' I heard the alarm in my voice, but before I'd even finished speaking, she turned pink and filled up with life as if someone was pouring it into her. The first line of a Plath poem jumped into my head: *Love set you going like a fat gold watch.* I'd always thought it was a great line, but now I totally got it.

The relief in the room was palpable; everyone was smiling, and at least two of the nurses had tears in their eyes. As Adrian leaned over to kiss me, it felt like nothing could ever hurt us again. I was aware of the grin spreading across my face as they dangled her over the drapes. I held my arms out, and the moment I touched her warm, slippery body I knew she was going to be all right. 'Hello, Harriet,' I said, and she looked back at me. Such an old, wise look, as though she knew everything there was to know already. I was humbled by my seconds-old daughter, and I wondered how she'd felt about the intrusion, about the surgeon's knife invading her safe little world. Maybe I shouldn't have insisted on a caesarean, but one day I'd explain about her brother, and why I couldn't go through a 'normal' delivery again.

Adrian cupped her damp head in his hand; there were tears on his cheeks. 'Hello, Harriet,' he said. 'I'm your daddy.'

Harriet and I continued to look at each other, cementing our connection, until one of the midwives came and whisked her away for her checks.

CHAPTER THIRTY-THREE

Now

Three weeks before Christmas, my phone goes on the Friday morning. 'Leah, listen, I'll be there in half an hour, but could I ask you a massive favour? I was wondering if there's any chance you could have Ollie for a few hours this afternoon while we get some Christmas shopping done. Me and Luke, I mean. He's not working today, so it's a good opportunity.'

'Of course,' I say, my spirits lifting instantly. 'No problem.'

'I'll leave him with Luke this morning while I come and clean. He can give him lunch and drive him over after that. We'll only be a few hours – say until about five or half past?'

'You don't need to leave him with Luke. Just bring him with you as usual – I've got loads of stuff I can give him for lunch. And hey, what about if I have him overnight? Then you and Luke can have an evening out. It'd be no trouble.' There's a pause, then a muffled sound as Cassie turns away to talk to Luke.

'Do you know what?' Cass says after a minute. 'That'd be brilliant – if you're sure you don't mind?'

'Of course I don't mind. I love having him here, you know that. And his . . . I mean, the box room's all set up for him from when he was going to stay before.'

'Really? Oh, that's so kind of you, Leah.' Cassie's voice softens. 'You're so good with Ollie, and I know it can't be easy for you.'

I swallow the lump in my throat. 'No, no, it helps, actually.' I take a breath. 'Tell Luke it's really not a problem for me to rustle up some lunch.'

'No, honestly – they're in the middle of some computer game I can't drag them away from, so I'll just come on my own.'

There are only so many times I can argue, but I can't let it go entirely. 'Isn't Ollie a bit young for computer games?'

'Oh, no, don't worry – it's age-appropriate. Well, age-appropriate for Oliver, anyway.' Cass laughs, and I hear Luke make some jokey comment. I can picture the three of them in Cassie's living room, Luke and Ollie sitting next to each other on the sofa, Cassie sitting opposite, watching them, smiling fondly. Like a family.

'Thanks again for having him today,' Cassie says as we drink our coffee. 'It'll be so much easier getting round the shops without Ollie wanting to stop and look at everything. How are you getting on with your Christmas shopping? Have you got much to do?'

I shake my head. 'Not much. I have a small family, as you know. Just my two nephews, really, A . . .' Shit. I so nearly said *Adrian's brother's boys*. 'A few other people.' Have I rescued it, or did that sound odd? 'I always buy for my father-in-law, and I'll probably get a little something for . . . I was going to say his "ladyfriend", but I suppose I should start calling Helen his partner – it's looking like she'll be around for a while.'

'Really? Do you think they'll get married?'

'Not sure, but it'd be great if they did. Helen's lovely. So it's not that many – the boys, Paul and Helen, and Ollie, of course – I'll check with you first, so we don't end up getting the same thing.'

'Oh, that's sweet of you, Leah. You don't need to buy him anything, though – Ollie does very well for presents.'

'No, really – I'd like to. I love buying for children, but I don't even know what my nephews are into, now they're older – the eldest is fifteen, so it's not the same as buying for little ones.' I seem to have got away with it, even though I'm sure my face must be burning red.

'You're lucky,' Cassie says. 'I've got tons to do. Not including Ollie, there are at least five kids, then there's—' She stops dead. 'Oh, God, Leah, I'm sorry, I didn't think. Christmas must be a shitty time for you.'

'Yeah, it can be a bit tough when everyone's saying

Christmas is for children, and there are Santa's grottos, and reindeer and pantos everywhere you look.'

'That was so thoughtless of me.' Cassie looks mortified, and apologises again. 'I'm always opening my big mouth without thinking.'

'Cass, it's okay. I didn't mean to make you feel guilty. It is a crap time, though. I always dreamed about being able to make a magical Christmas for my own children, like when I was a kid. We used to go my grandma's in Scotland. There would be paper chains, a huge tree, tinsel, a proper iced Christmas cake and loads of Christmas chocolate. Chocolate things on the tree, chocolate stars, chocolate Santas.'

Cass smiles. 'Chocolate mice, that little net of chocolate coins.'

'Ooh yes, I loved those.' I wasn't allowed much chocolate at home, but I always got loads at Grandma's. One night, after I'd gone to bed, I deliberately got up again to listen by the banisters, hoping they'd be talking about my present. Instead I heard my dad's voice: 'It'll rot her teeth, Meg. She'll end up with a mouthful of fillings.' Then my grandma's. 'Och, a wee indulgence won't hurt the bairn, Gerry. The lass has no mother; will ye not let me spoil her at Christmas time?'

I feel a swell of emotion as I remember those Christmases. We went up there every year until Grandma died when I was sixteen.

'Actually,' I say, 'I might try and make Ollie watch a Christmassy film with me this afternoon. *Miracle on 34th*

Street is on Netflix – the new one, I mean. Or is he too young for that?'

'I don't think so,' Cass replies. 'He hasn't seen it, but he loves anything with Santa in.'

While Cassie finishes the cleaning, I get the wood burner going in the sitting room, then pop out in the car to buy mince pies, Christmas biscuits and hot chocolate. It's going to be a wonderful afternoon and evening. I'll tell Cass not to rush back in the morning – I can easily give Ollie lunch, or maybe take him out for pizza. I'll let him choose.

But when they arrive, Ollie is still in a state of high excitement, and the way he goes on about the game he's been playing with Luke makes it clear he probably won't be snuggling up with me to watch *Miracle on 34th Street*. He needs to burn off some of that pent-up energy if we're going to do something relaxed and Christmassy later.

'Ollie,' I interrupt him mid-flow as he's going on about Luke and his bloody computer games. 'Shall we go to the park for a little while?'

'Can I go on the swings?'

'Yep. And then, when you've had enough of that, how about we go into town for pizza, and then go and get a Christmas tree? You can help me decorate it. Would you like that?'

His eyes widen and he nods enthusiastically.

'Come on, then.' I smile. 'Let's get your coat on.'

As I push him on the swings, I realise I'm looking forward to Christmas for the first time in years. Last year, not only was it my first without Adrian, but I'd only just found out about Oliver. The whole thing passed in a blur of cigarettes, alcohol and sleeping tablets. I probably slept through the worst of it. The Christmas before that was the one where Adrian had come home on Christmas Eve with a scraggy little tree he'd seen outside a greengrocer's. 'I relented,' he said. 'I thought we should start making an effort again.' So we put it in the window with a string of lights and a few baubles, and all I could think of was that all over the country, parents were filling stockings and wrapping presents and tucking wide-eyed, excited children into bed, and I would never, ever have that experience. On Christmas morning, the tree lights had gone out. A fuse, probably, but we didn't bother to replace it.

By the time we've decorated the tree, watched the film and eaten the pasta I made for dinner, it's gone eight. I help Ollie to wash his face, brush his teeth and get ready for bed. He looks adorable in his red flannel pyjamas with the teddy bear pattern. I tuck him into bed and read him *The Night Before Christmas*, and by the time I've finished the poem, his eyes are almost closed. 'Night-night, Ollie.' I kiss his forehead. And then, because it's true and because I've heard Cassie say it, and because, at this moment, it feels perfectly natural, I say, 'Love you.'

'Love you too.' He turns over and snuggles down. I smile and turn the light out, then I go back down into the sitting room. Spider is washing himself on the rug in front of the wood burner. I settle myself in the armchair, then lean over and lift him onto my lap; he purrs as he allows me to stroke him for a minute or so, then he jumps down and stalks out of the room. A few seconds later I hear the clatter of the cat flap.

CHAPTER THIRTY-FOUR

Now

As I'm about to get up, I hear the loo flush and then a few seconds later my bedroom door opens and Ollie's little pyjama-clad figure appears in the doorway. 'Hello.' I smile. 'Did you have a lovely sleep?'

He nods and rubs his eyes. His hair is sticking up at the back and there's a red crease in his cheek from the pillow. He moves nearer to the bed. I ache to put my arms out and invite him in for a cuddle, but would that be weird? The dark feeling starts to spread through me again, the certain knowledge that although I love this child, I can't guarantee his continued presence in my life.

I turn back the covers and swing my legs round to the floor. 'Ready for some breakfast?' Again he nods. 'Come on, then.' I stand up and put on my dressing gown, then hold out my hand, which he takes immediately. Momentarily, I'm choked by how natural this all is, how he's relaxed enough here to get up and come straight into my bedroom, just as he probably goes into his mother's room in the mornings at home.

'What's in there?' he says, pointing.

'Stairs. Leading up to the attic.'

'What means "attic"?'

'It just means a room right at the top of the house. I only use it to keep things in, like the Christmas decorations and old things I don't want to throw away.'

'What things?'

I bite my lip as I help him down the stairs. 'Oh, I don't know. Bits and pieces, things that are special.'

'Can I see the special things?'

'They're things that are special to me, but they might not seem very special to anyone else. Although . . .' There's a box of children's books up there, I remember. My dad gave them to me when I was expecting Thomas. He'd kept them, he told me, because he liked to see things passed down, and because he knew it would be next to no time before I'd be having my own children. I tell Ollie I'll pop up and get them after breakfast.

'Can I come?'

His little face is so alight with interest, so alive, I can hardly bear to say no to him, but I do. 'Another time,' I say, 'when you're a bit older.' When I tell him about his half-siblings, I want him to be old enough to understand who they were and what his relationship to them is, and then I'll take him up there and show him the things that were theirs.

I make myself some coffee and sit opposite Ollie at the kitchen table, watching him swinging his legs as he eats his cereal. I love the way he dips his spoon into his bowl so purposefully, lifting it to his mouth with care and occasionally wiping a stray dribble of milk from his chin. The spoon goes from bowl to mouth and back again almost rhythmically, then he tips the bowl so he can scoop up the last few Cheerios and drops of milk. When there's nothing left, he clatters the spoon down and announces, 'Finished! Can I get down please?'

'Good boy. Yes, of course you can.' It still thrills me when he asks me for permission to do something, when he talks to me as if I'm a parent.

I help him dress, then leave him playing with his train set in the sitting room while I go upstairs to locate the books. I haven't looked through them since my dad gave them to me. I lift the box down from the shelf and blow the dust off before lifting the lid. Some of these will be much too old for Ollie, but right on top is *The Giant Jam Sandwich*, and there are bound to be others. The box is heavy, so I carry it carefully downstairs and set it down on the rug. Ollie immediately leaves what he's doing to come and have a look. He reaches for *The Giant Jam Sandwich* straight away.

'That was one of my favourite books when I was little. I think my grandma bought it for me when I was about your age, but I read it again and again, even when I was older.

Shall I read it to you?' I open the cover. 'Oh look, I've written my name and age in it, see? I was five, so a bit older than you are now.'

Ollie points to the words written in purple crayon. 'Where does it say Leah?'

'Good point. You know how your name is really Oliver, but we call you Ollie? And when you write your name on the pictures you do at school, you write Oliver, don't you?'

He nods.

'And you know how when you talk to your mum you call her "Mummy", but when I talk to her, I call her Cassie or Cass?'

'And Luke.'

'Luke?'

He nods again. 'Luke does call Mummy Cass.'

'Oh, right. Well, anyway. Your mummy's name is really Cassandra, did you know that?'

'Yes, but Mummy says people can't say it because they've got their mouth full.'

I laugh. 'I see. I think she meant that when a word is quite long, sometimes we say "it's a bit of a mouthful".' He looks at me as if he's thinking, *yes, isn't that what I just said?* 'It's because it can be quite hard to say. So, Leah is short for Cornelia. That's my full name. Everyone calls me Leah now, and a few people called me that when I was little, too, but when I had to write my name, I always wrote Cornelia. See?'

Oliver nods again, then moves closer so he can look at the pictures while I read. After I've read it twice more at his request, I say, 'Shall we see what else is in the box?' I unpack the books. Most are too old for him, although one or two pique his interest. Right at the bottom are my dad's books. 'Ah, now this,' I lift out the *Boy's Own* annual 1948, 'is very old – older than you, and even older than me! See how some of the pages are loose? That's because it's so old, we have to be very, very careful, because we don't want the pages to fall out or get torn, do we?'

'No.' Ollie shakes his head as he takes the book from me ultra-carefully and places it reverently on the carpet in front of him. I open it and point to the writing inside the cover. 'That says, *Happy birthday, George, love from Auntie Doll and Uncle Bob, 4th December 1947.* George was my daddy, but he was only a little boy then.'

Ollie turns the pages with great care.

'Ollie . . .' I hesitate. 'Do you . . . What do you know about your daddy?'

At that moment, the doorbell rings. I'm tempted to ignore it, but Ollie springs to his feet. 'That might be Mummy.' He runs out into the hall.

'I don't think so,' I say. 'Mummy said she'd pick you up at lunchtime, but it's only just gone eleven.' I open the door, and there are Cassie and Luke, smiling, Luke bearing a huge poinsettia with a Christmas bow tied round the pot. He hands it to me. 'Just to say thank you,' he says as they follow me in.

I want to throw it at him. 'It's lovely,' I say, 'but there's no need, really. You know I love having him.'

'I know,' Cassie shrugs, 'but why not? We really appreciate it.'

'How's he been?' Luke says.

I open my mouth to answer, but an unexpected flash of anger renders me speechless. Ollie isn't his child – who the hell does he think he is? I look at Cassie, but she's smiling down at Ollie, unconcerned. 'Had a nice time, mister?'

I am gratified to see that excited nodding again. 'We did watched a film, with Father Christmas, the real one! And,' he pauses for dramatic effect, 'guess what?'

'What?' Cassie plays along.

'We did get a big huge Christmas tree! And I did help to decorate it!' He grabs Cassie's hand and pulls her towards the sitting room. 'Come and see.'

Luke and I follow. 'My goodness.' Cassie looks up at the tree. 'That looks lovely. And you helped to decorate it?'

He nods, grinning.

'You have had a nice time, haven't you? What a lucky boy.' She ruffles his hair, and turns to me. 'You're so good. I haven't put ours up yet, and I won't let him anywhere near it anyway, in case he messes up my plan.'

Luke laughs. 'I didn't think you'd be a Christmas tree control freak. Don't tell me you go for those soulless, trendy arrangements – white trees with purple lights, or something? Christmas trees should be chaotic and messy and covered with every bauble and bit of tinsel you can lay your hands on. Right, Leah?'

He's relaxed, hands in his jeans pockets, apparently

friendly. I'm not sure if he genuinely likes the overdecorated tree – I let Ollie have a completely free rein, lifting him up to hang baubles on the upper branches. 'I think I was going for traditional.'

'I like traditional,' Cass protests, elbowing Luke gently. 'I just like to do it my own way, that's all.'

Luke looks at me again, casts an exaggeratedly resigned expression in Cassie's direction and mouths, *Bossy*.

Cassie laughs and punches him playfully.

I can feel my own expression tightening on my face. Luke's attempt to include me in their banter makes me feel all the more excluded. There's only three years between Cass and me, but suddenly I feel much, much older, like some dried-up old spinster. I am forty-one. Is my life as a woman over now? It's hard to imagine loving a man again; even harder to imagine a man loving me. And I'll never be a mother, not now. Yet here I am in the same room as my husband's child, as this happy couple, in love, probably had sex this morning before they drove over here. It's as if I am suffocating under the weight of something cold and black and slimy. It's only when I notice Ollie and Luke exchange a smile that I realise what this dark, insidious feeling that has crept over me is. I am jealous.

'Look,' Ollie is saying, pointing to the books. 'There are some books from olden days.'

I take a breath. I have to rise above this darkness that is pushing through me. I manage to smile. 'Books from my childhood. And my dad's.'

Luke and Cassie both kneel down to look. 'Oh, cool,' Luke says. 'Look at this.' He shows Cass the *Boy's Own*. 'And look! *The Giant Jam Sandwich*! I loved this when I was a kid.'

Ollie steps forward and takes the book from Luke to show Cassie. 'Look,' he says, pointing to the writing inside the cover. 'This was Leah's when she was five. I'm going to be five soon, aren't I?'

'Well, I don't know about *soon*. It's not that far away, but you need to get to four first, then five comes next.'

'And you know what, Mummy?'

'What, Ollie?'

'You know Leah?'

'Yes.' Cassie smiles. 'I think I know Leah.'

'Well, her name is really called Cor . . . Cor . . .' He turns to me. 'How do you say it?'

'Cornelia.'

'Cor-nee-leah,' he repeats. 'Like how I'm really called Oliver, but sometimes my name is Ollie.'

'Really?' Cassie turns towards me. 'I didn't know that. I just assumed you were christened Leah.'

'No, but I've been Leah since I was about ten. Cornelia was a hell of a name to be stuck with at school. I used to get called Corny, or worse, Corn Plaster. That's why I started calling myself Leah.'

'Cornelia,' Luke says. 'Unusual name.'

'According to my dad, it comes from a poem my mum read while she was pregnant. "Cornelia's Jewels" – the jewels were her children, apparently, and my mum got a bit obsessed with it.'

'Cornelia,' Luke says again. 'I keep thinking I've come across a Cornelia before, but . . .' He shakes his head. 'Maybe not. I can't put a face to it, in any case.'

'Perhaps you've read the poem?' Cassie suggests.

Luke laughs. 'Nah, poetry's for girls.'

CHAPTER THIRTY-FIVE

THEN

It hurt a bit to walk, so I took it slowly, holding onto Adrian's arm while he carried Harriet in the car seat in his other hand. As we walked through the hospital corridors, everyone was looking at our new baby and smiling – hospital staff, old ladies, a teenage boy, even a huge, fierce-looking man with tattoos all over his neck and face. It seemed the sight of a newborn could melt any heart. On the drive home, I realised I was smiling, too, as if I'd soaked up some of the good feeling that was already pouring towards us.

'Home at last,' Adrian said as we turned into the drive. I'd only been away a few days, but it felt good to be back. He drove right up to the door and parked in front of the garage so it wouldn't be far for me to walk, then came round to help me out of the car. 'Okay?' He smiled, making sure I was steady on my feet before he let go. He handed me his keys. 'You get the door open. I'll bring her in.'

I turned my key in the lock, but as the door swung open, I was taken aback by a horrible, black memory of coming home from hospital without Thomas, of opening the door and walking into the house, silently, just the two of us, no baby. Instinctively, I rested my hand on my scar to quell the new emptiness in my belly. I had to turn round and look at Harriet to remind myself that this time, everything was okay, that the hollow feeling in my womb was normal and could be soothed instantly by the comforting weight of my baby daughter in my arms.

The house felt warm and the hallway looked tidy and newly vacuumed. Adrian ushered me into the sitting room, where the lamps were lit and there was already a fire blazing in the wood burner. The moses basket – a new one, bought specially for Harriet – stood in front of the bookcase, a white cotton shawl folded inside. 'You sit down,' he said, 'I'll make some tea. Shall I leave her in the car seat for a minute, or do you want her out?'

'No, leave her while she's sleeping.' I noticed how he automatically deferred to me, and how I automatically supplied the response; it was as though we both accepted that somehow, I knew more about what to do with a new baby than he did. We'd talked about how we were going to manage childcare. It made sense for me to stay home, at least for the first year. Adrian wanted to be as involved as possible, working from home when he could, and so on.

But as I sat there looking at my three-day-old daughter, I realised that no matter what Adrian did, Harriet was *my* baby, *my* responsibility. As he set a mug of tea down on the table beside me, I shivered, despite the room being suffocatingly warm.

Over the next few days, it snowed on and off, but we had the heating turned up and I was enjoying the feeling of being cocooned, safe and cosy, the three of us together in our warm house. I lost count of the number of visitors, but gradually, the pile of baby gifts grew higher – sleepsuits, dresses, gift sets, soft toys – so many of these that they filled the shelf we'd put up above the cot in her room. There were little fluffy teddies in various colours, a silky-soft elephant with furry ears, a hand-knitted pink rabbit and a big golden teddy bear wearing tartan pyjamas. We had so many congratulations cards that before long, there was no room to display them all. There were some lovely messages inside, especially from friends who'd shared our pain eighteen months ago. Half an hour after we got home, an enormous floral arrangement arrived from work – pink roses and carnations with delicate green ferns and white sprays of baby's breath. The card was signed, it seemed, by everyone in the department.

We'd been back a week when Diane next door, who'd already dropped in with a card and flowers, popped round again with a pink woollen outfit she'd knitted herself – a tiny long-sleeved dress decorated with rosebuds and a pair of matching leggings, threaded with pink ribbon at the waist and ankle. 'It should fit her for the first few weeks,' she said. 'I thought, well, everyone puts them in babygros at this stage, but a little girl, well, you want to be able to dress her up, don't you?'

'Oh, Diane, it's gorgeous!' I ran my hand over the soft wool. 'It's exquisite.'

Diane flushed with pleasure. 'I always knitted for my boys when they were tiny, and for the grandsons. I've made some lovely jackets and cardigans over the years, but it's nice to have the opportunity to knit a little frock.' Then she rummaged in the big bag at her side. 'And I brought you a couple more things. Ah, here.' She handed me a large, expensive-looking box of chocolate pralines tied with a tasteful white bow. 'Bit of a treat for the new mum.'

'Diane, that's so thoughtful – thank you! We've had tons of presents for Harriet, which is lovely, obviously, but this is the only thing . . .' I got choked up then and couldn't continue. She waved my attempted thanks away and delved back into the bag, bringing out two rectangular Tupperware boxes, which she set on the floor beside her, and an earthenware pie dish covered with foil. 'I thought you might like to have this tonight,' she said. 'It's just a steak and mushroom pie. There's beer in the gravy but it's only a splash so it won't do the baby any harm – you're feeding her yourself, aren't you?'

I nodded. 'Trying to.'

She pointed to the Tupperware. 'Then we've got chicken

and vegetable casserole in this one – there's potatoes in it as well, so it's a complete meal – and the other one's just some pasta with a spicy sauce. Save you cooking for a couple of nights.'

Adrian came into the room wiping his hands on a tea towel.

'Diane . . .' I tried to thank her, but I was so tearful with gratitude, I couldn't speak.

'Diane.' Adrian beamed. 'You are a total star.'

Again that little flush of pleasure.

'I'd like to say you shouldn't have,' he continued, unable to resist charming her. 'But having tasted your cooking before, that would be particularly stupid of me.'

There was a beat, during which we all remembered the reason we had tasted her cooking before, then she said, 'Well, I'll let you get on. But remember, I'm only next door if you need me.'

My nipples were so sore that the relief when Harriet stopped sucking was immense, even though I suspected she hadn't had enough. I looked down at her perfect, angelic face. Her eyes were closed, long lashes resting on her cheeks. I slipped my little finger into the corner of her mouth to detach her from my nipple, and the rush of cool air on my skin was soothing as her head sort of fell away. As gently as I could, I wiped the line of milk from her chin and laid her carefully in her moses basket. She made a few more automatic sucking motions, then she was asleep. I stood there for a minute or so, just gazing at her, in awe of her sheer perfection. The sadness for my lost babies would always be there, but I was aware of it beginning to fade, more a mist now than the all-consuming fog it had been at first. At that precise moment, I was purely, simply happy. At almost exactly the same time as the thought clarified, another chased it away; the certain knowledge that my happiness was as fragile as my baby's delicate bones. I leaned over and touched my lips against Harriet's silky skin, my face so close to hers that I could feel her breath on my cheek. I tucked the cot blanket around her so she'd feel snug and safe, and tried to recover the contentment I'd been feeling just seconds ago; but instead I felt heavy and uneasy. Adrian would be back from the shops any minute, so I made a conscious decision to try to pull myself together. He only had two weeks' paternity leave, and I didn't want to spoil this magical time.

When he got back, he went into the kitchen to put the shopping away and I could hear him whistling. It seemed loud. I wished he'd whistle more quietly. I got up and wandered over to the window to look out at the snow. It wasn't particularly deep, but it was enough to turn the lawn completely white except for a line of paw prints from one of the neighbourhood cats. A magpie landed on the terrace just outside the window. *One for sorrow.* I looked up into the trees for its mate, but another two landed within seconds. I smiled. *Two for joy, three for a girl* . . . They flew off again, probably aware of me watching them. A huge crow swooped down from the trees and stood just the other side of the glass, cawing so loudly it sounded as if it was right here in the room with me. It turned its head to one side and looked at me, then flew off. As I stood there staring out at the white expanse of lawn, the most terrifying thought came from nowhere, presenting itself in my head so powerfully that it was as if it was really happening and I could see it unfold in front of me: there was a car, and I watched myself lift Harriet out of it, still strapped into her car seat. I placed her on the ground and then I got back in the car, drove towards the car seat and ran right over it.

'Leah! My God, what is it? What's happened?' Adrian was crouching down beside me, his face and voice sharp with alarm. 'Can you move? Can you get up?'

My heart was pounding, and for a moment I felt as if I couldn't breathe, but then my head sort of rocked and I came back to myself. I didn't remember falling but my legs were twisted under me and I was clutching my abdomen as pain seared across it. I looked out at the garden but there was nothing but cat and bird footprints in the snow. 'I don't know what . . .' I tried to move but I felt my stitches pull, making me cry out in pain.

'Stay there, I'm calling an ambulance.'

'No, no, there's no need. Just help me up.'

I checked my scar, worried that there would be a gaping wound. One of the stitches looked as if it had popped but apart from that, it all looked okay.

'What on earth happened?' Adrian looked shocked. 'I heard you scream and I thought—'

'I screamed?'

'Well, I suppose it was more half-scream, half-groan. Look, are you sure we shouldn't call someone?'

'No, I'm fine, honestly. I just . . . I don't know, I felt a bit weird for a minute, that's all.' He still looked worried, but I couldn't tell him what I thought I saw.

CHAPTER THIRTY-SIX

Then

My breasts were still tender and my nipples felt raw, but I was determined. I gritted my teeth as Harriet latched on, then I settled back and tried to relax as she fed. As I watched her, I marvelled again at her utter perfection. It was hard to believe that she'd only been here for ten days. In that time, our lives had changed completely. Everything, from when we ate, drank, slept, even went to the loo, revolved around the baby. In every room there were baby clothes drying on radiators and open packs of nappies and wipes lying around. Adrian was tidying up around us in preparation for the midwife's visit. 'How can someone so small take up so much space in life?' he said cheerfully.

'I was just thinking the same thing. But when you look at the size of the hole we were left with after Thomas died, it doesn't seem so odd.'

He nodded. 'True.'

His smile faded and I wished I hadn't said that out loud. He hardly ever talked about Thomas now. I stroked Harriet's hair, silky black just like her brother's.

The doorbell rang, followed by two sharp knocks. 'That'll be the midwife,' Adrian said, going to the door to let her in. She was a big woman, not enormous, but sort of . . . hefty and big-busted. Older than the midwives at the hospital – in her fifties, maybe. 'I'm Liz.' She held out her hand. 'Sorry you've had to wait so long, but we're all over the place at the moment. Everyone's off sick with colds or flu. It's a flaming nightmare.' She sank into the armchair opposite, filling the space around her as she unpacked her bag, spilling files and notes across the floor and coffee table. 'Now, where . . .' She rummaged in her bag. 'Ah!' She pulled out a flowery glasses case, which she put on the table next to her pen. 'There we are.' She looked up at Adrian and beamed. 'Tea please, two sugars. I assume that's what you were about to ask?'

He smiled and went off to make the tea while she examined my scar, which she said was looking a little inflamed, but nothing to worry about.

'Got your red book to hand?'

'On the bookshelf there.'

She put her glasses on to peer at my record book. 'How is everything going? Harriet feeding well? Any problems?' She leaned forward to look at Harriet. 'Feeding on demand?'

She was slightly schoolmistressy, brisk and efficient rather than soft and soothing like the hospital midwives. But I liked her. She made me feel safe. I nodded.

'Good. How often?'

I tried to remember exactly how long Harriet went between feeds, but it was blurry. 'She seems very hungry. And she cries a lot if I'm not feeding her. I think it's about every two hours, two and a half if I'm lucky.'

'Oh dear. Rotten luck. Nothing to worry about, but hard going for you.' She looked at my record again. 'How are your nipples? Still sore?'

'Yes, very.'

'Get hubby to pop out for some lanolin cream. That should help, but it might be down to technique. If she's latching on properly, you shouldn't have a problem.'

I looked down at Harriet. As if to demonstrate the point, she appeared to be chewing on my nipple. 'Am I not doing it right?'

'It's a myth that women were born knowing how to breastfeed. Is there someone who could help show you what to do? Mum, or sister, perhaps?'

I shook my head. 'My mum died when I was seven. I have a sister-in-law, but she's in Cambridge, so no, not really.'

She took her glasses off and looked at me properly for the first time. 'You poor duck. It's tough, not having your mum at a time like this. New mums need mothering as much as the new babies, if you ask me.' She put her glasses back on, glanced towards the door and lowered her voice. 'Hubby looking after you? Doing his bit?'

'Oh yes. I've been expressing, so he gives her at least one of the night feeds.'

She nodded. 'Good, good. Now, show me how she latches on.'

Liz watched as I attempted to get my nipple into Harriet's mouth. Sure enough, I was doing it all wrong. Liz showed me what to do and gave me a list of organisations offering breastfeeding support, but the disruption had upset Harriet, and instead of dropping off to sleep, she started first to grizzle, then to yell. I stood up and paced the room with her, jiggling her up and down and gently patting her back. Adrian came back with the tea and biscuits, and I was aware of Liz watching me. *Please stop crying*, I pleaded silently. I didn't want the midwife to think I was incompetent, but instead of quietening down, Harriet cried even louder and more vigorously, her little face turning pink with the effort. I was on the verge of tears.

'She does this for most of the night,' Adrian was telling Liz. 'Is it normal for her to cry so much?'

'Some babies cry more than others,' she said, still watching me, observing.

'I don't know what I'm doing wrong.' My voice wobbled, barely audible under Harriet's cries. 'I'm feeding her whenever she wants, changing her so often that half the time, I find the nappy's still dry, but she still . . . Sometimes I think she doesn't like me.' I hadn't meant to say that, and, to my shame, the tears I'd been holding back spilled over. Liz stood up and came over to take Harriet from me. 'Come along, now,' she said, and at first I thought she was talking to Harriet, but then she said, 'Let's not be thinking like that. You're the most important person in her world. If anything, she's probably picking up on the fact that you're worried, and that's what's upsetting her.' She held Harriet out in front of her, then turned her over so that Harriet's tummy was cradled in that big, capable hand, then she gently jigged her up and down, almost as if judging her weight. Harriet stopped crying instantly and appeared to be looking around the room.

I should have been grateful for the sudden peace, but instead I wondered why this woman, a complete stranger, could stop my baby from crying when I couldn't do it myself.

Then she took the shawl from the moses basket, laid it out on the sofa and showed me how to wrap it around Harriet so that she was tightly swaddled in a little cocoon.

'I wish you'd been here at three o'clock this morning,' Adrian said.

Liz turned to me. 'How much sleep are you getting?'

'Not a lot, to be honest. She wakes up so many times. We take turns, but Adrian has to be back at work soon.'

'It gets easier, but I know that's not much help at the minute.' She looked at Harriet, whose eyes were closing now. 'There.' She laid her back in her basket. 'When you've been up half the night, it might seem like she's only sleeping for five minutes, but it's likely to be much longer than that. She looked at me sternly. 'Now, I want you to take some advice: she *will* sleep, even if it's only for half an hour at a time, and when this baby sleeps, you must make sure that *you* sleep, or at least lie down and rest.' Then she looked at Adrian. 'Make sure this mummy does as she's told, okay, Dad?'

He nodded. 'I'll do my best.'

'Good. Now, I need to run through a few things with you.' She told me about the baby health centre, the six-week check, when Harriet's vaccinations were due and so on. 'It's all written down in there.' She pointed to the red book. 'But sleep-deprived mums don't always remember to check. I'm going to put you down for another visit from one of the health visitors, but realistically, we're so short-staffed I don't hold out much hope, so you might be better dropping into the centre.' She put her glasses away and began to gather her things. 'Any problems at all, contact the centre, or your GP. Anything you want to ask before I go?'

Yes, I thought. *How do I get this right? Why does she cry all the time? Does she think I'm a useless mother?* 'I don't think so. Except . . . when did you say I need to take her to the clinic?'

'As often as you like – there are drop-in sessions every day. It's all in your book, but give us a call if you're not sure.'

And because I couldn't think of another reason to keep her here, I said, 'Okay, thanks.'

She gave me a big smile and squeezed my shoulder. 'You'll be fine.'

I felt a lump rise in my throat. I walked with her to the door and had to stop myself from bursting into tears and falling into her big, capable, confident arms.

CHAPTER THIRTY-SEVEN

Now

The following week, Cassie turns up alone. 'Where's Ollie?' I try not to sound too disappointed.

'Luke's watching him for me. They're both still in their pyjamas, so they're just slobbing around, playing some computer game.'

'Oh, right. Should he—' I stop myself from making another comment about computer games. 'Never mind. Luke not working again, then?'

'No, I thought I told you – his Friday job came to an end a couple of weeks ago. It was only a six-month contract. He's still got all the other stuff, so he's not going to bother looking for anything else until after Christmas.'

'Oh, I see. It's just that I bought some iced fingers.' I realise straight away how ridiculous that sounds, so I laugh. 'It doesn't matter. We can have one with coffee, and you can take the rest home with you. Shall I make it now?'

Cassie hesitates. 'You know what? I think I'm just going to crack on without a break today, if that's all right.' She opens the cupboard under the sink and starts taking the cleaning things out. 'We're going to Luke's mum and dad's for the night, and I've got a few bits to do before we go, plus I need to get our stuff ready.'

'Okay, if you're sure.'

She hasn't made eye contact since she arrived. 'Cass, is everything all right? You seem ... I don't know ... preoccupied.'

'Leah ...' She pauses, standing there with a bottle of bathroom cleaner in her hand, and it feels like she's about to say something non-cleaning-related. But after a second or two, she says, 'Listen. I've got so much to do before Christmas, do you mind if I skip next Friday? I'll give it a really good go this week, so you won't need to do much.'

I can't think of a reasonable objection. 'All right, if you can't make it.'

'Great, thanks. Do you want me to do the paintwork upstairs this week? The bottoms of the doors are looking a bit grubby where Spider pulls them open.'

I nod, not trusting myself to speak. At least having Spider means there's a bit more work for Cass to do. Without him, it's sometimes difficult to find enough to fill two hours. Ollie's interest in Spider is waning lately, but I find myself increasingly glad of feline company. I now encourage him to sleep on my bed, enjoying the warm weight of him on my legs and the feel of his smooth head butting against my hand in the morning. I don't delude myself, though; I know that if I were to disappear, Spider would simply move on to another source of food and shelter. He's the same as Ollie – he quite likes me if I happen to be around, but he doesn't need me; I'm not necessary.

The Wednesday before Christmas, I drive out to the café as usual. Cass smiles and says hello, but instead of waving me to a table and bringing over my coffee so we can chat, she busies herself tidying around the coffee machine, so it's the new girl who serves me. I settle to marking a pile of level four essays as I drink my latte. After a while, I order another coffee, and this time it's Cassie who brings it over. 'There you go,' she says, putting the cup and saucer down on the table. 'How's it going? Work and everything?'

Is it my imagination, or is she avoiding my eye?

'Not bad, thanks. I think I'm getting back in the swing of it now. In fact, I'm quite enjoying it.'

Cass nods. 'So how long were you off work before? After your accident?'

I freeze. She's never asked about the accident before, so why now? I reach for my cup and it rattles in the saucer as I pick it up. 'Quite a long time, in the end. I lost my confidence, you see. I'd only been back a few months when A . . .' I stop myself and fake a brief coughing fit. 'Ooh, something went down the wrong way.' I thump my chest. 'Sorry, what was I saying?'

'You were off work a long time. And you'd only—'

'Ah, yes. I was saying about how I'd not been back long when Clive was killed and, well, as you can imagine—'

Cass's face softens. 'Oh God, yes, of course. I'm sorry.'

'It's more than fifteen months now.' I feel the familiar stab of grief, tempered only slightly by the knowledge that at least I have Ollie. 'A lot of the time it feels longer ago than that, but sometimes it still feels raw, like it's only just happened.'

Cass nods. 'My David died five and a half years ago, and sometimes I still wake up wondering how I'm going to carry on without him.' For a moment, it looks like she's about to cry, but then she smiles and says, 'Not so much since I've known Luke, but it still happens now and then.' She sounds more like her usual self now. 'The first couple of Christmases are shit. Did you say you're going to your father-in-law's?'

'Yes, Christmas dinner with Paul and Helen. I'll probably stay with them for the afternoon, but it'll be low-key. We weren't that big on Christmas anyway, not after . . . Well, with no kids and such a small family, it was never a huge celebration. I'll probably have a brandy and a mince pie on Christmas Eve – after you've picked Ollie up, of course. Where is it you're going again?'

But Cassie's face changes and her eyes flicker down to the table. 'We're . . . um . . . we're supposed to be going out with some of Luke's mates for a drink, maybe a bite to eat. I'm not that bothered about it, really.'

'Oh, I thought you were looking forward to it?' She asked me weeks ago if I'd babysit on Christmas Eve, and hadn't she said it was a proper night out? Definitely more than a drink and a bite to eat. 'I thought you were going to an Italian restaurant – carols by candlelight after the meal, and all that?'

She shrugs and looks away. 'I don't think they could get the booking. I'm not too fussed. There's so much to do on Christmas Eve, isn't there? I might not go. I'll see. Whatever happens, I'll let you know in plenty of time. I'd better crack on. See you later.'

I watch her walk back behind the counter. Have I said something to upset her? I rack my brains, but can't think of anything to explain this . . . not coolness, exactly, but . . . distance. That's it. Cass is unusually distant. I pick up the next essay and try to read it, but I'm three pages in when I realise I haven't taken in a word. It's no good, I can't concentrate. I gather up my things, call 'See you soon' to Cass and head out into the cold.

The pasta ready meal is mediocre at best, and I can't really be bothered to finish it, so I scrape the remains into the bin and pour a glass of wine before pulling the pile of Katherine Mansfield essays out of my bag. I'm halfway through marking the third one when my phone rings. Cass. 'Hi Cass, what's up?'

'Hi Leah. I . . . er . . . I thought I'd give you a quick call now, rather than leave it until the last minute.'

'Oh yes? Leave what until the last minute?'

'You know when I saw you today? How I was saying about that Christmas Eve thing with Luke's mates? Well, I don't think I'm going to go, so thanks for agreeing to do it, but we won't need you for babysitting after all.'

There's a thudding sensation inside me, like a heavy weight falling from my chest down into the pit of my belly. I open my mouth to speak but my voice catches and tears spring to my eyes. I swallow. 'Oh,' I say after a moment. 'I don't have any other plans, so no need to decide now. You can—'

'No. Thanks, but I'm definitely not going. Luke's parents are coming for Christmas dinner, and I've got shitloads to do, so—'

'But when am I going to see Ollie?' I blurt it. I sound desperate, if I'm honest. 'I mean, if you're not coming on Friday and I'm not babysitting after all, when can I give him his present?' My voice sounds higher than usual.

There's a pause before Cassie answers. 'I expect we'll see you before Christmas.'

'But it's only a few days away.'

Another pause. 'We'll sort something out. Well, I'd better get on. Talk soon. Bye.'

And she rings off.

Ollie's presents – a remote-control car, some Lego and a big hinged wooden case full of art materials – are all waiting under the tree. I was going to give them to him on Christmas Eve – one when he arrived, the next one after dinner and the last one later in the evening when he'd be getting bored. I made a point of checking with Cass that it was okay, and she said he was bound to have loads on Christmas Day, so having one present – I haven't told her there are three – on Christmas Eve was fine. I imagine Ollie in his little red PJs – the plan was for me to get him ready for bed here, then he could stay up as long as he liked in the hope that he'd be good and sleepy by the time they picked him up, and if he went to sleep in the car, they'd just lift him in and straight to bed when they got him home. I've been looking forward to a magical Christmas Eve ever since Cass asked me. I'd planned to give Ollie hot chocolate, watch something Christmassy on telly. My throat tightens as tears threaten again. I really must get a grip on myself. It isn't as though I won't see him at all. Cass knows I want to give him his presents before Christmas; she said she'd sort something out.

Tomorrow is Christmas Eve, and I still haven't heard from Cass. I pick up my phone a couple of times, but stop myself from calling. Something's wrong, and I can't work out what it is. Maybe I was being too full on with Ollie; I shouldn't have let on how upset I was when she cancelled the babysitting. Although thinking about it, I'm fairly sure this coolness started before that. It flashes through my mind to come clean about who I am so Cass'll understand why Ollie is so important to me, but there's every chance it would freak her out completely. I go into the kitchen to make coffee, but I'm too agitated to sit still and drink it, so I pace up and down the kitchen, wishing for the first time in months that I had some cigarettes. I can't pace for long with Spider rubbing round my legs, and anyway, it'll make my back hurt. Perhaps I should just put the gifts in the car and drive round there. There would be nothing wrong with that, would there? But what if they're out? Worse, what if they're there but don't invite me to stay? They could just be on their way out, or . . . 'Oh, for God's sake,' I say aloud and reach for my phone. 'Cass, it's me. I was just wondering when I could see you. I'd like to give Ollie his present, and I've got a little something for you and Luke. Perhaps—'

'Oh, that's sweet of you, Leah, but I'm not sure when we're going to be able to get together. It's all a bit mad here at the moment.'

'But . . . do you mean I won't be able to . . . I mean, I know you're busy, but . . .'

'Look, I'm sorry, Leah.' There's a pause. 'I can't really think straight right now. Things are a bit hectic, you know? I'll be in touch after Christmas, okay?'

The following morning, Christmas Eve, I wait until half past eight, then pick up the phone and, not trusting the stability of my voice, send Cassie a text: *Can't believe I forgot 2 ask yesterday – would U 3 like to come over on Boxing Day? Proper lunch or evening drinks and nibbles? Whatever's best 4 U. Let me know! L xx*

The reply comes just after ten. *Thanks for the invite, but we've got some friends coming over. Have a good one! xx*

I stand looking at the message, especially the bit that says, *some friends coming over.* Usually Cass would say, *some other friends*. As in, *other than you, Leah, who are also my friend*. This has to be something to do with Luke, surely. Unless I've done or said something to upset Cass, but what? Just then, another text comes through. *How about lunch here on New Year's Day? It'll just be something light, but we could give each other presents then.*

The relief that I'll be able to give Ollie his presents in a week's time almost counters the disappointment that I'll have to wait so long. I feel bereft, robbed of the promise of a little joy this Christmas, but what choice do I have? I tap out my reply, glad that Cass can't see the tears streaming down my face: *That wd be lovely – see u then!*

So that's that. I haven't seen Ollie for more than two weeks, and now I have to wait another week. Spider is pressing himself against my shins, purring loudly. I pick him up, and bury my wet face in his warm fur.

CHAPTER THIRTY-EIGHT

THEN

It wasn't even ten o'clock, but I couldn't stop yawning. Adrian put his arms out to take her. 'Go on,' he said. 'You go up. I'll give madam her next feed so you can get some sleep.'

'You sure?'

'Of course. As long as you're okay doing the night feeds.'

He was back at work now and he had to be up at six tomorrow, so he couldn't be up with her half the night. 'Thanks.' I kissed them both goodnight and went into the kitchen for a glass of water. The steriliser, bottles and big tub of infant formula were lined up on the work surface as if they were reproaching me.

As I brushed my teeth I caught sight of myself in the mirror. My face looked greyish and there were dark circles under my eyes. I tried to remember when I'd last washed my hair. As I undressed and pulled on my pyjamas, I thought about the pictures in the baby magazines I'd sometimes flicked through at antenatal appointments – the smiling, radiant mothers holding naked babies to their plump, full breasts. That's what you're supposed to be when you have a baby, isn't it? *Radiant.* I laid down on our bed and sighed with relief as the softness of the duvet enfolded me. The pillow was cool against my cheek and I felt as though I was sinking, being sucked right down into the mattress, then down through the slatted base, through the floorboards, down through the sitting room below, through the cellar and down into the foundations of the house, then down, down even further into the clay soil on which the house was built. I wondered if I would ever stop sinking, or if I'd fall right through the centre of the earth and out the other side into space, into infinity.

I woke again at midnight as Adrian was settling Harriet into the moses basket. I tried to go back to sleep, but the thoughts were going round and round in my head along with little bits of music, snatches of tunes that I couldn't quite catch. I dozed on and off until just after two, when Harriet started to make those snuffly, pre-crying noises that meant she'd be properly awake soon. I could feel myself becoming anxious already. Adrian was so good with her, so calm. I wished I could be like that, but I was obviously doing something wrong or she wouldn't cry so much. The moses basket moved as she kicked her legs and wriggled around before starting to cry in earnest. 'Shush, sweetie, shush.' I picked her up and kissed her forehead. I loved the silky texture of her skin, and I had to stop myself from stroking her cheek all the time. I still couldn't quite believe she was really here.

I passed the room where she'd sleep once she was in the big cot, and I climbed the stairs to the attic where we'd set up the rocking chair and a little changing station. I liked to come up here because sometimes the change in air calmed her without me having to feed her again. I sat in the rocking chair, holding the shawl around her so she didn't get cold. I tried singing softly to her as I rocked the chair gently back and forth. 'Rock-a-bye baby, on the tree top . . .' She stopped crying and looked at me for a few seconds, and I thought maybe it would be okay, but then she turned her head away and started again. 'Oh, Harriet, I wish you could tell me what's wrong.' Her furrowed forehead and screwed-up eyes made her look cross, impatient. 'You're not hungry again, are you?'

As I said this, I felt my whole body tense up in anticipation of the pain I knew I'd feel as soon as I put her to my breast. Maybe that was why she was crying; maybe she sensed my reluctance.

'All right, sweetie.' I made a conscious effort to relax as I prepared to feed her, but she was rooting frantically, almost desperately, as if I'd been starving her. Then she found my nipple and clamped her hard mouth round it. I gritted my teeth as she twisted and pulled and stretched it like a bird pulling a worm from the earth.

I seemed to be feeding her almost constantly. Her face was filling out and she was gaining weight, but it was as if at the same time she was draining the life out of me. I felt I was Harriet's *Picture of Dorian Gray*, except that instead of ageing while my counterpart grew younger, I was fading like a photocopy of a photocopy while Harriet became stronger and sharper. Sometimes I felt as if Harriet was taking me over.

She made contented little noises after each swallow and for a while things were peaceful, but when I moved her to the other breast, she started screaming again. I held her against my shoulder to bring up her wind and then I tried to swaddle her like Liz had shown me, but her arms were waving around too much. 'Shush, sweetheart,' I whispered. 'Shush, shush, shush.' Maybe she needed changing. I checked her nappy, but it was still clean and dry. The screaming settled to a less urgent crying and I stood up so I could jiggle her. I wandered over to the dormer and looked out. It wasn't as bitingly cold as it had been the last few days, so I unlatched the window and flung it open to the night air. It worked. For a moment, Harriet seemed startled by the chill breeze and she stopped crying. She blinked, and I noticed the real tears wetting her eyelashes, then she gave a shuddering little sigh. Why was I making my precious child so unhappy?

Now she'd stopped crying, she was looking at me, and again I saw that wisdom, that ancient intelligence living behind her eyes. I held her up to the window. It was a beautiful crisp, clear night with a bright moon lighting up the garden and the woodland beyond it. 'Look, Harriet,' I whispered. 'Look at the stars up there in the sky, twinkling away like little diamonds, like in the song.' And I started singing it to her, softly. She burped, dribbled some milk and then yawned. Her eyes were starting to close and there was a change in the feel and weight of her body as the tension began to leave it. I kept on singing, gradually quietening my voice. *Twinkle, twinkle, little star,* over and over. I was scared to stop in case it brought her back to wakefulness.

After what felt like hours, I crept back downstairs, tiptoeing across the carpet to where the moses basket stood next to my side of the bed. Adrian stirred with a half-snore and I froze, terrified she'd wake, but her breathing didn't change and I was able to lay her down, carefully sliding my hand out from under her head before covering her with the fleecy blanket. I slipped back under the duvet and noticed Adrian's warmth. I'd been up with Harriet for so long that my side of the bed had gone completely cold.

I woke to the sound of crows cawing in the tree just outside the bedroom window. They were so loud it was almost as if they were deliberately trying to wake me. I felt as if I'd only been asleep for a few minutes. It was just getting light and Adrian was still sleeping, so I guessed it was still quite early. I leaned over to look at Harriet and she was just lying there, wide awake, looking up at me. I reached in and lifted her onto my shoulder, breathing in the warm, salty smell of baby sweat. Her head felt hot against my chin. Was it too hot? Maybe she was ill. No, she didn't look ill. Perhaps I was putting too many blankets over her at night. I worried she'd be cold, but what if she overheated? She started to grizzle so I leaned back, ready to feed her.

Adrian stirred, then leaned up to look at the clock. 'Shit!' He threw back the covers. 'It's almost seven.'

The mattress bounced as he leapt out of bed. Harriet started at the sudden movement, twisting her head away from my breast and dragging my nipple painfully at the same time. The floorboards shook as he hurried along to the bathroom. I heard him pee and flush, then turn the shower on and start singing, not one thing but little bits of several different tunes. 'Oh, shut up,' I said aloud. He'd probably had seven hours of unbroken sleep, whereas I'd been up three times with Harriet, once for over an hour and a half. I knew I shouldn't resent it, but I did, so much so that tears stung my eyes. I braced myself as I tried to get her to latch on again, but she chewed at my nipple half-heartedly then let it fall from her mouth. 'Come on, sweetheart.' I tried again, but she turned her head away as if my milk disgusted her. Adrian came in towelling his hair and smelling of shower gel, then he made more noise opening and closing the dresser drawers as he looked for underwear and socks. It was only then that I noticed the empty bottle on the dressing table.

'When did she have that bottle?' I asked.

'About half five, I think.' He put the heavy cotton check shirt I bought him for Christmas on over his t-shirt, then grabbed his jacket from the back of the chair. I must have been so deeply asleep I didn't hear him get up. Now I felt guilty for being cross with him. I was a bitch.

'I was going to stay up, but she went down again quite quickly,' he continued, 'so I thought I'd try and grab another half hour. Forgot to set the bloody alarm.' He smiled down at Harriet, who looked back at him and burped. 'How was she before? Did you have an okay night?'

I was about to run through all the times I'd been up with her, tell him that I fed her every time but it never seemed to be enough, and then I realised how whiny and ungrateful it would sound. Not only that, but I didn't want him to know how crap I was turning out to be at this, so I just nodded. 'Not too bad, thanks.'

'Great. See you later, then.' He kissed me, then he kissed Harriet on the top of her head. 'Bye bye, baby girl. Be good for Mummy.'

The snow had mostly cleared now, and although it was cold, it was a crisp, bright day, and now my stitches had healed and I was feeling stronger, I was itching to take Harriet out in the pram. The first week or so after leaving hospital, I felt safe and cosy just staying at home, but it had started to feel claustrophobic.

I didn't want to risk her getting hungry again while we were out, so I gave her a bottle of formula. I still kept hoping she'd reject the bottle in favour of breast milk, but yet again, she gulped it down like cold water on a hot day. Her head wobbled as I sat her up to burp her. She looked drunk. I couldn't stop myself from wondering whether there was something about me that wasn't meant to be a mother. Although I knew rationally that it wasn't my fault, two babies had died inside me, as though my body had poisoned them. And now, having finally given birth to this beautiful, perfect baby girl, I couldn't even make enough milk to satisfy her hunger.

She was fractious as I zipped her into her red snowsuit and tucked her inside the pram, but as soon as we were outside in the fresh air, she stopped crying, and as I pushed the pram along the road towards the park, she lay there, eyes wide open and looking up at the sky and the trees overhead. After a while, the movement of the pram lulled her to sleep, and I started to relax as I walked, but then I noticed that, even though Harriet was quiet for once, it seemed that everyone we passed was looking at me, as if they *knew* I was incompetent.

When we got to the park, the mothers pushing their children on the swings turned towards me as I passed, and I could feel their disapproving stares. After about five minutes I swung the pram around, suddenly feeling the need to be back at home with the doors closed so no one could see me. I started to walk faster. I turned into our road, where wheelie bins lined the kerbside waiting for collection. A huge crow swooped down in front of me to peck at a black bin bag that had already been torn open and was spilling rubbish into the gutter, then another joined it. They were searching for food, probably to take back to their babies.

I thought again about that poor little crow I hit before Christmas. As I passed the birds, they stopped their foraging and turned their heads to look at me. There were another three crows on the telephone wire, I noticed. They were all looking at me, too.

CHAPTER THIRTY-NINE

THEN

We were getting ready to go out – we planned to pop in on both dads, then do a bit of shopping on the way back. Adrian was just strapping Harriet into the car when she suddenly turned red in the face and noisily filled her nappy. 'Typical,' he laughed.

I lifted her out while he picked up the car seat and carried it into the kitchen. The greenish poo had come out of both sides of her nappy and she was absolutely covered.

'It's all over the car seat, too.' Adrian said. 'Have we got a scrubbing brush anywhere?'

'Cupboard under the sink.'

I held Harriet's ankles and gently lifted her so I could wipe her bottom, but the poo had gone right up her back. I pulled wipe after wipe from the pack and tried to clean her, but it seemed never-ending.

'Shall I use bleach?' Adrian called across the room. 'Or just some washing-up liquid?'

I sighed. 'I don't know. How bad is it?'

'There's not a lot, I suppose. Will it stain?'

'How should I bloody know?' I didn't mean to snap, but I just wanted him to deal with it. 'Try scrubbing it with washing-up liquid and see what happens.'

Finally, after God knows how many wipes, Harriet was clean. I placed a fresh nappy under her bottom. 'Do you think I should put some cream on her? She's not sore now, but if she's got diarrhoea . . .'

'I think that's done the trick,' Adrian said as if I hadn't spoken. 'It'll take a while to dry out, though. I'll text them both and tell them we'll have to leave it until tomorrow. I'd better go and do the shopping myself, hadn't I?'

Neither of us liked supermarket shopping, but it flashed through my mind that if I were to go, at least I'd be on my own for a while. Then I had a darker, more frightening thought, that if I were to leave this house without Harriet, I might just float away, with no control over what was happening and no idea how to get back to my baby.

'Leah? I said, are you okay?' Adrian was standing right next to me.

'What? Yes, why?' I still had my hand on Harriet's tummy.

'You looked a bit, I don't know, vacant.'

'Sorry. I was just trying to decide whether to put some cream on her. What do you think?'

'Won't do any harm, will it?' Just like that. He made the decision. Why couldn't I think like that?

'I'll be as quick as I can.' Adrian leaned over and kissed me. 'I've got the list, but text me if you think of anything else.'

I heard the front door open and close as I smothered Harriet's bottom with Sudocrem. She was starting to grizzle now, because the whole process was taking so long. I fastened the nappy and kissed her tummy, then I slipped on a clean vest and did up the poppers underneath. I was just about to feed her arms into a clean lemon-yellow babygro when her legs went rigid and more poo exploded out of her nappy, covering everything. With tears streaming down my face, I bit my lip and started all over again.

Harriet had been sleeping soundly for over an hour. She'd gone down easily tonight, but I was still tossing and turning and my brain wouldn't switch off. There was a cacophony in my head – parts of songs, a jumble of conversations, all running at the same time. It was as though someone had left three or four radios on different stations, all playing simultaneously. I was still awake when she started to make snuffling sounds just after four. I gave her a breastfeed and then a couple of ounces of formula and she settled again, but still I couldn't sleep. I finally started to doze as it was beginning to get light, but soon I was aware of Harriet's cries, which seemed to be coming from a long way away. Adrian stirred, so I put my hand on his arm and shook him gently. 'Adrian? I've barely slept. Could you do her feed?'

'Yeah, course.' He sounded sleepy as he sat up, pausing for a second or two before getting out of bed. He yawned and stretched, and then I heard him whispering to Harriet. 'Come on, baby girl, let's go and get you some milk, shall we? Let your poor mummy get some sleep.' And then I heard the bedroom door open and close softly. The birds were starting to sing, the sound dominated by the crows in the tree right outside the window. I was sure there were more of them each day. *For God's sake*, I thought, *just go away and let me get some sleep*. My head and limbs felt heavy, and somehow I managed to tune out the racket outside and doze off again.

I dreamed I was in the woods, pushing Harriet in her pram. In the dream, it was a beautiful day, shafts of sunlight filtering through the trees making big patches of light on the ground, like spotlights. I could smell pine trees, damp, leafy earth and the sweet wet grass, as if it had just rained. I was singing to Harriet as we walked, and I smiled at the wood sounds – birdsong, a woodpecker hammering away and the deep cawing of the crows. It began to get dark quickly, reminding me of the eclipse when I was at uni, when we all stood outside to watch as the sun hid behind the moon, silencing the birds and chilling the afternoon air. It grew colder in the dream, too, but the bird sounds got louder, especially the crows.

In the newly darkened wood, the trees twisted into ugly, shadowy giants and the sound of crows tore into my head. Then I realised I wasn't holding onto the pram any more. But despite the noise and my missing baby, I felt strangely at peace.

Soon the light started to flood back, spilling down through the trees and pooling on the forest floor. Then I saw a big, dark patch in front of me. It was moving. A writhing black mass of crows, all clustering around something, diving in and out, worrying at it until one by one they began to fly off, still cawing loudly. And there in the clearing, standing alone and surrounded by an ocean of bluebells, was Harriet's red corduroy pram.

Still unconcerned, I wandered over and looked in. It wasn't Harriet, it was Thomas, but he was in pieces. At first, I couldn't see any blood, and it was just that he was broken. His head, arms and legs had come apart from his body, like a doll, and I couldn't work out how to put him back together. But then the crows started cawing again and flapping their wings around me and I realised they had torn him apart. I managed to beat them away, and when I looked back in the pram, the broken baby's face was Harriet's, and she was looking up at me, pleading with me to mend her and make everything right. I was crying and the crows were getting louder and then Harriet started to cry. That was what woke me, of course. Harriet really was crying.

As I stumbled out of bed, I could hear the crows. In reality, I mean. Not in the dream. I picked Harriet up, breathing in her sweet baby scent and holding her warm, silky head against my cheek. I lifted the edge of the curtain. Adrian's car had gone and it was completely light. There they were again, in the tree outside the window. I could see four, no, five of them. Then another one swooped down from the tall beech and came to rest in the plane tree with the others. Six of them. I held Harriet a little tighter as my heart thumped against my ribcage. It was only a dream, I told myself, but a cold draught from the window chilled me and I shivered as it occurred to me that I was looking at a 'murder of crows'. I reminded myself that there were a number of other collective nouns for crows: a horde, a hover, a muster, a parcel, a parliament. Yes, I decided – this could definitely be a parliament of crows. I could see seven of them now, and they looked like they were in charge, like they made all the rules. They reminded me of judges wearing black gowns.

To start with they just sat there, not making any sound apart from the odd caw, but then I pulled the curtain aside so I could close the window, and as soon as they saw me, they went berserk, cawing frantically at me, heads thrust forward, black beaks screaming open. I pulled the window shut and closed the curtains again as quickly as I could, and with both arms protecting Harriet, I hurried downstairs and moved from room to room, checking that all the windows and doors were locked.

CHAPTER FORTY

Now

I wake early on New Year's Day after a broken night of disturbing dreams. Maybe it's that sense of new beginnings that is always tied up with apprehension – the sense that whatever might go right this year, there's plenty that can go wrong.

I stand under the shower and turn the temperature up so the hot water can ease the pain in my back. I wonder what I'd be doing now if I'd never found that email? And if Adrian hadn't died, I wonder how long it would have been before he told me about Ollie? I've been thinking about it a lot. At first I imagined him visiting Ollie in secret and then coming back to me and this big, childless house. But the more I think about it, the more certain I am that he wouldn't have kept it from me for long. He couldn't have. Maybe he was still coming to terms with it himself, or maybe he was waiting until he thought I was strong enough to take it. Whatever the reason, I'm convinced he would have wanted me to know. We could have shared parenting with Cassie, had Ollie over here regularly – every other weekend, perhaps, and maybe half of the school holidays. I imagine a beach, Adrian helping Ollie build sandcastles; me teaching him to swim; the three of us eating ice creams with flakes stuck in the top. How wonderful it would be to be on holiday with my husband and my stepson. There's definitely more of Adrian in Ollie than there is of Cass. He has Cass's skin tone – fair, slightly freckled – but that's about it. I look at my own reflection as I apply mascara. My eyes are the same as Adrian's and Ollie's: so dark they're almost black. Harriet's eyes were blue, but they were just starting to darken. She'd be a year older than Ollie is now, and when I look at him, I can't help but imagine what she'd look like.

I paint a little colour on my lips and force myself to smile. It'll be a nice day, and I'll get to see Ollie open his presents. I wish I could shake this gloomy feeling. I've bought Cassie some Neal's Yard goodies in a little wooden chest, and a voucher for a spa day. At the last minute I dashed out and bought one of those coffee-and-chocolates gift sets for Luke. The spa day is for two, and when I bought it, I'd hoped Cassie might ask me to go with her, but it seems unlikely now, so I write *To Cassie and Luke* on the envelope. Then I go into the study for some paper, cut out a small rectangle and write, *Gift Voucher* in large letters in the middle. Then underneath, *This voucher can be exchanged for one day's babysitting (can be extended to overnight on request) with love, Leah.* I slip it into the envelope with the spa voucher.

As I follow Cassie in, Luke comes out of the kitchen with a half-full glass of white wine in his hand. 'Happy New Year.' He kisses my cheek. 'What can I get you to drink, Leah? There's red or white, and there's some fizz open. Or do you fancy a G&T?'

He looks relaxed, very much the host, and I wonder vaguely if he's been staying here over the whole Christmas period.

'White wine, please.' I follow them into the kitchen, assuming I'll chat to Cass while she's cooking, but Luke takes the wine from the fridge and steers me back into the living room. Ollie is sitting on the sofa watching television with his thumb in his mouth. 'Telly off, please, Olls,' Luke says. But Ollie is too engrossed to hear him, so Luke reaches down and picks up the remote control, points it at the TV and switches it off. 'Just until after lunch.' Ollie's face falls and his bottom lip plumps forward as if he's about to cry. I'm about to protest on his behalf, but then Cass comes in with her wine and sits down next to him. 'Shall we do presents before lunch?' she says, and Ollie cheers up immediately.

I notice Cassie and Luke exchanging glances as Ollie unwraps his gifts. 'I bought the art kit ages ago,' I explain, 'and I totally forgot I had it, so I went out and bought the Lego as well. But then I spotted the remote-control car on a special deal and I couldn't resist it.' I laugh. 'So you got lucky this year, Ollie.'

Ollie is gratifyingly pleased with his presents and says an enthusiastic *thank you* after each one without even being reminded. After he's opened them, I notice Cassie whispering in his ear, and the next moment he's handing me a little box wrapped in gold paper. 'It's from me and Mummy and a little bit from Luke.' He grins as I give him a big thank you hug.

I open the box to reveal a silver bracelet made of tiny ivy leaves linked together on a delicate chain. 'It's beautiful,' I say, genuinely thrilled. I thank them again as I fasten it around my wrist.

'Leah, I got millions of presents in my stocking.' Ollie takes my hand. 'They're from Father Christmas. Do you want to see?'

I stand up to follow him, but then Luke says, 'Stay here, please, Ollie. Lunch'll be ready in a minute.'

'It's okay.' Cass checks the time on her phone. 'It'll be about another ten minutes or so.'

Does Luke look a bit put out, or am I imagining it?

'Come *on*, Leah.' Ollie pulls me towards the door.

'Okay, okay, I'm coming.' I laugh.

'Don't let him bully you,' Cass says. 'Ollie, you can show Leah your new stuff quickly, then you need to come down and get your hands washed ready to eat, okay?'

Ollie nods, and carries on pulling me towards the stairs. Up in his bedroom, he proudly shows me the rest of his present haul. He's still excited about having been to see *Snow White and the Seven Dwarfs* on Boxing Day, and he tells me how he went onstage at the end with some other children and sang a song with Snow White herself. But when, eyes shining at the memory, he tells me how Luke took him up on the moors to watch Santa's sleigh flying over the rooftops, I have to turn away to hide my miserable jealousy. The table is laid with a red cloth, napkins and sparkling glasses. There are even candles, despite the winter sun pouring in through the window. I feel a tiny fizz of pleasure at the trouble she's gone to.

'Lunch isn't very Christmassy.' Cassie sets a large earthenware dish of lasagne in the centre of the table, then a bowl of salad leaves. 'But it's something I know we all like.'

'Looks lovely.' I take my seat next to Ollie. Cassie serves while Luke opens a bottle of red. 'So,' I say as we start eating, 'how was your Christmas?'

We chat about how much work the Christmas meal is, and how turkey is overrated and expensive if you buy free range. Cassie says they might go for capon next year, because Luke knows someone who rears them.

Next year. Looks like he's here to stay, then. I'd sort of guessed that, but this confirms it. To think that I once hoped that Cass, Ollie and I might live in the same house.

'So, how was *your* Christmas?' Cassie asks.

'Surprisingly nice, actually.' I tell them about my day with Paul and Helen, how Chris and Judy and the boys came up for the afternoon and how we ate loads of chocolate and played Cluedo and Pictionary and even a couple of rounds of charades. At one point, when the boys were playing on the Xbox and we were all sitting round eating Christmas cake and drinking Baileys, it occurred to me that I hadn't thought about Adrian, or about Thomas or Harriet, or even about Ollie, for a good two or three hours. It was only much later when I let myself back into the house and looked at that ridiculously overdecorated tree with my presents for Ollie underneath it that the good feelings started to wear off.

After we've eaten, Olliie goes into the living room to watch one of his new DVDs. There's an awkward silence, and I sense something is about to happen.

'Thing is, Leah,' Cassie says, not quite meeting my eye. 'We . . . Luke and I . . . we have some news.'

'Oh yes?' I try to make my voice sound upbeat, but all I achieve is a squeak. *Don't be pregnant*, I think. *Please, please don't tell me you're pregnant.*

'We've decided to move in together. Permanently.' Cassie glances at Luke, who takes her hand. I notice the little squeeze he gives it, as though he's reassuring her.

I take a sip of my wine. Moving in together. My stomach gives an uncomfortable lurch as I realise this is a turning point, that it's going to affect me and, more importantly, that it's going to affect Ollie. They're both looking at me, waiting for a reaction.

'Well,' I say, 'that makes sense, I suppose. Two can live more cheaply than one, and all that. Have you told Ollie?'

'Of course we have,' Cassie says. 'It's partly for his benefit, to be honest. I don't really want him to grow up in a single-parent family.'

'But that was what you intended when you got pregnant with him, wasn't it?'

The words are out before I can stop them. Cass and Luke both look shocked at my bluntness, and I feel a bit shocked myself. 'I'm sorry, that sounded rude.' I reach for my wine and take a big mouthful. 'I didn't mean to be so . . . so blunt. It's just that . . .' I think quickly. 'I was so impressed when you told me how determined you were to have a baby, and I remember thinking how brave that was, to choose to do it alone.'

Luke gets up to open another bottle. He looks uncomfortable, embarrassed, possibly annoyed. Cassie is still looking at me. 'I know what I said, Leah,' she says quietly. 'I *was* determined, and I did plan to do it alone because I'd lost my husband, and because Oliver's father—' She shoots a quick glance at Luke, and I wonder how much she's told him. 'Oliver's father was a fling. He meant nothing to me.'

Her words sting, though God knows why, because it's not as if I *want* Adrian to have meant anything to her, but I still don't like to hear him dismissed, as if he was just some anonymous guy she picked up for the purpose of using his seed.

'I meant what I said,' Cass continues. 'But I didn't mean I was determined to raise him to adulthood entirely on my own, no matter what happened or who I met in the future. And now I've met Luke, and we're happy, and we can make a proper family for Ollie. Do you see what I mean?'

I nod. 'Of course.' I find I'm biting my thumbnail, so I

put my hand in my lap. Luke pours us all more wine. 'And Ollie . . . Ollie's okay about this?' Maybe I shouldn't even be asking, but surely they can't expect me not to be concerned.

'He's totally fine about it,' Cass says. 'He adores Luke.' They smile at each other again and I feel a pang of envy. 'Be happy for me, Leah,' Cass says, her face sadder and more serious than I've ever seen it.

'I am happy for you,' I say. 'Really. I say things without thinking sometimes, and . . .' I shrug. 'I'm sorry. Anyway, I'm happy as long as you and Ollie are happy.'

'In fact,' Luke says, 'Ollie's quite excited. He can't wait until we—'

Cassie touches his arm. 'There's something else I wanted to mention,' she says, 'before I forget.'

My heart starts to thump, because I doubt I'm going to like what I hear next.

'I . . . Oh God, I hate anything like this, so I'm just going to come out and say it. I'm going to have to give up the cleaning job.' She glances at Luke again. 'I don't mind doing the next couple of weeks, give you a chance to find—'

'But . . . you can't stop completely, surely? What if you came every two weeks instead?'

'No,' Luke says. 'Cass has been working too hard for a long time, but she doesn't need to do two different jobs now.'

'But when will I see . . . I mean, I've got used to . . . to us having coffee and a chat, and Ollie enjoys it, too. He likes playing with Spider, and there are all his toys and things and—'

'Yes,' Luke says. 'We wanted a word about that, as it happens.'

I notice Cassie touching his arm again and giving a tiny flick of her head, as if warning him. 'No, Cass,' Luke says. 'We might as well tell her now, give her time to get used to it.'

'Tell me what? What do I need time to get used to?'

Cassie sighs. 'We're moving.'

'Moving?' I parrot like an idiot. It takes a moment to sink in. 'You're moving house? Where? When?'

'Oh, not immediately,' Cassie says. 'A few weeks, at least, but we want to be settled before Ollie starts big school.'

'Cornwall,' Luke says while Cassie's still speaking. 'We've had an offer accepted on a little house in Boscastle, near to Cassie's parents and not that far from the sea.'

CHAPTER FORTY-ONE

THEN

It was the third night in a row that I hadn't been able to sleep. I sat up and leaned over the side of the moses basket.

'Leah? What are you doing?' Adrian propped himself up on one elbow. 'Is she all right?'

'Yes, I think so. She keeps going quiet. I was just checking she's still breathing.'

'I know you're anxious,' he sighed, 'but I honestly don't think there's any need. The health visitor said everything's fine, didn't she? Come on, lie down and get some sleep.'

I tried to relax, but it felt as if all my nerve endings were twitching. He was soon snoring softly, and I could hear Harriet's little snuffles, so I should have been able to sleep, but I couldn't switch off for some reason. Then the curtain moved – the window was open. I jumped out of bed and went to close it. It was mild for March, and I knew Harriet needed fresh air, but I'd rather take her outside so she could see the trees at the same time. What Adrian didn't seem to understand was that it meant the crows could get in. If I told him I was worried, he'd say I was being silly, but the other day, while I was ironing, that big crow was there again on the terrace, looking in at me. I mentioned to Adrian that I'd wondered whether it might be the mother of the baby crow I ran over, but he looked at me as if I was barking mad. He said I should tell the doctor I was having 'strange thoughts', so I pretended I wasn't serious. I suppose it does sound a bit bonkers when you think about it, but if he was here all day like I was, if he could see the way that creature looked at me . . . It made me realise that I needed to be careful what I told him. I used to think that Adrian understood me perfectly, that he and I were the other half of each other. But now I knew that it was Harriet who was the other half of me, and sometimes I wondered if Adrian was jealous.

I climbed back into bed, and now I knew the window was closed and we were all safe, I managed to drift off. Soon I was dreaming about them again. I knew I was dreaming this time, but I couldn't control what was happening. I was back in hospital and the crows were my family, crowding round my bed, smiling and friendly, cooing and cawing over Harriet. Then I noticed one that wasn't smiling. It gripped my arm with its wing and started shaking me, then it put its big, black beak right up to my face and said my name. 'Leah, Leah.' I knew this was definitely the mother crow. I tried to tell her it was an accident, that I didn't see her helpless baby falling into the road, but I couldn't make any sound come out of my mouth. I told myself I was dreaming, that I just needed to open my eyes and the dream would melt away. But the crow-mother spread her big dark wings and opened her beak and screamed right at me, blaming me still.

When I opened my eyes, Adrian was stroking my hair, his face close to mine. 'Leah,' he whispered, gently shaking my arm. 'Leah, wake up. You're having a bad dream. It's all right now. Everything's all right. Are you okay?'

'What?' My heart was racing as I forced myself properly awake. 'Oh, oh yes, I'm fine. Just another bad dream, that's all.' He kissed my forehead and turned over again. I leaned over to check on Harriet, to make sure she was still there, still breathing, still safe. She was lying on her back, wide awake and looking right at me. I dipped my hand over the side of the bed so it could rest gently on her stomach. Once Adrian was breathing deep and steady, I slid out of bed and tiptoed across to take my dressing gown from the back of the door. I slipped it on and lifted Harriet out of the moses basket, grabbing a shawl to wrap around her. We went up to the attic, where I settled in the rocking chair by the dormer window so we could watch the sun rise. The birds started up while it was still dark, the crows loudest, as usual, and before long, the sun peeped up over the black treetops, turning the sky pink and yellow and orange. I could see three crows settled in the branches of the plane tree and silhouetted against the fiery sky, and I remembered my dream with a little shudder.

As I watched, more of them settled in the tree, adding to the deafening racket. They were all facing this way, towards the house, and their deep cawing seemed to be aimed just at me. I watched, mesmerised, until suddenly I knew they were trying to give me a message. I couldn't work out what it was, but I was sure it was something to do with Adrian, because now I came to think about it, he'd started watching me all the time. Perhaps they were trying to warn me. I looked down at Harriet as she fed and I saw that she knew something, too, and I knew she was trying to communicate it to me because instead of having her eyes closed as usual, they were wide open, and in each one I could see a tiny black crow shining back.

I finished feeding her and sat her up, my hand cupping her chin so I could gently pat her back to bring up her wind. She did a little burp and regurgitated some milk, then she turned her wobbly head towards me and looked right at me. She said – not in the outside way, not in actual words, but quite distinctly nevertheless – *Be on your guard, Cornelia. Be careful who you trust.*

Adrian was upstairs, packing for the Learning and Technology conference. It didn't start until tomorrow, but we'd agreed it would be sensible for him to travel up tonight rather than risk a broken night with Harriet and then have to get up at five thirty. As usual, he was rushing about as if he was in a hurry, and as he clattered down the stairs, he knocked over the pile of washing I'd put there ready to go up. He picked it up but he shoved it back on the stair in a haphazard pile, so I'd have to fold it all again. Harriet was fractious this evening, grizzly. I tried to feed her but she pulled away. Maybe the sounds of Adrian getting ready to leave were bothering her, too. I'd told him I'd be fine while he was away, but I suppose I was a bit apprehensive about being on my own with her for four days.

'Have you seen my wallet?' he shouted from the kitchen. 'I thought I'd left it on the dresser.'

'In the dining room. On the table.'

'Oh, thanks.' The glasses in the cupboard rattled as he stomped across the dining room floor. A few minutes later, he came into the sitting room, keys in one hand, laptop in the other. 'Right, sure you'll be okay?'

Like I could say *no.* 'Of course,' I said. 'I'll be fine.'

He wanted to be out of here, away from Harriet's endless crying, my endless tiredness. He leaned over and kissed Harriet's head, then he kissed me quickly on the lips, then a second time, more lingeringly. 'Make sure you do what the health visitor told you,' he said. 'Sleep when the baby sleeps.'

I nodded. 'I'll try.' It sounded sensible in theory, but she rarely slept for more than an hour and even then, when she was asleep was the only chance I had to take a shower or have something to eat, never mind all the other stuff that needed doing.

'It'll be too late to call when I get there, but I'll phone tomorrow, okay?' He kissed me again, then headed to the door.

Amazingly, Harriet dropped off to sleep in my arms. After Adrian's noisy departure, the silence in the house was more noticeable. I was used to being alone with Harriet during the day, but on the rare occasions she was quiet, there was always some other sound – birds in the garden, next door's car crunching the gravel on the drive. It was odd for it to be so still and quiet in the evening.

I took her upstairs and put her in the moses basket and still she didn't wake. I should have followed the advice and got some sleep before the inevitable crying session later. I knew the continued lack of sleep was doing funny things to my head, but it wasn't yet nine and the idea of having some time to myself was appealing. Maybe things were slowly improving, because I definitely hadn't felt quite as strange for the last couple of days. I told Adrian I'd been feeling a bit weird, but I didn't give him details. He wanted me to talk to the doctor or health visitor, but there was no way I was telling them – or him – that my baby spoke to me, and that I thought the crows had talked to me as well. They'd think I was crazy. It even seemed a bit mad to me now, but it didn't at the time.

I considered going to bed. I undressed, put my pyjamas on and went into the bathroom to brush my teeth, but as I padded back into the bedroom, I realised I probably wouldn't go to sleep yet anyway. I wasn't used to the house being so quiet, for one thing, and for another, I was still hungry. So I switched on the baby monitor, went back downstairs and put the television on for a bit of background noise while I made some tea and toast. I was buttering the toast when I heard snuffling sounds from the monitor. I froze, holding my breath, knife in mid-air, but she settled down again. I took the monitor and my tea and toast into the sitting room just as some panel show was finishing. Next was a nature documentary, *The Life of the Crow.* Was that a coincidence? I'd had so many dreams about crows lately, I was becoming obsessed with them. I picked up the remote and went to the menu, but there was no point because I knew I had to watch the crow programme. And because I knew I *had* to watch it, that I couldn't *not* watch it, I felt afraid. I don't know why; all I knew was that adrenaline was coursing around my body and my heart was beating too fast.

After the crow programme, I turned the television off and sat for a while, thinking about what I'd learned. I wasn't imagining it; the crows *had* been speaking to me, just as I thought, but I'd misunderstood what they were trying to tell me. I thought they were angry, still blaming me for running over their baby, but it wasn't that at all. Tonight, in the programme, they explained. They knew it was an accident, and they wanted me to understand that it was a sign of how fragile babies were; that if I wasn't careful, I might harm Harriet by accident as well. Of course I told them I understood that perfectly, and that it was the very thing that had worried me since the moment I knew I was expecting her. I told them about Thomas, and about my other baby, and they said they'd help me, that they'd be watching out for me and not to worry if I didn't know what to do at any point, because they would tell me. All I had to do was look out of the window and listen to what they said.

I knew I mustn't tell anyone about this. If I did, they'd think I was mad, and then the social workers would come and take Harriet.

CHAPTER FORTY-TWO

Now

It is as though I've been punched by the air around me. I stare at him until I'm finally able to make my mouth move. 'Cornwall?' I look at Cassie. 'You're taking Ollie with you?'

'Of course we're taking Ollie with us.' She snorts. 'What did you think we were going to do, leave him here on his own?'

'But you can't move to Cornwall. What about preschool? What about his friends? And Spider – he'll miss Spider if you . . .' I shake my head. 'You can't just up sticks and move to the other end of the country, just like that.' I feel cold all over, like when you have flu. This can't be happening. I can't lose Ollie; I can't lose him, too. I start to shiver.

'We can, Leah,' Cassie says, her voice sharper now. 'I wasn't going to tell you just yet, but as Luke says, you need to get used to the idea that that you won't be seeing so much of Ollie. I know you're very fond of him.'

'Yes, yes I am.' I can't say any more, because my throat has closed up completely.

'But we can't not move house because of that. And it's not like we're moving to the other side of the world, is it?'

You may as well be, I think, but I don't say it out loud.

'You can come and visit us, obviously. The house is much bigger than this – you could come for a holiday.' I notice the look Luke gives Cass at this point. This is all down to him. He doesn't like me for some reason, and he's determined to take Ollie away from me. 'Cornwall,' I say. It comes out as little more than a croak. 'It's such a long way.' I pick up my wine glass, but put it down again. My throat is so tight I don't think I can even swallow. My eyes are brimming, so I keep them lowered. Ollie is in the living room, watching *Frozen* again, singing along. Does he realise what this means, I wonder? He probably has no concept of how far away he'll be going.

'I know you've become attached to Ollie,' Cassie says, 'but this'll be good for him. He'll be able to have a proper relationship with his grandparents at last. And he'll grow up by the sea.' She looks at me, then rests her hand on my arm. 'Please don't be sad, Leah. We'll stay in touch. We can talk on the phone. We can FaceTime, too, so you can see Ollie and chat with him as much as you like.' She smiles and gives my arm a little shake. 'Come on,' she says. 'Even my sister isn't this upset, and she's his auntie.'

'Yes, but . . .' I stop. What am I going to say? *I'm his father's wife? I'm his stepmother, and I should have been his mother?* No, I know that's ridiculous, but I feel the bond with Oliver as strongly as if he were my own flesh and blood. 'I . . . I'm sorry, this is silly, I know.' I push my chair back. 'Excuse me. Must just pop to the loo.' I manage to get into the bathroom and bolt the door behind me before I let myself cry. After a minute I blow my nose, then wet the corner of a towel with cold water and hold it over my eyes so they don't go all red and puffy. I take a few breaths and try to pull myself together before I go back downstairs.

As I walk past the living room I can see Ollie, sitting on the sofa with his thumb in his mouth, looking sleepy. I go in and sit down next to him. 'How's my best boy? Are you having a nice day?' He nods without removing his thumb. I put my arm around him and he snuggles up against me. I want to ask him about Cornwall, how he feels about moving away from everything he knows and loves, but I'm not sure what that would achieve; they've clearly made up their minds. They're kidding themselves if they think it won't do him any harm to be wrenched out of his life like this. Maybe if I could get Cassie alone, without Luke telling her what to do all the time, what to think . . . I'm stroking Ollie's hair, playing with the little sticky-up bit at the back. I can hear them clearing plates in the kitchen, so I suppose I ought to go back. I lean down and kiss the top of Ollie's head. 'I love you, Ollie. You know that, don't you?'

'Love you too,' he says, but I know it's automatic, a response Cass taught him.

'Are you coming back in the kitchen for some apple crumble?'

He shakes his head. 'Don't like apple crumble. Please can I have ice cream?'

'I expect so. Shall we go and ask Mummy?'

He takes his thumb out. 'Please can I have it in here?'

I smile. 'I'll ask.' As I approach the kitchen, I realise they're talking about me. I can't hear everything, but I catch, '*not healthy . . . can't let her. . .*' (Luke's voice), and then, '*she's not dangerous*' (Cassie), then Luke again, '*realistic . . . can't be sure . . . take the risk . . . be trusted.*' My legs feel weak and shaky; I put my hand out to steady myself. *Not healthy?* Yes, I've become attached to him, but is that so unusual, to be fond of a close friend's child? And we *were* close friends, at least before Luke came along. Cassie's speaking again. Her voice is softer, but I can't catch it all. '. . . overreacting . . . not as if . . . been through . . . circumstances . . .' It sounds like she's trying to pacify him. Does he really think I might be 'dangerous'? God, he doesn't think I'm some sort of pervert, does he?

I don't get where all this can have come from. I can't think properly here, with Luke looking at me with that nicer-than-nice smile of his. I creep back along the hallway, then deliberately make my footsteps louder as I walk towards the kitchen. They're sitting at the table when I go in, smiles firmly in place. 'Ollie wants ice cream,' I say. 'And I think I'm going to pass on the crumble. I'm feeling a bit rough, actually. Start of a migraine, I think.'

'Oh no.' Cassie stands up, looking genuinely concerned. 'Do you want some painkillers? I've got ibuprofen, or paracetamol.'

'No, it's okay. Thanks anyway, but they don't do very much. I probably need to go home and get my migraine tablets.' I start to gather my scarf and bag. 'I'm sorry. Thanks for lunch – it was lovely.'

Cassie stands up. 'Leah, you're not going because of what we said about moving, are you?'

I attempt a dismissive laugh, though I notice Luke is avoiding my eye. He can't wait for me to go. 'Of course not.' I make a gesture to my head. 'This has been threatening all day. I just need to go home and lie down, I think.' Oddly, my head *is* starting to feel a little thick, as though I may be getting a headache after all. That'll teach me to make up a migraine. I move as quickly as I can now, anxious to get away so that I can think about what to do next. As I say my goodbyes, I touch cheeks with Luke and I embrace Cassie, who hugs me almost but not quite as warmly as usual. Ollie is grinning up at me. 'Bye, Leah,' he says, 'see you on another day.' I sweep him up into my arms and squeeze, burying my face in his warm, little boy neck. I have to bite my lip to stop myself from crying and hanging onto him too tightly.

CHAPTER FORTY-THREE

Then

Thank goodness I'd brought the waterproof cover with me. What had been little more than drizzle when we left the house was now a full-on downpour, and as I looked at Harriet, all snug and dry beneath the plastic, I felt disproportionately pleased with myself that I had managed to keep my baby warm and dry. I also felt a flash of envy. Why hadn't I worn my other coat, the one with a hood? My hair was plastered to my head and cold water ran down the back of my neck. I pushed the pram into the warm fug of the health centre where the entrance area was crammed with prams and buggies, some still dripping. I squeezed ours in with the others, unclipped the waterproof covers and lifted Harriet out. After giving her name at reception I carried her round into the waiting area, a big, bright space with toys for the older children to play with. I sat down among the other mothers, thankful that for a few minutes at least, Harriet was quiet. She wasn't asleep, she was just looking around, and I felt a sudden tremor of fear at her vulnerability and at my own inadequacy. Keeping her sheltered from the rain wasn't exactly an achievement – there were much more challenging threats to her safety and comfort than a few drops of water.

A few of the mothers were feeding their babies, chatting at the same time, making it look effortless. One of them caught my eye. 'Hiya.' She looked young, not much older than my undergrads, but she radiated confidence. She was blonde, healthy-looking, with rosy cheeks and bright eyes, and her baby was sucking contentedly at a full, creamy breast. She looked as if she'd just stepped out of a Thomas Hardy novel. 'Little girl?' she asked, leaning over to look at Harriet. 'How old?' I guessed hers was a boy, given the blue babygro and the blue padded jacket. A toddler with his thumb in his mouth snuggled in closely under her other arm and a few feet away, an older boy was randomly clicking bits of Lego together. 'Yes,' I said. 'Harriet. Just over five weeks.'

'What a pretty name,' she continued. 'You're so lucky to have a girl.' She looked around at the beautiful, healthy boy children she'd been blessed with. 'I thought it would be third time lucky. Couldn't believe it was another one. Not that I don't love him to bits.' She tipped her head to kiss her suckling baby, then gave the toddler a squeeze. 'And you, monster.' She kissed his forehead, then looked at me. 'But really – three of 'em! I might give it one more go, but if it's another bloody boy . . .' She shook her head.

I thought about my own bloody boy. My blue, still, bloody boy.

She detached the baby from her nipple and shifted him to the other side where he instantly latched on again and settled into a pattern of efficient, rhythmic sucking, then she turned back to me. 'First baby?'

'Yes,' I replied, because it was easier.

'And how was it?' She was smiling, trying to be friendly. I was so shattered I found it genuinely bewildering that anyone would want to waste precious energy talking to a stranger. 'Are you still in the *never again* phase, or are you one of those annoying first-time mums who pops them out in two hours flat and without stitches?'

'I had a caesarean, actually.'

'Oh? How come? Breech, was she?' Questions. It felt like she was poking at me. 'Or was it last-minute? My mate had an emergency caesar – she'd been in labour forty-two hours, and she was exhausted, so—'

'No. She wasn't breech, and it wasn't an emergency. It was elective.'

She frowned, then gave a sort of *oh well* shrug, and I assumed that was the end of the conversation.

'I'd have hated that. I mean, a natural birth is painful, and your insides are never the same again, but even so. It's a wonderful feeling, to know you've made all that effort, delivered your baby through sheer hard work, and—'

'Shut up!' It was out before I could stop myself. 'I know how bloody hard it is,' I snapped. 'You don't need to go on about it because I know. I've been through it myself, all right?'

'I thought you said this was your first?'

'Yes, well, I lied.'

She looked as though I'd slapped her face. At that moment, the health visitor came round into the waiting area. 'Harriet Blackwood,' she called, as if Harriet was going to jump up and walk over there by herself. 'Could we have Harriet Blackwood next, please.'

As I got to my feet, the woman turned to another competent-looking mother. 'Personally,' she said, deliberately making her voice loud enough for me to hear, 'I'm in favour of natural childbirth.'

Natural childbirth. I turned towards her again. I wanted to reach out and grab her by the shoulders, look into her eyes and tell her what happened. I wanted to tell her there was nothing natural about spending a day and a night pushing out a dead baby.

The noise was starting in my head again as I followed the health visitor to one of the open doors, snatches of music and talking, as if someone had left a television on. Everything around me was too big, too bright. I had to look away from the red fire engine painted on the wall, because it hurt my eyes. The health visitor smiled, but it was one of those smiles that neither reaches the eyes nor stays on the mouth. She was thin, beady-looking and pointy-faced, with big, old-fashioned round glasses that made her look like an owl.

'Undress her for me and pop her on the scales, please.'

I did as I was told, but I didn't like her, this woman, and I could tell she didn't like me. When she'd measured Harriet and recorded her weight, she started the questioning – how often did I feed Harriet, how often did she have a wet nappy, what did her poo look like. I nearly said, *it looks like baby shit, what do you think it looks like?* Then she wanted to know all about her sleep patterns and whether she was still crying a lot at night. I told her things were better now, thank you. I didn't want anyone telling me what was best for my baby, because how could they possibly know? Harriet wasn't like those other babies they saw all the time. Of course, I didn't tell the health visitor that. I had to be careful, just like Harriet said.

I realised I must have tuned out for a minute, because she was looking at me, the annoying health visitor woman, and she was still asking questions, about me this time. How was I sleeping, she wanted to know, was I getting enough rest, how was I coping, yada, yada. But I gave her the answers. And there was nothing she could do, because they were the *right* answers.

CHAPTER FORTY-FOUR

Then

It was a bit chilly this morning, so after I'd fed Harriet and brought up her wind, we wandered over to the window so I could check the weather. The crows greeted me as soon as I drew back the curtain. I didn't quite understand *how* I knew what they were saying, only that I did. Somehow I'd been able to interpret their calls, and I was grateful for the privilege, especially as they were giving me such good advice. Now I thought about it, it seemed so obvious. When Harriet wouldn't settle, it was simply an indication that she wanted to be outside breathing the beautiful, oxygen-rich air that came from the trees. All I had to do was wrap her up and take her out and she'd become calm straight away. It had been mild this week, but there was a light dusting of frost on the grass today. It was cold, but not freezing, certainly not bad enough to keep us inside, so I dressed her in her red snowsuit, which made her look like a mini Santa, settled her in the pram and tucked the blankets around her. As soon as we stepped outside I felt a sense of relief that she was breathing fresh air at last. I'd have loved to take her into the woods, but it was still quite muddy underfoot from last week's rain, so we headed for the park instead. The late winter sunshine was so bright it hurt my eyes, and everything appeared more vivid. The postbox at the end of the road was such a startlingly bright red, I wondered if they'd just repainted it, and as we passed, I put out a finger to touch it, expecting the tacky feel of fresh paint, but it was bone dry.

We pressed on to the park, and I noticed Harriet was awake and looking at me. I smiled. 'When I was a little girl,' I told her, 'my grandma used to take me to the park. She taught me the names of all the trees, and of lots of flowers and birds, too. She knew all the different birds just by listening to them.' I laughed. 'I only know the crows.' We turned in through the wrought iron gates and I pushed the pram along the tree-lined path. 'You see these trees above us, sweetheart? Well, these two are beeches, like we have in the garden at home. This one's a plane tree – we have one of these, too.' Harriet looked up, her little eyes screwed up against the light. 'This great big one we're coming up to now, this is a horse chestnut. In the autumn, it'll produce beautiful fat, shiny conkers – we'll collect them when you're bigger.'

As I pushed the pram past the children's play area, I

realised there was a woman waving at me. She had a baby in a sling on her chest and a large double pushchair parked by the railings.

'Hello! It's Harriet's mum, isn't it?'

How did she know? 'Yes,' I said cautiously. 'That's right.'

'I saw you at baby clinic, remember? I think we got off on the wrong foot.'

Ah. The *natural birth* woman. I snapped at her last week. I attempted a smile. 'Oh yes, hello. How are you?'

'Oh, you know – run ragged, no time to put a comb through my hair and this lot driving me bloody insane. Just the usual.' She rolled her eyes. 'Ethan! Alfie!' she yelled at her two little boys, who were laughing with delight as they stepped in and out of a puddle near the swings. 'Stop that this minute, or you won't be going to Jessica's party.'

They were both wearing wellies, so I couldn't see what she was cross about.

'I'm dropping this lot off at their granny's in a minute, then I'm meeting up with a couple of other mums for coffee. Fancy joining us?'

I was surprised by the invitation, because I'd been quite rude to her at the clinic. I felt guilty about it, but how could I be friends with a woman who didn't appreciate her children? 'Thanks for asking me,' I said, 'but I've got some things to do.'

'Oh, go on – I'm sure it's nothing that can't wait.'

I shook my head. 'Thanks, but I need to get back.'

'Look, I can see I upset you the other day, banging on about natural birth.'

I shrugged. 'No harm done.'

'I know I can be a bit evangelical about it,' she went on. 'You know – the medicalisation of childbirth and all that. I sometimes forget that not everyone feels the same. So anyway, I'm sorry if you took offence. It wasn't intended.'

'I'm sure it wasn't.' Sorry I 'took offence'; not sorry she gave it, then.

'It's just something I'm passionate about.'

I nodded, attempting to move the pram round her, but the enormous pushchair she'd just pulled towards her was blocking my way.

'So, if you'd already had a natural birth, what made you go for a caesar the second time?' She looked at me brightly, as if it was perfectly all right for her to interrogate me like this. I wasn't sure what irritated me most, her relentless probing or the way she abbreviated *caesarean*, as if she was using her familiarity with the word to demonstrate her superior experience and knowledge of all things maternal.

'Look, I'm sorry, but I don't really want to talk about it.'

She shrugged, untying the sling that was fastened around her middle. 'Suit yourself. How old's your first one, then?' She let down one side of the double pushchair and tucked the baby inside, but before I could answer she said, 'Right, hopefully the little bugger'll stay asleep for half an hour.'

Something inside me screwed up tight and I had a powerful urge to hit her. I couldn't remember ever feeling this level of anger before. 'How could you call him that?' I said.

She looked up, startled, then smiled. 'I call them all little buggers. Or little sods.' She was still grinning and I wanted to slap her, to wipe that smile off her face.

'Well, you should be ashamed of yourself. You have three beautiful boys and all you can do is insult them.'

'Oh, come on, it's only—'

'I don't know how you can be so bloody ungrateful.' I was aware of my voice getting louder and of some of the other mothers looking at me, but I didn't care. She had to be told. 'Each one of those babies is precious and you should treasure every single moment. People like you make me sick. You don't know how lucky you are to have three live children.'

Her face changed and she said something else, but I didn't hear it because I was frantically trying to manoeuvre the pram round her and her pushchair and her two little boys, who had stopped playing in the puddle and had come over to stand next to her. They were looking up at me, and I realised with horror that I'd frightened them with my shouting. 'I . . . I'm sorry,' I muttered as I pushed the pram round them and headed back along the path.

I walked home briskly, not really taking anything in, and I was still shaking as I felt in my pocket for my keys. It took me a moment to fit my key in the lock, then the door swung open and I pushed the pram into the hall. My anger had subsided, but I still felt odd, as though I didn't quite know myself. Perhaps I'd overreacted. The woman was annoying, but she probably wasn't the only mother who took her children for granted. I looked at Harriet, sleeping now, and wondered if I'd ever take her for granted. The idea was inconceivable.

Adrian unwrapped the pizza and slid it into the oven while I finished feeding Harriet. 'Do you think she's likely to go down quickly?' he said, tearing open a bag of salad leaves. 'It would be nice if we could eat together tonight.'

'She'll be fine.' I sounded so unusually confident that he did a double take. 'I've worked out two things while you've been away. One is that I think I was getting so worried about her crying that I was making her nervous – I think I was actually causing it, because since I've stopped worrying so much, she's been crying less.'

He nodded and, to his credit, resisted what must surely have been a temptation to say *I told you so*.

'And the other,' I continued, 'is that when she *does* cry, I now know what to do if she won't stop. I just take her outside; it's the fresh air she needs, the oxygen. She needs to be near the trees, you see.'

He was searching noisily through the cutlery drawer, probably looking for the pizza cutter, even though I've told him dozens of times we keep it in the utensil pot next to the cooker. He was half-smiling, and he looked at me a little oddly. 'What do you mean, *she needs to be near the trees*? Obviously fresh air is good for her, but she's not exactly starved of oxygen, is she?' And then his skin went pale and he straightened up, his expression suddenly anxious. 'There isn't something wrong, is there? Like asthma?'

'Of course not. I'd have told you.'

He relaxed again. 'Thank God for that. It was just you saying, you know, about the trees – I thought the doctor or the health visitor or someone might have told you to take her out near trees or something.'

'No, it was the crows.' I almost started to tell him about how they'd used that television programme – clever birds! – to get the message to me, when his head whipped round as if he'd heard a loud noise. 'The crows? Leah, what are you talking about?'

My heart started banging against my chest, and Harriet sensed my alarm and pulled away. I'd forgotten. It was only me that could understand them, me and Harriet. Sometimes, when I was doing normal, human things, like laundry or cooking or shopping, it went completely out of my head that Harriet and I had been chosen, that we were unique. And I forgot that to anyone else, it would seem unbelievable, even a bit mad to think that the crows understood all this. So I decided to keep quiet, keep it to myself. It wasn't so unusual. After all, a few hundred years ago women who used herbs to cure illnesses were considered witches, weren't they? And all because people were too narrow-minded to be open to new possibilities.

'Sorry, I meant ...' I paused to help Harriet latch on again and to give myself time to think. 'I meant that it was watching the crows that made me think, you know, about the fresh air and the trees and everything.'

He shot me a look and I braced myself for another question, but at that moment the oven timer pinged and he turned his attention back to the pizza.

CHAPTER FORTY-FIVE

Now

As I drive home from Cassie's, I try to find the positive side of what they've told me. Luke isn't a bad man. He plainly doesn't like me, but maybe that's because he wants Cassie to himself. They clearly love each other, and he does seem to care about Ollie. It'll be a good thing, I tell myself. Ollie needs a male role model. And he'll see more of his grandparents, of course. Cornwall is beautiful and unspoilt, and he'll be growing up near the seaside. He'll have lovely fresh air and he can learn about nature and . . . and . . . the pluses peter out. Cornwall. Yes, I can go and visit, but how often, realistically? It takes hours and hours to drive there – seven or eight, I think. Adrian and I once ruled out a weekend there because it was too far to go for a couple of days. What would he think about them stealing his child away from me like this? I press my foot down harder on the accelerator, realising at the same time that I'm not that far from where he had the crash. It occurs to me that I could just duck out of all this right now. I could find something, maybe a tree, maybe a wall, and I could line up the car, flatten my foot to the floor and drive myself to oblivion. For a few seconds, maybe longer, that is exactly what I intend to do. My heart thuds so hard it almost hurts; adrenaline is zipping around my body, my knuckles are white on the steering wheel as the landscape flashes past. No trees, no walls, nothing solid enough. It is only when I see another car in the distance that the madness of what I'm doing shakes me back to my senses. The car is solid enough to smash me to pieces, but I must not hurt anyone else, not again. I take my foot off the accelerator and slow to a reasonable speed, and I try to focus my thoughts more clearly so I can make a plan. There's got to be something I can do. What, though? Something, something. I'm drumming my hand on the steering wheel. *Oh, for God's sake, Leah, get a grip on yourself.*

I arrive home in what seems like no time at all. Apart from that scary moment when I considered lining myself up with that other car, I've barely registered the drive. Without taking my coat off, I throw my bag down in the hall and go into the kitchen. Spider rubs himself around my legs and miaows at me aggressively until I've opened a bag of moist salmon chunks and squeezed it into his bowl. He eats, purring loudly, and I wonder where he'd have gone and who would have fed him if I hadn't come home. Still in my coat, I pour a large glass of wine and drink half of it down quickly.

How long would he wait for me before going out of the cat flap and finding somewhere else to live?

Go with them. It jumps into my head. *Move to Cornwall.* Why not? I don't need to live in this big house, and I've been told often enough that it would sell quickly in such a desirable area, and for a good price. I could find something lovely in Cornwall – a little cottage on the coast, perhaps, not too near to Cassie and Luke but near enough to babysit now and again. I could probably get some teaching work, enough to keep me ticking over. A fresh start. A tingly sensation runs through me at the thought. Maybe I should have done this before, got out of this house, started again somewhere completely new. I top up my glass and take it through into the study.

Boscastle, they said. I type in *Boscastle and ten miles around.* There are plenty of nice properties I could afford. I click on a few, look around the rooms, the gardens, how close they are to the sea, how near to schools – I'd have to be near enough to pick Ollie up if necessary.

For twenty minutes or so, as I sit there sipping my wine and scrolling down the list, I kid myself that I might actually do this, sell up here and move to Cornwall to be near my stepson. That's what he is, I remind myself. My husband's child. But by the time I've almost emptied my glass, I know it's not an option. Not only is this house my only connection with my own babies, but how would Cassie and Luke react? I'm not so deluded that I don't know it would look odd. What if I told them the truth, explained why I care for

Ollie so much? Would Cassie understand? She knows what it's like to long for a baby, after all, and she lost a husband she loved. But I can't think how I'd even start that conversation. I top up my glass again and I try a few opening lines in my head, but what becomes clear is that I have been a total bloody idiot, spinning such a complicated web of lies that I've trapped myself completely. If only I'd told Cass the truth right at the start. She'd have been wary, obviously, and it might have taken a while, but it's possible she'd have come to trust me eventually. As it is, I've basically lied through my teeth for nine months and now I don't know what to do; I don't know how to get out of the mess I've got myself into. Adrian was always the first person I'd ask if I was struggling with how to deal with a difficult situation – he always had an idea for a tactful and sensitive approach. The irony is cruel. I finish my wine and drink another glass, or maybe I have another two, I'm not sure. But by half past eight I'm properly drunk. I crawl into bed, clutching the teddy bear Ollie cuddles when he stays here. Harriet's teddy.

At ten past one, I wake with the threat of a hangover. I take a couple of paracetamol, drink a full glass of water and then drift off again. I sleep fitfully for a while, then I sit bolt upright, suddenly wide awake. It's a memory that's woken me, as harshly as a loud alarm or a thump on the shoulder. That day a few weeks before Christmas, when I had Ollie overnight so Cass and Luke could go Christmas shopping. We were all in the sitting room where Ollie and I had been looking through the books, and we'd had that discussion about names being shortened. I can see Luke's face, a crease in his forehead as he concentrated when he thought about my name; the way he kept repeating it, *Cornelia*; how he kept saying how unusual it was. I'm out of bed and downstairs in seconds. *Come on*, I murmur. Why is this bloody internet connection so slow? I haven't googled my name since I first came home from the unit. Adrian was cross with me for doing that – he said we'd never be able to move on if I was going to dwell on the trash they'd written about me. Now I hold my breath as I wait for it to load. First, I type in Leah Blackwood. There's a Dr Leah Blackwood in Brisbane. I scroll down the first three pages, and the only other Leah Blackwood that comes up is a teenager who lives in Sweden. I keep scrolling until it moves on to a Leah Blakewood. Then I go back to the home page, and with shaky fingers type in *Cornelia Blackwood*. And there they are, the headlines from when it happened.

CHAPTER FORTY-SIX

THEN

When Harriet woke just after two, Adrian sat up and swung his legs round to the floor, throwing back the duvet and sending a cold draught over my bare shoulders. Normally I'd have been mildly irritated by the way he did this with no thought as to how it might disturb me. But the new me was calm; the new me knew what to do. I put my hand on his arm, noticing the warmth of his skin. 'It's okay, you go back to sleep. I'll do it.'

'No, it's all right. I'm awake now.' He yawned and rubbed his eyes. 'Or I will be in a minute.'

'Really, it's fine. Go back to sleep.'

Another yawn. 'Are you sure?' He waited for me to nod. 'All right then, I can't say the idea of going back to sleep doesn't appeal.' He reached for my hand as I started to get out of bed. 'Wake me if she won't go down. My first meeting's not until ten thirty, so I don't have to be up until eight. No point in us both being knackered.' He flopped back onto the pillow, pulling the covers up around his shoulders.

'Come on, sweetheart,' I whispered as I lifted Harriet out of her little nest. I grabbed one of the blankets and wrapped it around her, then went down to the kitchen to make up a bottle of formula. She grizzled as I moved around the kitchen, but quietened down as soon as we started climbing the stairs, probably because she knew her food was coming. She took the bottle the same way she always did, guzzling it as if she was starving, but even after she'd finished, she still wouldn't settle, and soon started to cry again. I tried pacing up and down, patting her back, gently jiggling her in my arms. I tried singing 'Rock-a-bye Baby', but nothing would soothe her. Maybe it was time we went out.

I put her snowsuit on over her babygro and tucked her into the sling, then I put my big coat on over us both and slipped my bare feet into my boots. The cold air hit me as soon as I opened the back door. It was crisp and sharp, and I knew immediately that this was what Harriet needed because she stopped crying as soon as we stepped outside. I was halfway to the gate when I realised that walking in the woods was a stupid idea – the paths were difficult to negotiate even in daylight, but with nothing but the weak light from a pale quarter moon, all those gnarled and twisted tree roots lurking in the ground would make them treacherous.

'Never mind,' I told Harriet, 'we'll take the pram instead.' I went back into the house, moving quickly so she didn't start crying again, and as soon as I'd got her tucked into her pram, I opened the front door so she could smell the night air. I flicked the switch on the wall and the lamp at the end of the drive came on. Not many of the roads around here had street lighting, so I grabbed a torch from the hall cupboard, just in case, then I closed the door quietly behind me and we set off into the night. It wasn't as dark as I expected, because a few of the drives were well-lit and there were several lamps on in people's gardens. No one around here seemed to worry about their electricity bill – or the environment – and with golden light spilling over the silvery grass and frost-dusted holly bushes, it all looked very pretty. It was quiet inside my head for a change, so all I could hear was the sound of my own footsteps and the brush of the night air against my ears as I moved through it. We were a long way from the main road here, so even if there were any cars passing at this hour, we wouldn't be able to hear them. There was almost complete silence. Harriet was wide awake, mesmerised by the night. As I walked further away from the house, I was aware of a lightness in my step; I felt as if we were surging forward, my daughter and me, cutting effortlessly through the hushed darkness.

Soon, Harriet was fast asleep. But I didn't want to go back yet, because I was enjoying the beauty of the navy-blue sky, the frosty trees silhouetted against it and the almost-silence, punctured occasionally by the hooting of a distant owl. I was enjoying the solitude, too – we hadn't seen a single other human being the whole time, and I had this amazing feeling of . . . it was hard to describe . . . *significance.* I knew that Harriet was part of it, too. It was as though all those long, sleepless nights where she cried and cried had made me stronger. In fact, the exhaustion I'd felt just before we came out had faded away and right now, at this precise moment, I felt full of energy, acutely and magnificently powerful.

I wasn't sure how long we'd been out because I wasn't paying attention to the time, only to this amazing feeling of lightness and freedom. To think I used to be nervous about going out after dark! I kept walking, striding forward, aware of the smile on my face. I didn't even notice the route I was taking as I pondered this new way of feeling, but I must have walked in a circle because the next turning was our road. Harriet was still sleeping soundly and I could have carried on walking with her all night, but as we were so close to the house now, I thought we might as well go back.

As soon as I saw the lights on in almost every window, I remembered Adrian. It was quite a shock to realise that, while we'd been out, I hadn't thought about him at all. I'd completely forgotten his existence. How odd. How very, very odd.

We were only halfway up the drive when the front door swung open and Adrian appeared, phone in hand, wearing trainers and a jumper over his pyjamas. 'Leah! Thank God. What's happened? Are you okay?' He came hurrying down the drive and reached out towards the pram. 'Is she all right?'

'She's fine,' I said, in what I hoped was a calm, reassuring tone. 'Everything's completely fine.'

He looked at me strangely as he unclipped the carrycot from the pram base. 'But where were you? Why on earth would you . . .' But then he shook his head. 'It's bloody freezing out here. Let's get her inside.' He carried her in while I collapsed the wheels. 'Leave that,' he snapped. 'Christ, Leah. Just come inside before you get pneumonia.'

I shrugged and followed him in. 'She's absolutely fine,' I said as he peered in at Harriet and fiddled with her blankets. 'Leave her. She's sleeping. I just thought she needed some fresh air, that's all.'

'Fresh air?' His hand shot up and sliced through his already ruffled hair. 'For fuck's sake. It's half past three in the bloody morning.' I noticed the catch in his voice, an emotional break in the anger.

'Is it? Sorry, I'm not wearing a watch. And I forgot to take my phone.'

'I know you forgot to take your bloody phone.' He held up his own and shook it at me. 'I tried calling you. I've been worried sick.'

'I'm sorry. I should have left a note, but I wanted to get her outside quickly so her crying didn't disturb you.'

'Oh, come on. You make it sound like I'm some tyrant, shouting at you to keep the baby quiet.' He shook his head and sighed. 'I offered to get up with her earlier, but you insisted.' His voice was softer now. 'Want some tea to warm you up?'

I wasn't cold, but I said yes please, because I could see he'd feel better if he had something to do.

He put the two mugs of tea on the table and pulled out a chair, then ran his hand through his hair again. 'Look, I'm sorry I shouted, but you must understand how worried I was.'

'There was no need to worry – I was just getting her to sleep.'

'But don't you realise how . . .' He looked exasperated. 'How fucking *weird* it is to be taking the baby out in the middle of the night without telling me?' He was raising his voice again. 'Did it not occur to you that I'd worry? Especially given how you've been?'

'What do you mean?'

'Exhausted, tearful, snappy, confused – I know it's all supposed to be normal in a new mother, but that doesn't mean we should ignore it.'

I knew what was coming next.

'Have you made an appointment at the surgery yet?'

I sighed. 'And say what? I've got a new baby and I'm tired? I get a bit tearful and snappy when I'm sleep-deprived? She's going to say yes, you and every other new mother who ever lived.'

'Look, I'm not having a go at you. It's just . . . well, like I said before, I think you might be depressed. It's not uncommon, is it?'

'I'm not depressed. I don't even feel sad. The reverse, in fact.'

'Really?' He looked up, his face brightening slightly.

'Well, that's good to hear. I've been so happy these last few weeks, and I thought you would be, too, but you don't smile any more.' He sighed and looked at me with those glittery eyes I used to love so much. 'I think I've been a bit naive. I assumed that everything would be wonderful the moment she was born, but I can see that was unrealistic, especially after all we've been through. And you've copped for most of the work, haven't you? I try to do what I can when I'm home, but I know it's not enough. It's been killing me to see you looking so . . .'

'Yes, well, I'm okay now.' Such an understatement. I wished I could tell him how elated I felt now I knew how to look after Harriet properly. But if I tried to explain, I'd have to tell him about the crows, and how they were helping me. And then he'd think I was crazy.

He reached over and took my hand. 'I'm glad you're feeling happier now, I really am. I know it's hard for you being here with her on your own. In fact, I was thinking, maybe we could get someone in to help? Not a nanny, necessarily, but perhaps—'

'No, I don't want anyone else here.' I knew I sounded defensive, but the last thing I wanted was someone like that, one of those health visitor know-it-all type women watching me, telling me what I should be doing. I *knew* what to do now.

'All right, all right, but keep it in mind as an option. Just if things get difficult again – if you're on your knees from lack of sleep, if she's crying too much and you can't settle her.' He gave a half-laugh. 'After all, you don't want to have to wheel the pram through the streets in the middle of the night too often, do you?'

I was about to tell him she needed to be outside more, that she'd weaken and fade away if I kept her inside where she couldn't see the trees and the sky and the sun and the moon, but before I could open my mouth he said, 'I still think it wouldn't hurt to have a chat with the doctor. Just so that, I don't know . . . so they can keep . . .' He shrugged, and I could see he'd failed to find a good argument. 'I don't know, I'd feel happier knowing you'd talked to them, that's all.'

'I talked to the health visitor,' I lied. 'When I went to the drop-in centre.'

'That was a couple of weeks ago, though.'

'I went again today.' And then I took a chance. 'I told you.'

'No, you didn't.'

'I did. When you were making dinner.'

And then he had to concede, because he knew he didn't always listen.

CHAPTER FORTY-SEVEN

Now

I sit staring at the screen, unable to move. They know. Cassie and Luke; they know what I did. Luke must have googled my full name, seen all these stories.

. . . speaking outside the couple's £400,000 home, Blackwood's husband Clive, 43, also a university lecturer, insisted his wife was a loving mother and vowed to stand by her.

I'm aware of the tears leaking out of my eyes and running down my face, but apart from that, my body feels numb, as if it's shut down. But then the adrenaline starts flooding my system and I'm on my feet, pacing up and down the room, breathing fast. I pick up my phone, then throw it down again. What would I even say? Those little snatches of conversation I overheard when they were talking in the kitchen earlier come back to me, and at last I understand. Luke was telling her I couldn't be trusted. But Cass was defending me, because I definitely heard her use the words 'not dangerous'. Although that obviously means Luke thinks I *am* dangerous – he said something to Cass about not taking a 'risk', presumably of leaving Ollie with me. Cass will have thought about it, considered potential danger, weighed up whether I was likely to hurt Ollie. Oh my God, that's why she cancelled the babysitting on Christmas Eve, and why she's been so distant. She *has* been avoiding me.

More tears come, great, wrenching sobs from deep down inside me, until I start to feel as if I'm choking. I know I need to calm down but I can't seem to stop. I wish I still smoked. It's months since I've even thought about it, but right now I feel desperate for a cigarette. I lift the back of my hand to my mouth and bite down, hard. Maybe physical pain will distract me from the emotional pain. At the same time, I try to consciously slow my breathing. As the sobs gradually subside, I look at the deep indentations my teeth have left in the skin of my hand. It seems to have worked, though, because although I'm still crying, I don't feel quite so out of control. Taking a few deep breaths helps, too.

As I'm making my way downstairs for a glass of water, I remember there's an unopened half-bottle of brandy in the dresser. Adrian's dad gave it to me at Christmas. I'm not a huge fan of brandy, but I unscrew the lid and take a big swallow, feeling instantly calmer as the fiery heat burns its way down my throat and into my stomach. I pour an inch or so into a cup and take it back up to the study.

The photos they've used are quite grainy, especially the old one of me that they must have taken from the university website. As I lean in to look at the other pictures, my heart starts beating harder. Cass will have seen these; what if she recognised Adrian? I can feel the panic rising again. There are a couple of shots taken around the time of the trial, but you can't really see his face. Surely she'd have confronted me if she'd made the connection? I scan the story again. The papers only referred to him as Clive, and come to think of it, he looks different here. His hair had grown longer by then and he hadn't shaved since it happened, but by the time Cassie met him, it would have been six or seven months after this and he'd have been more or less back to normal. Then I scroll down to a photo of us on our wedding day; it's quite blurry because we were both laughing and trying to shake off a snowstorm of confetti. I don't know who took this shot; which one of our so-called friends gave it to the papers. I peer at the photo. No, she can't have recognised him. She'd have said. If she knew I'd been deceiving her, lying to her for almost a year, there's no way she'd have invited me over to lunch and defended me to Luke, and there's no way she'd have given me that beautiful bracelet. But just because she doesn't know now, doesn't mean she won't find out. More importantly, she does know what I did. And now she's taking Ollie away from me.

It's a few days into the new year, but I can't settle to anything. I've barely slept since New Year's Day, and I find myself moving from room to room, pacing the hallway, walking upstairs and then back down again. This constant movement is playing havoc with my back, but I can't keep still. I go into Ollie's room and lie down on the bed, looking up at the animal frieze that runs around the walls. The train set is still in the corner, its carriages parked in the sidings, waiting for him to return and weave a story around it. She can't really think I would harm him, can she? I run my finger along the bracelet they gave me, she and Ollie, and I go over everything she said about when they move – we could FaceTime, talk on the phone; I could go down for a holiday. But will I ever be allowed to look after him again? And even if Cassie's still speaking to me, even if *she* wants to stay in touch after they move, what about Luke? I can't see him being happy about me going down there.

I read the reports again, trying to work out what they will have thought when they read them. Maybe they managed to get past the *Mail* piece that refers to me only as 'Blackwood' and read some of the more sympathetic reports in the other papers – *Earlier stillbirth may have been factor in tragic mum's breakdown, says doc* . . . And in another: *Lifetime of loss had 'devastating consequences' for loving Sheffield mother* . . .

But Luke won't be swayed by any of that.

I find myself trudging up the narrow stairs into the attic. For a while, I just stand at the window, looking out at the trees. This is where it happened. I still can't recall it properly, only snatches of the hours and minutes leading up to it. I remember bolting the door downstairs and being aware of Diane next door shouting through the letter box, then Adrian, too. The doorbell ringing and ringing, my phone going constantly, and that frantic pounding on the front and back doors. At the time, all that noise and commotion only served to convince me that I was right, that they were coming for Harriet. The last thing I remember about that day is hearing the glass smash downstairs as they broke the kitchen window to get to me.

My phone rings and for a moment, I think it's part of the memory. Then I come back to the present. As I reach for my phone, I know there's no point in me hoping it'll be Cassie. In fact, it's Judy. I remember saying I'd call her in the New Year, but I can't face talking to anyone, so I ignore it.

It's completely dark outside now, so I go around the house closing curtains and blinds and switching on lamps. The heating has been on all day, but I'm cold; cold inside, as if my bones have chilled. I put my dressing gown on over my clothes, but it doesn't help. Maybe I should eat something, but the thought of food makes my stomach churn. I had toast this morning, but nothing since. Did I eat last night? I can't remember. I make a mug of tea, take it into the sitting room and huddle by the fire, but the only warmth that spreads through me is an unnatural heat, almost like a fever. I give a little shiver, enough to make me spill my tea, and after another ten minutes or so, I give up trying to stay upright and curl up on the sofa, where I stay until morning.

*

When I wake, my back is more painful than it's been for ages and I'm aching all over from sleeping scrunched up, so I need my stick to help me walk up the stairs. I run a hot bath, and soaking in it for a while eases the pain, but I still feel cold and shivery. It's only as I'm dressing afterwards that I remember that the holidays are over and Ollie will be back at preschool today, which means Cass'll be back at work. Tomorrow would be my usual day to go to the café. Should I just go? Pretend nothing's happened? No, idiot. Maybe I should text her, tell her I know that they know about me, offer to meet up and discuss it, try to explain. Not that I've ever been able to explain. But I've got to talk to her somehow, on her own, away from Luke.

I feel a yawning ache deep inside me as I wonder what will happen now, when I'll be able to see Ollie again – or *if* I'll be able to see him again. If Luke has his way . . . It comes back to me how he tried to stop Ollie taking me up to his room on New Year's Day. Oh God, if Cassie listens to him . . . And why wouldn't she? He's her partner, after all. I think back again to what she said about staying in touch, and visiting after they move. What if Luke persuaded her to fob me off? What if it was a ploy? Or maybe it was genuine on her part, but once they've moved, Luke will talk her into cutting off contact with me. What if . . . Oh my God, what if they're planning to just move one day, to just disappear without telling me? No; I shake away the tears that start to bubble up. No, I can't let myself think that. Ollie . . . but the cruel truth is, Ollie would forget about me.

As I move around the kitchen wiping down surfaces that are already clean, I become more and more agitated. So much of my life has come to revolve around Ollie and Cass; so much of my life *is* Ollie and Cass, I can't picture a future without them in it. I should be thinking about work, getting on with some planning – teaching starts again at the end of January – but I can't concentrate with all this going on. How can I even think about anything else? How can I possibly *care*? Maybe I'll drive out to the preschool after lunch – at least I can talk to Ollie through the fence. He'll mention it to Cass, but what else can I do? I have to see him; I *have* to think of something.

It's only when I'm walking down to the Spar to buy some cat food that an idea begins to nudge its way into my thoughts. It's vague and ethereal, rolling across the back of my mind like a fog. But by the time I'm on my way back home, the idea is beginning to take on a more clearly defined shape. Could I really do this? A quick glance at my watch tells me it's already past midday. And that's when it clarifies in my mind; this is my only chance, my only opportunity. I have three hours.

The man in Halfords shows me how to fit the child seat. It's much simpler than I thought; just a question of feeding the seat belt through the back, then using pressure to set the base properly and pulling the seat belt in tight to secure it. Back home, I start to pack, but I'm not really concentrating on what I'm doing, just rushing around throwing random items of clothing, toiletries and food into bags. Then I load up Spider's dish with food and fill his water bowl. I feel a pang about leaving him, but the cat flap isn't locked, so he'll find someone else to feed him quickly enough. I'm working feverishly, aware of the clock ticking.

It's only when I've half-filled the boot that I realise it's pointless. As soon as Cassie reports us missing, every police patrol in the country will have my registration number. Idiot. *Idiot.* How could I not think of that? I'd planned to head for the motorway, but maybe a train is better all round. If I'm not driving, I'll be free to reassure Ollie. I'll tell him it's a little holiday at first. It'll seem normal, but it all depends on moving quickly. Preschool finishes at three fifteen, but Cassie's never there until almost half past, so we should get a good head start. I take everything out of the car and repack a rucksack and a couple of bags, then I check train times. There's nothing from Dore until almost four o'clock, so I'll have to drive to Sheffield. With a bit of luck, Cassie'll come to the house first. In fact, she's bound to, which means there should be time to park the car a little way from the station so it won't be spotted immediately. By the time anyone works out that we're on a train, we'll be miles away. My hands tremble as I turn the key in the ignition.

I join the group of parents who always arrive early. One of the dads presses the button and speaks into the silver box, then the metal gates swing open immediately and I follow them in. I feel a flash of anger at how lax they are about opening the gates without checking each person, but I smile as naturally as I can at the teacher and hope she recognises me from when I've collected Ollie before. The woman returns my smile, so my intentions can't be scrawled on my face in fluorescent ink, which is how it feels. When Ollie sees me, he runs and throws his arms around my legs. I bend down and hug him tight, lifting him off his feet and wondering if he can feel my heart thudding through my ribs. 'Have you had a lovely day?' I ask, setting him down again. 'What did you do today?' I ask the same questions every time, and every time he shrugs and says he can't remember. 'Where's Mummy?' he says as I zip up his anorak.

'Mummy's still at work.' I take his hand and steer him towards the door. 'Say bye bye to Miss Taylor.'

'Bye, Miss Taylor,' he says, skipping along next to me.

'Bye, Oliver.' The teacher waves. 'See you tomorrow.'

'Guess what? I've bought you your own car seat to keep in my car.'

He grins in response. Then, just as we get to the car, he suddenly pulls his hand away and starts to run back towards school. 'Ollie! Where are you going?'

His head whips round at the tone of my voice. 'I forgot my lunchbox.' He looks a little scared.

Be calm; breathe. 'We've got to hurry today, Ollie. We'll leave your lunchbox until tomorrow.'

'But I need it for—'

'Tell you what, how about we buy you a brand-new one?'

He appears to weigh this up.

'Only we really do need to hurry now. Bet you can't get into my car and into your new seat before I count to ten. One . . .'

It works. He runs, laughing, towards the door I'm holding open and starts to clamber into the new seat. 'Two, three, four, five—'

'I'm in!'

'My goodness, so you are! Let's get you strapped in, then.' My trembling fingers fumble with the clasp but eventually I work it out and click it into place. 'There. All done. Let's go.'

'Will Mummy be at home?' he says as I start the engine.

I glance up and down the road; still no sign of Cassie's car. 'How would you like to go on a train, Ollie?'

CHAPTER FORTY-EIGHT

Then

The crows came as it started to get light, their thoughts crowding in through the open window and surrounding me. As I sat up in bed feeding Harriet, I looked at Adrian sleeping next to me and I tried to remember what I used to feel. Whatever it was, it seemed to have gone. I kept wondering if I was in the wrong life, if Harriet and I belonged somewhere else. It was confusing. I couldn't explain it. I couldn't talk to Adrian about it because he already thought there was something wrong with me. He wanted me to go back to the doctor's and I told him I would, but I wasn't going to, because sometimes I wondered if there *was* something wrong with me, and if there was, they'd take Harriet away, and then I'd die.

'I'm fine,' I promised Adrian.

'It's just that sometimes, you seem . . . I don't know, not down exactly, but not yourself.'

His face was clouded with concern, so I gave him what I hoped was a reassuring smile. 'Yes, I'm sure. Now go to work or you'll be late for your meeting.'

'All right.' He kissed me. 'Look, try and take it easy today, okay? I'm not sure these very long walks are a good idea. It's less than two months since you had major abdominal surgery, after all.'

'Exercise is good for me. And the fresh air—'

'. . . *is good for Harriet.* Yes, so you keep saying. But . . .' He was frowning. 'Don't take this the wrong way, Leah, but I'm worried about you. You're starting to sound a bit, I don't know – obsessive about it.'

I had to be careful, because whatever I said, he could twist it so that it made me look bad. 'She likes being outside,' I said eventually. 'It calms her.'

'Yes, but not for hours on end. And it's still only March, don't forget.'

'It's April in a few days. And anyway, so what? It's mild and sunny – look.' I pointed towards the window.

He glanced outside and sighed. He couldn't argue with that.

Finally, reluctantly it seemed, he left the house. I waited until I heard the car pull away and then I hummed to myself as I tucked Harriet into her pram, which instantly relaxed her because she knew it meant we were going outside. It was a beautiful day, and as we took the path into the woods, I saw that not only were the primroses along the bank flowering, but the daffodils were starting to open, too. As we went deeper into the wood, I noticed the colour of the grassy areas, a brilliant emerald green, sharp and vivid in the early spring sunshine. I heard a woodpecker in the distance, as well as the usual twittering birdsong, but most of all I could hear the crows. They were watching me, I knew they were, because I could feel their chatter poking into my head. I took Harriet out of her pram and put her on a patch of soft, tickly new grass so they could see her, and she lay there, moon eyes blinking up at the trees.

For a moment, I saw myself out there in the middle of the woods with my seven-week-old baby and I wondered what I was doing, whether I'd misunderstood something, got it all wrong. But then Harriet – my clever little daughter – said that as long as I trusted my instincts, kept her by my side the whole time and listened to what the crows told me, everything would be all right. I looked as hard as I could into those sharp, coal-black eyes and I promised that I would keep her safe, that I would protect her from people who didn't understand her, that I would die before I let anyone take her from me. Harriet smiled. A fleeting, lopsided ghost of a smile, but definitely a smile, and then she closed her eyes, ready for her nap.

She was sound asleep when we got home so I left her in the pram, and as I stood there gazing down at her and trying to work things out, there was a knock on the back door. Diane. I tried to fix a smile on my face as I opened the door.

'Hello, love.' Diane smiled.

I waited for her to tell me what she wanted, but she just stood there, grinning. I realised she was expecting me to invite her in, so I opened the door a little wider, and sure enough, in she came. I folded my arms and leaned against the sink.

'I thought I'd pop in to see how you were getting along.'

'Fine, thanks, Diane. I'm fine.'

'You know, I've hardly seen you since the baby was a few days old.' She paused. 'But I suppose you have a million and one things to do.'

'Yes.' I nodded. 'I'm quite busy.'

Her eyes were roving around the room. 'Baby asleep?'

I nodded.

'Good timing on my part, then.' She gestured towards the kettle. 'How about a quick cuppa? I'll make it – give you five minutes to put your feet up.'

'Well . . .' I knew it would look odd to refuse, and she might tell Adrian, which would only give him more ammunition. 'A quick one, then.' I pulled out a chair and sat down, allowing her to bustle around my kitchen.

'So how are you coping?' she asked as she set the two mugs on the table. 'Are you getting much sleep?'

'Not much at first, but it's better now.'

'That's good. Still feeding her yourself?'

My face felt hot. Why does she want to know? 'She's a very hungry baby, so I'm combination-feeding.'

She pretended she didn't disapprove, but then she went on to tell me how she'd fed both of hers until they were at least six months. 'The first few weeks are the worst, you know, but if you can get past that, it gets much easier. I remember when I had my Robert . . .' And she started telling me all about when she was a young mother in the 1970s. It was only when she reached for my hand and said, 'And how are you feeling in yourself?' that I realised. Like Adrian, she was trying to catch me out, trying to make it look like I couldn't cope. I knew what they wanted, all of these people. They wanted Harriet. 'I'm fine, Diane. Thanks for asking.' I stood up. 'Well, I must get on. Nice to see you.'

She looked startled. 'Oh, right.' She drained her cup, the loose skin at her throat wobbling like a chicken's, and then said, 'I was hoping for a peep at the little one.' Her eyes roved around the room as if I'd hidden Harriet in a drawer somewhere.

'She's sleeping. I don't want to disturb her.'

'I won't disturb her, love. I just wanted a quick look. I haven't seen her since just after you came home.'

She was lying. 'You saw her the other day,' I said. 'We bumped into you as you were coming back from the shops.'

I saw by her expression that she knew she'd been caught out. 'Oh, yes, but she was all bundled up in that little puffy suit, so I couldn't see her face.'

'Well, like I said, I need to get on now, so maybe another time.' I made to open the back door. I wasn't sure what I'd do if she didn't leave, but there was no way she was getting her hands on Harriet.

'Right you are, love.' She looked at me strangely, but eventually got to her feet, thank God. Just before she stepped outside, she put her hand on my arm. 'Having a baby can make you go a bit funny sometimes, you know. Probably down to hormones, and not having enough sleep. If you ever feel like that, if it gets too much in any way, I'm only next door, remember.' She gave my arm a squeeze. 'You've only got to shout and I'll come over, or you could bring her to me. I'll have her whenever you like.'

'Thank you.' I tried to sound normal, as if I hadn't guessed what she was up to.

CHAPTER FORTY-NINE

Now

I barely take in the destination, because what I respond to is the first part of the announcement: *the train about to depart* . . . 'Come on, Ollie.' I try to turn the anxiety in my voice to excitement. 'That's our train – let's have a race to see who can get up the stairs first. Ready, steady, go!' That works – laughing, he bounds up the stairs as fast as his little legs will allow. 'Okay, now we need to run straight along here to the next lot of stairs, and then down to the platform, ready?'

He nods and we run at about the same speed, because hurrying up the stairs has set my back off, so I couldn't run any faster even if I didn't have a small child to consider. As we hurry down the steps I can see the rail staff spaced along the platform, one holding a large paddle and one about to blow his whistle. 'Hurry up, love.' He holds up his hand to signal to the others. Pain shoots up my spine as I lift Ollie over the gap and onto the train. The second we're on board the door slams behind me, I hear the whistle and the train begins to move.

The pain has silenced me temporarily but I keep a reassuring hand on Ollie's shoulder, steadying him as we try to make our way through the packed carriage. Ollie looks up at me, plainly alarmed by the number of adult bodies surrounding him and the threat of being squashed. 'Come on.' I reach down. 'Let me give you a carry.' He holds his arms out and I lift him, causing such a surge of pain in my back that I actually cry out. Ollie looks terrified. 'Sorry, sweetheart. My back's hurting a bit, that's all.' I can feel the sweat break out on my forehead. Ollie is clinging to me, people are shoving at me, trying to get past although there are clearly no free seats. The pain has triggered a wave of nausea, and just as I think I might faint, a girl with pink and purple hair stands up and takes out her earphones. 'Excuse me,' she says in a cultured voice. 'Would you like to sit down?'

'Thank you.' I could weep with gratitude. 'Thank you so much.' As we settle in the window seat she's given up, the girl beams a smile at Ollie, who smiles shyly back, then buries his face in my neck.

Now he's not in danger of being crushed, Ollie starts to enjoy the novelty of being on a train. 'Look!' he says, pointing out of the window as he spots things of interest in people's back gardens – a trampoline, two motorbikes, a dog playing with a football. Then, as the gardens give way to fields and hills, he asks, 'Is Mummy coming on the train?'

'No, I don't think so. We'll probably see Mummy later, when we get there.' He looks uneasy. He's picked up on the hesitation in my voice. 'And if we don't see her when we get there, we'll see her tomorrow.'

'Am I sleeping over?' he says, animated again.

'Yes, but not at my house this time. We're going to a hotel. Have you ever been to a hotel before?'

His face drops again. 'Where is Hotel?'

'There are lots of hotels, but we'll find a nice one when we get there.' Wherever 'there' turns out to be. I still have no idea where this train is going. At that moment, there's an announcement: *Please have your tickets ready, as a full ticket inspection will be commencing shortly.* Several people laugh out loud. The girl who gave us her seat says 'Good luck with that', and there's a general muttering about how this train is always the same, and it's disgusting, and it wouldn't be legal to transport cattle like this. Ollie perks up a little with all this camaraderie, especially when the pink-haired girl smiles at him again.

The first announcement is quickly followed by another, saying that due to this service being very busy today, there won't be a ticket inspection after all. The next station, the guard says, will be Stockport, and after that, Manchester Piccadilly and Manchester Airport. *What are you doing, Cornelia?* The voice sounds so clear and real that I look up. I flick my head. I have abducted a child, and I'm on a train hurtling away from his mother.

'Leah, will Mummy come when we're at Hotel?'

I turn my face to the window and lean it briefly against the cool glass. The darkening sky is an ominous greyish-blue, making the pretty countryside that's flashing past seem bleak and gloomy. 'I . . . I'm not sure, Ollie. We'll phone her when we get there, shall we?'

He seems satisfied with that. It buys me time, at least. By now, Cassie'll know that I collected him. I slip my hand into my bag and unlock my phone. Three missed calls. She'll probably drive straight over to the house, which could take anything from ten minutes to half an hour, depending on traffic. I zip up my bag and smile at Ollie. 'Are you hungry?'

'A tiny small little bit.' He's cautious, but his face lights up when I produce a packet of Quavers and a Freddo Frog. Cass never lets him have sweets or chocolate before his tea, but why deny him? It's such a small thing. I open the Quavers and hand him the pack. He immediately picks one out and offers it to me.

'No thanks, Ollie, but you're a good boy for sharing.'

While he's eating his crisps, I try to think. Stockport? Or stay on until Manchester? Stockport's first, and I had a boyfriend who lived there when I was a student, so I vaguely remember my way around. We could stay there tonight, find a Travelodge or a B&B, and then I can plan where to go tomorrow. I'd better get some cash out . . . Shit! I should have done that in Sheffield. But at least if we're moving on tomorrow . . . Ollie is struggling to open his Freddo Frog. I open it for him, aware that my hands are sweating and clammy. I can feel the sweat pricking my underarms, and as I hand him the chocolate, I realise I'm breathing quite rapidly. Ollie twists round to look at me, his mouth surrounded by orange crumbs from the Quavers. 'Leah, why have you got a sad face?'

'I'm . . . I've got a bit of a tummy ache, that's all.' An all-purpose explanation I know he'll accept. Cassie told me once that if Ollie was feeling anything from actual tummy ache to tiredness, grumpiness or real unhappiness, he was likely to say he had a tummy ache.

'I've got tummy ache, too,' he says now, handing me the half-eaten Freddo and slumping back against my chest. 'I wish Mummy was here.'

'I know, sweetheart.' *What are you doing, Cornelia?* That voice in my head again. *This is not your child. His mother will be out of her mind with worry.* It's unsettling because it doesn't feel like my own voice. Maybe it's my conscience. I'm holding him with one arm, but now I slip the other arm around him and give him what I hope is a reassuring squeeze. He relaxes against me for a while, but soon he sits forward again and says, in his best 'I'm-being-a-good-boy' voice, 'Leah, please can we phone Mummy now?'

There's a lump in my throat the size of a walnut. 'Ollie, sweetheart . . .' My voice sounds scratchy and dry, and I can hear my own anxiety running beneath the words. 'I don't think Mummy will be able to answer her phone at the moment. She's probably driving.'

'In a minute, then?'

'Yes, okay. In a minute.' Perhaps he'll forget if I distract him. 'Look, Ollie, can you see the sheep?' He sits back against me and looks out of the window. We're hurtling through the Hope Valley, and there are sheep dotted about in the patchwork of fields stretching up the hillside. Ollie just nods, and I rest my cheek against his head, feeling the silkiness of his hair and recognising the faint scent of Johnson's baby shampoo. I lift my head so I can admire the thick, dark hair and the little whorl at the back, the same as Adrian's. The same as Harriet's.

This is not your child, the voice says again. *He can never be your child, and he cannot replace your lost babies.* No, of course he can't replace Harriet, or Thomas, but I can love him. I have so much love left over and I can pour it all into him. Cassie's bound to have a baby with Luke, then poor Ollie will be left out. He shouldn't have to make do with a share of his mother's love. I'm doing the right thing; I can give him so much more.

'Leah, why are you crying?'

His voice isn't particularly loud, but I'm aware of other passengers right next to us. 'I'm not crying, sweetie. I've got a bit of a cold, that's all.' I try to smile, but I'm not sure it works. He looks worried, and to my horror, his bottom lip starts to tremble and his eyes fill with glistening tears. 'I want to go home.' His face crumples. I try to give him a cuddle but he pulls away from me and it's as though I've been punched in the gut. 'I'm sorry, baby. Please don't cry. Tell you what, how about if we send Mummy a text, then when she isn't driving she can call us back?'

He stops crying instantly and his face brightens. 'Okay. Then can I talk to her?'

'When she calls back, yes.' I pull out my phone, check it's still on silent. Twelve missed calls, two voicemails and a text. I open the text first. *Where r u? School said you picked O up, but I'm at yours now & yr not here??*

I type, *Ollie is fine. Safe and well. Be in touch later.* 'There,' I say. 'We'll send that, and we'll talk to her soon, okay?'

'In how many minutes?'

'Ollie, please. I don't know.' I see his bottom lip come out again. 'Sorry.' I kiss the top of his head and give him another hug. 'I'm not cross, just tired, that's all. Now sit quietly like a good boy while I listen to these messages, okay?'

'Okay.' He nods gravely and does as he's told.

I press the phone tightly against my ear so Ollie can't hear. *First new message, received today at three thirty-two:* 'Leah, it's Cass. Miss Taylor says you've picked Ollie up today. I was a bit surprised because I don't remember asking you to collect him. Anyway, I'm just on my way to yours now. See you in a bit.'

She's worried, but she's trying not to sound worried.

Second new message, received today at three fifty-one: 'Leah, can you call me the minute you get this, please? I'm outside your house and you're clearly not here.' This time, she's not bothering to disguise her fear. She sounds on the verge of panic and I feel a stab of guilt. Poor Cass. Still, she'll see the text next time she picks up her phone.

'I can't see your car anywhere. I'm getting a bit concerned

now, because I didn't know you were picking Ollie up. I expect you've driven him home to mine, or maybe you've gone somewhere for a treat. Can you call me, please, Leah. Just let me know where you are and I'll come and get him, okay? Thanks.' *End of messages.*

As I'm putting my phone back in my bag, Cass's name flashes up on the screen. I could answer it, tell her I'm taking Ollie on a train for a treat, apologise for worrying her. We could just get off, go home and it would all be over. My finger hovers over the answer button.

But then I'd be back to square one, facing a life alone in that house with only the cat for company. I glance down at Ollie, patiently waiting as he was told to, gazing out of the window until he can speak to his mother. I feel guilty again, because he trusts me and I've misled him. But he's bound to forget soon enough. He's not yet four, and young children forget and move on quickly, don't they? I remember spending quite a bit of time with my Auntie Gail – my dad's sister – when I was little, but she moved to Spain when I was six, and sixteen years later, when she came to my graduation, I didn't even recognise her. On the other hand, I can remember having a mum, even if I don't remember much about her. Although Ollie's quite a bit younger, so maybe . . . But can I risk it? Just because you don't remember something doesn't mean you're not damaged by it.

Another voicemail. 'Leah, for God's sake, where are you?' Cassie sounds different now; frightened, but still holding onto her control. 'You need to bring him home, Leah, right now. Wherever you are, just turn around and come back. I . . . I'm not angry, but you need to check with me before you take Ollie out for the afternoon. Okay? So just come back now, and there's no harm done.'

There's a definite wobble in Cassie's voice this time. *Turn around and come back.* So she assumes I'm driving. Has she called the police yet? Even if she has, she's unlikely to remember my registration number, so they'll waste a bit of time tracing that. It might not take long to find the car, though – I should have disguised the number plates.

My mind keeps leaping into the future – finding somewhere to live, a school for Ollie. That'll have to be a priority. But what about when he asks for his mum? What if there's a television appeal, and someone recognises him? I slip my arm around his shoulder again, and as he turns to look at me, I remember that last day, the certainty that they were all working together, all conspiring against me – Adrian, the health visitor, the neighbours – and my fervent belief that they were coming for Harriet, that after all the loss I'd already suffered, they were coming to take my precious, uniquely gifted daughter.

CHAPTER FIFTY

Then

It was almost ten, and Adrian was still in the study on the phone. I could hear the murmuring through the walls but I couldn't make out what he was saying or who he was talking to. I popped my head round the door. He was between calls, standing at the window with his back to me. 'Aren't you going in to work today?'

He turned, startled. 'Not until eleven, and then only briefly for that meeting. I told you – I've arranged to work from home for a while. Just until you're . . . so I can help you with Harriet a bit more.'

I nodded, aware that I should be pleased. A few weeks ago I'd have jumped at this, but now it didn't feel right. I used to think it was good that Adrian wanted to be more involved with childcare, but that was before I realised that he didn't understand her needs, not the way I did. He didn't even like me taking her out in the woods, but I wanted to take her there more often, not less. I'd begun to feel certain that we belonged there, Harriet and me – outside, among the trees. Everything inside the house felt wrong. Too big or too bright. When I looked at the kitchen table, it seemed enormous. I knew it hadn't changed size, but I felt dwarfed by it. And if I looked at the white tiles on the wall behind the worktop, I had to screw my eyes up so they didn't dazzle me with their bright whiteness.

When Adrian finally left the house, I listened for the sound of his car pulling out of the drive, and when it didn't come, I went upstairs and peered out of the window. There he was, standing in next door's porchway, talking to Diane, no doubt asking her to spy on me again. After a few minutes, he got in his car and drove off. I went back down to the kitchen and when the doorbell rang, I ignored it, assuming it would be Diane. I glanced at the moses basket, but Harriet was still asleep. It rang twice more, and that was when it occurred to me that Diane usually came round the back, through the garden. I opened the kitchen door and looked along the hallway to the front door. I could see the shape through the glass. It wasn't Diane, but I couldn't think of anyone I wanted to see, so I stayed still, hoping the bell hadn't woken Harriet.

When the figure finally moved away, I nipped quickly up the stairs so I could look out of the window. There was a red car parked on the drive, and I recognised the woman as one of the health visitors from the centre. Thank goodness I hadn't opened the door. I watched as she leaned on the roof of her car to write something. Then she tore off a sheet, folded it and dropped it through the letter box before getting back in her car and driving away.

I went down and picked the note up from the mat. *Called today 11.30 as arranged, but appears no one at home. Please contact the centre urgently to arrange further appointment (six-week check, mum and baby now two weeks overdue).* And it was signed *Christine Cooper, Health Visitor.*

I screwed the note up and threw it in the kitchen bin. *As arranged* – I hadn't arranged any visit. It must have been Adrian. Thank goodness Harriet had warned me about this sort of thing – I could so easily have let that woman in. I was in awe of my clever daughter and her ability to communicate with me. At first I thought this was what mothers meant when they talked about a special bond, but this was different: Harriet and I had been specially granted this ability to communicate so that I could help her. They said all babies were born wise, didn't they? I'd noticed it in Harriet the moment she was born. But we adults swept away that wisdom. Within a few weeks they became vulnerable, innocent, helpless, and they had to start all over again, learning through mistakes and misery. The more I thought about it, the more puzzled I became. Why didn't other mothers try to stop this from happening? How could they bear to see their toddlers humiliated day in, day out? Laughed at because they'd misunderstood something, or they'd fallen over, or used the wrong word while they were learning to talk? All because the wisdom they were born with is destroyed in those first few weeks and their mothers do nothing to stop it.

Harriet made a little noise as she started to wake up, and the moses basket wobbled on its stand as she kicked her legs. I went to pick her up and found her already wide awake and staring. *I trust you, Cornelia*, she said with her clever eyes. I liked the way she didn't call me 'Mummy'. *You know what to do.* And all at once, I understood everything. It was so clear, I couldn't think why I hadn't seen it before. The urge to go into the woods, the crows coming every day to talk to me. That was what they'd been trying to tell me all along. Harriet wasn't just an ordinary baby, and she mustn't be shut away in this house, a box made of bricks where there was no wind and no rain. I had been *chosen* to be her mother and my purpose was to protect her, to keep her safe from all of them – Adrian, Diane, that health visitor woman. They were all in touch with each other, all making plans to snatch my baby from me and suck away her wisdom. But I wouldn't let them. The sense of responsibility I'd felt when she was born was nothing compared with the mighty sense of duty and purpose that surged through me now.

I held Harriet against my chest with one arm as I moved around the ground floor, humming 'Rock-a-bye Baby' to her as I locked and bolted the doors and windows with my spare hand. Sure enough, as I closed the window in the dining room, I could see Diane coming down her garden path and reaching for the gate that connected her garden to ours. 'Don't you worry, sweetheart.' I rested my lips against

Harriet's downy scalp. 'No one's going to take you from me.'

I was perfectly calm as Diane rapped on the back door. 'Go away,' I said, but she obviously didn't hear because she knocked again. I raised my voice slightly so she could hear me, but I didn't want to shout. 'I said, *go away*. You're not taking my baby.'

There was a pause, then her voice. 'Leah? Leah, are you all right? No one wants to take your baby. Come on, love. Open the door.'

'No, because I know what you're planning, all of you.'

'Leah, we're just concerned, that's all. Adrian's proper worried about you, that's why he asked me to pop round. Come on, love, just open the door and we can have a nice cup of tea and a chat.'

I chuckled. She must have thought I was stupid. I carried on humming as I walked up the stairs, because Harriet liked the song. I glanced out of the back landing window and saw that Diane was on her phone. Thirty seconds later, after she ended her call, my phone started ringing. Adrian. I hesitated, wondering whether to answer it, whether to try to explain. After all, he was her father. But I knew he wouldn't understand. It wasn't his fault; he hadn't been chosen like we had. He wouldn't believe me if I told him how special Harriet was, how special we both were, and how we had these extra powers. So I put my phone on silent and sat down on the stairs for a minute or two, watching his name flash up as he tried again and again. Harriet squirmed in my arms, and I realised that the sound of Diane banging on the door downstairs was disturbing her, so I started to hum the song again as I got to my feet.

CHAPTER FIFTY-ONE

Now

My back hurts and my headache is becoming increasingly intense; it feels like my body is screaming at me, stopping me from thinking properly. The man in the seat next to us has dozed off and is leaning against my arm, which I'm keeping rigid so he can't lean against Ollie. Every now and again, he snores, but that makes Ollie giggle, so I don't mind. I glance at the people standing within earshot – everyone seems to be wearing headphones or an earpiece. I speak quietly anyway. 'Ollie, do you remember meeting your daddy?' He looks at me blankly. 'A man called Adrian?'

He thinks for a minute. 'Adrian did come to my house. Adrian got me a farmyard set but not for my birthday.'

I nod. 'That's right. Well, didn't Mummy tell you who Adrian was?'

Again, he looks blank.

'I thought Mummy said she'd told you that Adrian was your daddy?'

He shrugs.

'Adrian *was* your daddy, Ollie, even though he didn't live in the same house as you and your mummy. You see, he was my husband.' I hesitate. Now I think about it, why would Ollie know the word *husband*? Although maybe he does, because his eyes widen at this information.

'He had to look after me because I was very poorly, so he wasn't able to see you as much as he'd have liked.' Ollie blinks and waits to hear what I'm going to say next. 'So,' I continue, 'because . . . because I was married to your daddy, you know, he was my husband and I was his wife, like most mummies and daddies who live together, so because of that . . . well, you see, I'm your *step*mummy. Have you heard of stepmummies and daddies?'

He nods gravely. 'Paris has got a stepdad.'

'There you are, then.' I try to smile, but my face feels tight and scared and I can't move it properly. 'You see, it's perfectly normal to have a stepmum or stepdad, and some people have stepbrothers and -sisters, too. I expect you'd like a brother or sister, wouldn't you?'

'Just a brother,' he says.

I'm guessing Cassie and Luke have talked about this, then. I want to tell him about his half-brother and -sister; I have wanted to tell him many, many times. But I have no idea what a child of his age is likely to understand about death. What will any of this mean to him, I wonder? My thoughts trail off, and that voice comes into my head again, screaming at me this time. *You can't keep him. The police will be searching for you by now.*

I look out of the window and realise we're nearly there just as the announcement comes: *We will shortly be arriving at Stockport. Stockport is our next station stop . . .* 'I love you, Ollie,' I whisper into his hair as I savour the warmth and weight of his little body. The sky is darkening rapidly as we pull into the station. I sigh and give him a quick hug. 'Come on, sweetheart. This is our stop.'

I check in both directions as I lift him down from the train, half-expecting to see the police waiting for me, but there's no obvious sign of police uniforms, just the station staff in their bright red puffy jackets.

'Leah?' Ollie allows me to take his hand. 'Will we see my mummy soon?'

This time I can't answer him. I can't find the words, can't locate them in the jumble inside my head. I glance along towards the viaduct. There are two black shapes on the platform edge – crows. 'I had my own little boy once, Ollie,' I tell him as I zip up his coat. 'And a little girl, too. They were called Thomas and Harriet. They both looked a lot like you, you know.' I can't see his reaction to this because tears are blurring my vision. 'If they were here now – Thomas and Harriet, I mean – you could all play together, couldn't you?' He doesn't answer straight away, then he says, 'Can they come and play at my house?'

I look at his sweet, innocent face and wonder what the hell

I think I'm doing. In my imagination, the three of them are all about the same age, the two boys so alike, and Harriet, with the same dark hair and eyes, a bit more grown up than her brothers. How I'd love to watch them play together.

Those crows – it can't be coincidence. There was a time when I believed they were communicating with me. Still holding Ollie's hand, I start to walk towards them, as though I'm being pushed in that direction, but then something happens in my head, a clunk, like a heavy object falling to the floor. *What are you doing, Cornelia?* And this time I recognise that voice. It's Harriet. Always so wise. I stand still for a minute, taking in Ollie's pale, uncertain face, then I turn back to the busier end of the platform. There's a café, its golden light welcoming in the near dark. 'I know, how about a cake and a drink, Ollie?'

Usually he'd be nodding enthusiastically, but he still looks hesitant – worried, almost. I hate that I've done this to him, to this child I love. 'And some crisps,' I add, my voice cracking, 'while . . .' I take a breath, '. . . while we wait for Mummy.' The words are like magic. He nods and the tension lifts from his face.

I buy him a fruit drink, a chocolate brownie and a packet of cheese and onion crisps, and we find a table next to a woman with a little boy about the same age and a baby in a high chair. The woman smiles as she spoons food into the baby. The little boy is playing with a tiny Thomas the Tank Engine, which he's running along the table edge. The two boys eye each other, and the other boy runs the blue engine down the table leg. Soon Ollie is eating his crisps, swinging his legs and grinning happily at the other child. I attempt to scrawl a note to Cassie on one of the papery serviettes. It's as if I have forgotten how to write, but eventually I make my hand work enough to write an apology and the briefest of explanations. It's barely legible, but Cass should be able to make enough sense of it. I tuck it into my bag and glance again at my phone. More missed calls. I stand up, scraping my chair back, my whole body tingling and straining to move. 'Ollie.' I put my hand on his shoulder. There are so many things I want to say. But instead, I turn to the mother at the next table. 'Excuse me, will you be here for ten minutes or so?'

The woman looks up at the monitor. 'At least another forty minutes. Although knowing my luck, it'll be longer.'

'I was wondering,' I say quietly, nodding towards Ollie, 'if you'd mind keeping an eye on him for five minutes? I need to find the loo, and,' I lower my voice further and glance around as if I'm embarrassed, 'I might be a little while.'

'No problem.' The woman smiles.

'Thank you so much.' I swallow and turn back to Ollie. 'Ollie, I just have to pop out of the café for a few minutes, but I've asked this lady to keep an eye on you until I get back.'

'We'll look after you, Ollie.' The woman smiles, and pats the seat next to her. 'Come and sit with us. This is Rufus, and this greedy little girl is Maisie.'

I move his drink and brownie to the other table while Ollie climbs onto the chair next to Rufus and offers him a crisp. I lean down and kiss him on the top of his head, savouring the moment. 'Wait here,' I whisper, but Ollie is already more interested in the Thomas the Tank Engine, which Rufus has shyly pushed towards him. After a moment's hesitation, I am out and onto the platform, hurrying along in the opposite direction, against the wind. It's easy. No one is paying any attention as I head away from the main part of the station.

CHAPTER FIFTY-TWO

Now

I need to let Cassie know that Ollie is safe. She must be out of her mind with worry. Out of her mind. Am I out of *my* mind?

She answers before it even rings. 'Leah! Thank God. Where are you? Where's Ollie?'

'Stockport station,' I croak. 'He's in the café on platform two. He's fine, Cass. He's safe – he's with a mother and her two children.'

'But what—'

'I . . . I'm sorry.' I end the call before Cass can speak, then I hoist myself up and swing my legs round so that I'm sitting on the viaduct wall. It's higher than I realised. I can feel the wind on my face and neck, so I pull my collar more tightly around me. I feel bad for causing Cass all that distress. She's been a good friend to me; I shouldn't have put her through this. I look at my phone – she's calling back. I reject the call. I look further along the wall and I see my two crows, still waiting.

Tentatively, still hanging onto the wall, I turn and start to lower my right leg towards the narrow ledge that runs along the other side. I stretch my foot down and search for the flat concrete, but it's further away than I thought. My hands feel sweaty, even though it's getting chilly now. I know it's silly, but I don't want to slip. I don't want to do anything by mistake – I want to be fully aware. I'm not ready to put myself down on that ledge just yet, so I try to pull myself back up but pain shoots from my back through my hip and down my leg. I grit my teeth and try again, but it hurts so much, I cry out.

As I stand here, clinging onto the wall, waiting for the pain to subside, my thoughts stray to Paul, who has been like a father to me almost from the day I met him. I'm glad he has Helen now. Then I think about Ollie, and Cassie and Luke, and what I've done to them. And I think about Thomas, my firstborn, and Harriet, my beautiful daughter – my lost babies. My thoughts are leaping about so much in my head that I'm surprised I'm able to stand still. Am I in my right mind now, I wonder? I wasn't back then, that's for sure, when I thought we were escaping, me and Harriet. In fact, I wasn't *in* my mind at all; it was as if I was completely disconnected from that version of myself. Even now, I still don't remember exactly what happened that day – I don't even remember the pain of fracturing my hip and spine.

All I know is what I was told, much later, after weeks of medication-induced oblivion.

Now, though, as I stand here, high above the ground and with the breeze on my skin, I find I can remember those moments immediately before with a crystal-sharp clarity. It is as if it's happening right now. I can actually feel myself back there: I am standing in the attic room with the music in my head, holding Harriet against my chest, certain that the hammering on the door downstairs is because they are coming to tear my beautiful baby daughter from my arms.

I feel Harriet's tiny heart beating close to my own. I am the only one who understands, the only one who knows why we need to be free. This room full of sunlight is the only place where we even stand a chance of being able to breathe, or to think. I am the only one who knows that Harriet isn't an ordinary baby. Until now, I have failed to realise that I'm not an ordinary mother, either – no wonder everything felt wrong when that was what I tried to be. I'm not sure what will happen next – all I know is that we can't stay here, trying to live the wrong life. How will Harriet ever learn to fly if we stay in this brick house? How will she thrive and grow strong? How will her feathers grow long and lustrous and ready to carry her over the rooftops?

Of course, they weren't coming to take Harriet away, I know that now. If only I'd gone downstairs and opened the door, maybe . . . But I was too far gone by then. According to the expert witness at the trial – a perinatal psychiatrist, a kind man with a soft voice and a serious face – I'd been suffering from a particularly severe post-partum psychosis when it happened. It was treatable, once diagnosed, he told the court, but it was a rare condition, and could be difficult to recognise.

'Harriet, look!' I point to the big plane tree. The crows are waiting for us. 'Listen, sweetheart,' I murmur as I release Harriet from the stupid clothes I dressed her in this morning, 'our favourite song.' I open the window and step up onto the window seat, then I tuck Harriet snugly between my breasts and gently fold my wings around her. I raise my head up towards the trees and position myself so that we can soar up quickly towards the others. And as we fall forward, I know that in seconds we'll be free, gliding and swooping through the air, happy, safe from harm, finally able to breathe.

I don't remember much about the trial, only part of the judge's summing-up, and then only because I read it in the papers afterwards: *'Although the consequences of Mrs Blackwood's actions resulted in the loss of her baby daughter's life, I am satisfied that the tragedy that occurred was not a criminal act in the way we would normally understand such activity. I unreservedly accept that Mrs Blackwood was a loving mother, and that when these events took place, she was suffering from a severe mental illness that had not, at that time, been recognised. Mrs Blackwood is in many respects a broken woman, who will have to live with the consequences of her actions for the rest of her life.'*

Everything looks beautiful from up here, especially now it is almost completely dark. The woman in the café must be wondering where I've got to, but perhaps the police will be there by now – Cass will have called them, I'm sure. I glance down and everything tilts. The pain in my back is easing off, so I bite my lip, grip onto the concrete and with an almighty effort, I manage to heave myself back up and twist round so that I am sitting on the viaduct wall instead of standing precariously on the ledge.

Paul has Helen, Cassie has Luke, but who do I have? I thought I had Ollie, but I've been fooling myself, ignoring the plain truth of it. Ollie may be Adrian's child, but that doesn't give me any right to him. I *have* to let him go, but I can't bear the thought. Nor can I bear the thought that, after today, he won't be able to think of me as someone who loves him and cares about him. Instead, I have become the person who tried to separate him from his mother. Cass won't let me meet him again. How will she feel when she finds out I've deceived her from the very first day we met, that I took advantage of her good nature, abused her trust? Even if she never finds out about my connection with Adrian, she knows I tried to steal her son.

There are golden lights everywhere, in shops and houses, in buses and cars. People are going home from work, back to their families, women to their husbands or boyfriends, mothers to their children. I lift my head up to allow the wind to blow my hair back from my face, and I stay like that for a few moments, enjoying the sensation. I look along the ledge and smile as I see the two crows there. They're watching me, their feathers fluffing up in the breeze. Rationally, I know it's coincidence that they seem to be hanging around, waiting for me. They are not some reincarnation of Thomas and Harriet, and I know that, but it does feel like some sort of sign. I like to think Adrian is with our babies, taking care of them, and that I'll be with them all again soon. Maybe that's a load of rubbish; I don't know.

Quite suddenly, I am absolutely certain that it doesn't matter; that it's all right. I smile, and even allow a small laugh to escape my lips. It really is all right. I am content, almost happy. A sense of profound and absolute calm is spreading through me, like soaking my aching body in a warm, scented bath. And from nowhere, long-buried memories start to take shape in my mind – my mum, stroking my hair when I was a little girl to help me sleep; reading me a story when I was in bed with tonsillitis; cuddling me after I fell off my tricycle. I'm surprised by these memories, but I feel as if I'm being soothed and comforted from all sides, almost as if my mum is here, looking after me again. It's time. I lower myself onto the ledge below, easily now, and as I look down, I no longer feel any fear. Still smiling, I close my eyes and tip my head back, then I spread my arms like a bird, and with the soft breeze of my babies' breath on my skin, I let myself go.

AUTHOR'S NOTE

Postpartum psychosis (or puerperal psychosis) is a serious mental illness that affects thousands of women in the UK each year, occurring in slightly more than one in every thousand deliveries. It's much less common than postnatal depression, which affects ten to fifteen women in every hundred. The symptoms, which come on suddenly in the first few days or weeks following childbirth, are varied, and can include high or low mood, confusion, hallucinations and delusions. Symptoms may come and go and can change rapidly. The woman herself may not display any outward signs that anything is wrong, but postpartum psychosis is a psychiatric emergency and it's important to get medical help as soon as possible. Once recognised, the condition is relatively easy to treat.

In the novel, Leah sometimes realises that the strange thoughts she has and the things she thinks are happening would seem 'mad' to other people, so she deliberately keeps them to herself for fear that Harriet will be taken away from her. This is not uncommon in real life cases. But it's important to stress that the other actions Leah takes as a result of her psychosis are entirely fictional, and although some real cases have had tragic consequences, these are relatively rare.

Postpartum psychosis can affect any woman after any of her pregnancies (although there are a number of risk factors – a previous diagnosis of bipolar disorder, for example, or having a mother or sister who suffered postpartum psychosis). If you think you or someone you know might have this condition, it's important to get help as quickly as possible.

If you'd like more information, including symptoms and risk factors, contact APP (Action on Postpartum Psychosis). Their website is www.app-network.org

Finally, I'd like to reiterate that the scenario I created for Leah – a scenario which, after a great deal of consideration and deliberation I decided was the right one for my fictional character, given the circumstances she finds herself in – is an extremely unlikely one for a real person suffering postpartum psychosis.

ACKNOWLEDGEMENTS

I am deeply grateful to both my editor Jo Dickinson, and my agent Kate Shaw for their insightful editorial suggestions on the various drafts of this book, as well as their continued support and encouragement. Thanks also to my ex-editor Clare Hey, who was there at the start but moved on to ever greater things before *The Flight of Cornelia Blackwood* was finished. Her enthusiasm at that early stage helped me make it through the later drafts. A big thank you also to my copy editor, Jenny Page, and to the wonderful team at Simon & Schuster, for everything from the cover design to the layout to the marketing of the finished book – writing the story seems a small part in comparison!

I am indebted to consultant perinatal psychiatrist Dr Nusrat Mir, for giving up his precious time to talk to me about postpartum psychosis and the feasibility of Leah's story as I imagined it. Any remaining errors are entirely my own.

Thanks also to Cherished Gowns UK for answering

my questions about the period immediately after stillbirth. Cherished Gowns provides bereavement packs containing gowns (or wraps for the tiniest babies) made from donated wedding dresses to fit babies who are stillborn from twelve weeks onwards. I feel privileged to have been able to donate my own wedding dress, which was turned into ten beautiful gowns by one of their wonderful volunteer seamstresses.

Grateful thanks to the Francis Reckitt Trust for providing financial support for two writing retreats, enabling me to work on this novel undisturbed by domestic responsibilities and distractions.

My thanks to my wonderful friends who listen patiently while I bang on and on about aspects of the plot: Iona Gunning, Sue Hughes, Annie McKie and Ruby Speechley, and particularly to Russell Thomas and Marian 'Dill' Dillon who go above and beyond the call of duty when it comes to constructive criticism and plot discussion. A special thank you to Russell Thomas for allowing me to give my fictional village the name he created for his own fictional village.

As always, the biggest thank you is to my husband, Francis, for the love, support and encouragement. This is all for you, really.

QUESTIONS FOR DISCUSSION

1 When we first meet Cornelia/Leah in the novel, we know she has done something bad in the past. Did this affect the way you related to her at the start? Did you find your feelings towards her changing as her story unfolded? How did you feel about her by the end of the novel?

2 Adrian appears to be a good man who loves his wife – he could possibly even be seen as 'too good to be true'. How did you feel when it was revealed that he had also done something bad in the past, and at a time when Leah was at her most vulnerable? Given the circumstances, could his behaviour be excused? Might Leah have been able to forgive him?

3 What do you think about the way the first few days and weeks of motherhood are portrayed in this novel? Do you think that Leah's initial experience (before the psychosis really kicks in) is typical for some mothers? How easy is it for new mothers to speak up about the difficulties they are experiencing?

4 Was Adrian a good father and husband? Should he have noticed there was something wrong sooner? What could he have done differently, if anything?

5 How do you think mothers, fathers and people who don't have children might react differently to this book? Does it make a difference if your children are younger or older?

6. The novel covers some distressing themes including miscarriage, stillbirth and postnatal psychosis. It is not an 'uplifting' read! Do you think addressing these sorts of topics in fiction can be useful in raising awareness generally, or are these discussions more useful in a factual context such as print, online or broadcast journalism? Why?

7. Crows are a recurring metaphor throughout the novel. How effective was this in creating atmosphere, and in reflecting Leah's state of mind? Did the crows suggest anything else to you in terms of themes?

8. How might things have been different if she hadn't taken Ollie? Might her friendship with Cassie have survived? How might Leah have rebuilt her life?

9. Could there have been an alternative ending for Leah, even after she has taken Ollie?

10. Leah and Adrian had a whirlwind romance; Adrian's grandmother fell in love the moment she saw his grandfather; Cassie knows within days that Luke is 'the one'. Do you believe in love at first sight? Might Leah and Adrian have still been happy together fifty years on had they not been beset by tragedy?

11. In some ways, Harriet only has a small part in the novel, but of course her significance is huge. How strongly did you feel her presence throughout the story?

12. Does every book deserve a happy ending? Or is a 'truthful' ending, consistent with the character and his or her experiences throughout the narrative, more important?

Loved *The Flight of Cornelia Blackwood*?
Read on for an extract from
Susan Elliot Wright's compelling novel,

What She Lost

Available in print, eBook and eAudio

PROLOGUE

Marjorie, October 1967

Marjorie didn't know how long she'd been in labour. There were no windows in the delivery room so she couldn't tell if it was day or night. It had been twelve hours with Eleanor, but she felt as though she'd been here twice that long already. She wondered if it was still pelting down with rain outside. When they said on the wireless this morning that there was likely to be some flooding, she'd gone straight downstairs to check the basement. Sure enough, there was already about an inch of water pooling in the area at the bottom of the back steps, so she took the stormboard from the old scullery and tried to wedge it up against the back door. Her bulk made it difficult to manoeuvre and the rain pounding on her back felt sharp and cold. She should have waited and let Ted do it, but she was sick of being huge and slow and useless, and she wasn't going to be beaten by a silly plank of wood, so when, after the fourth attempt to fix it in place, one side popped forward again, she put her hands on the door frame to steady herself, drew back her right foot and gave the board a sharp kick, slotting it perfectly into place. Whether it was the violent movement or whether it would have happened anyway, she didn't know, but it was then that she'd felt the unmistakable gushing between her legs.

There were three midwives in the delivery room now, and a doctor, too. 'We need Baby out, Marjorie.' This was the older midwife, the one she trusted. 'I want you to use all the strength you have. You've done this before, so you know you can do it again.'

'I can't,' she whimpered. She didn't want them to have to cut it out, but she couldn't go on any longer, she just couldn't. She wondered if Ted was still outside, pacing the corridor. Or maybe he'd gone back home to see to Eleanor. They'd dropped her off at Peggy's on their way to the hospital. Eleanor had been more excited about sleeping at Peggy's house than she was about the new baby. That seemed like days ago now. Another pain started to build, and she knew that within moments she'd be in its grip, consumed and unable to speak. She needed to say this quickly. 'Can't do it. Please. Caesarean. Just get it out.'

'Nonsense,' the midwife said. 'Come along, one more almighty push.'

Then more voices: *Push! Come on, push! You can do it, push!* So many of them shouting at her; she wanted to scream at them to shut up, but she didn't have the energy.

'I *can't*,' she cried, dragging the word out. Had they no mercy?

Just as she was certain she couldn't take any more, she felt the intense burning she remembered from before.

'Okay, that's the head. Stop pushing now and—'

But all at once she felt the little body slip out in a watery rush.

'That's it! You've done it!' The midwife sounded triumphant. 'Your baby's here. You have a little boy.'

A boy. Ted would be pleased. They'd call him Peter. If it had been another girl, they'd have called her Eloise. Eloise and Eleanor. She'd have quite liked another girl, but it didn't matter; so long as it was healthy.

She craned her head to see, barely aware at first of the hush that had fallen over the room. Then she realised her baby hadn't made a sound. 'Is . . . is he breathing?'

Before anyone could answer, the silence was broken by a weak cry, more like a kitten than a baby. He was alive. She fell back against the pillows, relief flooding through her. Why didn't they bring him to her? They were on the other side of the room, clustered around him, speaking in hushed voices. 'Can I hold him?' she asked. 'What is it? What's wrong?' She could hear his grizzled cry and her arms ached to hold him. One or two of the faces looked across at her, but still no one said anything. Then the older midwife – she was called Lily, Marjorie remembered – came to her side. She wasn't smiling. 'Baby . . . Baby has some mucus in his airways, so we need to clear that out for him, help him breathe a bit more easily.'

'Oh, I see.' She strained to see what they were doing. But it looked as though they'd finished clearing his airways. 'What are they doing now?'

The midwife opened her mouth then closed it again. Marjorie saw the anguish in her eyes, saw that her face was heavy with bad news.

'Tell me,' she said. 'Tell me what's wrong with my baby.'

The midwife nodded. There were tears in her eyes. 'One moment, Mrs Crawford,' she whispered.

It was the doctor who brought the baby to her, wrapped in a shawl. She could see a tuft of dark blond hair sticking up from the top of the bundle. She held out her arms to receive him. 'Mrs Crawford,' the doctor said, 'I'm afraid your son appears to have some . . . some problems.'

'Let me hold him.' She almost had to pull her child out of the doctor's arms. She saw it instantly. Those same frighteningly wide-spaced eyes she'd seen once before, a very long time ago. She looked into them in order to greet him, to welcome him to the world the same as she had with Eleanor nearly four years ago. She remembered that moment as if it were yesterday, the way Eleanor had looked back at her when she'd said, *Hello, baby*; the look in those moment-old eyes that said, *I know you; we are connected.*

But these tiny, too-round pools of blue were shallow and empty. She unwrapped the shawl. His scrawny body was too small in proportion to his puffball head, and the skin was pale and opaque-looking, with a delicate network of blue-green veins showing through. She ran her finger down his right leg to his foot, where the two middle toes were joined by a stretch of pink skin. She moved to the other foot, which was completely webbed, making him look like a little mer-child. He started to cough, his fragile chest heaving.

'He . . . as you can see,' the doctor was saying, 'this baby has a number of . . . abnormalities. There's likely to be a degree of mental handicap as well. We'll need to take a proper look at him.' He stopped speaking and seemed at a loss as to what to do next. Marjorie wrapped her limp-limbed baby in the shawl again, swaddling him tightly so he'd feel safe. He was still making that weak grizzling sound. 'Is my husband here?'

The midwife appeared at the doctor's side. 'Mr Crawford's gone home to try and get some sleep. He was dead on his feet. But he said he'd be back at about nine.'

'Are you on the telephone at home?' the doctor asked, and Marjorie nodded. He turned back to the midwife. 'The number will be in the notes,' he muttered. 'Get someone to ring him up and tell him to come and see me as soon as he arrives. I'll break it to him.'

Marjorie looked down at the child in her arms. If she kept her gaze away from his face and focused on the white, shawl-swaddled bundle, she could kid herself for a moment that he was normal, like any other newborn.

'Doctor needs to have a proper look at Baby, dear,' the midwife said, her voice so much softer now. 'I'll bring you a nice cup of tea in a minute, and then we'll get you onto the ward. You need to get some rest yourself.' She patted

Marjorie's hand. 'You've had a . . . Well, it's been a long night, hasn't it?' She tried to smile, but failed.

*

Marjorie was sure she wouldn't be able to sleep, but somehow she did, deeply and dreamlessly. When she woke, not on a ward as she'd expected but in a room on her own, Ted was sitting in the chair next to her, his face twisted with distress. On the end of the bed was a large bunch of white chrysanthemums, wrapped in blue paper and tied with matching ribbon. She hated chrysanthemums, and she felt momentarily annoyed with Ted for forgetting. But then she remembered why she was here.

She couldn't bring herself to look at Ted properly just yet, so for a moment she allowed her gaze to rest on the paper the flowers were wrapped in. It was so pretty: a soft, dusty blue covered with storks in flight. From each strong beak dangled a brilliant white nappy with a pink, plump, perfect baby nestled inside. Tears blurred her vision.

Somehow, eventually, she managed to lift her heavy eyes to Ted's. 'Have you seen him?'

Ted nodded.

She wondered now whether she should have told Ted about Maurice. But there was nothing to be done about it, so what was the point? Until today, she'd managed to do what Mother told her the one and only time she'd met him: *Now you must forget about this, Marjorie, and promise me you'll never, ever tell anyone. Never, do you promise?*

Ted was sitting in the chair beside her bed, not looking at

her, turning his pack of Embassy over and over in his hands. He looked up when the door opened. The doctor from the delivery room attempted a smile but then allowed it to die on his lips. He sat down in the chair on the opposite side of the bed. 'I understand how difficult this must be for you, Mr and Mrs Crawford, but you have yourselves and your daughter to consider. There are some excellent establishments that can care for Peter. It's unlikely he has much awareness of his surroundings, or indeed that he will survive beyond early childhood. My advice is to go home, try to put this behind you and look to the future. You're both young – plenty of time to have another child.'

She closed her eyes and leant her head back against the pillow, but she could feel Ted looking at her. Another child. How could she possibly risk another child? She took a breath and opened her eyes again. 'No. We'll take him home.'

'Marjorie . . .'

'I can do it; I've experience, after all. It was my job. I was a nurse before I had my first, and I worked with plenty of retarded children.'

'Mrs Crawford,' the doctor paused. 'I'm sure you were a highly competent nurse, but I fear that caring for your own child in your own home, where you would be "on duty", as it were, twenty-four hours a day, well, it's a rather different kettle of fish, don't you see?'

She turned her head to the pillow. 'I'm tired. Please, I need to sleep.'

She heard the doctor sigh; Ted, too. With her eyes still

closed, she pictured the look that was probably passing between them. Then she heard the doctor's chair move as he got to his feet. 'I'll come back when you've had some rest,' he said.

And he did come back, twice more, to try to persuade her to let them find somewhere suitable for Peter to be 'cared for'. 'Your intentions are admirable, Mrs Crawford, that goes without saying. But I urge you to consider the effect on yourself and your family.'

There were some very good places these days, he told her, but she didn't believe him. Things were better than in Maurice's day, and there were some kind and dedicated people working at the home where she'd been a nurse, but nevertheless, she'd seen children neglected, lying on their backs in their cots for hours, tied to the bed if they were restless, even slapped for emptying bowels over which they had no control. No, she had seen it too often. Her son was not normal, but he was still human.

The Secrets We Left Behind
Susan Elliot Wright

It was a summer of love, and a summer of secrets . . .

She has built a good life: a husband who adores her, a daughter she is fiercely proud of, a home with warmth and love at its heart. But things were not always so good, and the truth is that she has done things she can never admit.

Then one evening a phone call comes out of the blue. It is a voice from long ago, from a past that she has tried so hard to hide. Scott knows who she really is and what she has done. Now he is dying and he gives her an ultimatum: either she tells the truth, or he will.

And so we are taken back to that long hot summer of 1976 to a house by the sea, where her story begins and where the truth will be revealed . . .

'Tense and emotional drama'
Daily Express

Available in print, eBook and eAudio

The Things We Never Said
Susan Elliot Wright

The past shapes us all. But what happens when it hides a secret that changes everything?

In 1964, Maggie wakes to find herself in a mental asylum, with no idea who she is or how she got there. Remnants of memories swirl in her mind – a familiar song, a storm, a moment of violence. Slowly, she begins to piece together the past and the events which brought her to this point.

In the present day, Jonathan is grieving after the loss of his father. Then a detective turns up on Jonathan's doorstep to question him about crimes he believes Jonathan's father may have committed long ago . . .

As the two stories interweave, the devastating truth long kept hidden must emerge, and both Maggie and Jonathan are forced to come to terms with the consequences of the shocking and tragic events of over forty years ago.

Available in print, eBook and eAudio

SIMON &
SCHUSTER